Fiddlers Creek

by

Steve Taylor

Fiddlers Creek

Contact Information: info@thewildrosepress.com

Cover Art by *The Wild Rose Press, Inc.*

The Wild Rose Press, Inc.
PO Box 708
Adams Basin, NY 14410-0708
Visit us at www.thewildrosepress.com

Publishing History
First Edition, 2022
Trade Paperback ISBN 978-1-5092-4072-2
Digital ISBN 978-1-5092-4073-9

Published in the United States of America

Toad didn't bother to put on the holster but checked to make sure his gun was loaded. Rex returned topside. Toad was right behind him, heaving his huge bulk through the opening. Both thugs had their eyes on the companionway, but they were too late. From three feet Toad fired one shot into the face of nearest one and two shots into the torso of the other. The first died instantly. The second thug moaned and squirmed around on the floor. Toad stepped over and shot him one more time in the head.

"What the hell are you doing?" Rex shouted. "Have you lost your mind?"

With a condescending look, Toad responded in the same calm voice he would use to order his beloved escargot. "I'm trying to salvage an operation that's about to go to shit. I don't know who these two assholes are, but they were not La Coco men. My guess is the La Coco guys are vulture food somewhere in the mountains."

"Okay, hit man, what's the plan?" Rex shot back.

"They're probably part of a hijack operation on our delivery later tonight. Killing us was part of the plan. We gotta take delivery from La Coco and get the fuck outta here before the rest of them show up."

"We can't leave in the dark, or we'll run aground. Nobody in this shithole maintains anything. Most of the lights are out on the channel markers.

Dedication

To Val Mathews, my editor and mentor, without you, I would still be floundering around.

PART I

Chapter 1

Scrap

Early Fall, 2011, Mt. Pleasant, South Carolina

I'm the fox chased by the hounds to exhaustion. I come to the base of a rock cliff I cannot climb. Hounds on both sides are closing in. Soon they'll tear me apart. I will continue to fight, but eventually one will get me by the throat.

"Mr. Scruggs, Mr. Parks will see you now."

I took my place in the begging chair across from Howard Parks, only his clean desk between us. Like a mongoose, I focused on the pasty-white, pockmarked face of the fifty-year-old president of Cordgrass National Bank and anger overcame caution. "Howard, I know you have a gun in the right drawer. You might as well pull it out and shoot me. I'm dead anyway."

For a moment, Howard looked like a raccoon caught eating from the dog dish. After his brief wild-eyed survey of the room, his focus settled on a paperweight, which was the only thing on his desk. I wasn't sure if he was confused or if maybe he was actually thinking about shooting me.

"Mr. Scruggs, believe me," he said. "I understand how hard this is. Times are tough. We have to protect the bank."

"So now it's 'Mr. Scruggs'? This time two years ago it was, 'Scrap, old buddy, come on my big fishing boat, drink my bourbon, eat my steaks, and let me help you with your business.' "

Howard pushed his chair back a few inches. His face twitched. "I'm sorry. This isn't personal. It's business. I'm feeling the pressure too. I know why they call you Scrappy—you'll find a way. I have faith in you, but right now, it can't come from this bank."

"Shit, Howard, you sound like the mafia when they drop a friend overboard wrapped in chains. 'It's just business.' "

Howard reached into his shirt pocket, took out his pen, rolled it in his fingers, and frowned. Stretching his neck, he leaned forward, elbows on the desk. "The bottom line is the bank cannot extend Scruggs Construction more credit when your unpaid balance is ten million."

I could feel my face getting red. I slapped the desk, and Howard bolted upright. "Don't give me that ten million shit. Not so long ago, you threw money at me when I didn't even need it."

"Your credit was good, and you were highly qualified. You signed the notes. It wasn't my place to ask if you needed it."

"You remember the quail hunting lease your bank had over in Barnwell County back in 2006?"

"We had some good times there. You were a good shot." He relaxed with the change of subject, but I was in no mood for reliving old times.

"Well, there's something you may have forgotten," I said. "In the midst of lubricating me with liquor, you handed me a T-bone steak and asked if it wasn't time for another four million bank loan to expand my business and capture the hot market."

"Yes. Those were different times. I—"

"I'm not done. You also said the bank was my partner and would always have my back. How soon people forget."

His shoulders sagged like a puppy realizing it was being scolded. "It's the economy. The bank is in a squeeze right now."

"Can't you understand? Cutting me off will force bankruptcy. This isn't the housing meltdown when all of us should have been hunkering down. Things are starting to turn. I can see it. I can feel it!"

"The bank doesn't lend money on speculation."

I could see where this was going. He was scared, and I was getting pissed.

"All you banking bastards do is look in the rearview mirror, always using yesterday's news."

He opened and closed his hand several times and stared past me at his artificial plant. "This meeting is getting contentious. Believe me, I understand your frustration."

I gave it another try. "Cordgrass Bank works with me, and I'll eventually pay you. But if you don't loan me enough to keep my business afloat, you're going to end up with my real estate. Is that what you want?"

Again, Howard's face twitched. I noticed several rapid movements of his lower lip.

I smiled. I could read his thoughts. With bank examiners all over the place, the last thing Cordgrass National Bank needed right now was more real estate carried on the books at an inflated value.

"You have no idea the people nipping at my ass. Right now, my hands are tied. Try to sell some property, assets, personal stuff...raise a little money...show some good faith. Pay us something, and maybe we can take another look."

Fuming, I stood up from my chair and planted both hands on the desk. I leaned forward, towering over him. "Good faith?" I asked. "Good faith? I have been doing business with you in *good faith* for eight years. All that time, you people took my money and heaped praise on me about my good faith."

I always knew he was a sycophant to success. As long as you were on top, old Howard Parks was your friend. But I wasn't on top anymore, and he was about to throw me to the bank's legal meat-eaters. He was a weak man, and weak men will always take the safe way out. I knew my argument was fruitless—I was last night's leftover wine.

Head bowed, shoulders hunched, Howard looked like a miniature version of himself.

I straightened up and walked to the door. Before I closed it behind me, I looked back over my shoulder and smiled at him. "And by all means, please share these words with your bank buddies. Fuck you. Fuck you all."

For a long time, I sat in my aging truck, overdue for its 100,000-mile maintenance check. That SOB referred to me as "Scrappy." I always hated Scrappy. It's a mutt's name. I was fine with Scrap, but not Scrappy.

My anger turned to panic about where I stood on this disaster scale. The truth was, if I could have raised more cash, I would have. Howard had no idea how bad my finances were. I'd hung on too long. My construction company had been hemorrhaging for four years. The experts at Stanford and Wharton made predictions, and I had diligently heeded their advice and held on. In the end, they were wrong, and I bled out like a stuck pig. But I had a wife and child depending on me, and they had no idea of the pain ahead. The grim reaper of bankruptcy was approaching.

There was a large freshwater pond next to the bank parking lot. I reached to open my truck door but froze. Through the trees on the back side of the pond, it spread its menacing six-foot wings to dry—an anhinga. This snakebird had struck fear in my heart ever since my youth when tales were told about its doomsday prognoses.

I called my secretary and told her I would not return to my office. I pulled into the garage under my house without remembering the drive home. The door banged shut behind me, and instead of my normal feeling of contentment on arriving home, I felt like a bear discovering the cage door had closed.

Chapter 2

Rex

Jacksonville, Florida

Rex Morgan sat motionless in the cool room and sweated. Like a trapped animal, his eyes darted from the horror about to take place to the torture hooks on the wall. His gaze zoomed to the only door where he could escape. Two slabs of thick oak with soundproofing sandwiched in between made up the single-entry door. It had a double rubber seal at the bottom to decrease the sound of screaming from reaching the rest of the building.

Despite the cleanliness of the room, a faint odor of blood and stale urine persisted, like a New York subway after a stabbing. Dark bloodstains had soaked into the framing lumber making up the front wall. The thick wood continued over a quarter of the ceiling, where a block and tackle dangled. A tarnished pair of leg shackles hung from a steel ring attached to the front wall. At first glance, it might create the image of a clean garage or a hospital operating room, except they all knew this place had nothing to do with fixing cars or curing ailments.

The rest of the room was painted Confederate gray. The concrete floor near the front sloped to a drain under a stainless-steel table. A man was restrained on top with tie-down cuffs.

Rex and Toad, along with three other drug-dealing henchmen, sat in a row of chairs facing the table as if they were at a concert. A couple of them were so scared they couldn't speak. The others made nervous jokes.

Toad, who had witnessed the show before, turned to Rex. "Meatman don't look so tough right now. He's peed all over the table."

Toad's breath smelled like an overused portapotty. His fat bottom and bloated sides encroached on Rex's space. No wonder he was called Toad. Rex looked at him with disgust. "Why do I have to watch this?"

"'Cuz, flyboy, it's about compassion, so you don't someday screw up like Meatman and end up on that table yourself."

"Compassion? Nobody here gives a rat's ass about Meatman, just like they don't give a rat's ass about me. This is about fear. Okay, I'm scared, so let me leave."

"I'll tell you what you need to do, Rex. You need to shut the fuck up, or Snake will spit venom your way."

Rex turned his attention back to the show. Snake, a North Florida wholesale narcotics king, addressed the audience. He walked in front of the torture table as though he were the maestro on opening night. He appeared to be in his late forties, about five feet eleven, and maybe 180 pounds. A well-tailored gray suit, matching the room's color, gave the impression he was meticulous in dress and at creating distress. He had a swarthy Italian complexion and coal-black hair, slicked back for speed. The only jewelry was what looked like a college ring. To his dismay, Rex thought he witnessed

Snake's eyes go from blue to a steel glint complementing the somber setting. The room grew quiet with anticipation and horror as the show began.

"Gentlemen, what we have here is a failure to communicate."

Snake glared for a few seconds at his audience. Toad whistled under his breath.

"Betrayal, mendacity, or misappropriation of my funds will not be tolerated. And this lowlife—" He tilted his head toward the man trembling on the table. "—has ripped me off to the tune of four hundred thousand dollars."

Toad whispered, "I bet Meatman wishes he was back in Gonzales, Texas, peddling Hog's Head Cheese."

Rex had the desperate feeling he didn't belong here. He had made a mistake. Except for the terrifying man running the show, everybody in the room seemed to be bigger than he was. True, some of the audience members appeared nervous, but they tried to laugh or act nonchalantly.

He had a fleeting thought of Mona. She was why he was going to do this. As maître d' at an exclusive restaurant in Jacksonville, she came in contact with numerous high rollers. She liked high rollers and thought Rex was one. It thrilled her he flew airplanes and sailed, but what thrilled her most was he spent money. It had occurred to him her values were twisted, but who was he to judge? And besides, when she took off her clothes, he would have spit in Snake's eye if she said that's what it would take to keep her. He even named his boat *Mona*. Their last tryst prompted him to change it to *Mona More*.

A man Rex only knew as Gut stood next to the torture table. He probably weighed three hundred pounds, but he didn't look overweight. He would have looked right at home in an NFL locker room. A skull tattoo contorted on his huge right bicep as if it were alive. He didn't smile and spoke only with nods and grunts. He seemed to relish the show. He served double duty as torturer-in-chief and consigliore for Snake. Gut's sausage-sized fingers attached to hands as big as Porterhouse steaks. He wore a thick gold chain around his neck and a diamond ring on his left pinky, which caught the reflection of the bright overhead light.

Though Gut and Snake were coarse and cruel, Rex had been told both had law degrees. Rex clasped his hands together to keep from showing the tremble in his fingers. Gut hefted his huge frame to the back of the table. Without the slightest expression, he listened to Snake, and with a flicker of what appeared to be satisfaction, he looked at the quaking victim.

Rex had heard snippets of the story on Meatman but didn't understand exactly how he had ended up going from his own Texas butcher shop to being strapped to a table in Snake's butcher shop. Meatman whimpered a last-minute plea. "Snake, don't do this. I'll make it up to you. I'll pay back twice what I took."

Snake looked at him as if what he said were sounds from an inanimate object. Meatman moaned, and his body shook. Sweat trickled down his face, and a dribble of drool departed the corner of his mouth.

Snake casually put on rubber gloves, picked up a small beaker of fluid, and motioned for Gut to grasp Meatman's hair. Snake's alias, *The Acid Man*, became clear.

There was a slight sizzle and an ugly smell. Meatman's screams rivaled the sound of a braking locomotive.

Snake patiently waited for the screaming to subside, and Meatman progressed into a sniveling state of semi-consciousness. He surveyed his audience, seeming to focus on each grim witness in turn.

"And that, gentlemen, is what happens, and it can be worse—much worse." Snake turned to Gut. "When Meatman stops whining, tell him he will still pay me back twice what he took, or we will come for his other eye."

Chapter 3

Dee

Washington, DC

Agent Derrell "Dee" Boyd hated these meetings with the big dogs of the FBI, but he had hints this one might hold some real potential. Sitting across a large desk from him was Hal Bennett, the executive assistant director for the FBI's Criminal, Cyber, Response and Services Branch. Whatever he was called, without question, he could make or break Dee's FBI career.

Bennett picked up a file and studied it. "Agent Derrell Boyd, I'm told you go by Dee."

"Yes, sir. I hardly know my real name. It's a southern thing. At The Citadel, I was sometimes known as Deeboy, but of course as a Black man, that wouldn't work at the FBI."

Bennett laughed and warmed to the conversation. "Well, Dee, you have distinguished yourself and the FBI in an amazing and successful operation while you were undercover for the past year in Atlanta."

Dee looked around the clean, organized space—all the distinguished pictures. It was hard to imagine the degenerate lowlife characters who had been his associates for the past year. "Thank you, sir. I must say it was stressful, and many days I wasn't sure I would live to be here, but we rolled up a large drug operation of the worst sort. I'm glad to be away from the trash I've been dealing with."

"I want to give you my personal thanks and relay for the FBI their thanks. Your dedication and service are a large factor for our decision to promote you to Assistant Special Agent in Charge of the field office in Columbia. You'll be second-in-command for the FBI for all of South Carolina."

For a moment Dee couldn't speak. A tear progressed down his cheek. He had expected praise and maybe a promotion, but for a Black kid from Six Mile—

"Sir, I am honored," Dee said.

"Say no more. Normally, you would be getting the next month off to relax, recharge, and make your move to Columbia, but you have a new job you need to get up to speed on. Take a week to visit home, clear your head, and come back to DC for some high-level procedures and indoctrination. Of course, your promotion was deserved on performance alone, but there's an added plus to your Columbia position. We're having a narcotics increase in the Southeast. You're an expert on the drug trade, and we need you there."

Dee flew straight from DC to Charleston. He needed to tell someone. He thought of his ex-wife and was sad that part of his life was gone. But, what the hell, she didn't like the FBI anyway. Of course, his mom would be happy for his success, and he looked forward to the feeling of pride when he told her, even though it would give her another opportunity to caution him about being careful. His best friend, Scrap, was where he could unwind and celebrate his promotion.

Scrap was the most honest and principled man he knew. Man, he couldn't wait to relax in an environment a light year away from the sleazy undercover operation.

He spent Friday night in Six-Mile and called Scrap Saturday morning. "Hey, dumbhead, you not sleeping in, are you?"

He loved to call him dumbhead, smack, doowilly, or knob. Throughout the history of The Citadel, these words were the accepted way for an upperclassman to address a freshman. When he was a plebe, Scrap was a sophomore and used to lay them on heavy.

"Well, I'll be a suck-egg dog, if it ain't a voice from the past. I thought you had died, and the FBI was covering it up."

God, it felt good to hear his voice.

"Truth is, where I've been, I could've died. And they probably would've tried to cover it up."

"Are you here, or is this some mystery call that can't be traced?"

"I'm here and armed with news of my superior skills and talent. I'm ready to go shooting and drinking."

"You're on. Come by the house for lunch, after which I'll wax your conceited ass on the range."

At lunch he filled Scrap in on the part of his Atlanta operation that was public. "All I can tell you about it is what was in the papers."

"I didn't see anything about it. I'm so covered up I mostly skim the paper. Guess you'll have to tell me in your own words."

"If you're so covered up, you must be making a lot of money."

Scrap grimaced. "Not really. Just busy."

Following a great two hours of shooting at the indoor range, they sought out the sleaziest bar they could find. The place had several wooden booths along with a seated bar. It smelled of stale beer, peanut hulls, and wood shavings on the floor—and maybe a whiff from the latrine.

With two beers, they sat at the bar. Scrap turned to him and smiled. "So, what did the feds do for you after you risked your life for a year?"

"They gave me a week before I have to be back in DC. That's why we're sitting here drinking beer."

"Bullshit, come on, I know there's more."

Dee reached over and scooped a handful of peanuts. "You're looking at the number two guy with the FBI in South Carolina."

"Holy mother of a mule. This is the same Black man from Six Mile. The same cadet whose ass I saved at The Citadel?"

"The same—hopefully. And I still owe you, my friend." In his junior year, Dee was about to be expelled on an honor violation created by a vindictive female cadet. Scrap, as his company commander, had investigated the charge and defended him. He was acquitted and went on to graduate with distinction.

Dee would not have noticed the two men sitting in one of the booths if it wasn't for the one facing him was shifting his eyes all over the bar area. He had both hands under the table and leaned in when he talked.

"I'll still be in Columbia," Dee said, "and the secretary you talked to when you were trying to find me before, she'll now be my private secretary."

"Damn, that's good news. Another round on me."

The shifty-eyed man turned toward the inside of

the booth, and Dee got a flash of a concealed weapon. He doubted it was legal. He clearly saw one of them passing something under the table. The shifty-eyed man then brought his hands up and began openly counting money. *Damn, they're making a trade, right here in my hometown.*

Dee scrolled through his phone contacts. "God, how I hate drugs."

"What's up?"

Dee turned to Scrap, who had a puzzled look, and spoke in a low voice. "Scrap, listen to me. This is the Mt. Pleasant police number. Call it and tell them to get over here. Tell them I'm holding three drug dealers for them."

He got off his barstool and walked past the booth as if he were on his way to the head. Passing the booth, he turned and threw down his badge, raised his shirt, and put his hand on his Glock 23. "FBI. Hands on the table."

The man on the far side obeyed, but the one across from him scooted off the seat, trying to run. Dee hit him in the jaw so hard the man's head snapped back, and he fell unconscious into the booth. Dee heard a scuffle behind him. He turned in time to see Scrap standing over a man who evidently was the recipient of his friend's famous right hook.

"Pull that gun and you're a dead man."

Scrap held his little pocket .380 on a surprised thug who was halfway into the act of drawing his gun while he was still on the floor.

The third man—a sleeper. I should have known.

"Now you guys might have noticed—" Dee motioned for the third man to get in the booth and put his hands on the table. "—I have not drawn my gun because when I draw, I usually shoot. One more bad move, and some, or all of you, will die."

Four Mt. Pleasant police arrived. "Great response time, guys," Dee said. "I am Agent Boyd with the FBI. My badge is on the table. I don't want to be involved in this pinch. I have not made an arrest. You guys can read them their rights and take full credit. I believe you'll find drugs and money."

The three thugs were cuffed and moved out of the booth. Underneath, the police found cocaine and the purchase money. They were read their rights and escorted out. Dee joined Scrap, who was watching from the bar.

"Well done," the bartender said, "drinks on the house."

Dee took a sip of beer and gave Scrap a good hard look. "I probably shouldn't have done that. I'm on vacation, and it was a local problem, but I've been tainted. I hate drugs. I hate what they did to some of my schoolmates. I hate the lowlife bastards dealing in them. I hate the dirty money. And these sonofabitches were doing it right under my nose, in our hometown. This is our town."

"Okay, my friend, I get it, but I think these assholes would say you are one mean, uncompromising mother."

"I wouldn't say that. When I was undercover in Atlanta, I had to compromise my principles every day to get to the greater good. Many times, I've thought of The Citadel honor code: I will not lie, cheat, or steal, nor tolerate those who do. I violated the code every day because my responsibility was to lop off the heads at the top. You're fortunate, Scrap. You don't have to sleep with that. You still have the luxury of a clear-cut right and wrong."

Dee was happy his old friend never had to face the same conundrums he had faced on his undercover work. He hoped he never would.

Scrap drained his beer, caught the bartender's eye, and held up two fingers for another round. "It was right what you did."

"Thanks, buddy, and thanks for what you did. You're the real fighter. I still remember the time you cold-cocked the guy at Big John's for insulting your wife, and I had to save your ass from going to jail."

Scrap smiled. "Well, at the time, it helped that you were working for the Charleston Police. Your hot button is drugs. I guess mine is protecting Beth and Emma."

Dee savored his beer. "Truth is, ever since The Citadel, you've been the one who always had my back. Someday…maybe someday…"

He lifted his glass and touched Scrap's.

Chapter 4

Rex

Jacksonville, Florida

Rex stumbled outside into the heat. It was growing dark, and his hands fumbled for a cigarette, dropping it on the ground.

When he stood back up, Toad was standing there with a smirk on his face. He flipped open a Zippo with a steady hand. "Well, flyboy, did you learn anything from Meatman's screams?"

"I don't see any humor in this," Rex said. "How could Meatman have possibly cheated Snake out of four hundred thousand dollars?"

"You shouldn't ask too many questions, but just so you understand the lesson, I'll tell you a little about what he did. Snake was moving blow in sides of beef from Guadalajara, Mexico. Because the beef came from a USDA-approved packing house, it was not inspected again before it arrived at a butcher shop in Gonzales, Texas, which was owned by none other than our screaming Mr. Meatman Mancini. The problem was, it left Mexico with ten kilos in each side and arrived at Meatman's place with only nine."

The cigarette calmed Rex enough to speak without showing his fear. "So how do they know it was

Meatman that stole the drugs?"

"Snake sent a couple of his boys to follow the beef truck all the way from Mexico to its first stop just north of Laredo. They caught Mancini's punks in the act of removing one kilo from each side of beef."

Rex feared the answer, but he had to ask. "What did they do with Meatman's punks?"

"One was killed and hung on a meat hook in the refrigerator truck to give Meatman a hint that all was not well when he opened the door to the cooler. The other was forced to continue driving to the butcher shop, but on Snake's orders, he too died a slow, painful death while Meatman watched."

Rex nodded—reluctantly. "It's all about fear, isn't it? Everywhere that Snake and Gut operate, people are running scared.

"You got it, hotshot, and if you're smart, you should be running scared yourself."

Rex *was* scared, and it tested his courage to even ask questions, but he needed to better understand the lay of the land.

"So, Toad, you've worked for Snake a long time. Why is he called Snake?"

"Listen, Ace. I ain't about to tell you trash on Snake, but I'll tell you what you need to know and what Snake wants you to know. He has no feeling for anybody or anything. You ever seen one of them nature shows, where the Nile crocodile grabs the wildebeest?"

"Yeah, I've seen that. Pulls it into the river and drowns it."

"Well, you keep that picture in mind because that croc and Snake have the same amount of feeling. It's the eyes. When Snake is about to destroy some poor slob, he stares at them without blinking, like a pit viper about to strike. No joke."

Snake appeared at the door, giving Rex a jolt. He beckoned them to step into his office. Rex would as soon go to a cannibal convention.

Smoking a cigar, Snake took a seat behind his large, teakwood desk. He blew out a puff and placed it in a replica of a skull substituting as an ashtray. Rex and Toad stood in front, waiting to be addressed. Although Toad did not horse around with the boss man, he nevertheless seemed to be fairly comfortable around him.

Rex, now knowing the story behind Snake's alias, did not make eye contact. He sensed he had entered hell, and the devil was about to speak. His eyes wandered around the room. The dark wooden walls were fitted with full bookcases. A few gold-framed diplomas hung opposite them. Behind Snake's head was a painting of a gory medieval torture scene. Rex had seen something similar in a book once. It probably replicated Catholic judgment during the Spanish Inquisition. A man with his mouth open in a silent scream was being burned alive at the stake. Chills shivered down Rex's spine.

Snake's unblinking eyes bore into Toad, flicked once, and settled on Rex. "I have a mission for you two that should prove lucrative for all involved. Rex, I want you to sail your boat to Haiti's northern port of Fort Liberte and pick up one metric ton of one hundred percent pure Florida snow. You'll find a poverty-stricken town of about thirty thousand, not far from the border of Dominica. Anchor in the harbor well away from any civilization and wait for Toad to contact you."

The piercing gaze caused Rex to look away, feeling like a puppy that's peed on the carpet and afraid to make eye contact with his furious master. But Rex dared to speak, hoping to relieve the tension. "Will I be sailing alone?"

"You'll be alone on the trip to Haiti, but Toad will join you at your anchorage and supervise the loading of our cargo, which will arrive in waterproof aluminum suitcases. The two of you will sail from there to a small marina outside of Beaufort, North Carolina. Before you leave for Haiti, you need to position your plane at Beaufort's little airport."

Rex was surprised to see Toad frown occasionally at the instructions, and in a final show of courage, Toad actually interrupted Snake. "Boss, I think it's in South Carolina and is pronounced, *bew-fert.*

Snake pursed his lips and gave Toad an unblinking stare. "Try to display your ignorance outside of my office. It's pronounced *Bo-fort,* and it's in North Carolina. Both places are spelled the same.

Toad sniffed twice. "Sorry, didn't know about the one in North Carolina. Will I be making the flight back?"

"You fly commercially to Haiti, catch the local transportation that will be provided, and you'll accompany Rex on his boat to Beaufort. You'll also escort my money with Rex on his airplane. I'll give you detailed instructions later. In Beaufort, you'll swap the cargo for US currency arriving in waterproof aluminum suitcases identical to your cargo containers. You'll fly the money to a yet-to-be-determined destination in the Jacksonville area. Rex, I'll leave it up to you to plan your trip at sea and in the air. I want you to avoid all maritime traffic areas. Understand though, Toad is your boss. He will fill you in on further instructions. On completion, you'll receive five percent in cash."

Rex was still shaken from Meatman's torture. He was afraid of Snake and hated Toad. But this arrangement paid beyond his wildest dreams—and it would make Mona very happy.

"We will kick this off in about a week," Snake said. "In the meantime, get your boat and airplane ready to go when I say."

Rex would be responsible for transporting the drugs by sailboat and money by airplane, so he knew there were questions he should be asking, but having witnessed Snake's cruelty, he wanted to have as little interaction with him as possible.

Snake diverted his attention to a drawer in his desk. Toad looked uneasy, which caused Rex to momentarily panic, but Snake withdrew a notepad and studied it, leaving Rex with his brain racing.

My God, I'll make as much on this trip alone as the cost of my airplane and boat. A thousand kilos of cocaine would bring close to $20 million. His take should be about $1 million. He needed the money to keep Mona. Even now, he yearned for her. Rex was not sure he could hang on to Mona if she knew the truth about him. He had misled her, giving her the impression he moved in the circles of the rich. He had met her at a stopover on a shakeout cruise for a new seventy-foot Hatteras. The boat belonged to a rich dot-com entrepreneur who was on the trip. Mona believed the boat belonged to Rex.

During Rex's long and intense training to become a proficient pilot, he witnessed his contemporaries go on to become airline pilots and even a few rise to work for major carriers paying top salaries. Deep down, this caused him to feel inadequate, but if he ultimately made far more money than these successful pilots, it could make up for the prestige he otherwise lacked. And Mona would stay, none the wiser.

Snake turned to Toad. "Go tell Gut to come in my office, and when he comes, I want Bullethead to come with him."

"Roger that, I think he's finishing up with Meatman. The screaming stopped. Either he's done, or he killed him.

"That's all for now." Snake waved them off.

Rex nodded but kept quiet. He left scared—greedy and scared. *Who is this Snake demon, this sociopathic Acid Man?*

Chapter 5

Snake

Jacksonville, Florida

Snake worked on a spreadsheet for the numerous steps that needed to fall in place for a successful cocaine operation. Irritated that Gut kept him waiting, he couldn't concentrate. He cut the cap from a hand-rolled cigar, moistened the head, and toasted the foot. Propping his feet up on his desk for another smoke, he considered firing the crazy bastard but discarded the idea because he needed him. He knew Gut often inflicted some extra pain for his own pleasure when the show was over, but he usually didn't mind the add-ons unless it changed the desired effect.

Gut and Snake went all the way back to law school, where they met after Gut was accepted straight out of the state pen. The two things Gut got out of prison were law school credits and a huge, powerful, weight-trained body, but nevertheless, he was under Snake's control. Snake exercised his command over his thugs the same way he had seen a cowboy exercising command over a thousand-pound horse: he had the spurs and did not hesitate to use them.

He thought about the difference between himself and Gut. While growing up, Gut was severely abused.

He now drew pleasure from abusing others. On the other hand, Snake reaped no pleasure from pouring acid in Meatman's right eye. For Snake, torture was about cause and effect. The torture was a lesson to both Meatman and the audience. Snake didn't care about the agony he caused one way or the other. In fact, he had never felt sympathy for anyone's misfortune. The pain Gut loved to inflict served Snake's purpose of striking fear into the hearts of those that might be inclined to stray.

Gut entered the office and greeted his boss with no facial expression. "Good show in there, Snake. I think your boys get the picture, and Meatman will see that picture better with one eye than he ever did with two. I plugged him in for a little shock treatment. Right now, he's a mess, but he'll recover. I told him his new name was Rib-eye, but he didn't seem to make the connection to beef and his lost eye."

"If I wanted electric torture—" Snake rotated his cigar over the ashtray. "—I would have ordered it."

"Sorry, but I told him to stop whining about his eye, but he kept on until it pissed me off."

Snake returned to the computer spreadsheet for a couple of seconds but closed the lid.

Bullethead came in looking uneasy and stood next to Gut, his bald shaved head beaded with sweat. Snake was pleased he was uneasy. A strike could come without warning.

"Gut, sit down. I have a few things I need your take on."

He left Bullethead standing on purpose.

"Sure, Snake, you can trust me to help any way I can."

"I trust nobody."

Snake surmised Gut was probably in a good mood because he'd had the opportunity to give the traumatized Meatman another dose of pain. Being in a good mood for Gut did not mean he smiled or showed any expression. It meant he seemed to feel a certain sense of euphoria after someone else suffered.

"Do you think Meatman's howling is enough to send our message outside?" Snake said.

"Yah. This time tomorrow, word of The Acid Man striking again will be on the street."

Snake turned his gaze on Bullethead. "What do you think?"

Bullethead sniffed, wiped his nose, and sniffed again. "Man, it was enough to scare the devil."

Snake looked at him with disgust and continued talking to Gut. Even though he was responsible for destroying thousands of lives with his drugs, he despised drug use. Bullethead was known to be a few bricks short of a load, but Snake knew he was smart enough to know something wasn't right. Bullethead was like a rat that, every now and then, got a whiff of a cat.

"You know my rules, Gut. Number one is fear and respect. Otherwise, somebody will steal your business—rat you out. Right alongside the fear factor is the principle of never putting your fingerprints on anything. If things go wrong, somebody else takes the fall."

Gut was fucked up in the head, to be sure, but he wasn't dumb. He had a law degree, and Snake needed his input. But because of Gut's sick obsessions, there were times Snake wanted to make it clear what the philosophy was in running the drug trading business.

"Taking the fall. Guess that's my exposure, huh, Boss?"

"I pay you well. I have the contacts, reputation, and good credit. Besides, I'm the thinker. Thinkers always make the big bucks. I developed a unique smuggling strategy and didn't follow the rest of the trade. The Feds have never figured it out. We have ways of transporting that no one else does."

Gut scratched the back of his head, and his gigantic bicep all but split his shirt sleeve. "Okay, I get it. You got the organization, and I work for it."

Snake focused on Bullethead, who was shifting nervously from one foot to the other. Beads of sweat appeared on his shaved head. Snake noticed Bullethead's eyes were dilated. He glared at him and turned back to Gut. "That's right," Snake said. "And if my memory serves me right, you came here looking for a job because you lost your law license by tampering with evidence. I got no problem with hiding the killer's knife in the bar cushion, but you got caught. So, you're working for me."

Snake was always looking out for some miscreant to stab him in the back. He wanted to make sure Gut knew his place even though he was asking for his advice.

"I get your point. Now how can I help?"

Snake felt a trace of irritation. He let out a breath and continued. "Although we have done this Haiti route before, this time we will be moving one of our largest shipments. What do you think about it?"

Gut looked across the large desk to the torture picture on the back wall. His expressionless face seemed to light up. Snake knew Gut enjoyed the art, and Snake himself found the picture edifying to his business philosophy. Gut probably liked the realistic depiction of the victim's mouth open in an agonizing scream of pain.

"Last time, we had no problems," Gut said, "and we did it without Toad. It's good for another shot. It's so off the beaten path I doubt the Feds are on to it, and even if they are, we so rarely do it, they would have to be tipped to take the resources to cover it."

Still standing, Bullethead was ignored. The more the conversation discussed details of the business, the more his eyes darted around the room. He scratched his balls and cracked his knuckles and sniffed. Snake noticed but continued the suspense. It was his routine— the cat with a trembling trapped mouse.

"Okay, let's talk about something else," Snake said. "We need to start thinking of more ways to launder money. With this Haiti-North Carolina move, we will need to clean a lot of money. Also, I don't like that we are passing up millions on the opioid trade. I want you to see if you can develop some contacts."

"Opioids are a good business," Gut said. "And the markup's huge. I'll put out some feelers—try to find an operator who's not connected to a big cartel, kill everybody involved, and take over the business."

Unlike Toad, who killed for a reason, although it may be a small reason, Gut killed for pleasure, which caused Snake some apprehension.

"Be careful, Gut. I don't want a turf war, but I like the fact that opioids are so addictive. Once you get the market hooked, they're a cash cow until they die. Whatever we do, we need to keep it away from here in

Jacksonville. The users are the saps we depend on but keep them away from me."

Snake turned his unblinking gaze to Bullethead. "Do you have anything to say?"

Bullethead sniffed again. "Ah no, no, sir. I—I don't get—"

"That's too bad because those will be your last words."

Quick as a striking rattler, Snake pulled his gun and shot Bullethead between the eyes. Blood spattered onto Gut's right shoulder.

"Jesus, Snake. What the fuck?"

"He's a user," Snake said, his voice calm. "Bullethead's elimination is risk mitigation." Smiling at his rhyme, he looked over at Gut.

With his ham size hand, Gut wiped the blood from his ear. "Sonofabitch should've known."

Snake nodded his head toward the dead heap at the end of his desk. "Now drag him out of here and show him to the others."

Chapter 6

Scrap

Mt. Pleasant, South Carolina

Feeling caged in my garage, I thought over my meeting at the bank, and panic set in. What would I say to Beth? I dreaded facing her. Credit was my lifeline, but thanks to Howard Parks, I had failed. It wasn't that Beth knew this, it was I knew it, and she knew me. I was home early but unsure what to do next. I sat in my truck under the house for another half-hour. Brainstorming a lot of ideas, I came up with nothing short of winning the lottery.

I couldn't just sit there; Beth may have already known I had arrived. I placed my hand on the door handle feeling the excess acid in my stomach. Reluctantly I exited, but to delay a while longer, I stepped to the back of my house overlooking the marsh.

The marsh was soothing, and in times of stress, I was always drawn to it. I looked out at several great white egrets feeding in a small slew and thought how unfair my financial failure was. One of the egrets spread its great white wings and, with several bobs of the long neck, took flight. It only had one leg.

I always knew nature could be unfair, but I had never translated it to me.

I climbed the outside stairs to the first floor and entered the kitchen.

Beth greeted me with a kiss. "Well, Emma, look who came home early. Tonight, we will eat like a family."

For some reason, I felt guilty. I knew if I talked, Beth would ask me what was wrong. I needed to get away. I turned to my vivacious little Emma. "Hi, Pum'kin, what's up?"

"Daddy, you look sad."

Christ, even my daughter could tell. I had to get out of the house. I managed to utter, "Hey, ah…long tiring day, Sweetheart, but seeing your shining face makes it all better." I turned back to Beth. "I need some exercise. I'm going for a run."

"Well, ain't you the man? You all right? You look stressed."

"I'm fine. Be back in an hour."

By the time I got back from my run and showered, I felt more relaxed and able to have a normal family meal. After dinner I helped Beth with the dishes, but Emma pulled me away.

"Daddy, come see the picture I drew of a blue crab."

It was a good likeness. She had drawn the three legs behind the large claws and even had the swimmer legs at the back. "Sweetheart, you have your mother's talent. That is an excellent blue crab."

I occupied myself with scrubbing a dark spot on a pot. Beth casually moved a wet plate, allowing it to drip down my neck on the way to the dishwasher. I knew where this was going, but my heart was not in it. Instead of turning it into a normal grab-ass confrontation, I avoided the challenge by turning into a blue crab and chased Emma around the house. She squealed and bounced over the coach. I crab-crawled after her. So into the chase, I forgot my problems.

At bedtime I kissed Emma, and Beth put her to bed. I turned on the TV to watch some news, but now alone, my financial problems dominated my thoughts. Beth returned and watched the news, but ten minutes later, I could tell she was getting restless. I turned the TV off, and she gave me a look that I understood even in my preoccupied condition. By the time we reached the bedroom, I was turned on. She faced me inside the door and gave a mysterious little shudder, her skirt falling to the floor. We hit the bed together and undressed in seconds, but in the middle of our passion, disaster hit. She mumbled something about "sexy man…good provider…I feel so safe."

It was not exactly coherent, but it was enough to lock my mind on a feeling of insecurity for my family. The fiscal problems flooded my mind. My hands quit roaming, and I became quiet. She grew still. An agonizing minute passed—it got embarrassing, and I rolled off, looking at the ceiling.

I turned my head to see Beth also looking at the ceiling, but her face was contorted into a pained expression. Did she feel rejected? Maybe I was so sensitive it was my imagination. Maybe she thought I was diddling my secretary.

"What is wrong? Are you feeling guilty about something? Is it Sheryl?"

Now that she mentioned Sheryl, I did feel guilty because I had admired her ass and even fantasized from time to time. I got angry to cover my humiliation.

"Damn it, nothing's wrong."

There was silence.

"Well," I finally said, "yes, there is, but it's not your fault, and it has nothing to do with Sheryl. This isn't about you, and you need to get off this Sheryl thing." It came out a little too strong, and I instantly regretted my tone.

"Have you forgotten we were making love? I thought I was involved, and if you want to get off this Sheryl thing, you need to quit looking at her ass. Fire her."

I leaped out of bed and turned toward her. "I told you this has nothing to do with Sheryl."

With a defiant look, she stood and put on a silk robe. "Well, then it must be me."

I clenched my jaw and tried to get control of my frustration. I wanted to scream, lash out but not knowing where or at what. "C'mon, Beth. It's about how my mind seized on your 'good provider, feeling safe' mumbling."

She was silent for a good ten seconds—her face grew softer. "Oh. I'm sorry I was short. What's going on in that head of yours?"

I let out my breath in exasperation, feeling like a child being told it was all right if he missed the fly ball. I sat on the edge of the bed.

"It's the business," I murmured. "Money is short. The building slump has lasted much longer than I anticipated. I'm afraid I won't be a good provider."

She walked around to the foot of the bed. "We had a housing meltdown and a recession. You can't blame yourself."

"Beth, that's an excuse. Remember the most

poignant lesson from The Citadel: 'No excuse, sir.' No matter what causes you to fail, there's no excuse."

"This isn't The Citadel, and it's not the military."

Like Adam from the bible, I was ashamed of my nakedness. I got up, dressed, and sat down in a chair. "I know you don't want to hear this again, but you need to understand. There are two principles that were drilled into me there and that I live by—accept responsibility and follow the honor code. I'm committed to provide for and protect my family in an honorable way. Anything short is an excuse."

"I know, I know, you're an honorable man, but the housing meltdown isn't an excuse. Life is a lot more complicated than a few slogans you learned at military school. It was an economic collapse few saw coming, and even fewer thought would go on for years."

I was angry and frustrated, but I didn't feel like escalating the situation. "I'm just under a lot of stress right now. Things will turn soon."

She motioned for me to sit on the bed. Normally I would have felt like a herd bull, but now I was dejected, not only over the good provider thing but over failing as a lover.

"Maybe," she said, "I'll get the new job with the education department. It will pay well, and if I don't, I can always go back to teaching."

She didn't understand. I was in the hole for millions.

"The new job would be great, but if you don't get it, things will work out. If you don't get the new job, you need to stay on the school board. Your work there is too important."

"Well, maybe it would help if you fired Sheryl, and

I did the financial stuff too."

Shit, here we go, back to getting rid of Sheryl.

I shook my head. "She has a ton of stuff to do. No way would you have enough time to add her job to everything else you do."

She sat with me on the bed and rubbed my shoulders, insisting I tell her more about my stress. I told her about some but not all of the business problems. I didn't share with her the full magnitude of the financial disaster ahead, nor the impending doom I felt whenever I entered my office. I did not tell her how the loss of control made me feel like an airline passenger looking out the window at a burning engine on the wing.

Chapter 7

Beth

Mt. Pleasant, South Carolina

Beth had conducted many of these counseling sessions herself, but when it was about her own child, she was stressed. The school principal, Fay Norris, and Emma's primary teacher, Lara Trish, were at the meeting.

Norris opened the meeting. "Beth, let me take this opportunity to thank you for the good work you have accomplished in bringing us all aboard to fight bullying in the schools. Since you joined the school board, we all have benefited from your hard work and wise guidance."

"Thank you. But right now, I'm concerned about my child."

"Yes, I understand…Lara will explain what she has learned."

"Beth and I have already had discussions," Lara said, "but not about the testing. First, let me say that Emma is a charming, very bright girl. But all indications are that her brain is wired slightly differently than most children."

"Lara, are we talking about Dyslexia?"

Fingering her pencil, the teacher paused before

36

answering. "It does appear that Emma's test results show a strong indication of Dyslexia. You and I have already discussed other evidence of this condition."

Actually, Beth had pretty much determined Emma was struggling with some level of Dyslexia. She had studied learning disabilities in her graduate program.

"What is your advice?"

The teacher opened her hand in the principal's direction. "Mrs. Norris, you want to address that?"

"In the public school, we have programs to help, but if you can afford it, the Reynolds Guidance School concentrates on these problems with great success. This condition can be compensated for if attacked at an early age."

Her worry over the unknown money situation created pangs of fear.

"How much are we talking about?"

"Don't hold me to this, but I believe the total runs about fifty thousand a year."

Beth hesitated a few seconds and decided not to engage in more discussion. She determined that, if need be, she would quit her school board job and return to teaching.

"I'll talk this over with my husband. Thank you for showing so much interest."

Principal Norris added her thoughts as they stood to leave. "Beth, I feel I should relate my observation on children with Dyslexia. If treated properly, most children will have a normal outcome and eventually have no problem mainstreaming with everyday students. However, if the child is not provided with special education, the child will fall behind and become frustrated. There is a good chance she will be impacted for the rest of his or her life."

Even though Beth knew this, it still caused her chest to tighten. She was relieved to know Emma's condition was known and treatable, but she dreaded the conversation she was going to have with Scrap. No question, Emma had to go to the Reynolds School, but in the back of her mind, she knew there was some sort of money problem at home. Scrap was being evasive, and she wasn't sure what it meant. In the past Scrap was an open book, but lately Beth wasn't confident of her intuition. *If that bitch seduces my husband—I'll kill her.*

Beth arrived home deep in thought, stopped at her drive, and checked the mail. Her heart leapt. The heading on the letter read, Office of the State Superintendent for Education, Columbia, South Carolina. She ripped the letter open.

Dear Mrs. Scruggs,

You recently interviewed with this office for the job of Assistant State Superintendent for Education, state of South Carolina. We would like for you to return for a second interview at your earliest convenience. Please contact the above telephone number to set up your appointment.

This was it. Bar some unknown development, she was going to be hired. By the time Scrap arrived home, Beth was pacing the floor. Emma was home from school and had just come in from outside. "Mama, you look like an animal in a cage."

"Perceptive girl—now run along. Your dad just came home, and we need to talk."

"What does perceptive mean?"

Beth smiled at Emma and let out a long breath.

"Emma, I love you. We'll talk about it later. Go play in your room."

Scrap was in a sour mood. No, he seemed more dejected than sour, which was rare for him. It was almost as if he was losing his confidence, something that had always been innate to him.

"Give me a kiss and sit down," she said, "we have a lot to discuss."

"Jeez, Beth, are we going to do this financial thing again?"

This wasn't a good time, but this discussion had to happen. Beth took a deep breath. "I had the conference about Emma today."

"Ah, let me guess. She's too bright, and the school curriculum isn't challenging enough to stimulate her active mind."

"Well, that could be true, but she also has some Dyslexia, and it's causing her difficulty in school. It's not that something is wrong. Her brain is wired differently. She's a smart, gifted little girl, but she will need help learning to cope with her differences."

"What kind of help?"

She was so keyed up she couldn't sit. She moved a plate to the kitchen counter. "It's a special school called Reynolds Guidance School that teaches children how to read and write using their skills. Eventually, she will be able to cope well enough to go back to a regular school."

"Are you sure about this school change? She seems to enjoy her current school, and she has some nice friends."

"She doesn't just have *some* Dyslexia. She has a problem, and we need to address it."

"Okay, sweetheart, if you think that's what she needs, I'm all in. How do we enroll her in this special school?"

Beth went over to the kitchen window. It was starting to rain, the mood in the room was not right, but she couldn't figure out what she needed to do. "The school is private and will cost fifty thousand a year. I'm not sure we have the money for that. I know you're stressed over money right now."

"Oh, come on, it's back to the finance thing again."

He brushed her off as if finances were unimportant, but she saw panic cross his face. She knew he would cover it up by getting angry.

"Okay, okay, let's sleep on it." She handed him the letter. "I have some good news also."

He scanned the letter. "Wow, Beth, you're going to be a big shot. This is great. Now you'll have some horsepower behind your projects. Tell me again how this job in Columbia works from here."

"I'll have an office in Charleston and go to Columbia only once a week. About once a month, I'll spend the night in Columbia. It's only a two-hour drive. In the summer, when Emma's out of school, you and Emma could come with me if you have the time.

"Sounds like it would work. I'm excited for you."

But Scrap didn't look excited. He still looked different and a little defeated.

"There's one thing that bothers me," Beth said. "Remember we talked about the last interview and were surprised they asked me so many questions about your business. If something is about to change, it wouldn't be fair for me to mislead them. You know how sensitive these politicians can be. My boss over there holds an elective office."

Scrap's jaw muscles pulsed, his face grew red, and his eyes were slinging arrows. "Goddamn it, you do your thing and I'll take care of business. Tell them my business is sound and move on."

Chapter 8

Scrap

Mt. Pleasant, South Carolina

I woke up to an overhanging dread. Yesterday I fully intended to have a discussion with Beth about cosigning my bonding. But after she brought up Emma's school problem and her new job interview, I knew the timing was wrong. Like everybody else associated with the construction business, the bonding company was nervous. To secure the bond for a large school project, they required my personal signature—and my wife's.

I went down into my garage work area under the house to kill time until Beth took Emma to school. Tinkering in my shop was always relaxing. I had accumulated a lot of tools and prided myself on being able to make or fix anything. I especially enjoyed tweaking firearms and had actually made guns from various parts bought off the internet. Now my heart was not in it, so I went back upstairs and waited for Beth to come out.

"Hey," she said. "What are you still doing here? I thought you had left for work."

She seemed to be in a good mood, but I was still dreading something I considered a failure on my part.

Come on. You have to do this. "I had to wait for you because…because I forgot to get your signature on some paperwork."

Shit, that sounded phony. I had to tell it straight.

"Ah…Beth, I'm sorry about this, and I hate to ask, but the bonding company requires your signature to grant the bond on the school project."

She frowned and took the papers. "I know you're stressed over money problems, but I don't think it would be wise for me to sign this. Wouldn't that obligate any assets of mine as well as yours?"

"I never thought of assets as yours or mine," I said. "I thought they were ours. If we both don't sign, we won't get the bond, and with no bond, I'll lose the job. Our financial situation would be worse."

Tapping the pen on the table, she looked at the signature line like it was something about to bite. My face flushed with shame.

"But what about my parents' farm in Kansas? I'm an only child. It might someday obligate that."

I knew this was a real risk, but I had to secure the school job. I'd make one more try and then say fuck it. "Beth, I need this bonding now. Your farm inheritance is in the future. As soon as I get my finances stronger, I'll take your name off the bonding."

"First, I want you to tell me the truth about what is going on with the business."

I became frustrated. I wasn't going there now. "Look, this isn't about my financial situation. It's more about the holdover fear from the recession."

"Give me a day to think about this."

I jumped up and went for the door. "Okay, we'll talk tomorrow."

I hated to ask Beth to cosign the bonding. But in the end, though she didn't fully understand my crises, it was her I was trying to protect. On the drive to the office, my stomach was already causing pain. I took a detour and went to visit a job site and have a quick lunch. It was one o'clock when I arrived at the office.

Passing through the front reception area, I smiled and spoke to Sheryl, my efficient, sexy, thirty-four-year-old secretary who had a penchant for short skirts and dancing with herself while waiting for the copy machine, but today I noticed she had on some kind of thin pants outfit. Seeking the seclusion of my luxurious office, I closed the door behind me and sat in my leather swivel chair, looking at blurred raindrops on the window.

A gentle tap on my door. Sheryl came in and placed the mail on my desk. "You don't look happy."

"Just give me the mail and let me see what asshole wants money today."

She left, closing the door behind her. I opened a letter from the law firm representing my bank. Halfway through, I went to the john and threw up the chicken wrap I'd had for lunch. Returning to the protection of my office, I resettled into my position of gloom.

They're going to take me down. The lawyers are coming after me if I don't pay the bank. *And I can't pay the bank.*

That son-of-bitch Howard had to know about this letter when we had our disastrous meeting. I was the captain of a sinking ship and could hear the rats scurrying as they left.

I had to do something, and soon, or my whole construction business would collapse. All of the hard work of the last seven years would go swirling down the drain.

As usual, the banks were slow to see the gathering financial storm that would blow across the entire nation. Howard Parks and Cordgrass National Bank had continued to lend me money until I was swimming in debt. Then they turned mean.

The mail that had caused me to upchuck lay on my desk like a coiled cottonmouth. I eyed it as if it was about to strike. I could taste the stomach bile in my throat. Finally, I used my arm to sweep it off my desk into the trash. I turned back to contemplate the water trickling down the glass.

I picked up a picture of Emma and Beth on the beach. *I can't let this happen.*

The letter threatened to foreclose on everything mortgaged to the bank, which was about everything. I had thirty days to pay—impossible. They hinted at a lawsuit that would bring on the auditors, and there was no telling what illegal activity those eggheads could dig up. In short, the letter was a well-crafted threat: find the last three overdue bank payments of $263,000 each or face litigation with the possibility of incarceration. Years of building a stellar reputation are going to disappear in months. Beth and Emma will not have a good provider. I worried if Beth would still think of me as an honorable man.

Emma is going to need braces. The dentist said it at her last visit. What about her new expensive private school? She had to go. It was my responsibility to provide.

My manhood was being stripped away, and this fear about finances was tainting my values. I had already fudged some figures. My long-held and sometimes sanctimonious sense of integrity was disintegrating at my feet. Two years ago, I started doing what I had always preached against: making bank draws to cover expenses related to projects other than the one securing the loan. I was forced to build a project, not because it made sense, but to get more bank draws. I went from that to tweaking my financials to keep my bonding.

Sheryl returned, and without speaking, filed some no doubt unpleasant documents in my private cabinet. She was good, sensing when not to ask questions. I sat paralyzed, detached, unable to think clearly. My mind jumped from one episode to another. Underneath everything was the ever-present dread, as though it were the night before my execution.

Fingering my file drawer, Sheryl was only three feet away, and as she bent over, her butt entered my space—she was not wearing underwear. Under the thin pair of slacks, there was no line showing anywhere. *God, she has a nice ass.*

Sheryl was previously married to a golf pro who couldn't keep from diddling his female clients. I knew it was going on long before they talked about divorce. For the life of me, I could not see what the guy was thinking. Sheryl was smart and a knockout. She could have done better than the secretary of my company, except she had never finished college. Her selfish, womanizing husband made her quit as soon as she became his wife. I was lucky to have her as an assistant, and now she stayed during the worst of times because we both knew about the things nobody else should know. I trusted her more on business decisions and insider information than anyone.

There was one drawback, however: Sheryl had divorced three years ago, and it was commonly known, since then, she was fairly generous with her well-proportioned hard body. We had never talked about any kind of tryst, but I did fantasize from time to time. I deeply loved my wife, and any temptation was tempered by my desire to hold together a good marriage. As attractive as Sheryl was, however, there were times I had almost lost my head, but I knew an affair with her would be my undoing.

She did throw a suggestive glance my way every now and then. It was enough to let me know it was possible. But these glances were not so much that they interfered with our working relationship. Beth wanted her fired, but it was out of the question. Sheryl was too valuable. She knew who had to be paid and who could be put off. Now that we were hard up for money, she was right there with me on trying to make it work.

Her butt was there, too, like honeysuckle to a hummingbird. She turned her head and caught me staring. My face flushed. She smiled, and without changing position, resumed her work.

Sheryl left, and I went back into my stupor. Christ, I could be accused of sexual harassment. What the hell was I thinking? Was I losing my mind? *Come on, get a grip and quit acting like a lecher.*

Sheryl knocked lightly and came in again. She went to my file cabinet and gave me a sly look as if to say, I'm going to try this again and see what happens. I was the insect in a spider web paralyzed and waiting to be eaten, but maybe I was the one creating the web. Maybe it was all in my head. I felt a tinge of shame.

Of course, nothing happened. Leaving my office, Sheryl stopped at the door. "You look like you've been drugged. Do you need to talk?"

No, I don't need to talk. Just take off those slacks.

"Sheryl, I appreciate it, but I need to digest a few things. I'll be all right."

Five minutes later, Sheryl's sexy voice came over the intercom. "Your wife is on line one."

"Hi, just calling to see if you're hanging in and tell you I love you."

Chapter 9

Snake

Jacksonville, Florida

Snake had a lot of his chips on the table, but he could lose more than money in this smuggling gamble. He tried to isolate himself from direct contact by delegating to Gut, but because he was the one with good contacts, he had to do some things himself. Toad waited at the door for twenty minutes while Snake walked around talking on the phone. He hung up a special cell phone and motioned for Toad to sit. "We are close to beginning our operation. It will be the biggest shipment we have ever made. I don't want any screw-ups."

"Boss, do I have this right? We are contracting to drag two thousand pounds of cocaine across the entire country of Haiti, from the Caribbean Sea to the Atlantic Ocean?"

"Get some balls. I know it's tough, but I've thought it through. It will work. I have instructed Rex to stay away from traffic areas. This will require more sailing time, but I'll leave those routes to the macho boys with their fast boats. Our Caribbean portion of this trip will only transport from Colombia to the southern shore of Haiti."

Toad's eyes avoided Snake's stare, and though he was not known to be a user, he kept making a nervous sniff, noticeably uncomfortable with what had been described so far. Snake prided himself on meticulous planning, and it aggravated him to be questioned about the operation.

"I understand your logic," Toad said. "But it's also a long, unfriendly trip from the southern shore to the north of Haiti."

Snake sat back in his chair and focused his unblinking eyes on Toad, who shifted his fat butt around as if he were sitting on a cocklebur.

"I didn't hire you to complain; I hired you to get it done. Now listen. It's not easy, but we eliminate the U.S. feds, our biggest hazard. We have good contacts, and we have done it successfully before—without you. Once we get the contraband overland to the north shore, we can again ship by sea, traveling far enough east to avoid the Bahamas and most of the Gulf Stream."

"Okay, Boss, tell me what I need to know about this loathsome location."

Snake stopped his narrative and analyzed Toad. His concern was Toad's change in attitude, from questioning the trip to agreeing, might not be genuine. A stream of sweat trickled down the right side of Toad's face. He was always a sweater, but now his whole neck was wet. Snake got a whiff of BO emanating from the fat torso. He was pleased with the reaction. Word of the instant killing of Bullethead had increased everybody's anxiety.

"Haiti is a garbage dump reeking of corruption and poverty," Snake said. "The last thing anybody would normally elect to do would be to cross the whole country, but these conditions are the ones in which we know how to operate. I expect you to take full advantage of them. Everybody in Haiti is susceptible to bribes, including police and politicians, and it doesn't take much American money to buy them. They know the alternative is torture or death. Do you understand? I want to hear you are on board a hundred percent."

The truth was Snake did have concerns about the conditions in Haiti. It didn't concern him that Toad might suffer hardships on this trip, but it did cause him to reflect that these hardships might increase the chances of failure.

Toad leaned his big squishy body back. He ran his hands over his thinning hair and finally answered. "Yeah, I got it."

Snake continued his instructions. "We have contracted with an outfit known as La Coco to transport the cocaine from Colombia to Haiti and across land to rendezvous with Rex's boat in Fort Liberte. They will also meet you at the airport and provide your transportation.

"Like always, our biggest risk comes from U.S. agencies. It's always tricky entering or approaching the States.

"That is why I'm using Rex. Small pleasure sailboats leave and return unmolested to the U.S. east coast on a regular basis without bothering to contact customs. With this plan, I eliminate the duplicity and violence of the middlemen in the drug distribution centers of New York, Chicago, and Atlanta. Our product can be moved by my North Carolina contacts all over the eastern seaboard."

"Okay, Boss, I'll get it done."

"That's what I like to hear," Snake said. "The other part of my plan is getting paid. The airport at Beaufort is small, laid-back, close to the destination marina, and it will be easy to load the money unnoticed. Toad, you have been with me for five years and have been reliable, knowledgeable, and ruthless in carrying out my commands. You're my ace in the hole. I know you'll get it done."

Toad sniffed and shifted his shoulders. "Boss, changing the subject for a minute, this guy Rex Morgan controls the boat and the airplane. What do you want me to do if he strays?"

"What do you make of him right now?"

"Right now, he's scared, but if he got his ass in a crack, he would chirp like a jar fly on an August afternoon."

"Good that he's scared. Everyone should be scared—including you."

Snake paused and reached into his desk drawer. He was pleased to see a flicker of distress on Toad's face. Being unpredictable kept the fear level high. He pulled out a cigar, and relief showed on Toad's face. He lit a match, puffed several times, and looked back at Toad with unblinking eyes.

"If you feel Rex is getting out of line—"

"I understand. I'll watch him. If need be, I'll whack him."

Snake looked at the office wall where his law school diploma hung. He had no doubts about Toad's commitment to kill Rex if necessary. He had eliminated enemies and weak business associates without hesitation. His thoughts were on possible complications if Rex needed killing. "That's all for now."

Chapter 10

Rex

Jacksonville, Florida

Rex got a sinking sensation—it was Toad.

"Hey, Colonel Glen," Toad said, "time to light your rocket. Snake wants you to position your machine in Beaufort ASAP and call me as soon as you get back."

"Roger. I'm ready."

"And one more thing, Ace. From now on, you get all your instructions through me, and I don't take any deviation kindly."

Rex shifted his view to the open harbor and wondered if he was doing the right thing. "I told you, Toad, I'm ready."

He clicked off. *I hate that bastard.* Then he worried about the punishment if he screwed up. But he pushed those thoughts away and turned his attention to the money and Mona.

He quickly secured his boat and rushed to Jacksonville's Herlong Field. He arrived about 2:00 p.m. and filed an IFR flight plan to Beaufort's Michael J. Smith airport in North Carolina. It was over ninety degrees as he did a quick walk-around. On taxi out, Rex was so preoccupied with thoughts of the Snake's torture scene that he almost taxied to the wrong runway.

Scanning the gauges on engine run-up, he noticed number two oil pressure was low. He tapped the gauge to no avail. Jacking the throttle made the needle move, but it remained low throughout the range. It was still within limits, so he pressed on. Taxiing onto the runway, Rex added full power, giving his engine instruments another check, before releasing the brakes. Number two engine oil pressure gauge still did not line up with the left gauge. He pushed the throttles to take-off power and released the brakes. As always on lift-off, he got a feeling of euphoria, and tension of the past few days melted away. It felt nice to get into cooler air on climb-out.

Two hours later, Rex canceled his IFR flight plan with Beaufort in sight and landed at the small airport. He proceeded to the airplane tie-down area, anxious to get his fuel and pay any required fees before everybody left at dusk.

The attendant acted like he was ready to go home even though it was almost two hours until the published closing time. "If you want gas, you almost missed it. George is packing up to go now."

"I do want gas, and I want to pay for a parking spot for a month. Also, I need to rent a car."

"I'll call George and figure your fees, but next time, how about telling somebody to let us know. Car rentals are on the wall. Sometimes it takes a while until they come. You can wait on the bench outside. I'm locking up in an hour."

"Listen, asshole. Are you running operations or not? It says in the airmen's guide you're open until seven. So, do your fucking job, and tell your lazy friend, George, I want some gas, unless you want me to call the mayor of this hamlet and tell him he doesn't have an operational airport."

The attendant was speechless, but he called George and became much more accommodating. Rex settled his business at the airport, drove the rental car from Beaufort to New Bern, and caught a commercial airline back to Jacksonville, Florida.

He arrived back in Jacksonville after 10:00 p.m. Toad had instructed him to telephone upon his return, but he was bone tired and decided not to make the dreaded call until the next morning.

At 9:00 a.m., Toad answered the phone. "Listen up, Birdman. If you can't follow orders, you and me are gonna make a trip to the woodshed, and it ain't for chopping kindling."

"It was late last night. I didn't waste any time. It took what it took."

"I didn't say call me if it's not too late. I said call me when you get in."

Am I going to be able to put up with this despicable bastard? "Yeah, I know. Sorry."

"Tomorrow at midnight, Pigneck will deliver the guns for our protection, along with my personal guns. And listen, Rambo. You better be there, and it better go smooth, and for your own sake, all your talk about expertise with firearms better hold up. We are delivering a big gun with the others."

"Everything I told you is correct. Playing with guns is a hobby."

Rex suffered a sinking sensation in the pit of his stomach. *What am I doing?* He needed the money for Mona but felt that maybe it wasn't worth getting into this cesspool of psychos. These people were like parasitic wasps laying their eggs on another unsuspecting insect that will be eaten alive by the hatching young. And Rex joined the feast. "I need two days, counting today, to get ready to sail."

"What you need, Ace, is not my affair, but I'll meet you at Fort Liberte, Haiti, September fifteenth. Show up, or Gut will be happy to teach a lesson in responsibility back here in Jacksonville."

Rex's chest tightened on the reference to Gut and his madhouse.

At exactly midnight, a van showed up at the marina. A large ugly man approached. "I'm looking for a Rex Morgan."

"That's me."

"They call me Pigneck."

Pigneck looked like a thug. He had long wavy black hair descending to a thick, red neck that blended into his head—like a pig's neck. He wore a loose floral shirt with the top three buttons undone to show his gold chains. To Rex's relief, he was cordial and agreed to help load the guns. There was a lot he didn't know or understand about Snake's operation, increasing his anxiety. He needed to find out more about what he was getting into. Maybe this guy would fill him in.

They loaded the guns and ammunition in a dock dolly, covered them with a tarp, and proceeded to Rex's boat. "So Pigneck," Rex said, "you been working for Snake for a while?"

"Yeah, been around a couple of years."

"What is it about this torture chamber?"

"Ain't that some shit? I've seen these shows several times. Let me tell you something. Be careful around Snake. You get outta line, and he won't hesitate to put you on that table. He ain't got a heart—he'd kill his mama without a thought. Word is he set fire to the neighbor's cat when he was ten years old and was known in college for abusing the pledges in some fraternity he was in."

Rex nodded. After what he had witnessed with the acid in the eye, the cat thing was mild. But he needed to know more about the operation. "Did he really practice law?"

"Yeah, and at one time he was a county commissioner of a small county about thirty miles west. In fact, that's where he got into trading drugs. But, hey man, I ain't talking no more. It don't pay to flap too much about The Acid Man."

"Do you know anything about this cocaine haul we're doing?"

Pigneck went from a nice guy to a scared jerk.

"Listen," he said. "I don't know nothing, and I don't want to know nothing. If you're smart, you'll watch your fucking mouth."

Well, I guess that's all I'll get from this asshole.

Two days later, Rex was ready to sail. Because he had plenty of time for the planned rendezvous, he decided to take an extra day to check out the big gun Pigneck had delivered. Rex sighted in the .50 caliber BMG rifle to zero at eight hundred yards. He also adjusted the parallax for that distance. He was impressed with the accuracy and range of such a powerful weapon.

On the fourth day, Rex boarded his boat with a small carry-on holding a couple of changes of clothes. Due to threats from Toad, he gave himself two extra days to make the September fifteenth deadline. He cranked the little universal diesel and turned to release the stern line. The exhaust made an odd sputter, followed by a metal knocking sound from the engine.

Then the engine quit.

He cranked the diesel a couple of times, and it froze. Something was bad wrong, and he assumed it had thrown a rod. The engine was necessary to exit the harbor and enter the long approach into the harbor at Fort Liberte, Haiti.

Normally Rex did his own maintenance, but now he was panicked over showing up late in Haiti. The consequence was ominous. He thought about contacting Toad but discarded the idea. He found the mechanic recommended by the owner of the powerboat in the next slip and promised to pay him three times his normal rate if he would start work immediately.

Three days later the engine was running, but he was a full day behind schedule. He would need good wind conditions to make it on time.

Leaving Jacksonville late in the afternoon, Rex was soon doing seven knots on a beam reach, watching the setting sun disappear into the horizon over the last views of Jacksonville.

He had spent a great deal of time and thought rigging his boat for single-handed ocean sailing and felt confident to sail alone. He was an experienced, capable sailor with a U.S. Coast Guard Captain's License. His boat was a Pacific Seacraft, Crealock 37, one of the finest ocean-going sailboats made. It was equipped with a Monitor self-steering wind vane guidance system requiring no power.

Alone at sea isn't always lonely, but it's always a

time for reflection. It can be an almost spiritual event, even for a rogue like himself. Rex had this same feeling while flying, witnessing the grandeur of the firmament, as the famous pilot poem goes: *Oh! I have slipped the surly bonds of earth and danced the skies of laughter-silvered wings.* A large orange moon rose on his port bow, and it increased his pensive mood. He wondered how both of his interests had become slaves to his lust for riches.

Rex engaged the self-steering, took a turn on the sheet winch, and settled himself on the portside lazarette to continue his melancholy reflection.

He was doing well working for Snake, but deep within, he harbored an uneasy feeling as if somewhere out there, below the surface, was a partially submerged cargo container. And it was silently waiting to sink his boat. He looked at the phosphorescent sparkles coming from his wake and slowly shifted his focus to the distant horizon illuminated by the rising moon.

On land, he never thought about it—about what it all means—but alone at sea, his thoughts wandered to bigger things. *Is there a God, or am I in such violation that even thinking of Him is an abomination?*

He had made life-changing mistakes in the past and wondered if he wasn't tumbling headlong into another one. Once, he had longed to become an airline pilot, but by the time the necessary experience was accumulated, he also had a short rap sheet for small-time marijuana dealing. The drug bust ended Rex's dream to become an airline pilot, and after serving a short jail sentence, he never returned to college.

He joined into a partnership with two flying friends and bought a Beech Queen Air 70 airplane. They were always short on money. Fortunately for the business, Rex met Toad, and he was sucked into Snake's organization. In a short time, he made enough to buy out his partners. Although much of his flying time remained a legitimate business, Rex continued to work for Snake, which enabled him to pay off the airplane note. A year after his first job for Snake, he bought his boat. Now he loved sailing as much as flying.

He was getting a fifteen-knot wind out of the east to give him fast close reach. He made good progress, and the tension of arriving late subsided. Rex adjusted the steering five degrees to port and settled into the rhythm of the sea. This was what he loved—the gentle rush of water under his boat, the creaking of the rigging under pressure from the sails, the rising and falling of the bow to the cadence of the rolling sea, moving endlessly from horizon to horizon. He did not want to be a criminal, but crime made experiencing what he loved possible.

By10:30 p.m. Rex's boat was cutting through the swells at seven knots, and he was tired, so he went below to sleep. He had set a more easterly course in order to cross the Gulf Stream more quickly at right angles to incur less of the northern current. The radar alarm was set to go off if a ship came within five miles, and so he crawled into the center berth.

On the fourth day at sea, Rex had put almost six hundred miles between his boat and Jacksonville, but now the wind had dropped to eight knots, which was not enough to make it on time. Getting closer to his rendezvous with Toad in Haiti, this nasty business in Snake's torture room kept haunting him. And now he might be late.

He promised himself that at the end of this assignment, he would quit. But quitting was scary. How could he do it and not end up on Snake's chopping block?

Not all of Rex's reservations about quitting revolved around Snake, however. Mona was a driving force. He was first bedazzled on a 70-foot Hatteras he was delivering. He had shown her the boat the day after they met. Rex had picked her up in a rented Lexus at noon. She dressed in shorts, boat shoes, and a halter top tied at the waist. It caused him to stammer, and he worried he sounded more like a teenager than a tycoon.

"God, it's beautiful," Mona had said breathlessly in that sweet sexy voice of hers.

Rex jumped on board, spun around, and put out his hand. "All aboard for the captain's tour."

As they went inside, the exotic scent of new teak greeted them. Everything was clean and neat. Embroidered throw pillows covered the couches and chairs. Shiny hardware and fittings were everywhere. He went to a small refrigerator. "Can I get you a beer or some wine?"

"I better not. I have to work tonight."

Nervous as a racehorse in the starting gate, he took her hand again. "Like to see the master suite?"

"Sure."

Mona turned from looking through the porthole outlined in brass, and Rex kissed her. They fell into the king-size bed. In the middle of this passionate moment, she broke free and stood up. "Okay, Captain, it's time for the Mona tour."

She removed her clothes one piece at a time, and her spell possessed him like a junkie on crack cocaine.

From that day forward, he had been hooked and was determined to keep her, no matter what the risk.

This trip was for Mona, and he promised himself it would be his last. Rex's concentration refocused on his sailing with a new vigor for seeing it through and getting the money and somehow running away with Mona.

On the sixth day at sea, he noticed the wind dying with the setting sun. There were enough clouds in the west to turn the sky blood red, and soon the sea itself turned red. *Was this an omen?* He wasn't sure what lay ahead once he met up with Toad in Haiti. Toad had already promised he would have to face Gut if he was late.

He could run awhile with the engine, but it would only give him five knots, and he didn't have enough fuel to go all night. He decided to wait to see if the wind would pick up after dark.

Gazing at the smooth red sea in the quiet of the setting sun created a reverence for the wonder of nature and caused him to reflect on his life. Stooping to drink from the cup of temptation had cost him his airline career. The one thing he loved, wanted, and worked for was forever out of reach. Now here he was, working for a sleazy, bloodthirsty sociopath.

And what if Mona finds out I lied?

Rex went below and turned on his computer to check the weather. There was a weak tropical wave several days away that would bear watching but nothing immediate. He returned topside and contemplated the ocean. In some ways, the enigma reflected life itself. The ocean does not care how prepared you are or how irresponsible you are. If you sink, it gives no credit or criticism. You either live or die. The sea doesn't care. To it, you never existed. *And so it is with life.*

Rex watched the last of the red glow of the setting sun on the ocean of blood. How many millions of years has the sea looked the same? How many millions of creatures have lived and died without notice? He was one more of these forgettable creatures.

He focused on his little realm of time, knowing that he was nothing more than a raindrop on this red sea of eternity. But Rex loved the sea. Here he felt pure and clean—pure and clean on the way to do dirty.

There wasn't a breath of air. He moaned. *I'm gonna be late.*

Chapter 11

Scrap

Mt. Pleasant, South Carolina

I woke up Saturday morning tired from a week of stress. I was angry but not sure where to focus my wrath. Failure was chasing me, and I was running through a giant tub of molasses. Finally, I consoled myself by the fact at least I was still running. After coffee and breakfast, I looked at Beth and our seven-year-old Emma, who was still eating. "Emma," I said, "Tina loved your drawing of the blue crab."

She looked up, excitement on her face. "Crabbing! Daddy, let's go crabbing."

At first, I was too down to be interested, but her pleading eyes were convincing. I smiled for the first time in days. "It will be low tide in an hour. Let's do it. Dig out the chicken necks from the freezer. I'll get the nets."

Emma dashed for the freezer, but Beth grabbed her. "Whoa, young lady, finish your breakfast. I'll get the chicken necks."

"Momma, you don't know about crabbing. You lived in the little house on the prairie—you said that's what it was like in Kansas."

"I do know about crabbing. Your daddy showed

me before you were born. Now eat your breakfast."

I marveled at my little girl, bantering with her mother. Surely she was a shrewd prodigy from the loins of prodigies. And this made me feel better. My kid was great no matter what happened in the rest of the world. Crabbing was the right thing to do. My problems seemed lighter.

I gathered the nets and lines along with an old five-gallon plastic paint bucket. Beth and Emma showed up outside with the necks and a three-foot piece of broomstick. "Daddy, don't forget the stick. We need it when they try to get away."

"Do you think you can put the stick on one that is getting away and pick it up? Last year you got pinched."

She nodded in a confident manner. "I'm bigger now. I know how."

We put everything in a wagon and wheeled it to the dock. The dock was on a small creek in the marsh behind my house. The creek was home to lots of blue crabs. I purposely didn't bring a trap because it's less exciting than catching one or two in a net and transferring them to the bucket. Besides, a crab trap caught too many crabs. I knew from experience, Beth's and Emma's enthusiasm would wane, and I would end up picking most of what we caught.

Without my help, I let Emma and Beth go through the squealing and running back and forth with the bucket, stick, and net. I insisted they attach their own chicken necks. Emma chastised me. "Daddy, you aren't trying to catch any."

Beth gave me a coquettish glance. "Emma, Daddy's afraid of the crabs."

"Daddy, are you afraid one will pinch you?"

Both of them were bent over the dock rail, checking their nets. I took a crab out of the bucket and held it from the rear, claws extended, looking for anything to pinch, and snuck up behind them. With the crab in my right hand, I pinched Beth on the bottom with my left hand. She jumped and screamed. Emma turned, and I pushed the crab at her. She screamed along with her mother. Both of them dropped their nets.

"Just you wait," Beth yelled. "We'll get you! Won't we, Emma?"

"Yes, Daddy, you're gonna get pinched."

I smiled. "Girls, let's catch four more. That will be enough for each of us to have three nice crabs, and that's plenty."

"Daddy, I'm almost seven. I can pick as good as momma. Let's put some water in the bucket so they will stay alive."

"I don't think that's the thing to do. Crabs can get oxygen from the air and the water. If you put just a little water on them, they will use up the oxygen in the water and die because they cannot get to the air."

"Why can't we breathe in air and water like the crabs?" she said.

"We have lungs that don't work in water, but crabs have special gills that work in water, and if they stay damp, the gills can also absorb oxygen from the air."

We had caught about nine nice blue crabs when Emma pulled one up that caused her to squeal. "Eeeyuu, look at it. What is that yellow stuff coming out?"

"We need to throw her back. It's a female with about a million eggs. Maybe out of that million, two or three will become big crabs."

Emma looked at me for several seconds, and I got chills. It was the same look I loved so much about her mother. It was like I had said something noteworthy and it deserved thought before she answered. It made me feel relevant in a world spinning out of my control.

"What happens to all those other eggs?" she asked.

I sensed this was a great teaching moment. "A hundred different creatures eat the young until they get big enough to survive as crabs."

"Daddy, the world of nature is cruel."

"Yes, Emma, and we live in that world."

"Are we cruel?" she said.

Beth came to the rescue. "No, Emma, people don't need to be cruel. If I'm nice to you, maybe you'll be nice to me."

I looked at both of them interacting on the dock. Emma had eyebrows and ears like me, but she had this little dimple on the side of her mouth just like Beth. I knew this was my destiny. These two were my bottom line. Everything else was secondary. They were my responsibility. There was no excuse if I allowed my business to fail and bring them any resulting hardship.

I'm the wolf caught in the trap: do I continue to struggle to get free, or do I gnaw off my leg.

Chapter 12

Rex

Fort Liberte, Haiti

Rex was going to be late. He entered the long approach to the harbor at Fort Liberte but would barely make the harbor before dark. He jerked when his cell phone dinged. It was a text from Toad that had been sent eight hours ago. All it said was Toad's 6:30 p.m. arrival ETA at the harbor. *My God, it's 6:10 p.m. now, and I have an hour to go.* Toad would have made his grueling trip across Haiti with his La Coco transportation and two escorts. He would be pissed if Rex was not there.

At 7:05 p.m. Rex entered the harbor. He threw out the anchor and transferred to his dinghy. He could just make out Toad's fat blob standing on the beach. He beached the dingy, and Toad approached with two other men.

"Well, if it ain't Captain Bligh," Toad said. "How come I'm here waiting on you? I've been here fifteen minutes, and if these two knew what they were doing, I would've been here earlier."

Rex breathed a sigh of relief. *So he was also late.* "Hello, Toad. Are these two going with us?"

Toad hesitated and responded. "Only until the

work is done. Then that leaves just you and me between the Devil and the deep blue sea."

The four of them boarded the dinghy. Toad wrinkled his nose at the smell of an open sewer. "This place smells like shit."

The two thugs looked nervous, their eyes darting around like something was going to jump out at them.

"We're in the exotic Caribbean," Rex said. "You're just not accustomed to the smell of paradise."

Toad seemed to be deep in thought and didn't answer, but then he instructed the two thugs to sit up front while he sat in the back and looked at them. They seemed to get increasingly nervous. Rex eyed the drama before cranking the four-horse engine. *Something's wrong here.*

They motored out to the anchored sailboat and climbed aboard. Once again Rex noticed that Toad would not turn his back to them.

Onboard Toad grabbed Rex by the arm and gave him an intense stare. "Captain, back in Jacksonville, I had some merchandise delivered to your ship. I would like to see it."

Rex wondered if he was supposed to be playing some kind of part here. He took Toad below and noticed the two escorts looked at each other. Below in the storage area under the mid-berth, which was his favorite bed, Rex showed Toad two tricked-out AR-15 rifles in .223 caliber, each with a 50-round drum magazine. In a box alongside were ten spare thirty-round magazines. The costliest weapon was stored at the far end: a Barrett 107A1 extreme range rifle in .50 caliber BMG with muzzle brake and suppressor.

"I'll get to these later," Toad said. "Where are my

guns?"

Rex uncovered the box containing Toad's personal firearms.

Toad didn't bother to put on the holster but checked to make sure his gun was loaded. Rex returned topside. Toad was right behind him, heaving his huge bulk through the opening. Both thugs had their eyes on the companionway, but they were too late. From three feet Toad fired one shot into the face of nearest one and two shots into the torso of the other. The first died instantly. The second thug moaned and squirmed around on the floor. Toad stepped over and shot him one more time in the head.

"What the hell are you doing?" Rex shouted. "Have you lost your mind?"

With a condescending look, Toad responded in the same calm voice he would use to order his beloved escargot. "I'm trying to salvage an operation that's about to go to shit. I don't know who these two assholes are, but they were not La Coco men. My guess is the La Coco guys are vulture food somewhere in the mountains."

"Okay, hit man, what's the plan?" Rex shot back.

"They're probably part of a hijack operation on our delivery later tonight. Killing us was part of the plan. We gotta take delivery from La Coco and get the fuck outta here before the rest of them show up."

"We can't leave in the dark, or we'll run aground. Nobody in this shithole maintains anything. Most of the lights are out on the channel markers. The chart and the actual channel don't agree, and there isn't even a moon tonight. This boat draws six feet. I had a hard enough time getting in here in daylight."

"Listen, Magellan"—Toad pissed over the side—"I don't give a flying fuck what you have to do. You're getting paid to move drugs when I say move. This run aground shit is your problem, but we are leaving tonight right after we load. You got it?"

Rex threw up his arms in surrender. "Okay, we leave, but I guarantee we will hit bottom on the way out. What do we do with your two hunting trophies?"

"Help me put them in the back of the cockpit and throw a tarp over them until we are through loading. We can dump them at sea."

"Fine, but I need to wash all this blood off the deck, or your massacre will be obvious."

At midnight, the delivery boat arrived with three men aboard. They eased to the stern area and shined a light on the boat's name. *Mona More* served as the bona fides for the reception. They came alongside and flashed O-S-O in code.

"Okay, that's it. Get both of those AR15s," Toad ordered. "Give one to me and take the other on deck and cover this operation. Select full auto and be prepared to open up if these guys are more hijackers. I'm getting sick of this place."

Rex jumped through the hatch and fell on the cabin floor. He stood up with a bleeding knee. He was sure something would go wrong. Hyperventilating, he raced to the storage under the berth. *Come on, get a grip.* He checked the chambers and safeties on each weapon and returned topside, giving one to Toad. Toad calmly motioned with his head for Rex to stand on the front deck. Rex stood wide-eyed and nervous on top of the cabin, purposely not pointing his weapon directly at anyone.

The old cabin cruiser pulled alongside with six armed Haitians aboard. They tied their boat alongside and began transferring aluminum suitcases. Toad motioned for them to be stored in the forward V-berth cabin. In thirty minutes, the cargo was transferred. Toad paid the delivery crew. The men climbed back on their motor launch and departed.

Toad turned to Rex and handed him his gun. "Okay, Captain Drake, let's make waves."

Rex gave a nod of resignation, and the anchor was hauled on *Mona More* at 12:45 a.m.

They made it about three hundred yards before the depth alarm sounded. Rex turned the wheel without knowing which direction was better, and the boat made a scraping sound and lurched to a stop.

"Damn it! I told you this would happen. We've run aground, and I have no idea where the channel is."

"Well, Admiral Nelson, you had better find it because we may have the friends of our two shark-bait buddies on the way."

Rex slammed the little Universal engine into reverse. It moved three feet, and he went back to forward at full throttle. It moved another six feet. He spun the wheel and went back into reverse. With enough backing and turning, Rex finally found some eight-foot water but ran aground again in another hundred yards. He scanned the water for somebody sneaking up on them. *This isn't going to work.*

They were going to keep hitting the bottom. "I told you I had trouble approaching in the daylight, let alone in the pitch dark."

"Captain Cook, I'm not interested in your whining. I'm interested in getting out of here ahead of the rest of those assholes that want to kill us."

At first light, after wandering out of the channel three times, they were within a mile of the open sea. This time the sound was different—the boat made a sickening grinding noise, and the bow climbed.

Rex looked over the side and slapped his leg. "Shit, we're on a coral head. The motor won't get it off. I'll have to kedge off."

"Kedge? What the hell you talking about?"

"I need to take an anchor in the dinghy and set it and use the winch to crank us off."

On the way to fetch the anchor, Rex stopped in his tracks. In the quiet early morning, a motor buzzed in the distance. He raced to his set of binoculars and studied the bay in the weak dawn light.

"I believe our two reclining gentlemen have friends. They're maybe a mile away."

"Come on," Toad said. "Let's get this contraption underway before we have to risk Snake's *blow* in a firefight."

Rex released the breath he was holding. "Do you not get it? We are a sailboat. The most we can do is seven knots. That boat, which is headed right for us, is probably doing fifteen knots. The light is good enough now to barely make them out. They have something that looks like a machine gun mounted on the front."

Toad shrugged and gestured toward the inside cabin. "What can you do with that big, expensive rifle?"

"If I can get a steady platform, I can do damage."

In two minutes, Rex had set up the big .50 caliber on the life raft tied to the mast. With the bipod legs, the elevation was good. He tucked himself into a sitting position and peered into the scope. He calculated distance using the range markers in the scope against a man standing on the approaching powerboat. He loaded the magazine containing the five-and-a-half-inch shells and watched for the boat to enter his eight-hundred-yard area. *Mona More* rested hopelessly on the coral head, and the sea caused little movement.

Toad didn't say anything else but intently watched as Rex set up the rifle. Rex put the crosshairs on the man in the bow and put slight pressure on the trigger. As the crosshairs moved off and on the target, he paused and continued his squeeze on the trigger. An enormous blast ejected at the end and sides of the muzzle brake.

Rex watched through the scope. "Well, that takes care of the guy sitting next to the machine gun."

Rex spoke like a true killer, but he didn't feel it. His mind was reeling. Who could live after being hit from a .50 BMG? The bullet is four times the size of a 30-06 hunting rifle slug. *Is he dead? He has to be. He fell into the water.* There was a lot of moving and ducking. His next shot took out the gun itself, although it was a lucky shot. With the mind-numbing distraction of wasting a human, he absentmindedly shot at the center of the boat, directing his fire at the waterline. It evidently caused damage. "They're turning back," Rex said.

"Well, Hot Shot might be your new name. Now let's see if you can get this tub to float us out of here."

An hour later, Rex finally kedged off the coral head, but Toad was still agitated. "You need to turn on the speed," Toad said. "We're already running late, and if we miss our contacts in Beaufort, you and me liable to end up in Gut's little playground."

Rex didn't answer, but he had a sinking in the pit of his stomach. *I just killed a man. God, I've crossed over the line.*

Chapter 13

Dee

Columbia, South Carolina

Dee was hard at work trying to get a handle on the responsibilities of being second-in-command. He paced the floor of his new office, mentally organizing his actions. Long ago, going all the way back to The Citadel, he had learned there was a thin line between taking command and appearing to be a pompous ass. If you drifted too far on the friendly side, you could lose command respect, and if you were too overbearing, the morale of your subordinates would suffer.

His boss Ray Bowley appeared at his door. He did not look happy. "I got some *ah shit* news from Washington."

In his excitement over the rush of developments, Dee did not fully pick up on the seriousness of Bowley's mood.

"They made a mistake," Dee said. "Instead of a promotion, I'm supposed to go to Fargo, North Dakota."

"Dee, this could be serious. One of the guys you left alive in your takedown in Atlanta has filed a complaint with the Justice Department. Bennett wants you in his office in DC tomorrow afternoon."

At 9:10 a.m., Dee caught a flight to Reagan Washington National Airport, walked to the Metro, and arrived in time for lunch at 935 Pennsylvania Avenue. After lunch he showed for his 1:30 p.m. appointment at the office of Executive Assistant Director Hal Bennett. The receptionist instructed him to go on in.

Another man dressed in a blue suit was seated with Bennett. Bennett rose and shook Dee's hand and motioned to the man in the blue suit. "This is inspector Graham from the Inspector General's office. I think you have heard about the filing of a complaint. He has been assigned to investigate."

Dee squinted his eyes at Graham. *God, I hate these guys.* They were like the FAA, taking six months to second guess a pilot that had only ten seconds to make a decision.

Graham opened a notebook and turned on a recorder. "Please tell me in your own words what took place on the takedown in Atlanta."

Bennett showed no expression and did not attempt to get into the discussion. Dee was getting pissed but feared his new job was in jeopardy. "I will," Dee said. "But first you tell me exactly what you're investigating."

Graham shifted in his chair uncomfortably.

"The man we identify as Perp Four has filed a complaint with the Justice Department that you made an unlawful entry, without a warrant, killed Perp One, Two, and Three, and arrested him. If this is true, he would be exonerated, and you could be charged."

Dee forgot that he was standing in the hallowed halls of hierarchy. His mind went back to the takedown. Anger reared. "Inspector Graham, have you ever been in a situation where you feared you could be shot in the back of the head at any minute and where you were surrounded with scumbags that placed no value on life, whether it be man or child?"

Graham seemed to assume a superior air. "I don't see how this is germane to my investiga—"

"It has everything to do with it," Dee snapped back at him, not disguising his annoyance. "I was pretending to be one of these scumbags. For a year I had worked to earn their trust, and every day the risk grew that I would be discovered and killed. But I wasn't. I did not need a warrant to be in that house. I was trusted as one of them and invited to be there."

Dee was breathing hard when he stopped talking. Graham seemed to have gotten smaller. He didn't speak, and Bennett broke the silence. "Mr. Graham, that will be all for today. If you need more information, there's a full detailed report on this operation you can access."

Amazed at Bennett's response, Dee calmed down and wondered why it was urgent that he was even brought here.

Graham left like he had been whipped, and Dee dreaded the coming reprimand from Bennett for his impertinence, but he was surprised again. "Well," Bennett said. "I think that about covers it. This thing will drag on for several months, but everybody knows it's bullshit."

Bennett smiled, sat back in his chair, and motioned for Dee to take a seat.

"Sir, I appreciate that."

"There's one thing, though. Until this IG investigation is over, you will only be acting Assistant

Director in Columbia. However, I want you to aggressively do your work as though your position was permanent."

"Sir, I am at it hard already."

"There's another reason I brought you here today. After we all have had a chance to digest your undercover work in Atlanta, you're now recognized as one of the most knowledgeable we have on drug smuggling."

Dee winced. Instantly, he wondered if he had become so valuable that he would be shifted back to an undercover job, which he hated.

"Sir, I like my present assignment and believe that is my best place."

"I agree, which brings me to my point. I'm concerned that cocaine trafficking in the southeast is increasing. Your Atlanta operation confirms it. But there's much more. Did you ever come across a distributor that goes by the name of Two Finger?"

"Two Finger Willie. Yes, I know about him. He has a legitimate bar and grill in Atlanta, but he cooks crack and distributes it along with cocaine throughout the southeast—but not in Atlanta. My market was Atlanta. It was too risky to try anything with Two Finger while I was embedded in my Atlanta cartel. Willie is smart and experienced."

"Okay, I want you to track him down from your office in Columbia. And by the way, Bowley, your immediate boss, is on board with this. Do you know of a cartel in Jacksonville run by a sicko called Snake?"

"Yes, he holds a Florida law license and is strictly wholesale, imports from out of country and sells large hauls to distributors."

Bennett was pleased and threw out his hands in elation. "Great, figure out a way to get him. That's all I have. I'll let you know when this other thing is complete."

Chapter 14

Rex

At Sea, from Haiti to North Carolina

By eight o'clock, they had made it to the open sea. Rex set the wind vane steering on a northeast heading to pass well southeast of Grand Turk Island.

Toad stepped over and eyed the compass. "Captain Cook, this heading ain't going to get us to North Carolina."

"This route is longer," Rex said. "But passing through either the Caicos Passage or the Turk Passage increases the chance of encountering narcs."

"Well, ain't you Mr. Nautical Stealth. Just don't get us lost."

Rex pursed his lips but didn't respond.

With a fifteen-knot southeast breeze, Rex set the sails for a comfortable close reach. Late in the afternoon, about fifty miles out to sea, Toad's two quiet visitors sacrificed their bodies to Neptune.

After remaining on the northeast track for two days, Rex turned ninety degrees to port and took up a heading for the North Carolina coast 1,100 miles away. But he had neglected to keep up with the weak tropical wave. The last time he'd checked, the wave would pass to the south of their planned position. This, of course, was before Toad killed two men and announced the attempted hijacking. Bad weather seemed unimportant when they were slated to be shot. With everything now settled down, Rex turned to his normal sailor routine.

"I haven't checked the weather since we left," Rex said. "I'm going below to take a look."

"Thought you sailing types could look at the sky and tell. You know, red sky in the morning stuff."

Rex rolled his eyes, went below, and turned on his computer. He listened to a NOAA weather forecast, which talked about a strengthening tropical wave moving onto their planned track. He pulled up a radar image of the cloud cover in the location of the disturbance. No doubt about it, the tropical wave had turned north and was now unavoidable. In fifteen minutes, he returned topside. "Toad, sometime tomorrow night, things could get rough."

Toad answered in his usual asinine way. "Not my problem, Magellan. You're being paid to keep this thing upright and on course."

"Okay, but tomorrow night we are going to double reef and batten everything down. You do whatever you want, but if you're out of the cabin without a harness, you may join your Haitian friends as shark bait."

The next day they sailed into an increasingly cloud-covered horizon, and by night the wind shifted to the east and picked up to thirty knots. Toad was already in his berth. The genoa was rolled up, so only about twenty percent showed. A double reef was taken in the main, reducing it to one-third its usual size. Ten-foot swells were breaking over the deck. Exhausted, Rex checked the steering and went below.

He was awakened at 2:00 a.m. by the roar of a

storm. The boat pitched and rolled so much it was impossible to stand without a handhold. On his way out, he fell onto Toad's head in the quarter berth.

Toad woke up and yelled to make himself heard over the noise. "Get this sonofabitch under control. It's making me sick."

"We're in a storm. You want to come and help?"

"Not my job description, Admiral Halsey."

Rex hooked up the tether to his safety harness and stepped into the cockpit. Large waves plunged over the cabin. He checked the rigging and heard a loud pop— the roller furling line broke. The huge 160 percent genoa came flailing out into the gale.

The boat heeled to a dangerous degree. Wind and sea wailed like a jet engine on run-up. The big sail flapped back and forth as if it were a bullwhip wielded by the hand of God. The sail had to come down—now.

Rex cranked the engine, turned the boat into the storm, and engaged the electric autopilot. The excessive boat heel stopped, but the huge, loose genoa flailed like some trapped wild animal. After winching in the rogue sail from the cockpit, Rex clawed his way to the mast and loosened the halyard. On his way to the mast, the pitching boat brought him to his knees, and he crawled the rest of the way.

The sail only came down a couple of feet and became stuck. He tried to dash to the bow to pull on the sail during the falloff from a large swell, but he was caught during the following rise of the bow and he fell again, his face hitting the deck and busting open his lip. After pulling on the sail from the bow, it was necessary to go back to the mast to let out more halyard and return to the bow, which plunged and rose ten feet every few seconds. The sail had been attached and fed through a slot in the roller-furling rod; it would only come down a couple of feet at a time.

Due to the violent movement on the bow, he became sick, throwing up between the trips. Horizontal rain peppered his face. Fifteen-foot waves washed across the deck, periodically burying him underwater.

On his way back to the mast, a large wave rolled across, knocking him down and scooting him like a loose boat fender across the deck and under the lifelines. His safety harness saved him. The sail was flailing like an angry twenty-foot dragon. Pulling on the harness, he made his way to the sheet winch to try to control the beast. He tightened the sheets to tame the wild flapping, but he failed to cleat the second line after wrapping it around the winch. The line worked free and turned the sail loose once again. At the last moment, he saw it coming but too late. The large metal clew struck him in the temple.

The next thing he knew, he was dangling by his safety harness over the side of the boat while tons of water washed over him. He struggled to climb back aboard but was beat back by the waves. Finally, a wave thrust him upward, high enough for him to grasp a lifeline, and he climbed aboard.

An hour later, Rex had secured the sail. He stumbled down the stairs. Toad was in the quarter-berth with his head over the edge, where he had barfed all over the floor. For a few seconds, Rex considered killing him, but he was too tired and fell into the center berth, wet clothes and all.

At daybreak, Rex woke to a loud beeping noise. He bounded for the boat cockpit with the right side of his head throbbing. He was already faulting himself for sleeping so long without checking conditions. Out of his exhaustion-created coma, he tried to focus his mind.

Toad sat up. "What's that noise? Are we sinking?"

Rex opened the hatch. "It's the depth warning," he yelled. "Something's wrong."

The wind was still blowing about thirty knots, but on exiting the cabin, he noticed a less threatening sea. The depth gauge was periodically reading less than eight feet, which is where it was set to alarm. He looked down the companionway to the cabin and over the side and back to the depth gauge. The gauge bounced from six feet to a depth beyond its limit to read. The alarm stopped.

Rex studied their position on the chart and reported back to Toad. "It must have been a giant fish following under the boat."

Toad came on deck without his safety harness. "So, Captain Drake, you can talk to the fishes? How do you know we are not running aground?"

"Our position has us in five thousand feet of water. By the way, isn't it about time you cleaned up your barf on the cabin floor?"

Toad stood at the stern, looking out to sea. His loose hold on the self-steering was interrupting the guidance system.

"I'm not here to do sailor work," Toad said. "I'm here to shoot your ass if you get out of line."

Rex stepped up behind him. If he pushed the bastard overboard, he could say Toad was lost in the storm because he wouldn't wear his safety harness?

Toad turned, smiled, and stepped back into the cockpit. "So, Captain Cook, how're we doing on time?

If we miss our rendezvous with the money men, we both will end up on Snake's torture table."

They had another problem—they were way off course. Rex didn't answer but turned the boat to a corrective heading. He was reluctant to tell Toad they might be late.

"I asked you a question."

"We had an extra day to get there on time, but we've been blown off course."

"If you're so good at navigation, how did you get to where you didn't want to be?"

Rex gave Toad as much of a disgusted look as he dared. *Why did I even tell the bastard what I was doing?* "While you were barfing all over the cabin, I was saving the boat and I was exhausted," Rex said. "Ah…fuck it. Yes, we could be late."

"Don't be a wiseass, Captain Cook. The natives might get mean. But if you're late, I'll get real mean."

Chapter 15

Scrap

Mt. Pleasant, South Carolina

Monday morning, I got a call from my insurance broker. "Scrap, I hate to bring this up to start your week, but I got a letter from your bonding company yesterday. They say, due to insufficient supporting financial information, future bonding has been put on hold."

This was a punch in the gut right when I was beating at the fires of failure.

"Can you sow any magic over there?" I asked.

To make a stronger balance sheet, I had already fudged the percent of completion on my work in progress and delayed expense reporting. *I dare not do more.*

"Afraid not, Scrap. These people are all running scared."

Loss of bonding would kill my prospects for future work. At least now, Beth would stop hounding me over her exposure to the bonding, but it would be a small satisfaction if she knew the whole story of our financial situation.

I still hung on to the long-delayed school project, which finally had been approved and was now in full swing. Bankruptcy was looming—the birds had run out of the cover of marsh grass. Facing open water, the only chance was to fly. Like the birds, I was determined to go until the hunter fired his gun. He still had to hit the target.

I had laid off half my employees and tried to convince those who remained that we were now leaner and meaner—and stronger. We were making draws on the school project, although it wasn't enough money.

After the top structure was complete, and before the glasswork began on a unique viewing area, I received an architectural notice that changed the glass specifications. Along with routine guidance, embedded in the notice were some startling new glass requirements. I was pissed. It was obvious the architect and the engineer had overlooked the requirement for higher wind-resistance.

I called the architect. "What's this about the new glass specifications?"

There was a long pause. "It's a requirement," he said. "You will have to comply with it."

I slammed my desk drawer shut and sprang from my chair. "Well, I'll comply, but only if you give me a design change so I can work up a change order."

There was an even longer pause. "I'm sorry, Scrap. The owner has a tight budget. They won't accept a change order. They expect you to do the work without a design change."

I smelled the stench of bankruptcy. I clenched and unclenched my fists in frustration. This put my company in an impossible situation. I could not continue the job without a design change, and they would not give me one.

We stopped the job. Meanwhile, I was due a $240,000 progress payment on work already completed, and they held it up as further pressure.

I knew that stopping project work might cause the school district to call the performance bond on the job. Wednesday afternoon, I got the call. "Mr. Scruggs, this is Frank Harris representing Tri-State bonding."

"Yes, I have been expecting your call."

"As you know, Low Country Charter Development School has called your bond. I have been directed to gather the facts. The first order of business is to do an audit on the contract to see if we actually pay on their performance bond. This, of course, is time-sensitive because they want the money to complete their project. Later, we will do an extensive audit on your company finances."

My adrenalin peaked, followed by a sinking feeling. Shit, I had fudged the figures on income to get the bonding. If this came out in an audit, at best it would be embarrassing, but at worst it could be criminal.

About halfway through the contract audit, Harris informed me that he had enough information to justify putting a hold on paying the bond claim. This did not stop me from sweating about my pending company audit, but I was pleased those cheating bastards would not be getting their money for now. If I had anything to do with it, they would never get it.

The school district called a meeting, but I was not invited. I was the only one who was not at fault, so I was the enemy of all. After the meeting, I met with my attorney, Felix McCain. "What is going on?" I said.

Felix leaned back in his chair, turned his head

toward some diplomas on his wall, and turned back to me. "They say the cost overruns should be shared equally with the architectural firm, the engineering company, and you."

The total was a $900,000 increase in project cost.

I lost it. "I'm not paying those crooked sons of bitches a dime. I wasn't even at the meeting. I'll tell you what I'll do for them. I'll get my demolition crew together and tear the motherfucker down. I can probably get it done before they can get an injunction."

"Hold on, hold on," Felix said. "I'm your attorney and your friend. Let's work through this."

Felix called another meeting, which I did attend. The attorney for the mealy-mouthed architect addressed me. "Mr. Scruggs, the fact you have failed to perform under your contract makes you liable for these cost overruns."

I was like a lion sire looking at a strange male entering my pride. I leaped up, charged to his place at the head of the table, and grabbed him around the shirt collar. "Listen, you ethically challenged cur. Everybody in this room knows this is a sham. The bonding company said as much. If I'm going to be liable, it will be because I'm going to kick your ass."

I dragged him out of his chair by the collar before Felix raced over and hustled me out of the room. All eyes followed me in total silence except for the calm voice of my attorney coaxing me along.

Felix left me alone and went back to the meeting. He returned to present me with a reduced liability offer. I would pay only $100,000 of the increased costs. I wouldn't consider it. My lawyer was one of the good ones, and he gave me some serious advice. "If we litigate, we will probably win, but it will cost two hundred thousand to take it through the courts. What they're offering is a cheap way out. They even had the gall to say it. This is a form of blackmail, which happens all the time. Agree to pay the price to avoid an expensive lawsuit."

"What about the two hundred and forty thousand they owe for work I completed before the job was shut down?"

"That's another fight, but keep in mind, they will use the new contractor to obfuscate and hide the work you did. I doubt you'll ever get enough to justify going after it. It will be another expensive court fight."

I couldn't believe this kind of legal treachery was possible right out in the open and with no shame. If it hadn't been for Felix, I would have handed somebody his head.

"This isn't fair. How can they do this?"

"Listen. Fair's got nothing to do with it. You want fair? Go to the whorehouse—you pay your money; you get your pussy. That's fair. This is cutthroat legal manipulation."

"What the hell you talking about? Can they do this? I need to get me a mafia lawyer."

But Felix wasn't to blame. I could tell he felt my pain.

"Okay," I said after I cooled down, "let's try some manipulation of our own. Here's what we do. You had to stop me from fighting at the meeting, so they already think I'm a wild man. Go back and convince them I'm crazy, and I'll pull them all into a huge court fight if they keep insisting I pay another one hundred thousand. Tell them there will be enough adverse publicity to go around, and their court expenses will go through the roof. Convince them I'll go all the way to bankruptcy and even physical attack, but I will not pay—which, Felix, I won't. I don't have the money."

Felix agreed, and it worked. He returned to my place of solitude and informed me they would share all the extra expense.

So, I won that fight, but by the following Wednesday, it made no difference. Without the money they already owed me, I was a goner. Bankruptcy, Beth's new job, Emma's expensive school, and my reputation lay like roadkill at my feet.

Chapter 16

Rex

Beaufort, North Carolina

They were in sight of Beaufort a day late. Toad was agitated and Rex was scared. He was also sick of Toad's grunge and insults and looked forward to getting off the boat. He was tired, hadn't had a real shower in two weeks, and dreaded what might be ahead. He knew Blackbeard ran *Queen Ann's Revenge* aground near North Carolina's Beaufort Inlet. As he planned his sailing approach to Beaufort, these old calamities of wild and wayward men whispered to his blackened heart. He could see the news: *Florida boat suffers the fate of Queen Ann's Revenge. Runs aground with one thousand kilos of cocaine. Two drug smugglers arrested.*

The eleventh day at sea arrived with the boat close to shore, sailing well south of Cape Lookout. Toad appeared nervous, causing Rex's heart to pound. The only conversation came from Toad. "Listen up, Captain Bligh. If we miss the money exchange, we're both up shit's creek, but I'll see to it that you scream twice as loud and long as Meatman."

They turned north to line up with the channel leading into Beaufort. Motoring past the business area around the Town Docks, they proceeded to the less-populated Town Creek Marina, which had the added advantage of its location next to the airport.

The *Mona More* came alongside the dock, and Rex asked Toad to secure the bowline.

"Secure it yourself," he said. "Not my job. I got more important things." He pulled out one of his many cell phones and tried to make their delivery contact.

Rex threw his hands up in disgust and scurried to the bow to keep the boat from drifting away from the dock. Tying up his boat, he made a trip to the marina office to register for rent on a boat slip. He lingered at the marina and didn't return for an hour, dreading what he may face. He considered running away but decided he would be caught.

"Where the hell have you been?" Toad said when Rex finally returned. "If you think of anything close to crossing me or quitting, I have been directed to take you out."

"Toad, it took some time to reserve our space, that's all."

About midnight, a van showed up with three men, two of which were festooned with gold chains and tattoos. The third man was dressed in a suit, but not just any suit. This one was dark blue with green buttons and a bright green vest, the color of a chameleon on a new fern leaf. His hair was cut close on the sides and fitted perfectly on top was a blue fez with a yellow tassel. Tied to his wrist was a leather thong about eighteen inches long.

The dock was deserted. The man with the bright vest strutted up to Toad. "Okay, big fellow, they call me Suit Man. You're late and we was about ready to take back the money. We're here with twenty mil. You're supposed to have one thousand kilos for me."

Toad picked up the AR-15, cradling it so the barrel pointed at Suit Man's crotch.

"Don't 'big fellow' me, you fucking strutting gasbag. The amount is twenty-one million, and if you think you're going to cheat Snake that easy, you must not have heard about his torture room."

"Hey, man, I don't got to take your shit."

Toad raised the AR15 and pointed it at his chest. "Not only do you have to take my shit, but you're about to die in the process."

Rex thought Toad was going to kill all of them. Once he waved the gun around, it became obvious that Suit Man, notwithstanding all the peacock display and smart-ass talk, was now deathly afraid. "Hey man, don't shoot. I don't know 'bout no money. This is what they give me to buy your one thousand kilos."

Rex interceded. "Maybe we should call Snake and ask him to check with his contacts."

"Not gonna happen. Snake's priority is keeping himself removed. If anybody dies, I decide. You keep out of this."

"Man, please," Suit Guy said, "I ain't here for no war."

Rex could see these guys were ready to bolt and run. If that happened, he was sure Toad would start shooting. "Wait, killing these guys might ding our deal."

"Listen, Magellan. I want you to shut up. I'm going to kill two of these and let the third go back and pass the message. If they got the money, we take it and try to give the syndicate the correct amount of coke later."

Suit Man's voice trembled. "Man, don't shoot. We can work it out."

To Rex, the air felt charged, like it did before a lightning strike. One of Suit Man's punks backed away. Toad fired, and the man grabbed his leg and hit the ground, groaning.

"Toad, Toad—hold it!" Rex said. "Listen to me. I'll take my pay in fifty kilos of cocaine, which is worth about what I would make. Snake gets all his money, and if this bird of paradise is telling the truth, he should be happy to escape with fifty kilos less."

"That's a good deal, Captain Cook, and if you hornswogglers like it, we can start loading coke in the van. If you don't, you die."

Whether it was chicanery or a mix-up, the money men seemed happy now, with the idea they could make the transaction and get away with their lives. The man that was shot in the leg was allowed to sit out the loading.

Now that he had prevented a crisis, Rex gave some thought about what he would do with his cocaine. *Perhaps he could come out even better.*

The cocaine, including Rex's portion, was loaded into the van with the money. On the way to the airport, Rex worried about the weight to be loaded on his airplane. He kept looking at the suitcases full of money and counting them.

A night watchman was on duty at the airport's entrance. Rex showed him ownership papers of his Beech Queen Air. "We need to load the plane for an early morning departure," Rex said.

The guard looked at the papers and nodded. "Okay, you guys are keeping my miserable hours."

Snake had demanded the money be delivered in the same type of waterproof aluminum suitcases as he had shipped the cocaine. Rex counted forty pieces of the luggage, each containing $500,000. He was uneasy and chastised himself for not thinking this through. It never occurred to him they could overgross the airplane with money—but forty suitcases could be over two thousand pounds.

Everybody but Toad and the man with the bullet hole in his leg helped load the money and Rex's two suitcases of cocaine onto the airplane. The relieved thugs piled into their van. Suit Man turned to his wounded helper and demanded that he stop moaning until they passed the night watchman. The van sped away with the cocaine less the two suitcases Rex received for his payment. Rex confronted Toad. "I was not aware all the money would be delivered in twenties."

"What are you driving at, Bird Man?"

Arguing with Toad increased his apprehension, but Rex was in a tight spot. "This is a heavy load. We might be too heavy and—"

"Hey, Lindbergh, you'll just have to add more power. We ain't leaving Snake's money in Beaufort."

Rex surveyed the quiet airport. In the dim light of a runway marker, a coyote strolled across, no doubt looking for an easy mark for the evening meal. *Aren't we all?*

"Somebody should have told me the money was all in twenties. If it had been in hundred-dollar bills, it would be a snap."

"Well, General Mitchell, this ain't your end of the operation. Only about five percent of people ever see a hundred, and these boys who buy nose candy deal in twenties, so twenties it is. You just got to figure it out."

Rex gazed at the runway, which only had the edge lights turned on. He wondered what the overrun looked like. He was trapped. He wasn't sure until he did all the calculations, but he feared the worst. *I'd feel better if this sleazy bastard weren't aboard.*

"I can't make things weigh less, and this airplane is unsafe flying with more weight than it was designed to carry."

"Listen up, birdman. You're contracted to move Snake's money. My job is to kill you if you don't. Got it?"

Chapter 17

Beth

Mt. Pleasant, South Carolina

Beth opened the refrigerator door and realized she was holding the greasy spatula intended for the dishwasher. *I'm losing my mind.* The distraction over Scrap, and the cost of Emma's new school, had persisted all morning. Though he had downplayed their financial situation, she was sure it was more serious. She went to the study where Scrap was working on what he said was business details. "We need to talk."

He faced her, but his wild-eyed expression belied his soft demeanor. "Sure, morning glory. This can wait. What's on your lovely mind?"

She put her hand on her hips and noticed he folded his arms defensively across his chest. "Scrap, I'm serious, don't shut me out."

He unfolded his arms and toyed with a paperweight. "Okay, I'm serious."

"It's our finances. I'm concerned about paying for Emma's new school and misleading the Education Department in Columbia. I promised them there would be no surprises."

He bolted out of his chair. "I told you I have it covered. Yes, money is tight, but I'll figure it all out. I thought we had this conversation."

Beth left the study, still flustered.

Scrap left the house in a huff.

She went to their bedroom and absent-mindedly straightened the throw pillows on the bed more than once. Alone in the house, she considered the tension between them. It seemed there was some deceit going on. They had always confided in each other, but not lately. Now he seemed preoccupied and on edge.

It wasn't that she didn't trust him. She knew her husband. He was a good, principled man, but he was not a person of ordinary habits. Scrap was impulsive and could veer off the normal road without hesitation. She recalled the time he came home after 9:00 p.m. because he was at the police station over a confrontation with a man for whipping his dog. Incensed over the interference, the man resisted, and Scrap ended up beating him into submission and calling the police. In the end, assault charges were dropped on Scrap if he would drop his cruelty to animal's charge on the dog whipper.

She went back to the kitchen and heard his truck leaving the garage. Something was going on, which she couldn't quite get her arms around.

Beth called her friend, Tina. She needed to talk to another female.

"Hi girl, what's going on?"

She noticed her hands were sweating. "There's something going on in Scrap's head that I can't put my finger on. I feel like our marriage is being pulled apart."

"You think he's having an affair?"

Beth hesitated, picked up a pen, and started doodling on a notepad. "No, our marriage is too intimate for me not to know."

"You two have a wonderful thing. You can't let it slip away. Remember, I was there when you met Scrap after The Citadel parade. The day in front of number four barracks, with his trim, muscular physique and ready smile—the sword, the red sash, the shiny brass on white webbing. You actually said, 'He's the most beautiful thing I've ever seen.' He changed your life from a semi-recluse to an outgoing, vivacious charmer."

Holding her cell phone, she went out on the porch overlooking the marsh. A flight of fifty ibises flew overhead. Their only worry: Would the destination mudflat have too much water for their long, curved beaks to retrieve the tasty fiddlers? "Oh, stop it, Tina. You exaggerate everything."

"Really?" Tina said. "I know the racy things you said about him after just one date. In fact, I remember your words: 'With Scrap, it's animal magnetism. It's hard to describe. Although he exudes confidence, he's still polite and kind. But there's this aura about him, as if he's ready to pounce and devour anything life presents. He might be a little rough around the edges and even naïve.' And here, old girl, you giggled, and in your exact words, you said, 'I ache for him, I think about him constantly, I want him close.' "

Beth cried. "Oh Tina, I do remember. I fear it's all drifting away."

Trying to get control, she threw a handful of birdseed off the porch

"Don't let it happen," Tina said. "It's your job to get to the bottom of the problem. Men are too stupid to know how."

"Thank you, Tina, I needed the talk. We'll visit later."

The phone call caused Beth to wonder what could be done to improve their relationship. Maybe she was the problem. She had to admit she missed working and feeling productive. Maybe it was eating at her, and she was taking it out on Scrap. Being on the school board was not a paying job, but if she got the new job in Columbia, it paid well.

She walked aimlessly around the house and finally went to her closet and opened the drawer where she kept her gun. It was two hours before Emma got out of school. She removed her 9mm Lady Smith and one hundred rounds of ammo and drove to the gun range. Beth usually did her shooting with Scrap, but she had found when she was alone, the concentration and solitude cleared her mind.

She fired two clips at a silhouette target and stopped to reload and look at her target. Although Scrap didn't say it, she had a suspicion they may need the extra money. He had a way of always pushing to the edge of the envelope. In earlier years, the world seemed less complicated, and Scrap's unpredictable behavior was a thrill. It was one of the things she found fascinating, but now it worried her.

She fired fifty rounds and packed up her equipment, resolving to work on her marriage, but right now, her concern was on Emma. The prospect of the new job was exciting, but her daughter needed help, and the expensive new school was a must.

Chapter 18

Rex

Airport, Beaufort, North Carolina

Rex added up the weight at 6:30 a.m. and nudged Toad. "We're overgrossed."

Toad snorted himself awake. "What's that?"

"The airplane is going to be overgrossed."

"Ah, don't give me this gross shit," Toad said. "What does that mean?"

"What it means is money weighs one gram per bill. We have one million—in twenties—plus my cocaine, plus the weight of forty-two suitcases themselves at five pounds each, for a total cargo weight of 2,720 pounds. Add in your weight, my weight, our luggage, and 750 pounds of gas, and the grand total is 4,100 pounds. The empty airplane weighs 5,000 pounds. Add this up, and it weighs 9,100 pounds. But the max gross weight on this airplane is 8,200 pounds. Meaning we're 900 pounds overweight."

Toad actually seemed to listen, and he appeared impressed, but for only a second. "Well, General Doolittle, you better make this thing work on less gas, or throw your luggage and two suitcases of toot overboard, because we ain't leaving Snake's money."

"It would help if you removed your 320 pounds

plus your luggage and flew back commercially."

"No way, you'll get both of us on The Acid Man's table. And something else, Ace, careful with your slurs about my weight."

Rex had already seen Toad kill without warning, and he had just watched him shoot a man in the leg. The airplane would probably fly with an over gross weight situation as long as no other problems developed. Besides, any peril to the money delivery was an invitation to Snake's torture chamber. He knew, however, this was bad aviation. "If one of our engines quits on takeoff, we die. If one quits in route, the airplane cannot maintain altitude."

"Listen, Yeager. You need to keep 'em running. That's your job. It ain't my job to see this thing flies, but before I leave Snake's money, somebody's gonna die. Got it?"

Rex had developed a visceral hatred for Toad. It would be nice to see him on The Acid Man's table, but if anything went wrong, they both would be there. Being overweight increased the risk of not arriving with Snake's money on time. He wondered if losing Mona was worth all the risk he was taking to be rich. *Jesus, why did I get in this?*

"Okay, okay," Rex said. "But it would be nice if I knew where we are going."

"Don't be a smartass. I told you Snake didn't want to give that out 'til right at takeoff. If you got your shit together, I'll give Snake a call, and he ain't gonna be happy we're late."

With a new cell phone, Toad called. "Dos speaking."

Then what must be some sort of code: "Rome,

Georgia."

And finally ending the call with: "Seagull flying with full craw."

He clicked off and turned to Rex. "Okay, Colonel Glenn, your airport is named Herlong. Now see if you can get this bird to flap its wings, and I don't want to see another delay."

Rex knew the airport; it was where he had been keeping his own airplane. He cranked the engines. Oil pressure on number two was low. The distraction over his evil endeavor had caused it to slip his mind, and now it loomed. He tapped the gauge. No change. His anxiety increased. *Maybe it will increase some on engine run-up.*

He completed his checklist and turned to Toad. "You need to put on your seat belt."

"Don't tell me what to do, Lindberg. Seatbelts are a waste of time because if anything goes wrong, we both gonna die on The Acid Man's table."

"Suit yourself."

The mention of Snake's table brought back the horrible experience in the torture room.

The weather was clear, and they were the only activity at the small airport. The Queen Air taxied out at 7:30 a.m. before the scheduled attendant came on duty at eight o'clock. They had not filed a flight plan, which was considered careless, but not illegal.

On the run-up check, Rex was tense. Toad was in the right seat next to him like a coiled cobra. Jacking the power back and forth on the right engine attracted Toad's attention.

"Hey, Lindbergh, something wrong with your machine?"

A drop of sweat dripped from Rex's chin. "Number two shows low oil pressure."

"Well, quit fucking with it and let's go."

Rex lined up for takeoff, held the brakes, and applied full power. He released the brakes, and the plane roared down the runway. Agonizingly slow, the airspeed crept toward liftoff, and the end of the runway neared. "Come on baby," Rex murmured. "Come on."

They had passed the point where they had enough runway left to stop. Now it was either take off or die. Just prior to a grass overrun, they staggered into the air and did a slow climb.

They struggled out over the ocean on a south heading to avoid traffic at the Cherry Point Marine Air Base. Once clear, Rex turned southwest, direct to Wilmington.

It took ten minutes to reach the VFR cruising altitude of 4,500 feet, where Rex could reduce the strain on the engines. The oil pressure on number two was low but holding. Toad looked out the window.

No reports were made, and the transponder was off. Even if a radar operator picked up a skin paint, they would not know who or what they were.

As the Queen Air continued its journey to Jacksonville, the airway to Charleston gradually took it about twenty miles inland. Toad was sound asleep. The engines made their harmonic drone, and Rex rubbed his eyes to stay awake. His thoughts turned to Mona—how he longed for her. Was it just sex, or did he truly want to be with her? It was hard to tell because he wanted sex all the time. *What would she say if she knew what I was doing to earn the money she liked to spend?*

After this delivery he would contact his friend in

Lexington, Kentucky, and arrange a trade for his cocaine—and return to Mona. He could get $25,000 per kilo in Lexington, which would give him $1,250,000 for his fifty keys. This haul should be enough to satisfy them both.

But he wasn't sure how he was going get out of this Snake enterprise alive, or if God was going to punish him for the evil he'd done. He looked across Toad's sleeping fat body toward a change in the sound coming from the right side—and got his answer. There was a loud bang. Toad jerked but did not fully awaken. Oil pressure for the right engine dropped to zero.

Oil and smoke poured out of the engine, and it quit.

The Queen Air yawed thirty degrees right, and the left wing rose ominously in what Rex recognized as the entry to a spin. He knew engine failure with a high-gross weight Queen Air can—and has—caused an out-of-control spin and crash.

Rex immediately applied left rudder and turned the yoke to the left. As soon as he had control, he eased the left engine to full power. To prevent uncontrollable drag, he focused on making sure the prop was feathered, all the time feeding in rudder and aileron trim to relieve control pressure.

"Okay, got it under control. Shit. I'm losing altitude."

Smoke poured out of the dead engine. Toad woke up, and his eyes got wide. He looked over at Rex, who was sweating to maintain control. "What's going on?"

In order to halt the speed deterioration, Rex dropped the nose for a slow descent.

"Listen, bastard," Rex snapped. "I told you this whole thing was out of limits. Now the worst has happened. We are going down."

"What the fuck you mean we're going down? Aren't we still flying?"

"We've lost an engine, asshole. We can't maintain altitude. We're too heavy and need to throw something out."

Toad drew his gun and pointed it at Rex. "I told you, we ain't losing any of Snake's money. We can throw out your coke and our luggage."

"That's not enough. We need to lose at least five hundred pounds."

"You better figure something out. We ain't losing Snake's money!"

Rex glanced out the side window. "We just passed Georgetown County airport. I need to declare an emergency and land there."

"Bullshit, Yeager. If you talk on that radio, you'll do it with a bullet in your head."

Rex's priority now was to save his life and, if he could do that, stay off Snake's torture table. Getting caught with drugs was no longer his biggest concern. But Toad was a mystery. He either did not understand, or he didn't care. He was hung up on saving Snake's money.

Toad cocked his big revolver and aimed at Rex's head. "You gotta just keep this thing in the air."

"That gun won't do you any good. Shoot me and where does it leave you?"

"It's encouragement for you to do the right thing. I'll shoot you even if we both die. Don't test me, Yeager."

Rex knew Toad would probably shoot him right before impact if they were to crash. Under their present conditions, the airplane would not stay in the air. All the choices led to disaster. He considered trying to find water to land in, but Toad would still probably shoot him.

In his effort to control the airplane's asymmetric power, Rex had overcorrected, and the plane's heading had drifted to the east toward the ocean. The altitude was one thousand feet as they crossed a marsh area and into rain.

"Damn, I can't see anything up ahead."

Out the left side, he could barely make out that they were passing next to a large bay.

Toad still held the cocked 44 magnum at Rex's head. "Better figure out something, Ace, or this is your last dogfight."

"Fucking quit with the damn names!"

On the floor to his left, a leather bag contained flight manuals. Rex turned and looked down as if he had the saving information in the flight bag. With his left hand, he shifted some things around in his flight bag. In one lightning motion, he thrust a .38 caliber derringer into Toad's face and fired.

An ugly hole appeared at the base of Toad's nose from the hollow point bullet. The fat body gave a convulsive jerk, and his big gun fired. The bullet missed Rex and blasted through the side window. Toad's head popped back and fell forward.

Rex reached across the twitching walrus and unlatched the door. It fell open a crack and wind howled through the plane. Toad was not wearing his seat belt, and his weight slumped against the door. Rex used his right foot against Toad's rib cage and pushed him out the door. The blast of air caught the open door and slammed it closed so hard it latched. Toad fell toward the marsh.

There, I lost 320 pounds of ugly fat!

Rex wrestled the airplane back under control and checked to see if Toad's weight loss made a difference. He wondered how deep Toad would sink in the marsh below and when the vultures would arrive.

Chapter 19

Rex

Over the Marsh, South Carolina

The plane was down to four hundred feet. With the loss of Toad's weight, Rex was able to slow his descent but not stop it. He was too low now to try to throw anything else out. It was all he could do to maintain control of his descent.

The rain reduced visibility to only a couple hundred feet. He descended through fifty feet, and the nearness of marsh loomed out his side window. *This is it.*

In World War II, there were stories of airmen who made it home with a damaged engine by flying on a cushion of air that gave extra lift close to the ground. *Maybe—maybe?*

Descent slowed and stopped at twenty-five feet. Voila! Ground effect. Wet with the sweat of exertion and stress, he skimmed a few feet above the marsh.

He worked the outside observation into the instrument crosscheck, but his view there was partially restricted by the bullet hole from the final shot Toad would ever fire. Rex took some comfort in the fact that he was over the constant elevation of the marsh; however, it occurred to him there could be manmade structures ahead. The confrontation with Toad, his close proximity to the ground, and the heavy rain had caused him to lose track of his location. He stole quick glances through the forward windshield, but they revealed nothing but the driving rain striking the windshield. He worried about what might lie ahead.

The terrain immediately below abruptly changed from smooth cordgrass to black needle rush, red cedar, and scrub live oak. He looked up in time to see two seventy-foot slash pine trees appear at the edge of a hummock. Before he could react, the airplane went between them. The trees ripped off both wings, and the Queen Air plunged into the jungle ahead.

There was loud grating and ripping as the fuselage bounced and plowed through earth and vegetation. Rex was thrown forward against his shoulder harness with the force of possibly twenty times gravity.

****

Rex gradually began to perceive the world around him. Everything was quiet, except for the rapid rattle of early fall cicadas. He didn't know how long he had been out, and at first, when he came to, he thought he was dead. Then he worried about fire but remembered the wings had been torn off along with the fuel tanks.

Am I injured?

He tried moving body parts—some pain in the left knee and neck. He turned his head and found the pain wasn't bad. His jeans had a tear at the knee but no blood. Gradually, he realized there were no serious injuries, and his condition was much better than he had imagined. Taking stock revealed positive possibilities. He wondered if anyone had seen the plane going down. It was possible no one had, out here in the marsh, in a low-visibility situation, with hard rain. Snake's torture table was a sure thing now. Escape was his only avenue.

Rex didn't know where the plane was, but neither did anybody else. Without his help, the crash site may go undiscovered. He pushed aside a suitcase, which had come forward during the crash, and checked out the disarray in the back. Although some of the suitcases were dislodged, and at least one was busted open, it was unlikely any had been tossed out.

Toad is gone. I still have all the money.

He needed to get out, figure out where he was. He tried the door, but it was jammed. After several raps with his shoulder, the damaged door released. It hung down from hyperextended hinges, and he took in the lush vegetation outside. The rain had stopped. It was especially humid and hot for late September. Somewhere the distinct cackle of a pileated woodpecker pierced the silence.

The fuselage was three feet above the ground and resting on a solid undergrowth of saw palmettos. Rex slid to the edge of his seat. The gentle sulfur aroma of the marsh seeped in, and with it a flashback to the time in high school when he had made a marsh field trip with the Sea Scouts.

God, it's hot. This area was not the mainland. It was a small island called a hummock. Rex's fleeting reminiscence also triggered a vague sense of dread, for he knew how remote these little islands could be. The one they had visited as Sea Scouts near Jacksonville could only be accessed at extreme high tides.

He surveyed the steamy surroundings and sensed he was about to go from predator to prey. He jumped from the aircraft door far enough to miss a fallen cabbage palmetto trunk.

A half-second after Rex's shoes struck the ground, searing pain shot into his left calf. He screamed, but only a marsh rabbit stopped to listen, and a great blue heron, perched on a dead cedar, took flight. He looked down in time to see a huge snake slither away. It disappeared under some palm fronds nearby. He got a glimpse of the yellow-outlined black diamonds on a sleek, long body as thick as a man's arm. *Oh God, a diamondback rattler.* He had an overwhelming sense he was in trouble. "You son of a bitch!"

Panic set in.

"God, please no."

Rex hobbled to the edge of the marsh that confined him, alarmed to see the outline of the mainland a mile away. He wasted valuable time running to the other side of the hummock only to find land of a barrier island much farther away. He became more desperate when he looked at his swollen, discolored leg. The pain was like a hundred hornet stings in the same spot.

He remembered the airplane first aid kit. The FAA required a first aid kit to be on board. Racing back to the plane, he realized it was wasting valuable time. No way an aviation first aid kit would have anything for snake bites.

He retrieved the small backpack that had his personal items and dragged it across money that had spilled out from the busted open suitcase. Hesitating for a second, he stuffed stacks of twenties into his backpack.

Before leaving the airplane, his eyes focused on another suitcase. *I need more money for Mona.* He slipped on his backpack and snatched up the suitcase containing $500,000 and headed toward the mainland side of the hummock. With the backpack and a fifty-pound aluminum suitcase, Rex struck out across the stretch of marsh. He looked at his watch. It was after ten o'clock. The recent rain caused the humidity to spike. The sun came out and the steamy temperature climbed. His clothes stuck to his body with sweat, but the marsh was firmer close to the island, so good progress was made. The dark green outline of the mainland in the distance seemed to be getting closer.

I'm going to make it.

The marsh grass stung his arms and legs, and gradually, as if the marsh itself had a score to settle, the pluff mud grew softer, and he sank farther with each step, finally losing his shoes. He cut his feet on oyster shells, but he had to keep going. He could feel the poison. Tired and sick, he wanted to lie down.

He stopped and retched up the last of what was in his stomach and then kept going.

His thinking grew disjointed. He was getting dizzy. He sank to his knees with each step but still hung onto the suitcase. *The money, I need money for Mona. I can't lie down. Got to keep going.*

He arrived at the edge of a tidewater creek, but his stamina was spent and fell into the water. He struggled to keep his head above the surface and lost his grip on the suitcase. With a desperate attempt, he tried to retrieve it, but the tide was flowing fast and carried it away. The cooler water of the creek cleared his head enough for him to keep from drowning, but all he could do was flounder around helplessly.

In his fading awareness, there was the putt-putt of a

motor. A strong arm pulled him into a boat.
    Oh Mona, I'm dying. And his mind went blank.

Chapter 20

Scrap

Autumn on the Marsh, South Carolina

My depression overwhelmed me. I walked around my office in a daze. At times, I felt like saying fuck it and walk away. But, of course, I couldn't do it. My training at The Citadel was to take responsibility—*No Excuse, Sir.* You don't fold when too many enemies are coming over the hill. I would stand up and face what came and own up to all.

I got a fishing rod from the storage area in the back of my business and drove to the Mt. Pleasant Pier. I decided to give myself a week to figure out an orderly defeat, and then I would tell Beth and my employees.

It was almost dark when I departed with two nice sheepshead, still depressed but in better shape.

I came home from fishing late Friday afternoon. Beth was in the kitchen and greeted me with a big kiss. She was beaming and jumping around like a child. And it hit me. She had her interview in Columbia at one o'clock today. "How'd it go?"

"It went really well. In fact, they all but told me I had the job, but they also said that they could not commit until all of the due diligence was complete."

My heart sank. Panic gripped my chest. This job

meant so much to her, and I was about to sabotage it. I faked a big smile. "Great new...news."

"What's wrong? You act like you're about to have some kind of attack."

I closed my eyes and a tear squeezed out and trickled down my face. "I'm okay. I had a knock-down, drag-out fight with city hall and I'm still keyed up."

"If it was about money, I hope you won. The only stressful part of my interview was the disclosure statement I had to sign."

I gathered my wits. "What's that got to do with money?"

"I signed a statement that said I had no knowledge of any personal circumstances that could reflect unfavorably on the department, its employees, or their family."

I swallowed, kissed her gently, and turned away. "I'm glad it went well. I need to go for a run. Be back in an hour."

During my run, I realized Beth knew something was wrong and she knew what it was. It was time to chew my leg off. But not until my week was up.

Saturday morning promised to be one of those wonderful early October days in the Lowcountry. It had been hot, but a fast-moving cool front came through in the night. The temperature was forecast to climb to seventy-five degrees at 2:00 p.m. The new moon high tide would peak at over seven feet around 9:00 a.m. During this moon phase, with the sun and the moon in alignment, the pull of both would make a super tide. The promise of a fifteen-knot wind out of the northeast would make the water even higher and hold it in longer. Conditions were perfect, and it had been so long since I had been marsh hen hunting, I was eager to get out. It would take my mind off this endless financial waterboarding.

At 7:30 a.m., I launched my fifteen-foot Jon boat at Garris Landing off Sewee Road, close to my old childhood stomping grounds. I motored out to the vast marsh area south of Bulls Bay. Normally this hunting is done with two people, but craving solitude, I went alone.

The high-pitched cackle of the clapper rail can often be heard in the marsh behind my house, but these Lowcountry fowl are seldom seen. They can fly quite well but mostly run out of sight in the tall marsh grass. Beth does a great job of turning my hunt into a tasty meal from these birds, which are about twice as large as a bobwhite.

The peace of Fiddlers Creek brought tears. I throttled back and steered in the quiet rising water.

The time to actually see marsh hens is when the tide rises high enough to float them out above the grass. During the legal hunting season, these tides only occur a few days a year. Because the hunter's boat is poled through the thick grass, it's hard work and has discouraged most of today's softer hunters.

The temperature climbed to sixty degrees, but with the northeast breeze, it was chilly. As the sun rose over the marsh, it felt good. The smooth cordgrass, a.k.a. marsh grass, was mature and starting to tan. It would soon resemble the ripening of a giant wheat field in Kansas. Newly arrived green-winged teal streaked overhead like jet fighters. Rounding a bend in the creek, I caught sight of the partially hidden silhouette of a majestic great blue heron. It gave a complaining, froglike squawk and took flight with its six-foot wingspan.

The saltwater made its way into the upper reaches of the marsh, and finger mullet took the opportunity to feed on the rich nutrients. I glimpsed a ripple from the dorsal fin of a spot-tail bass following the mullet.

The nostalgia and tranquility gave me an endorphin high. I felt grateful, almost religious. This was how life was before it got complicated. But it wasn't long before my financial situation came rushing back to mind—a threat to my way of life and to my family.

I shut off the engine and waited for the tide. It kept rising until it was almost too high. The marsh hens had so little cover they were swimming toward any high ground they could find.

Hunting alone was difficult. I had to pole the boat until a bird flew, quickly throw down the pole, grab the gun, and shoot before it was out of range. I admit that sometimes my shot was made in what a game warden may classify as a legal gray area. I occasionally pushed the birds to fly while still running the motor.

The legal limit was fifteen birds, but after killing only six, it was obvious the birds were trying to find cover on higher ground. I figured I might be able to flush some birds off the edge of the marsh where they were hiding on a hummock about a mile from the mainland. The water was the highest I had ever hunted in, and I was able to motor right up to the island, which normally was surrounded by an expanse of marsh. I had viewed the small island from Fiddlers Creek many times in my youth but had never had a tide high enough to actually visit.

I tied up to a red cedar bush and waded in the

ecotone area of the hummock. The ecotone is a transitional area between the salt marsh and the highland. The vegetation there is different from both. It's made up of black needle rush, sea ox-eye daisy, marsh elder, sea-myrtle, and red cedar.

I immediately flushed two birds and shot one as it flew into the island vegetation. The interior of the hummock was made up of scrub live oak, pine, cabbage palmetto, yaupon holly, and saw palmetto. Searching for the bird, I walked to the middle of the small island. My heart skipped. For a second, it was hard to focus on the unlikely image—an airplane.

Approaching, I could make out a fuselage with the wings missing. Cautiously, I neared, wondering about causalities and survivors. I stopped short for a few seconds and tried to assess what had happened here in this remote place. Sensing danger—a feeling of foreboding—the hair stood up on my neck. Everything was quiet. No evidence of survivors. Slipping closer, I was wary as if something deadly were about to spring from the scene. I stepped onto an old palmetto log and peered through the side window. I noticed the glass.

A bullet hole.

How could this be? A crash I had never heard about and nobody at the crash site? And what about the bullet hole? Maybe there were bodies inside out of my view.

The cabin door was open about three inches and misaligned. Dreading what I would see inside, I opened the door. There was an odor of oil and electric wiring—a fresh odor. And another smell I couldn't place. Everything was eerily quiet. My eyes fully focused—

Money—lots of it—spilling from an aluminum

suitcase in bundles of twenties. Quiet money just lying there.

In the still air came a rustle and a sound like the wings of a giant bumblebee. It came from the log under my feet. A huge diamondback rattler slithered out from under the old dead palmetto I was standing on. A chill engulfed me.

Within seconds the rattler disappeared into the underbrush. My eyes refocused on a drip of fluid coming from the demolished wing. I checked closer. The area was wet with hydraulic fluid, and in some places, it was dripping. Torn vegetation was fresh.

This just happened.

They may be coming back soon. With heightened apprehension, I went back to the airplane cabin and leaned inside for a better look. There was luggage and a flight bag but no other evidence of humans. I climbed onto the pilot's seat and stood on my knees to study the cabin. The light was poor inside, but I could make out more suitcases, all of them identical. Far too many to be luggage. Two of them had been thrown forward and were partway open. My God, it was all money, stacks and stacks of twenties. The smell I couldn't identify was the odor of money. My hands were shaking. Maybe because I'd been living for the last few months so short of money, or maybe large amounts of money naturally inflamed humans.

I used my multi-tool to open several suitcases. *Money—more money.* I was breathing heavily when I got to the last two separated from the others in the back. One of these had also been sprung partly open. I looked inside, but my excitement was replaced with a sense of dread and disgust. It was full of small plastic-wrapped bundles of white powder.

Cocaine?

I left them alone and made my way back toward the front of the airplane. I had lost track of time. The receding tide would leave me stranded. I needed to get off this island.

I looked at the bundles of twenties—hesitating, trembling. Fleeting thoughts of Beth's new job, Emma's dyslexia and need for an expensive school, and my failing business in need of a massive influx of money to keep it afloat. But this was drug money. I thought of Dee and how we had lived by the code of honor. I moved one of the suitcases to the door area. I looked at it with both excitement and dread.

Could this be turned from bad money to good money? I picked up the suitcase and headed to my boat. I looked around like an animal that had made a kill and was worried another larger predator would take it. A marsh rabbit startled me as it bolted for cover. Although I had done nothing wrong, I felt guilty—like a dog eating the neighbor's garbage.

The tide was indeed going out and had already fallen a couple of inches. Several wood storks took flight from a roost on a dead live oak tree. Their long, black-tipped wings stood out in the morning sun. Fiddlers Creek was about three hundred yards southeast, and I needed most of the unusually high tide to make it back to deep water. Rushing back, almost in a frenzy now, I became a man on a mission.

I made a total of ten trips from the crash to my boat, each with a suitcase full of money.

Chapter 21

Rex

Hospital in Mt. Pleasant, South Carolina

Rex opened his eyes, and a fluid drip attached to his arm came into focus. There was a white ceiling—he was in bed. *I'm alive.* He turned his head left. His backpack was on a chair.

A nurse came in. "Oh, you're awake. Maybe you can tell us something about what happened and who you are."

"Where am I?"

The nurse took his vitals and smiled. "The question should be, how am I? And the answer is, I believe you're going to be all right. You're at Roper Hospital in Mt. Pleasant."

She finished her check—Rex caught her arm. "How did I get here?"

"Some big guy dumped you at the door. Said you had mumbled something about a rattlesnake. We took a look at your left leg and gave you most of the anti-venom we had in stock. Cool your jets for now. I'll be back with some paperwork after the doctor takes a look."

"Ah...before you leave, would you hand me my backpack?"

He had left most of his personal things on the boat. He took inventory inside the backpack. The money was still there. His wallet, Coast Guard Masters License, and commercial pilot's license were all there. There was a pair of shorts, a T-shirt, pair of socks, and a change of underwear. And that was it. No shoes. They were somewhere out in the vastness of the marsh.

He was wearing nothing but a hospital gown. His muddy jeans and T-shirt were rolled up under a chair. His cell phone was probably ruined, but he didn't dare use it anyhow.

Rex was scared. If Snake found him in the hospital, he would be tortured and killed. He had to get out ASAP. He had wanted to quit and now he could do it. Being on the altar of death focused his mind. Now he knew what to value. It was freedom, and life—and Mona.

Instead of the nurse, a hospital administrator returned. "Sir, I need to get you registered. The gentleman who dropped you off provided us with no information. I'll leave this paperwork for you to complete at your convenience. Someone will collect it later. I hope you're recovering well."

"Okay, I'll get it done later...feeling a little tired right now. Buy the way, on your way out, would you have one of the orderlies step in?"

After the administrator had gone, Rex fished $400 out of his backpack and stuck it under the sheet.

The orderly gently knocked and came in. "You asked for me, sir?"

"What time do you get off?"

The orderly looked confused. He shifted his body and gave a nervous nod. "At four, in about an hour…but I don't understand."

"You will. Come over and sit down."

He was hesitant but complied.

"You see, I have no shoes and no one to bring me any. I'll need shoes to leave the hospital." Rex pulled out the $400 and handed it to him. "I need a size 10E sneakers, nothing fancy. You can buy them at a lot of places. Should be able to get some for less than a hundred fifty. The rest is yours, but I want them today by five o'clock."

"Yes, sir! You want any particular color?"

"Whatever you like is fine."

Looking confused, the orderly lingered. "Is this on the level? I'll do it, but I ain't into no scam."

Rex heaved a sigh. "Listen. I got some important business, and I didn't fit getting snake bit into my schedule. Believe me, if you can do this, it's well worth it to me."

The orderly took the money and left. Five minutes later the doctor came, checked Rex, and said he would see him again tomorrow.

The shoes arrived at 4:50 p.m. Soon after, the nurse returned. "Thought I'd check on you. Heard you weren't feeling so good."

"Just don't feel like concentrating on the man's paperwork right now."

"Hon, I don't blame you, I hate all the damn paperwork, and when you've been snake bit, well, you just take your time. You're not going anywhere for a while. You can do it tomorrow."

Rex smiled and locked eyes with her. "Sweetheart, I need a favor."

"Hey, Romeo, getting bitten once oughta be

enough, but go ahead, I'll listen."

I can't bullshit this gal. "You see those wet pants over there? My cell phone is in them and it's ruined. I need to make a phone call. How can I do it?"

"The easiest is to use my cell, but don't do nothing illegal on my phone."

"Hey, nothing like that. Just need to catch up because of this hospital delay."

She handed over her phone and left the room. Rex called his old high school buddy in Lexington.

"Hey Flip, I'm visiting a friend at the hospital in Mt. Pleasant, South Carolina, and I dropped my phone in the John. I need you to order me an Uber to go to the Charleston airport. Can you do it?"

"Sure, tell me exactly where you want to drop the pickup pin."

"The far end of the east parking lot, at the Mt. Pleasant Roper Hospital. I need them to arrive at seven o'clock."

They chatted for a bit. Flip going on about flying for starvation wages and how they needed to get back into their own business somehow. "Flip, let me call you back later when I'm not jammed for time. Thanks man, for helping. I owe you."

He disconnected, erased the number, and waited for the nurse's return.

Once everything was quiet, Rex showered, dressed in shorts, T-shirt, and new sneakers, put his old clothes in a plastic bag, shouldered his backpack, and walked out. He went to the stairs at the end of the hall and exited to the outside. It was 6:30 p.m. He hid in some trees beside the parking lot. His Uber arrived at 6:55 p.m. Rex got in the front seat but hung onto his backpack.

"Are you Rex Morgan?"

"Yes, let's sit for a minute. I need to explain something."

"You going to the Charleston airport?"

Rex unzipped his backpack and turned to him. "I have a proposition for you." He reached into the outside pocket of his backpack and brought out $2000. "I want to go to Beaufort, North Carolina."

The driver put it in his GPS and whistled. "It's over five hours."

Rex pulled out another thousand. The driver agreed.

On the trip up, the Uber driver turned out to be a good travel companion. He came from India and was smart and ambitious. Rex had guilt over how he had squandered his American privilege, and now he was riding with a man who was grasping at the straws of the dream Rex had wasted.

But mostly he worried Snake might be checking on the boat. He arrived in Beaufort around midnight, and all was quiet at the marina. He made several quick checks on his boat and cranked the engine. He untied from the boat slip and motored out in the dark.

Rex arrived in Wilmington late the next day, exhausted. He slept six hours, provisioned his boat, and set out for the Cayman Islands late in the afternoon. His leg looked bad and it hurt, but he took some antibiotics from the supply he kept on his boat. His priority was escape, but he still yearned for Mona and knew he had to send for her before Snake got to her first.

He had gone to great lengths to keep their relationship from any of Snake's people, but he still would need to take great precautions. He would buy her a ticket to Atlanta and another separate ticket to the Caymans. Somehow, he would convince her to join him on a life-changing adventure around the world. They would pass through the Panama Canal and continue across the Pacific to the first Polynesian landfall paradise in the Marquesas Islands. He was free of Snake. God had granted him a second chance, and this time he and Mona would take it.

Chapter 22

Scrap

Hummock on the Marsh, South Carolina

Out of breath, I loaded the last of the suitcases I had time to retrieve. The bottom of my boat was almost touching the mud. It was time to leave—now—or become stranded. My fifteen-foot Jon boat could have hauled more if there had been enough water under it. Not sure how much the extra load would affect my escape, I was anxious to get away from the island. I didn't want to be the robber caught stealing more loot than he could carry.

The receding water, in combination with the added weight, caused my motor to kick up mud on the way back to the creek. I came to a slightly higher spot and had to use the pole. Fear over getting stuck out in the open marsh made my adrenaline kicked in, and I pushed on the pole hard enough to find deeper water.

Once in the creek, I shut off the motor and drifted with the current, trying to put all of this together. As I floated around a bend in the creek, hooded mergansers caused me to jump when they blasted off like planes from an aircraft carrier catapult. Making a half circle, they came out of afterburner and headed for the mainland.

The cocaine confirmed beyond a doubt that I had stumbled onto criminal activity. But where was everybody? Why had I never heard of a missing plane or a crash?

Not ten feet from my boat, I was surprised by the puff and surface roll of a bottlenose dolphin. It stood at the top of a food chain that began with the detritus and tiny plankton in the high marsh. It was a comfort to see one of my old comrades. Once I had seen these highly intelligent mammals herd fish toward a sandflat and use their great flukes to splash the fish onto the flat so they could literally come out of the water to partake of the meal. At the time it was only an interesting demonstration of dolphin intelligence, but now I could feel the life and death desperation of those small fish.

Now what do I do? What about the money— cocaine money—burning a hole in my boat, in my mind?

The Feds would love to know about this discovery, but I knew they would take the money as contraband or evidence. Of course, giving it to the authorities, whoever they were, would be the honorable way to go, but was I going to be happy with that outcome? What would Dee think about what I was contemplating? I had always prided myself on honesty, even under the temptation of trying to get much-needed work for my business. Taking this money was not the honest thing to do. Sure, the money would help solve the responsibility of caring for my family, but how does it fit: I will not lie, cheat, steal, nor tolerate those who do?

I recollected the excitement on Beth's face when she realized she might get her new job, and then I saw my little Emma thriving in her expensive new school. I saw the relief and satisfaction of my employees when they worked for a prosperous company.

Thoughts of my dilemma had plagued my pleasure of the hunt since I'd left that morning, and they influenced the excitement charging through my body when I discovered the money. Before I found the crash site, my thoughts caused a sinking feeling in my gut, so I tried with only partial success to concentrate on my hunting.

My last thoughts on Friday ended with *No excuse, sir. It's my fault.* I must find a way. I cannot give up. You have to be Scrap. Think of the badger taking on all adversaries, never giving up.

Damn it. I'll keep it, at least for now. I would tell no one about the crash site. I realized I was tiptoeing toward a line that would cross into some kind of criminal activity, even if I was merely associated with it.

But I desperately needed money, and it seemed too good to pass up—even if it made me shiver. I cut open garbage bags and covered what had become *my* contraband. Weighting the edges down with items from my storage box, I was the jackal trying to hide my kill.

I cranked the engine and motored back toward Garris landing. My mind was so distracted that half an hour later, it dawned on me I was dodging crab trap floats. *I'm lost.* I was on the wrong branch of the creek and not sure how I got there. I reversed and almost ran into a boat with crab traps stacked high. The guy eyed the garbage bags covering the suitcases. I panicked and looked back after passing to see more of his response. Of course, I was sure he thought I was stealing his crabs. He was not thinking of suitcases full of money.

I calmed down and found my way back to the right branch. My mind settled on a plan. I would tap some of the money to stave off my certain bankruptcy. The rest I would think about later. Yes, there was some guilt, but it was exciting, even exhilarating. This money was going to save my business, my family—my face. The Feds could kiss my ass, and so could the drug dealers. As they say in the real estate business, this money was going to be its highest and best use.

Chapter 23

Scrap

Charleston County, South Carolina

I arrived at Garris Landing with what everybody dreams about: a boatload of money. Somebody was backing in a twenty-foot fishing craft, decked out with trolling motor, steering wheel, and covered cockpit. My God, it was Bill Wise. I'd known him since high school. He recognized me and waved. I waved and cruised right past the launch ramp and disappeared up the creek. I shut off the motor and waited until there was the sound of him cranking his engine. Hoping he was going the other way, I cranked up. I had to move in case he came upon me and wanted to talk.

I motored back toward the landing. Around a bend in the creek, I came across him coming toward me. He slowed, but I waved and continued. I imagine he probably was thinking, what's the matter with that jackass?

I tied up at the end of the dock and went to get my truck. Another boat arrived at the slip, and a truck was backing in for the pull-out. I pretended to have a problem with my trailer hitch until they left.

On the way home, I was as keyed up about having this money in my possession as I'd been about what bankruptcy would do to Beth and Emma. But the excitement was different. Now instead of the feeling of having my back to the wall, I was thinking about new possibilities, unknown frontiers and, surprisingly, the thrill of violating the law.

I wasn't even sure what law I was violating. Of course, I could call my good friend Dee, but deep down I knew if I did, he would convince me to turn in the money.

A mile before the main road, I blew right through a stop sign. Man, talk about violating the law. That's all I needed—to get pulled over for a traffic violation and get busted for dirty money. *Come on, Scrap, pay attention.*

The money might be a solution to my problem, but it was going to be hard to inject a large sum of cash into my business without raising suspicion. The IRS would be a danger. New bank regulations cropped up every year in an effort to force them to report unusual cash transactions. There were authorities like the DEA and the FBI looking for drug money, which of course is what this was.

What would Dee think? I had witnessed how he hated anything to do with cocaine dealing.

I pulled into my driveway, half-expecting Beth to meet me in the yard.

It was best, for the time being, not to tell Beth. She knew we were under financial strain, but she didn't know we were on the road to bankruptcy. She would probably try to make me do the legal thing with the money. I needed to keep her out of this. If I were going to do something illegal, she would not be complicit in the activity if she didn't know. I didn't have the right to do something illegal and try to force her to go along with it.

I opened the garage bay where I kept my boat, feeling like someone hiding a body.

Throughout our marriage, Beth and I had been in agreement on our value system, but lately I was secretive, unsure of her reaction. Differences had developed. I was not always clear about what was wrong and what was right. I felt so much pressure to save face and protect my family from financial ruin that sometimes what was wrong seemed to be the greater good. Beth, on the other hand, was steadfast in her belief in the firm line between right and wrong. For a fleeting moment, I reconsidered my decision but then remembered the problems this money would solve.

It would behoove me to be careful with Beth. I'd been married to her long enough to know she could know something without having any way of knowing it; she felt it. She could hear a voice I could not hear. For this reason, I usually leveled with her and eventually would about this, too. But not now.

Tomorrow was going to be hectic. To start with, I needed to go get another load of money while these high tides continued. They would not last but a few days. I also had to find a place to temporarily store the suitcases.

I lived in Hamlin Plantation, a large development off Rifle Range Road at the north edge of Mt. Pleasant, South Carolina. Our house was on the marsh and elevated. It had four parking bays with garage doors underneath. I kept my boat under the house in one of the enclosed bays. A growth of trees shielded my house from the nearest neighbor five hundred feet away. The suitcases would be safe there.

I backed the boat under the house, closed the door, and took my birds out back to clean. It was a good thing, too—Beth showed up.

"How'd you do?"

I was rattled when she spoke behind me. "Uh…ah…not all that good, but I got a few."

"With such a nice tide, I thought you would limit out."

"Truth be told, the tide was so high the birds went to the shore."

"Scrap, what are you doing? You look guilty."

Like a chastised schoolboy, I shrugged my shoulders and concentrated on turning on the outdoor faucet.

"Do you have my good knife out here?" she said."

I moved the bucket like I was looking for a knife. "No, I need to get the knife…maybe that dull old knife."

Damn it. I need to shut up. Those little voices could start talking to her right now. "I'm going in the house to get a couple of pots and a knife."

She followed me in, stood at the sink a second, and reached to the knife block. She handed me the good knife with an accusing smile.

Under the house there were several stacks of leftover tile with a tarp thrown over them. I put the suitcases underneath with the tile. I stood for a long time staring at the tarp. *What am I doing?* I thought of the lives that must have been destroyed earning this money, the distraught loved ones wringing their hands in frustration over a habit they cannot control.

More rationalization: I did not destroy anybody's

life. And taking this money away from criminals is a positive thing for the world. This money was going to save all that I held dear. Using it for myself was like using it for the greater good, and tomorrow I was going for more.

Beth called from the stairs. "Scrap, what are you doing? I thought you were going to clean your birds. Do you need help?"

"No, no, I'm fine. There's something wrong with my boat trolling motor, and I'm trying to figure it out."

I had lied to my wife and planned to lie some more, but even so, I still was excited about the prospect of using my new money.

I cleaned the birds and took them upstairs, nervous over facing Beth. She didn't appear suspicious anymore, but sometimes it was hard to tell. She salted the birds and put them in the fridge for later. She grew up hunting with her father in Kansas, so she was used to the sight of wild game and blood. As she turned, I put my arms around her. "You think you can find a babysitter for tonight? I would like to take you out to dinner."

She opened the oven, and a wonderful odor permeated the room. "Are we celebrating something I don't know about?"

"No, but can't a man take his wife to dinner just to enjoy her company. What are you cooking this time of day?"

"I promised Emma some gingerbread, but should we be spending if the business is short of money?"

"I've been meaning to talk to you about that. I'm feeling better about the business lately. We burned through so many assets during the building dry spell, I was worried, but the economy is turning now. I think we'll be all right."

She gave me a peculiar look but didn't say anything.

We ended up going to dinner at Rue de Jean's, where we polished off a bottle of expensive top-shelf pinot noir.

She laid her hand on top of mine. "What's going on?"

Oh, shit, I knew it. This woman is a soothsayer. "Morning glory, I have had a hard week turning things around. Let's just enjoy. We can talk when I'm not at such a disadvantage. For now, let it suffice that I love you."

She laid down her fork and looked intently into my eyes. "Scrap, don't try that. I know you love me, and you know I love you, but that won't suffice. This time it's not going to shut me up. I have watched you come home for six months so stressed sometimes you couldn't eat. Yesterday when you came home, you looked terrible. You make little jokes and try to brush it off, but I know something worse is going on in your head than you're telling me."

"Okay, okay, I have been stressed. Do you remember when you were going to the College of Charleston and came to watch The Citadel parade?"

"Of course, I remember. I think I fell for you on the spot."

I leaned back and let out a long breath. "You're stealing my lines. That was when I fell in love with you, and from then on, I would have kicked the general in the shin if that's what it took to keep you happy."

"Are you trying to put me off again?"

The waiter came and checked on us. I was glad for a break in the tension.

"No," I said. "I'm coming to my point. I still feel the same way today, except now Emma has increased the pressure to provide a happy home. Today there's no general to kick. This business has been kicking me, and I have worried myself sick to protect my family, but things are going to get better now, I promise."

"I hope that's true. But I still don't feel like I'm in the loop. You can talk to me."

"Okay, okay, I'll talk more. It's that—you see…I…"

"What? Tell me."

I couldn't. I knew it would be a much bigger argument. I put it off. "Come on, you're trying to make me say something, and I don't know what it is. Believe me, everything is going to be all right."

Chapter 24

Snake

Jacksonville, Florida

Snake's eyes pierced Gut's. "Goddamn it, where is my money?"

Gut stood on the other side of the desk, clenching and unclenching his ham-sized hands. Outside the office, two henchmen peered inside in abject fear at the shouting.

"Boss, I can't get anything," Gut said. "I've tried all my contacts—nobody knows nothing. They just disappeared."

Snake glared at Gut with unblinking eyes. "Somebody has hijacked twenty-one million of my money, and you have no idea where to start looking?"

Snake kicked himself for not knowing more about where the money was at any given time. He didn't take pride in showing off big-name acquaintances nor friendships. Indeed, he liked to say he had no friends. He didn't take pride in his wealth, although his whole life was focused on obtaining it. He took no interest in politics other than how it affected his money. But what he took great pride in was his successful planning to move contraband without getting caught or cheated.

Snake cooled down—yelling and showing rage

was not his thing. It was both his unpredictability and what he actually did that struck utter fear in others. Was the call a phony contact? There had to be some kind of deceit here. "The last thing I got was the call from Toad's cell phone yesterday requesting the destination airport. I thought the money was on the airplane and they were about to leave. They could be anywhere by now."

Gut shifted his muscled hulk and gestured with an open palm. "I have scoured the news from Beaufort to Jacksonville, and there's nothing about an airplane crash. Yesterday, I had a man check for Rex's boat in Beaufort. It's there tied up at a marina, and the slip is paid for through the end of the month. But there's no sign of activity."

"Here's what I want. Contact Two Finger Willie and tell him I want to set up a meeting. Since he's the one that bought the drugs, he must know something. If he's clean, maybe he can help."

"I already contacted him. He said he delivered the money."

Snake let out a long breath. "Set up the meeting. I'll get to the bottom of this if I have to put him in our torture chamber."

Gut returned to Snake's office two hours later. "Boss, I talked to Two Finger again. Said he would help any way he could, but no way would he come to Jacksonville. He will meet you in his office in Atlanta."

Snake turned his head and scanned the spines of all his law books in the case on the sidewall. "The sonofabitch is smart. No wonder he's lived so long. Okay, set up security for my meeting in Atlanta."

Snake's flight landed at the world's busiest airport

at 1:20 p.m. His only communication with the passenger next to him in first-class was a nod upon taking his seat. He was picked up by one of the men assigned to his security detail, and they proceeded straight to Lucky Street in downtown Atlanta. "You got all my boys positioned?"

"Yes, sir. But I tell you, this Two Finger is wily. He's got guys watching us everywhere."

Snake nodded. "It's okay; I'm not expecting any trouble. Two Finger Willie has been scratching and clawing through the drug scene all his life. He's smart and at the top of his game."

"How did he lose his fingers?"

Snake gave his man a grimace. "Enough of this chit-chat."

He arrived at Willie's place on time at three o'clock. Snake sat in the black Lexis and surveyed the building for two minutes. He went inside and was immediately approached.

"Welcome. How do you prefer to be addressed?"

"Snake will do fine."

"Very well, Mr. Snake, I'm to take you directly to Willie's office. He is expecting you."

Snake cocked his head, like a serpent flicking its tongue, sensing the mood of the room. He recognized his men eyeing what must be Willie's men eyeing them.

He entered Willie's office, and the door closed behind him. Willie was standing behind a large desk. They took seats on each side, facing each other.

Two Finger opened the conversation: "Maybe you're unsatisfied with our last trade?"

"Yes, it was a disaster. Tell me how it went from your end."

"My men showed up with only twenty mil. He was given twenty-one, so he tried to cheat both of us, but I will get to the bottom of that."

Snake glared at him with steel gray, unblinking eyes. "So, tell me how the transaction went."

Willie shifted in his chair, wiggling his shoulders, and his gold chains caught the light. He waved his two-fingered right hand decorated with a diamond ring on the remaining thumb and forefinger. "Your man, the pilot, said he don't want money but wanted his pay in blow. He took fifty keys along with your twenty mil on his plane. What's the beef, man?"

Two Finger sat back and waited. Snake relaxed slightly, digesting what was said. He knew they had the money at one time; at least he knew Toad had said so, and of all people, he trusted Toad the most. If he could find Rex, he would deal with him later, but right now he needed help. He also needed to know—for sure—Two Finger had not killed his men and taken the money and cocaine.

He leaned forward and stared at Willie. "My beef is I didn't get jack shit. My money disappeared, Toad disappeared, Rex disappeared, and you got over two thousand pounds of pure grade snow. Now, what do you know?"

"I don't know nothing about your missing money."

"Can you find out? I'll make it worthwhile for you."

Two Finger cocked his head and gave a little smirk, but he avoided looking directly into Snake's eyes. "What exactly does worthwhile mean for me?"

"It means I'll pay five mil to anybody that can lead me to my twenty mil."

A slight smile appeared on Two Finger's lips. "Well, that's a lot of scratch. I put my boys on it and see. Me and you, we friends?"

"I have no friends, Willie. This is business."

Two Finger seemed tense and diverted his attention to an odd-looking trophy of some kind on the side of his desk. He turned it so Snake could see. There appeared to be a pair of taxidermized gonads attached to a wooden plaque. The wording underneath read *There are worse things than losing your balls.*

Etched on the top of the plaque: *NORTH GEORGIA FIGHT TO THE DEATH WINNER.*

Snake always wanted to be in control, and he didn't like interruptions, but he had to ask, "Whose balls?"

"The trophy I won with my prize pit bull, named Dazzle. He killed this here mutt for the championship."

"Okay, Willie, are we straight about helping with my money?"

"I got you, man. We be snooping from Jacksonville to North Carolina. Maybe I find your money."

"There's one more thing," Snake said. "I need to interview the men who were at the exchange."

"That's good with me. They're all here now. I'll have them come in."

While Willie rounded up his men, Snake had a short meeting with Pigneck. "Pay close attention to what these guys look like when they come to the meeting in Willie's office. Later I'll want you to grab one of them and bring him to the compound."

In the presence of Two Finger, Snake individually interviewed all three men that were at the transfer with Toad and Rex. They confirmed it occurred as Two

145

Finger had said.

"We give 'em the money," Suit Man said. "But if you ask me, that fat man, he crazy—"

"You glossy gasbag," Two Finger said. "If you don't know nothing, don't say nothing."

Snake listened with interest but made no comment. He would find out everything later. He needed to determine for sure nobody from Two Finger's outfit had anything to do with the heist. If Two Finger was cheating him, the interview they had with the men was worthless. What he really wanted was to have his boys see the three men that were at the exchange so they could identify them later. He glared at each man until the discomfort caused them to avert their eyes.

On the way back to his car, Snake motioned to Pigneck, who followed him to the car. "I want you to lay low for a day or so and grab one of these guys. Once Gut has a chance at him, we'll know for sure if Willie is being straight with me. Be careful. I don't want Willie to find out. Pay attention to that dandy they call Suit Man. He knows, and he will crack."

Chapter 25

Scrap

Fiddlers Creek, South Carolina

Sunday morning, I got up at 6:45 a.m. and tiptoed out with my shotgun. Remembering to include a tarp, I hooked up to the boat and eased out of our drive. There was still an east wind that should help bring high water. I launched early at the boat ramp but needed the extra time to think. At the point on the creek where I would depart for the little island, I shut down the engine, waiting for the water to rise—shivering, more from my thoughts than from the cold. I planned to take money belonging to criminals, the type who would kill for far less. I also planned on breaking the law, even though I wasn't sure which law I was breaking.

The tide moves with the moon phase, so it would be high about fifty minutes later each day. Around nine I cranked the engine and proceeded toward the hummock.

When I arrived at the island, the water still had a few more inches to rise. I broke off a limb from a dead Cedar and poked under the old palmetto log, but nothing moved. The diamondback must have been out hunting. The bullet hole in the glass of the partially opened cabin door caused me to hesitate. What kind of foul play was going on? There was a large stain on the right seat I hadn't noticed before in my excitement—blood, lots of it. No doubt, the crash was not the only drama that went on here.

I shook it off and grabbed a suitcase. *My God! How much money is here?* I calculated. The figure was scary. If all of these suitcases were full of twenties, there must be close to $20 million. I didn't need this much money, not to protect my family, not even to save my business. But overnight I had concluded it was safer to get it all away from the island, leaving the drugs for somebody else to find and assume it was the whole show.

This time I did fill up the boat. I took twenty suitcases and scraped bottom on the way out. At one point, it was necessary to get out and push. My boat was full, literally, from stem to stern. Counting the ten suitcases I took the day before, there were thirty-nine in all. This count included the nine still left on the airplane. I would have to make another run tomorrow.

Beth would give me a hard time when I got back home. She and Emma had to go to church without me. There was no telling what she would say about me going marsh hen hunting again the next day—during the work week—when I had already explained about my pressing schedule at the office.

There were no problems hauling out my boat for the return trip home. Pulling into my drive, it was evident Beth and Emma were still at church, which gave me time to figure out a place to stash the money. I waited in my drive for a few minutes and decided it would be best to split up the money. With the boat trailer still attached, I drove the truck to Keep Safe All Night Storage, which was only three miles from my house. The storage unit attendant jumped when I opened the door. It was obvious he had been asleep. "What do I need to do to rent one of your units?"

"Fill out your name and address, tell me what size, and give me at least one month's rent in advance."

I registered with a fictitious name and address and paid cash for six months' rent. He also sold me a lock but didn't ask for any identification. I was given directions, and I left. The area around my storage unit was deserted, so I unloaded what I estimated to be $10 million in twenty suitcases.

On the way back home, my hands were shaking on the steering wheel. Pulling into the driveway, I was still keyed up. Beth and Emma returned from church.

"Daddy, you missed church to go hunting and didn't tell anybody!"

Beth gave me the silent treatment. I tried to crack it. "Would you two like for me to take you out to lunch?"

"Emma and I have already eaten." Her reply was terse, her face unreadable, which to me meant angry.

Frankly, I was glad she gave me the silent treatment. It was a relief not to have to explain or make up more lies.

Grabbing a cold piece of meatloaf from the fridge, I slipped off to my shop downstairs, piddling until late afternoon. At five, I told Beth I had some work at the office and actually did go there to think about the money and how I could inject it into my business. I didn't come back home until eight. Beth gave me some leftover supper and sat down across the table.

Oh, shit. Here it comes.

"Keeping these types of secrets from one another

can damage a marriage."

"Come on, Beth, so you not only know I'm keeping secrets, but you know what kind of damaging secrets they are? And if you know what kind of secrets they are, are they really secrets? I always knew you could read my mind, and such a lovely oracle you are."

"Stop it. You're diverting. I'm serious."

"Okay, okay, listen, with all the business problems from last week, I needed some time to unwind, so I went marsh hen hunting again. We can talk more later, but not tonight."

"But you didn't bring back any birds?"

"I didn't shoot many, so I gave them away. We have more than we can eat anyhow. Most of the time, I drifted in the creek and relaxed."

She didn't challenge me, but it was obvious my answer didn't make sense. I tried to imagine what she might be thinking: either he's lying and didn't even go hunting, or he's doing something else with his boat he doesn't want me to know about. In either case, she would think it had something to do with my damn secretary. I hated the distance growing between us, and I promised myself I would somehow deal with it but not now. I told myself it was more important to do what was necessary for Beth and Emma than to clear the air between us. I was afraid Beth would get in the way of my plan. But there was a risk in not leveling with her. She had too much perception, and I was not a practiced liar. But I knew I better learn to be one—and quickly.

Chapter 26

Scrap

Mt. Pleasant, South Carolina

Monday morning, I busied myself working on job estimates, pretending to be getting ready to leave for work. Beth took Emma to school at 7:30 and said she was then going to the grocery store. As soon as they were gone, I hooked up my boat, ready to set out for the golden goose of Fiddler's Creek. My cell chimed. It was Dee. Feeling guilty, I answered. "Hey man, what's up?"

"Just wanted to let you know, I'm in the area for the day, had to check up on a couple of things in the Charleston office. Can you break away for a quick lunch before I head back to Columbia?"

I couldn't remember a time I didn't want to see Dee, but now I dreaded it. We had always been on the same team searching for the truth. But I was avoiding the truth. Converting drug money to personal use—it felt like a lie. I answered with fake regret. "I'm sorry, man. I can't do it. Tied up all day with problems. If I eat, it will just be fast food. Can you spend the night?"

"Got to get back. Lots of criminals and drug dealers to put in jail. I'll check with you later."

The statement sent a jolt through me. I wandered

back into the area under my house for something, but I couldn't remember what it was when I got there. Dejected, I sat down on my weight bench. What would my friend say if he knew where I was going today? Working undercover for a year, he had developed a strong disgust and hatred for drug dealers. Ever since then, he went after them with a vengeance. Would he consider me part of that world now?

He was my best friend and had been since he had been framed for an honor violation at The Citadel. I defended him, and during the stressful time of the trial, we bonded into a lifetime of friendship. I recognized in Dee a rare quality individual, and he often professed to be forever beholden to me for saving his bacon at The Citadel.

I was holding a hammer and had forgotten why, but I had to get going. Beth might soon be back, and I didn't want to miss the high tide I needed to approach my treasure island. Dee's call had dampened my enthusiasm, but I was up to my neck now. I had no choice but to see it through.

Once on Fiddlers Creek, I ran full throttle, making my way north until the exit point to the island. Once again, I was able to motor right up to the small island due to the unusually high tide. I eyed the wall of lush foliage with caution, half expecting something to come rushing at me for the encroachment. Silently I crept to within sight of the crash. All appeared quiet. Was it only the day before yesterday when I had discovered this place? So much had gone through my mind that it now seemed so familiar, but it still had an eerie aspect, as if ghosts replaced the missing people. I used an eight-foot limb to thoroughly poke under the old palmetto log. Out slithered my six-and-a-half-foot friend, like a sinister metaphor for the whole setting.

I retrieved the remaining nine suitcases, which left the two disgusting suitcases full of cocaine as the only evident cargo. I gave a sigh of relief to be leaving the island for the last time.

The tarp I brought was small because my large tarp covered the money back at the storage unit. In my haste to get underway, I had failed to secure the edges of the tarp to the boat, and on the way back to the dock, it blew to the side of the suitcases. I stopped and hastily secured the edges. I traveled several miles south on Fiddlers Creek and turned halfway through a 180-degree bend in the creek. The shift in wind direction caused one side of the tarp to blow off. Before I could correct it, I was almost run over by Fish Blount as he rounded the other end of the bend. I had met Fish a couple of times at the dock. He was always telling some bullshit story about fishing or the law getting somebody. Dee said, if Fish was talking, he was lying. Although Dee grew up in the same area of Six Mile, he had little in common with Fish. According to Dee, Fish was always out of money due to his habits of gambling, liquor, loose women, smoking Mary Jane, and occasionally, even snorting a little low-grade nose candy.

Fish waved as I swerved and passed within five feet of his old, leaky boat. He looked right at the suitcases. My heart leaped. I blindly raced up the creek. Once more alone, I shut off the motor and covered the suitcases.

Damn! That was stupid. What would Fish think? I sat in my boat drifting with the outgoing tide, deep in thought. Considering all the possible reactions Fish might have to the suitcases, I decided I was paranoid to think he could tell anything. Hell, what would Fish know? As a contractor, I could have been hauling supplies from a boat on the intercostal waterway. And who would pay any attention to Fish anyway? He was always lying and telling some unbelievable tale. I resolved to put the incident out of my mind.

Except for a few heart-stopping seconds passing Fish, the rest of my trip was uneventful. In keeping with the idea of splitting up the money, I took the nine suitcases to a different facility called Live Oak Storage, rented a unit, and stored them under the smaller tarp.

I was about to lock up, but the thought occurred to me I may need some cash today. I went to my truck and emptied my briefcase and took it into the storage unit. I switched $60,000 from a suitcase to my briefcase. Now that's what I called working capital.

I left the storage unit and went directly to my office, boat and all. Driving away from the storage building, I slowed on approaching the main road. I glanced through live oaks on the bank of a small finger of marsh ending at the road. I slammed on the brakes. Standing on a fallen tree, an anhinga turned its head toward me.

I returned the stare, hoping it wasn't a bad omen. As a kid, I once fell from a tree and broke my arm shortly after seeing one of these birds. And another time, as I walked next to a forested swampy area on the way to catch the school bus, I had another sighting: wings cocked open, its threatening head turning on its snake neck to look at me. That day I was suspended from school for fighting.

I drove away with a sinking feeling. At the intersection from the storage unit, I missed the stop sign. Two drivers laid on their horns. Superstition, that's all it was, but my mood had gone from excitement to dread, and I couldn't shake it. Trouble always followed that snakebird. It was true to its name: anhinga. It means devil bird.

Chapter 27

Beth

Mt. Pleasant, South Carolina

Beth had fought the school board all year over inserting a school assembly session once a month on bullying. Although the board members appreciated her passion, a majority rejected the idea because there were so many topics to cover at the assembly that they couldn't decide what to eliminate to make room for the lesson on bullying. One board member had a different reason to object. "Ms. Scruggs, we don't have a trained psychologist on staff in most of our schools. I know, back in February, you offered to do the sessions for free, but I fear you may not be available."

"Why do you think I won't be available?"

This blunt statement caused the board member to look away and shift uncomfortably in his chair. "Suppose," he said, "you have a more important position and leave the school board?"

Beth had a quick catch in her breath. *Columbia has been interviewing the board.* She wouldn't be surprised if everybody on the board knew about the possibility of her becoming Assistant Secretary of Education.

She pushed her chair back and stood. It was time to clear the air. She had intentionally been secretive because of her fear that the job may not materialize due to the financial stress that Scrap refused to acknowledge to her. If Columbia had interviewed the board, it was logical that they would also try to interview banks about Scrap's finances.

All the board members focused on Beth as if she were about to announce World War III. She took several moments to gather her thoughts. In clearing the air, she decided to also use the situation to further push her proposal. "I will acknowledge that I've been interviewed for a job in the Education Department in Columbia. But it's not a job; it's an interview. If, in the possibility, this job did materialize, I assure you that my desire to eliminate bullying will not decrease. I'll see to it that either I or some other qualified person is available to conduct these meetings."

She had not intended for her new job to enter the bullying discussions. But now that it had, she threw out the veiled threat that since she was a powerhouse in the Education Department, her bullying proposal would be pushed even more effectively. From the looks of the board members, the threat did not go unnoticed. The board adjourned for lunch, and as soon as they were out the door, Beth heard the chattering start.

Returning from lunch, the board voted to include Beth's bullying education sessions.

On Friday Beth drove home thrilled over her success at the board meeting. But as she arrived home, the agonizing question about their finances returned. She felt responsible for seeking out the truth and leveling with Columbia.

On Monday morning, Beth suffered a nagging restlessness after taking Emma to her school. When it came to Sheryl, *the wonderful secretary*, even though Scrap was too naïve to understand, Beth knew he was up against a one-sided situation. She had noticed Sheryl's coquettish behavior around Scrap at their company party last year, when everybody was drinking, and how he subconsciously looked at her butt. Scrap was resisting, but Sheryl was all in for an affair.

Beth returned from the grocery store and busied herself with putting things away, but her mind was so distracted she found herself storing the milk and bacon in the pantry. Finally, she decided to go to Scrap's office and see for herself how things looked. Confident of her excellent intuition, maybe she could get a feel for how bad the business was doing. If there were a crisis atmosphere, she would sense it.

Pulling up to the office, she didn't see Scrap's truck but that wasn't unusual; he often visited job sites. She armed herself with a reason for the visit and went inside.

Sheryl was not there, and neither was Scrap. However, three project managers were hard at work.

"Hey, Matt," she said, poking her head into his office. "I was driving by and thought I could pick up some office supplies Scrap promised me and never delivered. It looks like Sheryl is out also."

"Gee, Beth, neither one of them is here. Sheryl called in sick, and I think Scrap is at a job site. He hasn't been in this morning."

She gestured with her open right hand and gave Matt a fake smile. "No problem. Don't bother to look for the supplies. I'll call Scrap later. I don't want to interrupt a job site meeting. If either one of them calls or comes in, just tell them I was here. I will leave Scrap a note to get my supplies."

She went into Scrap's office and found his desk drawer unlocked. There was a legal pad with doodling and some illegible notes, but down near the bottom of the pad was a curious sentence: *need to stop this shit with Sheryl.*

Beth abruptly turned and walked out. She went home with an uneasiness she would not acknowledge. She hesitated but then called Scrap's cell phone. He failed to answer. For the next hour, she walked aimlessly from room to room. She unloaded the dishwasher, sometimes holding a dish like she didn't know where it went. She fluffed the pillows on the bed but picked up the last one and threw it across the room. Finally, she acknowledged her foreboding subconscious: *has Sheryl succeeded?* She was about to go back to the office and wait when Scrap called.

"Hi, morning glory. Sorry I missed your call. I was tied up at the office."

"Where? Did you say...*office*? Ah...never mind. Would you bring the supplies you promised me?"

She closed her eyes and a tear trickled down her cheek. She took the phone away from her ear, squeezing it in front of her face, but could still hear his distant voice.

"Sure, I'll bring them tonight."

Beth closed her hands into fists and paced the kitchen floor. Her anger turned to Scrap. If something were going on, it isn't just Sheryl. He's a grown man, and I've told him how I felt about her. *He should have fired her long ago.*

Chapter 28

Scrap

Mt. Pleasant, South Carolina

After talking to Beth, I went straight from the Live Oak Storage to my office, planning on returning the boat to the house at another time when Beth was away. My mind was racing through how I would find the time to get cash money into my business, make plans for my construction comeback, and put out the raging current business fires. All of this, of course, was the key to paying for Emma's expensive special school, satisfying snoopy bureaucrats about my finances so Beth's new position was a go, and making my employees secure in their jobs.

I parked my truck with the boat attached at the back of the business and went inside to discover Sheryl was not there. I stuck my head in Matt's office. "Where's Sheryl?"

"She said she was feeling punk but would be in later."

It put a kink in some of my plans. Too excited to wait for Sheryl to come in, I hurried back to my truck and called. "Hi, how you doing?"

"Oh, I'm feeling better, just my allergy acting up. I think I got it under control. You have something urgent? You can come over here, and while I shower and dress, we can talk about it."

Shit, I temporarily lost what I wanted to tell her. "I don't have time. Write this down."

"One day you might have more time," she said. "Okay, I'm ready. Shoot."

I got my mind back on track. "Tell the payroll company to figure all the employees' check deductions and deposit it as usual, but not to actually cut the employee checks. Tell me the amount, and I'll pay it personally. Also, stop my salary check."

"Wow! You been to Vegas?"

I gazed a second through my truck window and wondered if I would get everything done fast enough. I had a fleeting recollection of a Mario Andretti saying, "If things are in control, you aren't going fast enough."

"Something like that," I said. "I'll explain more later."

Next, I deposited of $9,820 in my regular bank and another for $9,760 at a new bank where I had previously established an account. These were under the bank's report limit and would only be a one-time relief. I did not want to get the IRS to pick up a pattern for money structuring, which they call depositing dirty money.

With my new wealth, I could afford to sue to get my money on the school project, but considering the time it would take and the possibility of exposing my dirty cash, I decided to blow it off, take my loss, and move on. Also, there was no way I could salvage my bonding in time to win any upcoming bids. For the time being, problems would be handled with cash, and I would concentrate on getting new work that did not require bonding.

I did, however, have a couple of ongoing jobs that could be salvaged. My company was constructing a new YMCA holding up a $200,000 draw because a plumbing sub would not sign a lien waiver. On many jobs, a mechanic's lien waiver must be furnished by all participants for work accomplished, before the general contractor can make his draw. Some unethical subcontractors take advantage of this system, especially if they sense the general contractor is hurting for money. The subcontractor dreams up an extra charge, and if you don't pay, the sub will not sign his lien waiver. This holds up the draw for the whole project.

In this case, my $200,000 was held up by a bogus $15,000 plumbing charge. He would be the type to want his $15,000 under the table, so I called him. It irritated me to cave in on the illegal charge and was something I would have never done in the past. But what the hell—a lion will eat rotten meat if he's hungry enough.

Then I returned the message left by a nervous bank officer and told him he could expect $200,000 in ten days. Moving faster now, I noticed my shirt was wet with sweat and my hand had a slight tremble. Next, I called an individual owner who had two building lots under a sales contract with my company, but I could not close on it because of a lack of money.

"Ward, if I pay you in cash for those lots, will you discount them ten percent?"

"If you're talking about today, you're damn right I will."

Feeling like I was on a runner's high, I made another call. A foundation company was thrilled to be paid in cash, and so was my sheetrock company. Part of their thrill may have been their payments were overdue.

A small sawmill had contacted me to sell framing lumber direct and at a better price than the bigger companies; however, I could not take advantage because he wanted payment up front. Previous to my money jackpot, procuring financing had become more important than saving money. But not anymore. I contacted the small lumber company.

"Buck, I'm reconsidering your offer to sell my company framing lumber. How about I pay you up front Monday morning—with cash."

"You got it! See you Monday."

Matt walked by my open door and backed up.

"Sorry, I forgot to tell you earlier. Your wife was here this morning. She said to tell you she was here to get the office supplies."

"Here at the office? Shit. Ah…sorry, Matt. I'm just wound up. Okay, I remember. She needs her supplies at the house."

Matt left with a puzzled look on his face.

Leaving the office to go home for the evening, I experienced an overwhelming sense of dread. I had lied to Beth and now she knew it. I was so preoccupied with my thoughts that I blew right through a stoplight. A momentary crunch, my truck moved sideways, and things went dark and quiet.

I came to, disoriented and in a panic. I kicked my door open and bailed out.

Two men immediately helped me to the ground. "Sir, you need to lie down and stay quiet until an ambulance—"

"I think I'm okay," I said. "A little shook, but I'm

not hurting."

"Listen to me. I'm a paramedic. You could be badly injured and not know it."

"Okay, okay. I'll be quiet until they come."

By the time I arrived at the hospital, I felt normal and called Beth. At first, she sounded cool, but all that changed as I explained what happened. "Scrap, oh Scrap, are you sure you're all right? Emma and I will be there in twenty minutes."

Under the cloud of being caught in a lie, I thought maybe it would be good if I hurt a little. "I won't know for sure until they check me out. I just have a little pain in my chest, and my head hurts some."

At least for now, the big lie was on the back burner.

A bunch of tests, two hours of observation, three grand in charges, and we went home. Beth could not have been sweeter, but now, I had another worry. "Do you know what happened to my truck?"

"Yes, I called the police and told them to have the wrecker take it to Mike's Body shop, where we had my fender fixed."

"I have to go there. I need to get my briefcase."

"Tonight? They will be closed. Can't you call them tomorrow?"

My fear was building. I didn't care about losing the money. After all, compared to what I now had, it was insignificant, but I was aghast at having the money news work its way through the underworld. "No, we need to go there now."

She gave me a curious look. I knew the danger here was tripping her back into her suspicious disposition, but this was too important.

They were closed, but I could see my truck where it had been offloaded in the back. I walked to the back. The passenger's side door had been demolished, and there was no way the truck could be locked. I pulled the squeaky door and looked inside.

The briefcase was gone.

Chapter 29

Snake

Jacksonville, Florida

Snake went out into the common area of his compound but abruptly returned to study the map opened on his desk. Seething over the missing money, he covered every possibility of deception or mishap.

Gut's huge frame appeared at the open door. "Boss, Pigneck just showed up in the van with one of Two Finger's men trussed up like a hog going to market."

Snake stopped cold and gave a hint of a smile.

"Which one did he nab?"

"It's the loudmouth dandy who was at your meeting in Atlanta. This guy actually came to him, claiming he had information on the money going somewhere in the Midwest. Told Pigneck he heard Rex say something. That's when Pigneck took him down."

Snake put his hand on his chin, hesitating long enough for Gut to get uncomfortable. "He's probably lying. Take him to the confession chamber. We'll find out."

An uncharacteristic smile showed on Gut's normally blank face.

Snake arrived in the torture room to find Suit

Man's hands and feet tied and him dangling from the ceiling.

He motioned for Gut and Pigneck to take a quick meeting out of earshot of the driveling Suit Man. "I want the truth about what Rex might or might not have said. I want to know exactly what took place at the exchange with Rex and Toad, and I don't want anybody else to know we kidnapped Suit Man. This cannot get back to Two Finger Willie. I need his cooperation. After the interrogation, get rid of Suit Man without a trace. Gut, when this is finished, come to my office and give me a report."

"Got it," Gut said.

Snake went back to his office and studied a map of the Southeast United States.

It was almost dark when Gut reported back to Snake. "Boss, I think I've got the truth and everything Suit Man knows."

"What did you do with him?"

"We ran him through our woodchipper and took the sacks to a place I know where the big fish are hungry. And don't worry, I ran some limbs through the chipper afterward."

Snake nodded slowly. *You're one sick fiend but necessary.* "Okay, tell me."

Gut's thick gold chain reflected a glint of the bright light illuminating the gory picture behind Snake's desk.

"To start with, you were right. He was lying about overhearing Rex say anything about taking the money to the Midwest. All he heard was Rex trying to keep Toad from killing them over the one million short. He said Rex saved them all by offering to be paid with cocaine."

"And Toad agreed to this?"

Gut scratched the top of his head, his bicep bulging like a possum in a sack. "Yes, according to him, Toad liked the idea. I'm sure Suit Man told us the truth. Once the pain was intense, believe me, he didn't want to lie."

"So why did he lie to us before about Rex?"

"I got into that pretty well. Took a lot of screaming before I was satisfied, but in the end all he wanted to do was get in front of Willie for the reward money. Also said he would like to get in tight with you."

Snake let out an audible humph. Best he could tell, Two Finger had told the truth, which left a bigger mystery: how could an airplane, fifty kilos of cocaine, $20 million, and Toad and Rex disappear from the face of the earth without a trace?

"Okay, I'll think this over and call you back for more later."

Gut left, but in ten minutes he returned in what for him would be an excited state. He waved his massive arms, his voice rising an octave higher. "Shit, you not going to believe this. I just got a call from the man who was keeping an eye on Rex's boat. He says it's gone."

"What the hell you mean, gone? I thought you had it watched."

"The guy said it was his day off at the marina. People at the marina said it was gone when they got to work at 7:00 a.m."

Snake felt his anger growing. "I thought this guy was living on the boat?"

Gut shifted his weight uncomfortably from one foot to another, opening and closing his crushing right fist.

"He was, but he spent the night with his girlfriend

and returned this afternoon to find the fucking boat gone. Said all his stuff is missing with the boat."

Snake became more methodical and calmer. "I want him punished. He didn't do his job."

Gut nodded. "Okay, okay. I'll take care of him, but what do you think this means?"

Snake took a deep breath. "I think if we can find that goddamn boat, we find Rex, and if we find Rex, we find my money."

At one time they were ready to take off. How did they get back to the boat? Snake went back to his map. The boat could be anywhere. He wondered if Rex had killed Toad or if Toad had deceived him.

"I want you to throw dragnet along the entire southeast coast. Find Rex. We know he's on the boat. Toad couldn't sail it. He may or may not be with him. Contact some boys in the Bahamas and the Virgin Islands. Find that sonofabitch and get him here to our compound."

Chapter 30

Scrap

Mt. Pleasant, South Carolina

The following Saturday I walked out on my porch with a new snap to my step. A great load had been lifted. I still worried about the morality of what I was doing and the deceptions I was laying on Beth, but it was all outweighed by the great relief of having money.

The unknown implications of my missing briefcase increased the pressure I felt over Beth bringing up my bald-faced lie. The accident had bought me time and sympathy, but I knew it wouldn't last.

Around 11:00 a.m. Beth, Emma, and I went on a bike ride through our subdivision. It was a typical cool but not cold October in the Lowcountry. Emma had insisted this was a special occasion. She had learned to ride with no hands, and now she was showing off by turning back and forth with her hands off the handlebars.

I felt comfort over having solved the expense of her new special school. The dyslexia worry was diminished to the point that I just enjoyed my wonderful child. I was proud of her coordination at such a young age. Beth laughed and gave me the credit. "Oh, Scrap, she's just like her old man—thinks she can do anything."

Emma made a swooping no-hands turn and overdid it. The front wheel cocked, and she flew over the handlebars. Beth screamed. Emma hit the pavement and her helmet strap came unhooked. She skidded for several feet without it, and her bare head struck the curb.

Beth got to her first. "Emma! Emma! Oh God no. Emma, look at me. Speak to me."

Emma's eyes rolled back into her head, and she was unresponsive.

Beth looked up. "We have to get her to the emergency room!"

"I'll call 911," I said.

Tears ran down Beth's cheeks. "No, Scrap, it will take too long. Tina is home. I'll call her. It will be faster."

Tina was there in five minutes. Beth sat in the back, and I carefully laid Emma on the seat so Beth could cradle her head. She was still unresponsive. Beth was sobbing but in control. I got in the passenger seat with Tina.

"Are we going to the emergency room at Roper here in Mt. Pleasant?" Tina asked.

"Yes," I said.

"No," Beth said. "Go to MUSC Emergency in Charleston."

I knew where it was, but it didn't make sense. "Hell no. That will take another fifteen minutes."

"Scrap, shut up and listen to me. MUSC has the only trauma center. If we go to Roper, there may be a big delay to transfer her to MUSC anyway."

I nodded my head, and we took off for MUSC.

On the way Emma was moving and breathing but still unconscious. As we arrived at the emergency entrance, she opened her eyes and immediately threw up. I scooped her up and dashed through the door where two hospital attendants met us.

They wheeled her into an examining room. With puffy red eyes, Beth looked at the doctor. "She's my little girl. Oh God, help her. Please help her."

After extensive tests, a solemn doctor appeared in the waiting room. "Mr. and Mrs. Scruggs, I'm Dr. Hammond."

Beth answered, "How is she?"

"She is stable, but she has had a concussion from trauma to the top right of her head. She needs surgery to remove a blood clot on her brain."

Beth's eyes grew wide. "How serious is the blood clot?"

It's serious, but indications are it's not increasing in size; however, it should be removed."

"How soon should she have the surgery?" I asked.

"It's time-sensitive. I'll have someone come out to guide you through the necessary paperwork. The surgery could be scheduled as early as tomorrow morning."

After filling out the insurance forms, permissions, and bullshit legal waivers, I had Tina take me home to get my car while Beth remained at the hospital. Back at home, I got a call from Matt, one of my project managers. "Scrap, what's going on? They won't take my insurance."

"Matt, I'm not sure what you mean. Is it an insurance problem? Are you okay?"

"I'm at a Doc-in-the-box place for a few stitches I

need from a sheet metal cut. They won't take my insurance and said it has been canceled."

My mind was rushing ahead. It was one of the delayed payments that I had not yet figured out how to cover with my new cash.

"Let me make a couple of calls and get back to you."

I should have had a grace period, but I had not checked what it was due to other pressing problems.

Before calling my insurance broker at home, I got an angry call from Beth at the hospital. "Scrap, something is wrong with the insurance. The operation has been delayed. Something to do with our insurance being canceled. What the hell is going on? What's wrong with our insurance? My little girl could die. You have to do something!"

She didn't call Emma *our* little girl; it was *my* little girl.

"Beth, I thought I was in the grace period. Somehow I missed this when a week ago I was trying to scrape together enough to make payroll."

"You always managed to pull something out of your ass, Scrap. Now is the time to do it. I'll never forgive you if Emma suffers because of your skating on the edge."

Jesus, she didn't even want to hear why I had overlooked the payment. She was reverting to the animal instinct of a mother. No wonder the most dangerous animal in the world is a mother grizzly sensing you're between her and her cub. But my danger here wasn't being clawed to death; the danger was the alienation of my marriage.

The all too familiar tightness in my gut returned.

I called my broker. "What the hell is going on with my company health insurance? I'm getting notices of policy cancelations."

"I just got the notice yesterday. I tried to call your office, but everybody had already left."

"How can they cancel my insurance? Isn't there some kind of grace period?"

"The grace period has passed. You have been cutting into the grace period on every payment. I'm sorry, Scrap, you just waited too long."

"What do I need to do to reestablish it. My little girl is in the hospital right now in serious condition."

"If you make the payment, I'll try to get it turned back on, but bear in mind, they will not go back and cover something retroactively."

"Forget the insurance. I'll cover it another way."

"You have to have insurance, and by the way, I did try again on your bonding, but they were adamant."

"I said forget the insurance, and you can forget the fucking bonding, too."

I called my project manager back. "Matt, do me a favor. Go ahead and cover your medical bill with a check or credit card, and I'll reimburse you with cash Monday morning. I'm sorry about the mix-up."

"Yeah, I can do that. You sure you want to do it this way?"

He was a good man and my best project manager; I needed to do what it takes to keep him. "Don't worry. I got it covered."

I hung up, grabbed a small backpack, and made a dash to my basement. Removing the tarp, there was a tinge of relief to see the money was still there. I stuffed twenty thousand in the backpack and headed to the hospital.

Beth had finally been cleared and was visiting Emma's hospital room. I demanded to see Dr. Hammond. The nurse told me I couldn't see him because he was getting ready for surgery.

"And what time is his surgery?" I asked.

She made a mistake by telling me it was in an hour.

"Is he already in the operating room?"

I caught sight of him down a hospital hall and walked past her as she protested.

"Dr. Hammond."

He turned but immediately tried to turn back and walk away. "I'm sorry, but I don't have time to talk right now."

"Not even to save a child's life?" I asked.

He paused long enough for me to open the backpack. "There's twenty thousand in here, and if it costs more, I can get more. Whatever the expense is to treat my little girl, I'll pay it in cash."

His body relaxed, and he unfolded his arms and smiled. "Mr. Scruggs, I can't walk around the hospital with all that money, but I do appreciate your seriousness. I'll get Emma on the schedule tomorrow. Please don't worry. Emma's prognosis is good."

Wow, the saying money talks isn't just a saying—it talks. "And Dr. Hammond, I'll make good on all the hospital charges with cash."

I returned to the hospital waiting area and ran headlong into Beth.

"Scrap, you're walking in a daze. You didn't even see me."

"I just talked to the doctor. He's proceeding with the operation and thinks Emma's prognosis is good."

Her face beamed with relief but turned to a frown of worry.

"Why are you so distracted?" she said.

It's an intuition thing; she read my mind. "I guess I'll worry until Emma's back to normal."

"Are you worried about things other than Emma? What did you do to convince the doctor?"

I can't tell her the truth. "I made out a cashier's check to him from our business bank account and gave it to him."

She raised her eyebrows skeptically. "But I thought you were short of money."

Here I go again, another lie. "I got a draw yesterday on one of our jobs. I'll have to juggle some things around, but I'll figure it out."

Thank God she didn't push it. The weather was cool, but I could feel the sweat under my arms.

A young woman came into the waiting room. She was crying. I motioned with my head for Beth to come outside with me. We walked as far as the short-term parking lot, and she stopped.

"I have something else," she said. "I got a letter about my new job with the state department of education."

"That's great."

"I'm not sure. I know they are interviewing anybody I have worked with at school and on the school board, but I think they have been doing some checking on your business. They want your accountant to send them a financial report."

I took a deep breath and watched a male squirrel sexually harassing a young female around a tree.

"Okay, I'll send them last year's. This year isn't

done yet."

Last year's financial report was the one I had juggled the job expenses and work in progress figures. Of course, that bit of chicanery would make this current year's financials look worse, but I'll fix that with laundered money.

She lightly wrapped her fingers around mine. "I know you can make the numbers look okay. I'm concerned about what is the real picture. I don't think you're leveling with me. I think somebody out there has sent them a red flag. I can't take this job and create a political liability for Columbia, to say nothing of embarrassing ourselves."

Wow, the second time in a day that my new money was going to bail me out. It caused stress but was paying off. I felt the decision to take the money was not only correct, but the only way out. Much of the time I was on an adrenalin high over my new wealth. It wasn't just that I was solving my financial problems, but it was also about using illegal money. I didn't want to admit it to myself, but it gave me a rush.

We went back in to see if both of us could visit Emma. I was elated with Emma's prospects but was now experiencing trepidation over how quickly I had been caught up in throwing money around. Carelessly showing cash was something I had promised myself not to do, but I had already exposed myself to numerous risks.

This was a recipe for getting caught.

Chapter 31

Scrap

Mt. Pleasant, South Carolina

Two fours and a deuce. "Hit me again…a jack. I'll play these."

A scantily clad waitress offered to get me a drink. "Huh…what…ah, no thank you."

I imagined the scene. Pretty cocktail waitress standing next to lecherous contractor playing blackjack. Beth thought I was on a business trip, at least that's what I told her. *Why should I feel guilty?* Actually, this *was* a business trip to launder money. It's just not what Beth thought. She wouldn't have understood.

The dealer turned up a king underneath with a seven showing. House rules required him to stick with what he had. I gathered my chips and went to the cash out. I had won $20,000 shooting craps and another $10,000 at blackjack. Of course, I had lost more on previous occasions, but I would register these winnings and pay the taxes. It would become clean money I could spend any way I wanted.

This money laundering spot was Tunica, Mississippi, which was easy to get to from Memphis, but I did Biloxi a couple of times also.

It was exciting while I was winning but now, I felt

like a diabetic that had eaten half a chocolate cake. I wasn't sure if I was doing this for a clear purpose or I was becoming addicted? I had the same winning thrill when I discovered the money. Maybe I was addicted to the thrill of walking on the edge. Dee and the Citadel entered my head, and a let-down feeling came over me. *I will not lie, cheat, nor steal...*

I left the casino for some fresh air. I walked the sidewalk and stopped for a light to change. Out of the corner of my eye, I saw a panhandler huddled up against a building. Normally, it pissed me off to be panhandled. I always expected a scam—some con artist on the street corner claiming to be a Viet Nam vet who probably was ten years old when the war ended. But this was a teenage girl holding a baby, and I had more money than I knew what to do with. I walked over to her, and she gave me a sullen look.

"Are you giving me money?" she asked. "Or are you like the rest and want to trade?"

"I'll give you money, but first I want to know why you're here."

She was a pretty girl, which told me she must not have yet crossed over to selling herself or she would not have to be begging.

"Why is anybody here? I don't have a job. No education. No money—and I got a baby."

I was tempted to try to help by assisting her to organize her life, but it was too risky. I had to remain anonymous. "Listen. I'm going to give you money—lots of money, but as soon as I do, I want you to forget what I look like."

Her eyes widened, but she didn't speak.

I pulled out my phone to look up an address. I

179

wrote down the name and address of a place I knew would help and handed it to her. "Promise me you'll go there immediately. They want to help. Open that bag you're carrying."

I had with me several $1,000 stacks of twenties. I crammed $2,000 into her bag and walked off. "Catch a cab—now," I said.

In some ways the girl reminded me of Emma, and it depressed me. *I'm glad I took the money.* It felt good to give some away, but I had the vague sense that the satisfaction I experienced was to assuage my guilt.

It was only noon and I had not planned on returning until tomorrow, but I decided to leave now. I walked back to my rental car and headed to Memphis with Beth and Emma on my mind.

I didn't always say it was business. Sometimes I was hunting. Lies, lies, and more lies. I was getting better at lying, but deep down, I doubted Beth was believing me. I feared, instead of getting confrontation, I was getting a slow erosion of my marriage.

I called airline reservations on the way to Memphis and paid extra to change my ticket. On the way to the airport, I wrestled with how to fix my deteriorating marriage.

This gambling activity started shortly after beginning my frenzy to launder money fast enough to save my business. I even became a big lottery player, although as a numbers man, I had railed about it being a tax on stupidity due to the bad odds. Now, even a small return on my tickets would at least pay money unnecessary to hide and hitting the big one was always possible. It was turning out that laundering money was stressful and hard. It was difficult to keep up with my needs, and I wondered if there was a better way.

I turned in my car and proceeded to the gate. Six months had passed since my hummock grand slam, and most of that time I had been going like a shrew on steroids. Now I was beginning to relax some about the illegal money. It had been a good decision to use it. I felt more secure. The reservations and restraints I first felt about spending the cash had mostly melted away, like fear in a chipmunk after the hawk had flown off. All I needed to worry about was injecting the money in a careful way. The money paid for Emma's surgery and her expensive school. Got us out of debt. Made us look good for Beth's new job. And I was trying to convince myself that it would save our marriage, but the thrill of using illegal money to save my family was offset by my domestic strain. My stress level had diminished, but it didn't go away. The nagging feeling remained about compromising my principals and morals. And there was uneasiness with Beth. She was too perceptive not to know something was fishy about my behavior and all the new money.

I called Beth to tell her I was returning earlier. She seemed pleased, but normally she would have asked why, and even this bothered me, because it was more indication of the wall between us.

Monday morning Sheryl came in my office. Although Sheryl knew I had managed to come across cash money, she didn't know the details. She didn't ask questions, but tried to deal, first with lack of money, and now handling all the mysterious cash. In some ways she seemed more cooperative and incurious than what I would naturally expect. At times I feared she was getting too close for comfort in my personal affairs.

The most important thing was she didn't talk out of school. I needed her now more than ever.

"Scrap," she said, "I think you made some kind of mistake with the cash salary payments. I got my regular pay envelope, but I found this other envelope, addressed to me, with an extra five thousand in it."

"That's not a mistake. From now on, you'll get this cash payment once a month. I don't wish to discuss it. You deserve it."

"Well, okay…as they say, don't look a gift horse in the mouth."

"That's one reason you're getting it."

"Thanks." She turned to leave but swung back around. "I know something is going on, but I am with you. You're a good man, and I'll help any way I can. Just tell me what you need—or want."

She gave me a little sideways smile. I forgot what I was about to say. She seemed to enjoy that.

Finally, I turned back to a notepad on the desk and asked her to sit down. "Starting this week, I'm canceling all insurance except what the law requires. I have already canceled health insurance, which as you know, has been a constant confusion. As much as possible we will use medical services that don't take insurance, paying cash, taking advantage of their savings because they do not have to file insurance claims. Our employees are encouraged to use these services and my company will be billed direct. The employees should like this because there will be no co-pay."

I was enjoying the unlimited cash, but I experienced a hard-to-define dread, like the family dog that stole the Thanksgiving turkey.

Although my generosity had to remain unidentified, it was still fun to give it away. I surreptitiously gave away envelopes containing $1000 cash. From time to time, I dropped one of these into my church plate, the Salvation Army pot, and occasionally, if the situation warranted, I left a goody, secretly, for a deserving individual. This was hazardous, because if discovered, I would attract suspicion from several directions, not the least was the criminals who were missing the money. I was dealing with all the cash by the seat of my pants, and realized I needed a more organized plan. I also decided, if I was going to give away money, I needed to be as cautious as a skilled thief would be in stealing it.

When I got home, Beth was distant but did not ask me anything about my trip. Sunday morning, I was in a good mood. "Emma," I said. "Go put on that pretty blue dress and let's get ready for church."

"Are you going?" she said.

I stood up from the breakfast table. "Yes, I'm going to get ready now."

Beth gave me a surprised look, but it turned into a pleasant smile. "Well, what do we owe this to? Did you almost have another wreck?"

Visiting in front of the church after the service, I was approached by someone from the Monday night men's group, and I promised to attend the next meeting.

At the meeting, Wilbur, our chairman, asked to go off the record. "Guys, what I'm about to tell you is confidential and sensitive. As some of you may know, our late member, Clyde Harden, was having financial troubles."

Another member piped up. "I'm not familiar with

183

this gentleman. Could you give some background?"

Wilbur nodded. "Clyde owned and operated a landscape company, and it's my understanding, he was having problems competing because he insisted on using nothing but American workers. Couple that with more small business regulation and the new healthcare laws, and he was squeezed."

Somebody else added, "His wife is Pam Harden. She quit her job at the bank to try to save the business after his death."

"Which brings me to my point," Wilbur said. "It turns out it was too far gone and now she's in a bad situation. She has four children, no benefits, and hardly any income."

Phil Brand piped in. "What about unemployment insurance from her bank job?"

"She's not eligible if she quits," Wilbur said. "Also due to the assets listed for the business now in her name, she's not eligible for any other government benefits."

This discussion went on until a resolution was made to come back next week with some ideas about how to help. I did not participate in the discussion but privately resolved to help her immediately.

I drove to North Charleston to buy a newspaper from a curbside stand. This precaution was to prevent any fingerprints already on the paper from causing an association with my area. Using rubber gloves, I cut out letters and arranged them to read: *USE THIS MONEY, BUT DO NOT TELL ANYONE.*

I turned onto her tree-lined street and slowed to allow the car in front to clear. I pulled up to her mailbox, acting much like a thief. I quickly placed an envelope with $1,000 along with the note and drove away, wondering what a suspicious neighbor might say.

The discussion continued in the men's group the following week, and they raised $500, but that was it. I continued to make the secret $1,000 mailbox deposits every week, until there was a strange coincidence.

After giving Pam a total of $11,000, I ran into a friend of hers at a car wash lounge. I was eager to find out how she was doing but had to keep my distance out of fear of any kind of association.

"She's not doing well. Yesterday she told me the stupid bank she had worked for was investigating her about some missing money."

"What? That's crazy. How could she have stolen it?"

"Pam said it makes no sense because she still has a bank account there. In fact, the bank account is what they're homing in on. Seems she made $11,000 in deposits she cannot or will not explain. Sounds weak to me, but I guess they're rolling over all stones."

I was stunned. Now I needed to take the dangerous step of confessing my involvement to Mrs. Harden. This was my fault, and I had to somehow relieve her of suspicion. At the same time, it was necessary to keep the confidentiality of the cash giveaway.

I called her the following day. "Mrs. Harden, my name is Daniel Scruggs. I'm a member of your church and in the men's group that tried to help with a small donation awhile back. If I could, I would like to have a meeting with you about your money situation."

"Are you with the bank?"

"No, ma'am, I'm a building contractor."

"Why do you want to meet?"

I knew I had to commit, or I would look like some sort of predator.

"Mrs. Harden, do these words ring a bell? *Use this money, but do not tell anyone.*"

There was a long pause. "Yes…oh my God, it's you."

"Will you come to Pickett Park, at the old Sullivan's Island bridge? Do you know where that is?"

"Yes, when?"

"In an hour. I'll be near or sitting on the first bench overlooking the marsh. I'll be wearing a green baseball cap."

Even though Mrs. Harden did not know me, I had already made the effort in the past to be able to identify her. She was about thirty-five with brown hair and a trim figure. There was someone already sitting on the first bench when she approached, so I walked toward her. She had a serious look on her face.

"Pam Harden?"

"Yes."

"Walk with me to the bridge."

She was hesitant but agreed. I was relieved to discover Mrs. Harden was informed and smart. She understood how money moved through the bank and how the bank examiners did their work. She was not hysterical but concerned. "Mrs. Harden, are you under suspicion for missing money at the bank you worked for?"

She looked out across the harbor to Charleston on the other side and then turned toward me. "Yes, it appears the suspicion was created when I made your deposits to my account at the same bank I was working for. These deposits evidently were for a similar amount that was missing. They were the deposits of the money you gave me."

"But it's my understanding you no longer work for the bank."

We were out of earshot of anyone else walking along the old causeway. We could see Fort Sumpter out in the Charleston harbor. She stopped and faced me. "That is correct, but I quit to take over my husband's business, and it cast more suspicion on me."

"Mrs. Harden, I'm so sorry. This is ridiculous. How do they think you took the money?"

She exhaled a deep breath and eyed two orange billed oyster catchers hunting on a mudflat.

"They have not told me of how the money was stolen," she said. "So, I'm not sure they even know. On your previous instructions, I resisted telling the bank about the mysterious mailbox money. But under relentless pressure, I finally did tell them. They didn't believe me. Even said my story sounded preposterous. Now they're more suspicious than ever."

Somehow, I had to take suspicion away from her. An hour-long discussion with Mrs. Harden finally formed a plan.

"Mrs. Harden, money isn't as important to me as remaining anonymous. I want you to hire a lawyer and tell him you did not embezzle money and you want to get the bank off your back. Stick to the story about the mailbox money and say you think it's somehow coming through the church. I'll increase your money to pay the attorney. At all costs, don't tell anyone about our meeting or that you even know me."

She agreed, but I did not tell her the rest of my unlikely plan. In order to relieve Mrs. Harden of suspicion, I dreamed up a scheme to repay the missing $11,000. The amount in twenty-dollar bills would weigh more than thirteen ounces, which is the post office limit for curbside drop off. I dared not expose myself to post office personnel and security cameras. Both fifty and one hundred-dollar bills would put me under the thirteen ounces, so I decided on a mix of these.

Using two different banks where I had an account, I withdrew the money in fifties and hundreds. I used gloves to remove the money from the tube and stuff it into an envelope, which had also been protected from my fingerprints. I created another message cut out of the newspaper. This time it read: *HERE IS YOUR STOLEN MONEY.*

The envelope was addressed to the bank president. A return address was used for a bank located in Summerville, South Carolina, which was an hour's drive from my house.

I pulled up to a drop off box in Summerville, feeling like a mail thief. I looked both ways to see if anybody was suspicious. The bank would know the money did not come from Mrs. Harden because they were watching her bank account.

The following week, I talked to Pam on the phone. "Have they let up on you about taking the money?"

"They have been talking to my lawyer, but he tells me that they still think somehow I'm connected. He's talking about suing them."

If this didn't stop, it would eventually get to me. Meanwhile, even though I was sure Pam was trying to keep it quiet, friends and bank tellers were talking. The next church meeting one member commented, "This

Pam Harden story is getting bizarre. I heard the bank got money that fell right out of the sky."

I was like a criminal trying to think of all the details in covering up a murder. What out of the way corner resided that little detail that would tie all this back to me? How long would it be before the drug dealers came calling?

PART II

One year later

Chapter 32

Snake

Jacksonville, Florida

Snake walked over to his bookcase and retrieved an atlas of Central and South America and the Caribbean. He needed to come up with a foolproof delivery plan. He could not afford to lose any more deliveries.

There was a knock and Gut stuck his head in. "Boss, I got Two Finger Willie on the phone. I think you'll want to hear this."

"Willie, you got something."

"I do. He goes by the name of Fish Blount. He's in Six Mile, a community outside of Mt. Pleasant, South Carolina. My boys say he's spending lots of money he found in a silver suitcase out in the marsh. He's gambling, snorting, and womanizing like he's rich. He even bought a new jacked-up blue Camaro and painted a big silver fish on the side."

Snake got excited at the prospect of retrieving some of his money. He needed it badly. "Thanks, I'll check that out."

"Okay," Willie said. "I do what I say for you. You do what you say?"

Snake would be glad to share what he had

promised to get his money, but first he needed to verify. "If it pans out, you'll get your money."

He sent Gut to investigate.

Two days later, Gut called. "We got him, and I think we can make him talk. He's scared shitless. It looks like he only found one suitcase, so the question is, does he know anything about the rest?"

"Bring him to the compound. We'll find out."

Gut arrived at the compound with a trembling Fish Blount. He was thin, small, and wore a baseball cap with a picture of a fish on the front. He shifted his eyes around as if any minute something would charge in to devour him. Snake looked at Fish and smiled. "Take him to our confession room and strap him in."

Gut and Pigneck dragged Fish into the torture chamber. Snake followed at a distance.

Fish's eyes darted wildly around the room furnished with torture equipment. His body quivered. "Please…wh-what you w-want with me?"

Gut jammed him into a chair resembling an old school desk, and Pigneck strapped his arm onto the rest.

Snake put on noise-canceling earmuffs and smiled. He nodded to Gut, who was holding a pair of pliers.

"No, no, man," Fish said. "Man, no… Please…don't hurt me. I'll tell you anything, but I don't know what you want."

"All in due time," Snake said. "But first things first." He gave a slight hand wave to Gut.

Quick as a burnt child removes a hand from the hot stove, the fingernail on Fish's right index finger was yanked out. His eyes bulged, and he screamed like he was on fire. Pigneck sprinkled it with salt. Snake waited patiently until the screams subsided. "Now, Mr. Fish, would you like for us to take away the pain from the end of your finger?"

Fish looked confused. "Yes, yes, yes. Please, yes."

Gut reached under the desk and came up with a meat cleaver and in one continuous movement chopped off the finger.

The lights were extinguished, and Fish was left alone, still tied to his chair screaming. An hour passed, the lights were turned on, and Snake watched Gut and Pigneck set up a video player. Snake grabbed the quaking chin and turned Fish's head so his tear-filled eyes looked directly into Snake's. "Mr. Fish, pay close attention to this video. Without your full cooperation, you'll become our next movie star."

They turned off the lights and left Fish with his movie. It depicted graphic pictures of a man being tortured to death.

The video ended. It was deathly quiet except for a sobbing Fish. Thirty seconds later, Snake entered, and the lights came on. Fish drooled and babbled. He had peed all over himself. "Mr. Fish, please tell me all you know about finding my money."

Fish couldn't get the information out fast enough. "I found one suitcase in the marsh. No more, only one. Oh, God, if I knew more, I'd tell. Please believe me! Please, I don't know about no more money—less Mr. Scruggs find some."

"What about this Mr. Scruggs?"

"About a year and a half ago, I passed him in the creek with some of them shiny suitcases in his boat. Please, I don't know no more."

"Tell me more about this Mr. Scruggs."

"He's a big-shot builder, lives in Hamlin

Plantation. Now and then, I see him in the creek or marsh. I think he likes to fish and hunt marsh hen."

"How many suitcases did you see in his boat?"

"Maybe he had seven, eight, maybe more. I just see him when he pass in the creek."

"You're a good honest man, Mr. Fish, and I appreciate your cooperation. Gut and his assistant, Mr. Pigneck here, will now take you home."

"Please just let me go. I find my own way home."

"Pigneck," Gut said, "get the boat keys."

Chapter 33

Scrap

Mt. Pleasant, South Carolina

By late spring, my financial problems were solved. After gradually injecting $3 million into my company, it was strong and doing well. Bank relations were better, although they still were not the same, and neither was my relationship with my wife.

Several more bank accounts were opened where I occasionally made cash deposits of under $10,000. I had a reliable group of suppliers and subcontractors that took cash from time to time.

Wednesday afternoon I left a job site and circled by a pawn shop in North Charleston. I had cultivated several of these places that sold me gold for cash. I deposited the gold at a major trading house, and after accumulating $100,000 worth I planned to sell it for a check that I could deposit. This was the third time I had successfully done this transaction.

The cash infusions I made in my business to pay for many expenses created large profits to show up on the bottom line. I gladly paid the taxes, and it became clean money. It was certainly a better plan than gambling.

Often, I didn't make it home in time for the three

of us to sit down and eat like a family. This afternoon I did, and I was nervous about what might come up. "Emma, what did you do at school today?" I asked.

"We did the same things, but we got a new girl today. She's very quiet. I tried to talk to her at recess, but she ran back inside."

"Emma let's play a game," Beth said. "Where Daddy tells us what he did."

Oh boy, she's using Emma to be snarky. It pissed me off—and worried me.

"Daddy, tell us what you did."

I knew I needed to stop this poison. "Daddy spent lots of money today," I said, "and lied to momma about where it came from."

"You're being silly, Daddy."

Beth shot out of her chair and threw her dish in the sink. It shattered, and she stomped out.

I felt awful. I resolved to go straight to her and tell all, but I couldn't leave my daughter in a state of confusion. By the time I talked things out with Emma, I had lost my nerve.

In these situations, I usually tried talking about Beth's job at the Education Department to gloss over my secrecy. In the early days of my gravy train, I considered telling Beth. I even told her I would, but there was always a lingering fear of involving her in something illegal. As days, weeks, and months passed, a cloud settled over our marriage and for most of this time, things didn't change. The promised talk was put off for so long I felt awkward bringing it up. Besides, I was afraid to face what she might try to make me do, but now her tolerance was running out.

I went to the bedroom door and stood. Beth was on

her back in the bed. "Beth," I said. "I'm probably doing this wrong, but whether wrong or right, there's one thing that will not change. I love you more than life itself. If there's nothing else, you can take that to the bank."

She rolled over on her side and looked at me. "I know that, but over time love can be eroded if couples can't confide, communicate, and share their emotions."

I was at a loss of how to respond for fear that anything I said would trap me into promising to do something I wasn't ready to do. There was something about Beth I found both fascinating and perplexing: I never knew for sure what she was thinking. Because of this, and her intuition, I often let a disagreement fester. From the beginning, she was more psychologically astute. Hell, it didn't make sense. I grew up fighting with an older brother. I had to learn when to bluff and how much I could get away with. She grew up as an only child isolated from this test by fire. But somehow, she learned far more about human nature and how people behave than I ever did.

I was fanatical about protecting Beth and Emma, but I imagined my perception of what I needed to do would be at odds with her. Finally, I gave up trying to come up with a response that would satisfy her. "I understand," I said.

"No, you don't."

The following Friday I made every effort to arrive early for a planned Easter weekend celebration, but Beth and Emma were not home. A week of successful returns on somebody's drug money put me in a good mood. I poured two fingers of bourbon and sat in the den. Beth and Emma arrived at seven and walked through. Beth glanced at me without speaking. Emma squealed, "Daddy, you're home."

I smiled. "Hi, girls, the man of the house came home early, but there were no ladies here to celebrate with. Have you been having fun? Where you been?"

"When you come home at seven or eight, I don't ask where you've been," Beth said.

"Hey, I'm not prying—just missing my girls."

She appeared angry, which confused me.

"Don't patronize me. If you miss us so much, why do we see you so little?"

Now I was getting mad. I took the time to sip my drink. "Sweetheart. If you had a bad day, you don't need to take it out on me."

"Don't give me that. You come home at a decent time maybe once a month, but you expect us to be waiting with bated breath. Your wonderful secretary knows more about what's going on or where you are than I do."

"I've worked hard to turn things around. We are doing okay now. I don't understand why you're so snippy?"

"There is more to *okay* than throwing money, especially money I'm wary about."

So, my financial deception was still the elephant in the room. She could see money came too quickly and easily. I operated in secret for the most part, but she knew there was too much cash washing around.

I had dodged a bullet with my finances and once again was a good provider, but now it was causing marital problems. Other than her psychological aloofness, Beth had not pushed me about the money. I worried, with her intuition and the unmistakable evidence of cash, she would figure it out.

Beth's face took on a more tolerant look. She even gave me a small smile as if I were a remorseful schoolboy bringing his pea shooter to school. "I know your heart is good," she said. "But I'm not sure your wild and erratic tendencies will overwhelm the goodness. You need to let me in, Scrap. I can help."

"Now who's patronizing? You need to understand, I'm in a conundrum, and you're part of it. Please give me some space."

Something else bothered me. Always priding myself on honesty, I had been unforgiving when others crossed the line. Since graduating from The Citadel, up until my financial stress, I had continued to live by the same honor code the school had ingrained in me. So, it was hard to shake the idea that even though it felt right to be saving my business and providing for my family, I was now a crook. *What would my friend Dee think?*

I always used to say a contractor could make money and stay honest, and thinking back, now made me depressed about my situation. I was bullshitting myself. I had to get a grip, had to establish some boundaries. Hypocrisy was crawling on me like fiddler crabs on a mudflat.

"So, this means you're not going to talk," she said. "What you're telling me is I'm not up to the level of helping with your conundrum. If you love me so much, where is the trust?"

The sun was setting. The tide was coming in, and the colors of the marsh would have brought a rush of creativity to Monet. "I'm going out on the porch."

I felt like I was going through a midlife crisis, questioning the foundation of my principles, and I was barely forty years old. Trying to rationalize away my improprieties, the expanse of gray encroached into territories once belonging to black and white. I thought more about the greater good and less about absolute right or wrong. I once read if you're starving, honesty is a luxury you cannot afford. I had scoffed at this, but now I wondered. If there were a pyramid of principles in life, was honesty the foundation? Or maybe it was more toward the top, after security and comfort were satisfied.

All of this reshuffling of priorities caused me angst. I sensed once the line was crossed, it was hard to know where the next line was. I could now see how the tainting of Scrap began. It was like mold growing in the shower. It starts subtly and gradually spreads.

Here I stand—a full-fledged fugitive, a liar, a thief, a money launderer, and a user of dirty money for personal use. Had I given up too much for my survival?

A marsh hen let out a staccato cackle, as if laughing. Wood storks settled in to roost on the scrub trees out on a small spit of land protruding into the cordgrass and pluff mud. I could smell it—the sulfur-tinged, Lowcountry fragrance harking back to the lazy days of summer of my youth.

Would it have been better to fail and start over? But then there was my family. Did I have the right to decide on my moral principles and ignore the hardships it would bring? I needed to patch what I could and move on. Once I got my business thriving, I would wean myself off the dirty money and be a straight arrow once again.

On the distant beach of Dewees Island, I could faintly hear the rumble of an unfathomable ocean. Like the creatures of the sea, I was nothing more than any other species struggling for the right to survive.

Chapter 34

Scrap

Mt. Pleasant, South Carolina

Thursday morning at nine o'clock, I was mulling over my little dance with a foundation company to see if the owner was amenable to receiving half of his bill in cash. This was touchy because I did not want to commit until I got some indication he was on board. His clear advantage would be not paying taxes on the cash part, so he would be dancing too. It reminded me of a tropical bird mating ritual.

I reached for my office phone, and my cell chimed with a call from Beth. "Scrap, come quick. My SUV is burning. All of Emma's things are in the back, my CDs, everything inside is destroyed."

"Beth, step back from the car."

"I'm not close to the car! It just burned by itself. Nobody is near it…It caught fire while I was still in my exercise class."

Not knowing the details, my immediate worry was a gas tank explosion.

"Stay away from the car. It could blow up."

"A fire truck just came. There's the police. Scrap, I need you here. You need to come. Now!"

"Where are you?"

"At the gym. How could this happen?"

Normally, Beth was not easily frightened, but I could detect an edge in her voice that worried me as if she was about to lose it.

"Go back inside the gym. I'll be there in ten minutes."

As I raced out, Sheryl tried to ask me something. "Sheryl, not now. Something's happened."

I jumped into my truck and spun the back tires as I left my office parking area.

I pulled into the gym parking lot. Beth's burned-out SUV had firefighters still huddled around it. I ran to the door of the gym, pushing a police officer to one side, and went inside. Beth was talking to a fire chief and another police officer. "You all right?"

"Yes, but I don't understand what's going on."

The police officer I had brushed aside had followed me with a determined look but stopped when he realized who I was.

I put my arms around Beth, and she cried. "I'm scared," she said. "This is strange. It just burned with nobody around. Did you see it? It was destroyed."

"It's okay," I said. "Where were you when it caught fire?"

"I walked out of the gym, and it was burning."

A police officer, who I had noticed was watching us, walked over and asked if we would step outside the gym.

At the front exit Beth and I were met by the fire inspector. He eyed us sternly, and I got the sense we were under some kind of suspicion. The police already asked Beth to provide her car plate information, which she couldn't do without going home, and they had asked to see her driver's license.

"Mr. Scruggs," the fire inspector said, "what type of business are you in?"

"I own and operate a construction company."

"Who is this SUV registered to?"

"It's in both our names."

What is it with these guys? I need to calm Beth before she says something that sounds incriminating.

"Do you have a loan on the car?"

I could see Beth was upset, and these questions were pissing me off.

"No."

"What type of insurance do you carry on this vehicle?"

He seemed satisfied about the money aspect when I told him there was no loan and we carried only the minimum insurance the state law required.

He stepped away from our conversation and conferred with a Mt. Pleasant police officer.

They approached together, and the inquiry turned to whom our enemies might be. Beth and I were uncomfortable with these questions for different reasons. She did not like the implication that somehow she was responsible for the fire. But I had other, more ominous, thoughts—a sense that something was sneaking up on me.

I became more irritated when they homed in on Beth, but because of my guilt, I didn't object.

"Mrs. Scruggs, driving over to the gym, did you notice anything unusual about your car?"

"No, nothing out of the ordinary."

"Have you noticed anyone unfamiliar hanging around your car?"

"No, but when it caught fire, I was in the gym."

Three curious teenage boys were being restricted by a police officer from getting closer to the SUV.

"Have you noticed an unusual smell in your car?"

"No."

I need to cut this shit out until I had time to think.

"Has your husband, or any of his friends, worked on your car lately?"

"No, it's been running fine so—"

I stepped between them. "Can't you see she's upset over the fire? Could we have some time to collect our wits before all of this interrogation?"

The fire was out, but I watched a firefighter spray it again.

"Mr. Scruggs, just a couple more questions for now."

I was nervous about this mystery, but still, I was getting irritated with these questions.

"Mrs. Scruggs, have you or your husband been threatened?"

"Not at all...Should I be worried?"

"We have no evidence of foul play other than the fact the fire in your car was not likely spontaneous."

The one thing I knew was I did not burn the SUV and Beth did not burn the SUV, but this investigation was beginning to worry me. "If there are no more questions, we need to go." I turned to escort Beth toward my truck.

"Mr. Scruggs, just one more question. It's unusual for a man in your position to carry the minimum amount of insurance. Could you shed some light?"

"I'm self-insured for an amount over the state requirement. If you find the insurance insufficient, take it up with the state legislature. They set the minimums."

Beth gave me a harsh look but said nothing. We were told to be available for more questions later and were released.

On our way home, Beth was still upset. I was concerned, but I wasn't sure what to be concerned about.

"This type of thing isn't normal," she said. "What is happening to us?"

She had good reason to say this. Of course, it's not normal. I needed to keep her calm until I figured this out.

I reached over and touched her hand. "Just because we don't understand the fire doesn't mean there's not a plausible explanation. We will probably figure it out with time."

She gave me a stern look and raised her eyebrows. "I'm not so sure. Could it be connected to all the extra money?"

"Come on, Beth. You're upset, I know, but don't bring up something unrelated. I don't know what you're talking about."

We arrived home and parked in the garage under the house. Before I could open the door, Beth grabbed my arm. "Something strange is going on in your life and has been for too long. I can't help but wonder if this is connected."

I didn't answer but got out to open the door for her. I arrived on her side as she bailed out and marched toward the house.

I followed her in. "Sweetheart, I'm concerned too, but let's not bring in unrelated things. There's no evidence of what this is."

She spun around and faced me. "I do have evidence. I have watched you become different. You're more evasive and unhappy."

"That's not evidence. That's a feeling. Intuition isn't evidence. I know you're upset and tired—"

"The hell you say. I may not know exactly what it is, but I know it's there, and if you patronize me again, either you or I will sleep in the guest room."

This was going downhill fast. I took a deep breath and softened. "Okay, I've been evasive and there are some things we need to talk about, but now isn't the time because they have nothing to do with your car fire."

"So you admit to being evasive, and yet you're not evasive about my car fire?"

Chapter 35

Scrap

Mt. Pleasant, South Carolina

I wasn't sure why, but at 10:15 a.m. the following day, I was intent on checking out the 9mm I kept in my desk drawer. The intercom clicked, and Sheryl interrupted. "You have a visitor who says he's a contractor. Says he has confidential business with the owner."

I hesitated for several seconds, put the gun away, and pushed the intercom button to answer. "Okay, send him in."

A large beefy man opened my door. I stood to greet him but immediately became wary when his huge bulk entered. His arms were almost too thick for his suit coat. He wore no tie, and gold chains hung around his neck. He turned and shut my office door as if he were in charge. When we shook, his huge hand engulfed mine. I noticed his diamond Rolex, and alarms went off in my head. If I had been a dog, the hair would be rising on my back.

He sat down. "You can call me Gut."

I started to object but hesitated when he reached for his briefcase. He opened it and withdrew a folder. I clenched and unclenched my fist, trying to control my fear mixed with anger. The SUV fire and now this. A knot developed in the pit of my stomach.

"Mr. Scruggs, I am not a contractor. I am a messenger here to discuss the safety of your wife and daughter."

The surprise on my face was probably discernible. "Did you say, my wife and daughter?"

He didn't answer but laid down a picture of my adorable nine-year-old Emma holding her bike not two blocks from my house. A van was stopped in the road, and she appeared to be talking to someone inside.

Before I could digest the picture, he produced one of Beth getting into her car at the grocery store. He kept throwing down pictures. The last one was Beth's SUV with her gym in the background. I could clearly read her license plate, but I focused on the back window—a sign: *BURN HERE TODAY*.

My face flushing hot, I slammed my fist on the desk. "What the hell is this?"

He put up his hand for me to wait and showed one more picture. It was taken inside my house.

"What do you want?" My voice sounded strained.

He reached into his briefcase and gave me an envelope.

"These are instructions from my boss. You are to follow them precisely. He sends his assurance, with your full cooperation, your family will not be harmed, but make no mistake about it, your full cooperation is necessary."

I was scared, but I couldn't allow him to threaten me and walk out.

"Listen, asshole. I don't know who you are, but I imagine the police would be interested that you burned my wife's SUV and now are threatening my family."

"Mr. Scruggs, you and I both know this is about stealing money from my boss. I'd advise you to read the letter and follow the instructions. Any other action will endanger you and your family."

He turned and walked out, once more closing my office door behind him as if to leave me alone to contemplate. I sat dazed for a few seconds looking at the closed door where he had departed. Like some zoo animal shot with a tranquilizer dart, I slowly turned my head and gazed outside. Finally, I fumbled with the envelope he had left. There was one typewritten sheet inside. It had no heading.

There will be a business meeting held in Jacksonville, Florida, at 2:30 p.m., Saturday, June 1. Attendance is mandatory. You should arrive at Marsh Creek Manor located at 14668 Duval Rd. at 1:45 p.m. Park in front of the hotel and remain in your car until contacted for transfer.

All the distress I had felt during my financial problems returned, except worse. This was not humiliation or loss of livelihood. It was about our survival. I experienced the prehistoric emotion of fight or flight.

Dizzy with this foreboding tidal wave of evil affiliation, I tried to think. A visit to the wolf's den, alone? No way, I was no fool. The gangster movies came to mind—the scenes where they put a bullet in your head and stuffed you into a barrel of cement. My God, the meeting is tomorrow afternoon, and Jacksonville is 250 miles away.

But I looked again at the pictures of little Emma—and reconsidered. This was not only about the danger of me going into their headquarters alone. This was about Emma and Beth. I had to take the chance, but somehow, I had to stay alive. For a moment I was overwhelmed with remorse over the enormity of what I had done. Taking the money to save us from financial ruin had now turned into a life-and-death struggle. The retribution of endangering the safety of my family was worse than I could've imagined.

I picked up the picture taken inside my house, and it hit me: *They found the money!*

Chapter 36

Scrap

Mt. Pleasant, South Carolina

As I came out of my office, Sheryl looked up from her work. "You look like you're going to a fire," she said. "Who was that brute?"

"I can't talk now." I rushed past her. "I've gotta go. I'll call you later."

From the ten suitcases of money I had stored under my house, there had been two left. Last week I removed the rest of the money in a third suitcase and buried the empty in the old microwave oven box at the bottom of our recycle can. The two that should still be there had been left for expenses and working capital I had grown accustomed to.

I drove home in a stupor, hardly aware of the road. I looked under the tarp in my basement—the suitcases were gone.

They knew. I was the key to their missing money.

But how did they even know to look for it?

Beth was out and Emma was at school. I stepped around my garage, turned, and stared at the tarp as if it would bring back the suitcases. Drug dealer stories flooded my mind. They will kill and torture with little provocation, especially if their money or identity is jeopardized. Once they think they have all the missing money, I will be eliminated and possibly my family. *I need to buy time.*

The more I considered my situation, the worse it seemed. I ran upstairs, thinking I would find some other evidence, but came up with nothing. They had magically invaded my sanctuary and left without a trace.

I thought about grabbing my family and fleeing but realized that would never work. No way would I pull it off without them knowing. They would follow us to the ends of the earth. In anger and desperation, I went to my gun safe feeling the need for a weapon to handle the threat. I picked up my AR-15 and got to the door. What or who was I going to shoot? I put it back, checked my concealed carry, and walked out in bewilderment.

My mind kept coming back to the missing money. I ran down and jumped in my truck, planning to check on the money in storage. I only got to the turnout from my street before it dawned on me. I could be followed. *Dumb idea.* I needed to stop and think. I drove back and went out on the porch.

Turkey vultures circled the trees to my left. I caught a tiny scent of something dead.

I shivered. Maybe I should give back the money I had left. It was too late. If I gave them the money, they would ransom my family until they got what I had used over the past eighteen months, and then they would kill us.

Across the miles of marsh, I could hear the deep tone of a tugboat horn, probably pushing a barge. The answer was out there somewhere.

It's all about the money.

The money! Maybe that's the key. I had to offer something they wanted, and at the same time convince them they will get all their money, but not right away. They needed to understand they will never get it if I died.

A plan took shape, but first I had to figure out how and what they knew.

More vultures arrived, homing in on some unfortunate creature to pick its bones.

The drug dealers had to have a suspicion even before they found $1 million under my house, but how? They now knew I had at least some of their money, but did they know how much? Did they know I took it all? Thirty-nine suitcases with $19,500,000.

My brain hurt with tension. I went over my movements during the discovery of the money. How did they know to come after me? Somebody had to see…*but who?* I thought back through the last eighteen months and relived each day from when I discovered and removed the money. Did somebody see something at the boat landing? Did they find my storage? But why would they even be looking? It didn't seem feasible they could figure it out by watching my business. I came up with nothing.

Maybe it had to do with the cash I had given away. I called Pam, the woman I had sent money to. The money had gotten her embroiled in the bank's embezzlement by an unknown thief. "Pam, did you ever get the bank off your back?"

"In a way I did. My lawyer threatened to sue them, so they dropped it, but it turns out that the amount stolen was not the same as my eleven-thousand-dollar deposit. Somehow, and I don't understand this, they got their money back, but it was more than what was stolen. They were so stupid. Instead of absolving me, they thought their audit department made a mistake. In any case, right now they're leaving me alone. Thank you again for trying to help."

So, it probably didn't come from the cash I had sent to Pam, but there had to be something. I had to use logic. My mind retraced every minute I could remember during the week I had discovered the crash site a year and a half ago. I mentally went back to the island each day and traced my movements when I stashed that day's money.

Tracing my action on the third trip, I came to Fiddlers Creek and Fish Blount. He almost ran me over. *That's it! The tarp.* It had blown off. Fish saw the suitcases. Somehow it had to come from him. On that trip there were nine suitcases. If it were Fish, those suitcases have to be all they know about connected to me. They probably don't know about the crash or how the money disappeared.

The thought occurred to me, why not tell about all the money? But after going through the thrill of finding the money and working so hard to integrate it into my business, I reasoned that at least some of it now belonged to me. If I could keep those scumbags from having it, I would. Besides, it was going to be security for my family if everything else came apart. To buy time, I must convince them the money they know about is tied up in my business.

I got another whiff of something dead and went inside.

Coincidentally, the $3 million, which I had sunk into my business, plus what they found in my basement, comes to $4 million, which would be eight suitcases— close enough to the actual nine I had. I was sure Fish did not have time to count the exact amount. The weak part of my assumption was even though Fish saw the suitcases, how did he know they were full of money? Also, I was assuming they didn't know the suitcases Fish saw came from the crash site. If these assumptions were incorrect, my plan would fail. It was, however, the only explanation that made sense, so it was the story I decided to go with.

I drove back to work, looking out the whole time to see if somebody was following. Sheryl confronted me as I entered the reception area. "Hey, Scrap," she said carefully. "Is there something I can do to help?"

"As a matter of fact, there is. Would you come into my office, please?"

She entered behind me, and I told her to close the door. She acted like maybe this was an invitation.

"I'm going to write a letter to Dee. You know who he is. I want you to hold it until 9:00 p.m. tomorrow. If I don't show up at your house by that time, I want it delivered. Will you do it?"

"Of course, I will, but I'm worried about you. Why wouldn't you show up? That sounds like something I should be concerned about."

"I can't tell you more. Maybe later—but not now."

She reluctantly left my office, and an hour later, I came out and gave her the letter.

"If I don't show up by nine o'clock tomorrow night, I want you to use a courier to send this letter to Special Agent Dee Boyd. The address is on the envelope. Also, I want you to use these instructions to send a backup email."

"I understand, but I'm afraid for you. Are you sure you're all right?"

I hesitated over how much I should tell her.

"Frankly, I'm afraid too. I have to caution you that it's possible you could get a call from me begging you to not send the letter—"

"Scrap, no, I—"

"Just listen to me, Sheryl. This is important. You have to ignore any request not to send the letter, including my own. Unless I'm here, alone, in person, the letter must go out."

She took the letter like I was handing her a snake.

The letter I gave her was sealed and told Dee everything—well, almost everything. The only part left out was the existence of the $10 million at Keep Safe All Night Storage, which was separate and undisturbed. That part was in a second letter I wrote to Beth, which hopefully she would never read. I told no one about the second letter. The envelope said for Beth only, personal, to be opened in case of my death.

I left Sheryl looking scared, and I raced to the bank to leave the letter to Beth in my safe deposit box. I went home to cancel the weekend plans I'd made with Beth. She would be mad, and I dreaded going through her questions followed by her cool silence.

I was relieved to find Beth in the study doing paperwork for her job. "Hi, morning glory. I'm home. I think I have time for a run."

"Okay, I'll be at this for another hour. I already got something for supper. Say hello to Emma."

Returning from the run, and still scared of facing Beth, I went out on my dock. Finally, I decided to tell her straight out. "I'm sorry, but I will not be able to go to the beach this weekend."

"What! Emma and I have been planning on it. What is it this time?"

Emma came running in. "Daddy, come see my lizard I caught on the porch."

"Oh no, you don't," Beth said. "Not until you tell me what is more important than our beach trip."

"I have an important business meeting in Jacksonville tomorrow."

She didn't let this one go, and even though I was irritated because she'd been following my activities more closely lately, it was understandable she was upset.

"I guess it's like everything else: we will do it without you. Must be a really important meeting. Who's it with?"

Without time to think, I came up with a stupid reply. "It's with the National Homebuilders' Association. They have a big meeting in Jacksonville."

I was the raccoon trapped in the barn and desperately searching for an escape. "I smell something good in the kitchen. I'm starved!"

"I should let you just smell it and not give you any. Why did you not mention the meeting when we made plans for the weekend?"

Digging a deeper hole, I gave another dumb answer. "Sheryl just reminded me. I had forgotten about it," I said. "I know what's cooking. It's spaghetti. I smell the garlic."

She put her hands on her hips and pursed her lips. "If Sheryl is as wonderful as you say, she would've reminded you sooner."

Exhausted from stress, I snapped. "Damn it! Why

do you have to pick on her?"

She gave me a curious look as if she knew there was something more to discover here. "Why are you so sensitive about it?"

I turned away and walked out to our back porch overlooking the marsh. I did my best thinking here because the marsh brought me back to my youth, to the molding of my character in my formative years.

Where am I going wrong? Beth and Emma were my world. If anything happened to them, my life would be meaningless. Yet, in trying to protect them, I was driving a wedge between us. Maybe I should have told Beth everything. But I had a feeling she would change my trajectory. In the end, their safety was my responsibility. Even if I violated Beth's trust, I had to protect them.

The next morning, I worked at getting my head into what was facing me, but Beth confronted me, her defiance radiating. "You're lying about something. I want you to understand I know you're lying."

Shit, I didn't have the balls even to answer. I went to the porch.

Pretending and deceiving for so long would cause me to lose stature in her eyes if I told her everything now. Besides, she may insist on going to the law. That won't work. The bottom line was Beth knew I was hiding something. She would find out there was no Homebuilders meeting. *Foolish.*

I came inside to get another cup of coffee. Tension still hung in the air. She was standing by the sink and turned. "I had a fitful night, and I noticed you seemed to have one also."

"I'm sorry. I—"

"Let me finish! You know why neither of us slept well. The problem is I don't know. I want you to tell me."

I let out a heavy sigh and looked at her angry face. "Okay, there's a problem that I'm trying to fix, but I'm running out of time to get Jacksonville and believe me, this meeting is important."

"Does it have to do with all this money I see sloshing around?"

Beth was pressuring me at a time I was already about to explode under the strain of my future visit to the den of drug dealers. "Goddamn it—I—I don't have time to do this now. I have to go."

"Okay, but believe me, you're caving to something that isn't as important as what you're leaving behind— unfinished."

At 9:00 a.m. I was in my truck, scared and angry, barreling toward Jacksonville, not even seeing road signs or the other vehicles. This trip could lead to my total demise. I could be kidnapped, or worse, my family could be. Going to the law was out of the question; I would surely end up in jail, and my family would still be in jeopardy. But I wasn't confident the drug dealers would go along with my plan.

I tried to imagine what I was facing, but I had no other experience in my life I could compare it to. I had always been a fighter, that's why I was called Scrap, but this was different. I was out of my element. Being a fighter was not enough. I had to be a thinker, be creative.

How did it come to this? Dee…I needed him. He was an expert on drug dealers. But I couldn't bring him into this. He would either need to arrest me or compromise his integrity with the FBI. Besides, how could I face Dee with such hypocrisy? *I will not lie, cheat, or steal.* And here I am barreling down the road to meet with a den of cocaine traffickers. The very thing he despised the most.

Damn, I had to slow down. I was doing ninety. It was like my foot was attached to my frustrated brain.

I knew they might torture me to death, but I had to face them and try to solve it. Surely, the bastards were not smarter than I was. The plan I worked out with Sheryl would buy me some time. But as soon as I was wallowing in feelings of confidence, the realization sank in. I was about to play on their home turf, at their game. The thought struck me: *An alligator isn't as smart as a raccoon, but many a raccoon has been eaten while drinking at the alligator hole.*

Chapter 37

Dee

Columbia, South Carolina

Dee shuffled through criminal files with the enthusiasm of a hog rooting for truffles. His secretary buzzed him on the intercom. "Got a Zack Miller from DEA on line one. Says he was instructed to talk to only you."

Dee answered with hope. "Agent Miller, tell me you know something that leads to Snake."

"You can call me Zack. We've got three guys in custody in Norfolk, but I can only hold one for criminal activity. The other two we'll have let go by tomorrow. They're somehow associated with this cocaine smuggling with cruise ships. It looks to us like a Snake operation with a Two Finger purchase, but they won't talk."

"Will you let us at them?"

"Yeah, we've exhausted our interrogators. I gave DC a courtesy call on it, and they directed me to you. If you send somebody up today, you can try on all three. One guy, we have dead to rights, but he's terrified to talk no matter what deal we offer."

Dee had hit the ground running at his new job. The IG investigation on entering without a warrant while bringing down drug dealers in Atlanta was closed. He had been fully absolved, and his position as second-in-command in the Columbia field office was made permanent.

As instructed by the DC hierarchy, he had been hot on the trail of Snake and Two Finger Willie. Trying to turn over a stone that would create a lead, he had initiated several smaller drug busts with nothing that lead to the big boys, but he was as persistent as a hyena smelling dead meat.

"I'll have two agents on a flight tonight. Try to come up with something to hold all of them."

Some of these DEA agents had a knack for sniffing out a drug operation. There was a good chance Zack could be right in his assessment of who was doing the Norfolk smuggling. In any case, it was as good as what he had. Dee had just completed a small-time drug bust in Florence, South Carolina, which turned out only to yield three small-time pushers.

Thursday morning Dee got a call on his cell from one of his men he had sent to Norfolk. "Dee, I got a thread but not much else. You wouldn't believe how scared these guys are, and they're not scared of us. One of them said he would do life without parole before he would rat on Snake. So, we do know it's his operation, but ain't nobody here going to roll over on Snake. What does this guy do to get such loyalty?"

The mention of Snake excited him. He thought about what he had heard about The Acid Man and his sicko sidekick.

"You probably don't want to know—it's that bad. You got anything else?"

"One more thing. One of them slipped up and

mentioned Aruba. We checked, and that's where the ship originated."

Dee clicked his ballpoint in and out and doodled on his day planner. "Good job. I knew you could squeeze out something the DEA had overlooked. Okay, both of you leave ASAP for Aruba. See what you can pick up down there."

Three days later he was sipping an Amstel Light at his boss's house, Ray Bowley. They were waiting for the finishing touches of what Ray claimed was the best barbeque in South Carolina. Chasing crime with a white collar sure beat the hell out of living undercover in the squalor of the underworld. He did miss the adrenalin rush of the takedown though, but he satisfied himself with the knowledge that eventually he would be able to eliminate more of what he despised.

It was 7:30 p.m. when Ray looked up with amusement to hear Dee's phone go off to the tune of "Nobody Knows the Trouble I've Seen."

"I got to get this," Dee said. "It's from our boys in Aruba."

Dee excused himself and answered. "Yeah, you come up with anything?"

"You bet. I think we hit pay dirt. We are holding a guy in the Aruba jail that wants to deal."

Dee looked over at Ray and gave him a thumbs up.

"Deal? What kind of deal?"

Ray lifted the grill lid. Smoke poured out and the smell was divine.

"Claims he knows all about the setup and how it's supposed to isolate Snake, but before he sings, he wants a guarantee of full immunity, a new identity, and enter into the witness protection program in the United

States."

"Sounds great, but I'm suspicious of why he's so willing when others absolutely refused."

Ray removed the beef brisket to a large board. The aroma was distracting.

"Well, it's like this, the Aruba authorities are fully on board to crack this guy. He's in an Aruba jail, and let's just say, they do things different down here than we do in the States. He's desperate to get out of here. I need authority to give him what he's asking for."

Dee walked into Bowley's backyard and considered the question.

"When will you be able to see him again?"

He was getting excited over the prospects of finally catching Snake after so many dead ends.

"We are scheduled to have another session tomorrow at 2:00 p.m."

"Ok, let me confer and I'll call you back."

Ray was reluctant. "We can't grant such a full blanket immunity to a third-rate Aruba criminal."

"This could be the nugget we have been looking for."

"But it could also be a hoax that sets us up for other criminals to demand total immunity. Come on. We'll talk about it over dinner. You ever cook brisket?"

"Growing up, we didn't eat much beef. Meat was mostly chicken and pork. My daddy butchered a hog every year. I tell you what, you never tasted anything so good as scrambled eggs and fresh hog brains for breakfast."

Ray was beginning to look a little uncomfortable until Dee looked at him with a twinkle in his eye and a mischievous smile. "But mostly, boss man, I likes brisket."

"You SOB, no wonder you're on a fast track with the FBI."

"I tell you what," Dee said. "The people in DC were adamant about nailing Snake and Two Finger. Let's lay it on them and let them stick their necks out."

Ray had started moving toward the back porch with the brisket, but he stopped and looked at Dee. He hesitated for a few seconds before answering. "You're a political genius. Let's do it."

By ten o'clock, DC issued approval, and Dee passed it on to his agents in Aruba. He was still making plans for the interrogation of the Aruba turncoat at three o'clock the next afternoon. By 4:00 p.m. he was getting anxious but didn't want to interrupt the negotiation.

At five o'clock he got the call. "How's it going?" Dee said.

"Shit, sir, bad news. We got the run around at the jail for a while, but in the end, they told us. He was found in the exercise yard this morning with his throat slit ear to ear.

Chapter 38

Scrap

Jacksonville, Florida

Late recognizing the backup of slow traffic, I jammed on my brakes so hard the truck's anti-skid cycled. *Jesus, Scrap, pay attention.* I passed a truck with a blown tire on the shoulder, and the traffic cleared. Thirty miles outside of Jacksonville, I tried to change lanes into a passing car. An alert driver swerved and shot me the bird. I arrived at the Jacksonville hotel early, but rather than pass the time there, I parked under a tree in a nearby shopping mall lot.

At 1:40 p.m. I pulled into a space at the front of the Courtyard, which was on the north edge of town. Five minutes later, a slick black sedan with tinted glass windows pulled up and two men got out. They approached each side of my truck. I rolled down my window and went eyeball to eyeball with the lowlife on my side.

"Mr. Scruggs, we have been expecting you. Would you please step out?"

I got out, and the other man came around and frisked me. I figured it was a waste of time to carry my gun, so it was locked up in the glove box. Everything in my pockets was thrown into my truck console, including my phone. I held the truck keys in my hand.

"If you're worried about somebody stealing your stuff, you can lock your truck. From here you'll be going in our car."

Determined to put up a brave front, I showed no visible fear, nodding like we were all on our way to a business meeting. I put the keys in my pocket and climbed into the front passenger seat of the black sedan.

No one spoke until the driver veered onto I-95 going south. The man in the back handed me a sack. I turned to see him holding a cocked .45 automatic. "Put it over your head," he said.

For about twenty minutes, we rode in silence. We stopped and there was a sound like a garage door moving. The car moved for a few seconds. The door noise again. My heartbeat increased. With a man on each arm, I was escorted through what seemed like a door into an air-conditioned space. I could hear muffled screams. *Was this what I was here for?*

We moved toward the sounds of agony. My pulse quickened. The screaming rose to the level of a braking locomotive, and a door slammed behind me. The sack was removed. Catatonic, mouth open, eyes bulging—I was held there for five minutes, witnessing unspeakable acts accompanied by blood-curdling screams. The victim was hung on the wall like a side of beef. Red hot irons were applied. I noticed the man administering the pain was none other than Gut, the same brute who had visited my office with pictures of my family. These bastards know where I live. They had pictures of Beth and Emma.

The two men grabbed me under my arms and half-dragged me out of the torture room. The screaming subsided. I assumed the victim had died. They roughly shoved me into a plush office, where a man with no expression stared at me with unblinking blue eyes from behind a large desk.

The blue eyes appeared to turn gray as they bored into my face—eyes as cold and unforgiving as a diamondback stalking a baby rabbit.

The door closed, and he motioned to a chair. "Mr. Scruggs, please sit down."

I maintained composure, but despite the air-conditioning, sweat trickled down my face.

A long thirty seconds passed. He broke the sinister gaze and picked up an aluminum suitcase at the side of his desk. I recognized the suitcase. It came from under my house. *Don't lose it. Hang in there.*

"Two of these were found in your basement," he said. "They belong to me. I would like the others."

Between the time of leaving the torture chamber and the suitcase display, I was trying to control my terror, revulsion, sweating, nausea, and yes, deep down, unquenchable anger. Now I focused on this inhumane monster: the piercing stare, cold smile, and confident, unnerving demeanor—intimidation radiated. Combined with the horrors I had witnessed, my fear escalated, and it took my full concentration not to show it.

He was trim and muscular but did not have the bulk or size to be threatening in a physical sense. A rattlesnake does not have the bulk or size to be intimidating, but a horse is afraid to approach or pass one coiled and ready to strike. This man was a snake, and his rattlers were shaking.

Although horrified, I tried not to show any expression. Somehow, I managed to speak with a steady voice. "A year and a half ago, I found eight suitcases in the marsh—"

He put up his hand like he could stop the rotation of the earth with a casual gesture. "Mr. Scruggs, tell me again exactly where you found my money."

"It was scattered out in a large marsh area north of Dewees Island."

Here I had to be careful. It was my intention not to identify the crash site, which was eight miles farther northeast.

He nodded and I continued. "Each suitcase had five hundred thousand for a total of four million. You broke into my house and took the one million left of this four million. The other three have been integrated into my business. The money's been invested in real estate and other business assets. I'll give you your money, but it will be impossible to produce it immediately."

"Mr. Scruggs, the pain you just witnessed is usually enough to make a man recover his memory and think things are more possible. I'm sure Mr. Leroy, who is now dead, would have been forthcoming with any information he could provide before he expired."

For a fleeting moment I wondered what Mr. Leroy had done to merit his horrible extermination. Did he steal from this man? Did he double-cross? Or maybe he was a nobody used for the shock value to soften me.

But I had been threatened with an equal experience, and it was time to present my defense— first the stick and then the carrot. I looked him in his evil eyes.

"I did not come to your crime den without thinking this through. A letter has been left for the FBI. You probably already know I have a close contact there. If I don't show up by nine o'clock tonight, this letter will be delivered, and I can assure you, the FBI will pull all the stops until you're dead or in jail. To cancel the delivery of this letter, I must appear in person. No other form of contact will suffice."

"And you're telling me that your FBI friend does not yet know about your predicament."

"That is correct. It would incriminate me to tell him. So, you can look at this situation like you might look at the Cold War nuclear weapons. To tell the FBI would be mutually assured destruction. The letter is in the form of both a hard copy and a coded email attachment. The FBI will be sent the unlocking code along with the email. If I show up on time, the letter will be destroyed, and the e-mail will be deleted. I will not only arrange to return your money over time, but it will be laundered, clean money, paid with a check."

His snake eyes seemed to be interested, and I detected a slight nod.

"How will you accomplish this laundering?"

"I have always been an honest man, but my business was failing. Your money turned my business around and now it's prospering. That three million gave me a lot of experience getting illicit money into a legitimate business."

Once again, his unblinking glare locked onto my eyes. "Mr. Scruggs, I'm missing much more money than the sum you mentioned. Your discussion about three million sounds interesting, but we need to talk about *all* of my money. Perhaps a visit to my discipline room will establish where the rest might be."

Fear and anger came frothing forth, overruling my caution. He'd torture Beth and Emma—he needed to die.

"Listen, you snake-eyed son of a bitch. If you put me in that room, you will never see even the empty suitcases. You'll have the Feds all over you like gold chains on your fucking thugs. I don't know about any other money. It's probably still out in the marsh somewhere. What I can tell you is I can launder the three mil I have, and for a fee, I'll launder more, including what you're talking about, *if* you find it. But it will take some time. If you must have some of the money quicker, I'll be able to squeeze out enough to raise a million in cash in about two months, but it won't be clean money."

He didn't respond right away. His face turned red, but it subsided, and he appeared to go into deep thought, his eyes going from gray black to pale blue. "Mr. Scruggs, my friends—and most of my enemies—call me Snake, not snake-eyed sonofabitch. Some of them, for good reason, also call me The Acid Man."

He paused to glare at me before continuing.

"I'm prepared to entertain your offer, but keep in mind it's not only yourself that you're trying to keep out of my discipline area. Remember, this meeting is about protecting Beth and Emma."

His mention of their names made my skin crawl. My anger rose, but I knew I had pushed him far enough. Though it would have been disastrous, I wanted to leap across the desk and go for his throat.

"If it's important for you to destroy me, hurting my family will do it, but I'll guarantee that you'll also be destroying yourself."

He gently nodded as he spoke. "I'll give you two months to get me a million in cash. Back at, what you perceive to be, your secure little nest, I would like for you to prepare a complete outline of how you can launder my money, how much you can handle, and a timeline for repaying me in clean money. Someone will come for this information in two weeks. And Mr. Scruggs, any conversation with the FBI and I will come for your wife and child."

Trying to digest this information, I was as nervous as a deer with coyotes nearby. The door opened and two thugs came in. They placed their hands under my arms and attempted to lift me out of the chair. Instantly I interpreted this as my trip to the torture room. I swung to my right and grabbed one of them in the groin. At the same time, I came out of the chair, lifting him up and backward. He screamed as his head hit the floor. The other thug hit me with something on the back of my head and the lights went out.

****

I woke up tied to a chair. Handcuffs squeezed my wrists, and two thugs stood over me. I was back in the torture room. The dead victim hung motionless from arm shackles on the wall. It was my turn. Not the first time my temper cost me. I tried not to focus on the dead victim. My mind raced to find a way to avoid what was coming.

Snake entered the room. "Mr. Scruggs, our meeting is complete. My two friends here will take you back to your car."

I was glad not to be taking the place of the man on the wall, but now I wondered if I was slated for concrete shoes.

They put the hood over my head, untied me from the chair, and guided me out of the building into a car.

We made the twenty-five-minute trip back to my car in silence, which struck me as odd. Maybe they were showing respect for the future dead. Arriving at my truck, I was assisted out of the car and pushed into the seat. The man called Pigneck removed the sack, released the handcuffs, and paused at my open door. "Man, you one lucky dude. If Snake hadn't stopped it, we'd be cutting you up for fish food."

Pigneck slammed the door, and I stared through the windshield, watching them leave.

I was drained and still had four hours of driving ahead. A hotel would have been nice, but my threat to Snake was not a bluff. Sheryl had to see me in person by nine o'clock.

39
Snake

Jacksonville, Florida

Snake opened a small box on his bookshelf. Inside was a police shield. He removed it and turned it over, remembering what it represented. It was the only time he found it necessary to eliminate an officer of the law. It came close to bringing him down. He wasn't confident about his recent actions concerning Mr. Daniel Scruggs. It was perilous to deal with a man who was friends with someone high up in the FBI. That's why he had let Scrap go. That and the possible money-laundering opportunity.

He put the shield back in the box and another thought gnawed at him. Throughout his crime-ridden career, he had been associated with cruel, violent men, but all of them had a weak point, something which made them afraid. He knew being violent was not the same as having courage. He feared Scrap was a man who would not buckle, a man of courage, a man who could be deadly.

Though Snake found his cruel ways an effective method of intimidation for most men, he recalled times it hadn't worked. When he was a teen, there had been a boy he could not frighten. With two accomplices, Snake demanded the boy's wallet. He refused, and Snake pulled a knife. The other two grabbed the boy's arms. Snake looked at him without blinking and described how he was going to carve him up.

"Fuck you," the boy said, and Snake closed in.

With a sweeping motion from the boy's foot, the knife was dislodged, and Snake's two accomplices ran. The boy was not only gutsy but also skilled. Although Snake was not afraid to fight, he was no match for his intended victim. After taking several sharp blows to the face, he was brought to his knees with a right cross. Without mercy he received a foot to the face that put him in the emergency room.

The memory made him feel weak. For this reason, Scrap both intrigued and worried Snake. Second to making money, he not only enjoyed breaking strong, courageous men, but he felt a need to do it—and do it well.

He stepped out of his office and motioned to Gut, who was on the phone gathering any information he could in Charleston County.

Gut came into Snake's office and closed the door. "You want to chew on this stuff some more?"

Even though Snake knew Gut was hopelessly sick in the head, he valued his advice. With such an unappealing personality, it was hard to believe he was smart, but he was—and with a criminal mind.

Snake went back to his chair and took his position of authority. He tapped his fingers on his desk.

"The loss of twenty million has knocked our dick in the dirt. Now this operation on the cruise ship has gone bad. What happened there?"

Since his unique route through Haiti and on to Beaufort fell apart, he had investigated other ways to smuggle. He had developed a working relationship with employees on several cruise lines making stops in the Caribbean, which originated and returned in Charleston, Norfolk, and Baltimore.

"Actually, a virus caused it," Gut said.

Snake was surprised. "You got to be shitting me."

A slight twitch of the lower lip was Gut's only expression of humor.

"Shitting is the correct terminology. Our inside man who was supposed to receive the tagged suitcases had the 24-hour stomach flu and was replaced at the last minute. The replacement got suspicious and contacted the DEA."

"You mean all those bribes we paid to grease things, all the way from Aruba, were defeated by somebody getting the shits."

Snake felt no humor, and Gut got more serious. "That's about it. If we had known in time, we could have gotten another one of our people, but the guy left after his work shift had started and the supervisor replaced him with somebody from the freight department. Speaking of Aruba, we had some boys eliminate one of the guys who was caught down there. I think that seals it away from the law now."

"And so, I lost another five million."

Gut shrugged his massive shoulders.

Snake started to berate him but had more pressing issues. He was running out of money. *I need the one million Scruggs has promised and anything else I can squeeze from him.* The million found in the garage underneath Scrap's house was an infusion Snake needed to preserve his reputation. But he had to have more, and he didn't care if it was laundered. It was going to pay bills that could be paid with dirty money.

"We need to tighten up," Snake said. "Send a message: not performing the job I pay you to do will not be tolerated."

Snake paused. "And I want Stomach Flu Man whacked."

"It's as good as done, Boss."

Scrap had agreed to pay another million in two months. If Scrap could not make payment, maybe he would have to undergo some encouragement, but something told Snake it would be a dangerous move. He had been both surprised and impressed with the way Scrap handled himself during their meeting and agreed with Gut's analysis: Scrap was not going to be easy to crack.

"Tell me the latest on the search around Charleston."

"I have people searching the marsh where the late Mr. Fish had found his money—"

"My money."

"Found your money. But this area was so large the searchers were not encouraged. It has an infinite number of saltwater creeks with fingers to nowhere."

Snake nodded. "What do you make of Scruggs?"

Gut scratched his massive head with his King Kong fingers. "He's a tough one. I watched him closely. Fear doesn't make him irrational. I have to tell you that grabbing Pigneck's balls and dumping him over amazed me, especially after he watched the demonstration. I will be glad to administer some encouragement pain, but my best advice is to hold off until we know more."

Snake pursed his lips in thought. "I think you're

right, especially because he was walking into an unknown situation naked, but I believe it has more to do with his desire to protect his family. Something we need to keep in mind."

"Yeah. It took balls to show up here. I frankly didn't think he would come."

Snake turned his head toward the office bookcase and focused on a picture of him breaking ground on a new library when he served as a county commissioner. Back then he made money through his political graft, but it wasn't enough. Drugs were more lucrative. He liked to look at the picture, which reminded him of the gullibility of people. But he didn't think Scrap was gullible.

"I agree with what you say, Gut, but right now I'm more concerned with this FBI connection."

"We need to know more about what's going on up there in Charleston," Gut said.

"Okay, let's find out. Get a couple of good men, not punks, men with experience. Place a locator on Mr. Scruggs's truck and the wife's car. I want to know where they go every time one of them moves, and also, if Mr. Scruggs has more of my money hidden, find out where. If he's visiting his friend in the FBI, I want to know."

"Got it, Boss."

"And Gut, I want you to be prepared to snatch the wife or kid if I say the word."

Chapter 40

Scrap

Road Trip Home to South Carolina

I was relieved to have escaped, but on my way home, diabolical thoughts raced through my head. I couldn't get over the vivid torture picture—or shake what this Snake person could have meant by the name The Acid Man. The interstate north was a blur. Numb and exhausted from a constant pumping of adrenalin, I tried to think of what I would tell Beth, but my mind was too frazzled.

As tired as I was, I still had to go to Sheryl's house. She would be getting nervous as nine o'clock approached.

Bright taillights appeared from the cars up front on I-95. I jammed my foot on the brake and slowed to a stop. The northbound traffic on I-95 had come to a halt. At first, I was thankful I had not plowed into the line of cars but sitting still for twenty minutes caused me to worry about what time I was going to get to Sheryl's.

A police car came roaring along the shoulder—then another—followed by an ambulance. I turned on the radio in time to hear about a bad accident on I-95 north. I checked my GPS but couldn't find an alternate route for over two miles. Time was ticking.

I beat the steering wheel in frustration. Thirty minutes later, the traffic still had barely moved. I called Sheryl. "Sheryl, listen. I'm stuck in traffic. I might not make nine o'clock."

"Don't do this to me. I have to follow your instructions. This is hard, and I'm sorry if this call is real, but that is what you said."

"I'm stuck in traffic...I can't—"

"I know you created this plan for a reason. Whoever is holding you, tell them it won't work."

"Sheryl...I...ah, fuck it."

I disconnected, and like a caged animal jerking his wild-eyed head around, I searched for a way out. Jamming the accelerator, I pulled out to the right and onto the shoulder, causing other drivers to honk. I raced along the side of the road for a mile, but another police car closed on me rapidly from the rear, lights flashing, siren blaring. The vehicles on the road to my left were bumper to bumper. I could not squeeze in. The police car apparently was going to the accident up ahead. In desperation to allow him to pass, I pulled over on the grass that sloped toward a shallow drainage area. Instead of passing, the police car pulled in behind me and got out, shouting as he approached.

"What's the matter with you? There's an accident, and you're impeding emergency vehicles. If I had time, I would take you to jail. Stay where you are until I can return and deal with you."

He got back in his car, backed up, and drove around me to the left.

As he sped away on the shoulder, I looked across the low drainage area to a grassy field with a country road on the far side. Slamming my truck into four-wheel drive, I took off down the bank toward the drainage. At the low point, all four tires were kicking up mud and spinning, but I made it across. I sped through the grassy stretch and joined the country road on the far side. No one followed. Arriving alone on the road, I triggered my GPS and got a new route back to the freeway on the other side of the accident.

Back on I-95, I accelerated to ninety and headed for Mt. Pleasant, arriving at Sheryl's house at 9:02 p.m.

The courier arrived right behind me. I dismissed him and banged on Sheryl's door.

"Is that you, Scrap?"

"Yes, stop what you're doing. Let me in."

She took one look at me and breathed a sigh of relief. "Thank God you're here. You really know how to scare a girl. I was getting ready to send the email."

I followed her in. She was wearing a house robe revealing a lot of skin as she moved.

My left hand kept shaking, and I noticed I was wet with sweat. "I didn't think I would make it. I've been driving ninety miles an hour."

"I don't know what's going on, but whatever it is, you have to stop. My stress meter is pegged, and you look like something my cat brought home."

"I'm sorry to involve you in my problems, but don't give me a hard time. Just cancel everything and forget it. Someday I'll tell you what's going on."

She went to the kitchen but soon returned, handing me a small glass half-full of straight bourbon. "You need a drink, and so do I."

"You're right, thanks."

She left to get herself a glass of wine. I nervously walked around, consuming half my drink before I calmed down enough to drop myself onto her couch.

She returned, sat on the couch, and crossed her legs, which revealed so much thigh I had to look away. With a hint of a smile, she leaned toward me.

"Last week there were several suspicious-looking characters outside our building, and I believe one of them was the brute who visited your office. Maybe you should talk to Dee anyhow."

"I can't, not unless this spins out of control."

Sipping my bourbon, I had an uneasy feeling about Sheryl's body language. The bourbon was magic, flowing through my tense, tired body like an elixir from the gods. She gently touched my arm. "Scrap, you need to unwind."

I had to face Beth, who was probably pacing the floor in agitation. It was time to leave.

I got up and walked unsteadily toward the front door. Sheryl went to an end table and retrieved the courier paperwork. "Take this with you." She handed it to me. Her breast was fully visible through the gap in her robe, and she wore a little smile. "You better be careful," she said. "This mystery stuff causes a girl's heart to skip."

I exhaled and hastened out the door. Now my worries turned to Beth, knowing she would be upset, and I still had not figured out my story.

Chapter 41

Scrap

Mt. Pleasant, South Carolina

I arrived home at 10:05 p.m. Beth came out of the bedroom and confronted me with a distressed expression on her face. One look and I knew she had been crying. My first thought was the thugs had contacted her. If they touched her or Emma, I would—

"Are you having an affair?" She turned and gazed at me with wide eyes, red with worry but full of hope.

I had driven eight hours, some of it at ninety miles per hour, spent another hour with a sack over my head, witnessed the most horrendous display of inhumanity possible, met with the scariest man I had ever seen, and barely escaped being tortured to death. Now my wife was accusing me of infidelity. I couldn't speak.

Finally, I recovered my voice and closed the distance between us. "No, Beth, I'm not having an affair. I've been through hell. Could we do this tomorrow?"

She slapped me hard across the face. "You son of a bitch, you've been drinking. You were with that whore secretary and don't tell me you weren't."

She glared at me, her face radiating anger and determination.

I was dumbfounded. How the hell did she know I had stopped at Sheryl's? It was that intuition again. "No, no, it's not what you think."

"Don't tell me what to think. I've been patronized and played for a fool long enough."

My frustration was building, which always turned into anger. "Goddamn it, you don't know what you're talking about—"

"I do know. Your truck—" Her face was red; her eyes were wide and on fire. "—it was at her house less than half an hour ago, and I also know there wasn't a home builders' meeting in Jacksonville. You didn't even go to Jacksonville. You were with that bitch."

The room was like a minefield where a misstep would cause it to explode. I went to the porch to get control.

Beth was pacing angrily inside the house. I had to tell her the truth. I went back in. She was in the kitchen. "Yes, I was at Sheryl's, but it's not what you think. I have been lying to you, both by deception and out-and-out lies, but it's not about sex. It's really because I love you so much."

"Ah, come on. You got the audacity to feed me this bullshit that you're destroying our marriage because you love me so much?"

With the amount of adrenaline that pumped through my body today, you would think it was used up, but no, it was charging through again as if I was standing on the scaffold and the hangman was reaching for the trap door release.

"Beth…Beth…stop. Let me talk."

Her frustration had peaked over these long-festering secrets. I sensed I needed to make this count. I paused, afraid about how she would judge the illegal money. I felt defeated in my attempt to protect her from any implication. Now she would be complicit if she knew and cooperated with my plan.

She was quiet, tears streaming down her cheeks, waiting for me to gather my thoughts.

"A year and a half ago, I was concerned about the business. I didn't tell you how bad things really were. I was about to be forced into bankruptcy. We were going to be ruined financially."

"What? Bankruptcy? I knew you were having a tough time, but bankruptcy? Why did you keep this from me? I told you not to keep information from me that would damage my position at the education department."

This wasn't going to be easy. "It was my responsibility to provide. I asked you to quit teaching and stay home, and I felt like I had betrayed you. It was too much humiliation for me to admit I was failing, so I kept struggling alone."

"But we are supposed to be a team…from this day forward, for better, for worse… Remember?"

Some of the tension seemed to leave her face. She looked me in the eyes and turned to gaze out through the darkness of the kitchen window.

I waited until she turned back. "The thing that caused me the most stress was deceiving you."

She frowned. "I'm not so sure that you're not still doing it."

I needed to save this personal stuff for later. "Hear me out before you make a judgment."

"I will, but I'm entitled to ask questions. I'm sorry you were suffering, and that you chose to suffer alone.

You're too proud and bullheaded. Maybe it's partly my fault because I always loved that about you."

She went to the fridge and poured herself a glass of wine. This was progress. "But now it's not pride," I said. "It's survival."

"So, what happened? Where did all the money come from?"

I hated lying again, but in case she was ever interrogated, she needed only to have the story that Snake had.

I sat down at the table, picked up the pepper shaker, and turned it around in my hand as if it were a fascinating thing. "I found it in the marsh when I was hunting."

"You must be joking." She sat back and gave a little mock laugh.

Finally, I got the courage to look at her. "Think back to when you got upset about me marsh hen hunting on Sunday and bringing home no birds. Do you remember?"

"How much money did you find?"

I did an involuntary swallow. "It was four million."

"Come on, there was four million scattered around the marsh, and you just gathered it up and brought it home?"

She laughed at her own description, but I didn't crack a smile.

"You're serious!" she said. "I don't understand. How could four million be sitting in the marsh?"

"It was in waterproof aluminum suitcases."

She opened her hands, and with a little fake smile, shook her head. "So, we have been spending money you found in the marsh? Did you also use this money in your business?"

Now I realized this was going to take some time. I had been at this deception for almost two years, and she was going to pull out all the details.

"I have used three million of it," I said.

"Wow. Okay, we will get back to that, but first I want to know why you were at Sheryl's. Does this have something to do with her?"

"No—except…this had to do with a letter she was to give to Dee if I didn't return by 9:00 p.m. I had to show my face so she would not send the letter."

She turned and glared at me with fire in her eyes. "Then why do you have alcohol on your breath?"

"I don't know…I mean…I don't know why I had the drink there. After racing back on I-95 for five hours, desperate to make a deadline, Sheryl thought I needed a drink, and with all I had been through, I did need one. I was only there a short time."

She finished off her wine, went to the fridge, and poured another. This time, surprisingly, she offered me a glass, which I gladly accepted.

I knew the explanation sounded weak, but shit, that's what happened. "I guess I could've come home for the drink," I said. "But that's hindsight."

She looked away and finally let it go. Thank goodness. But after I told her about the drug dealers, she became adamant I was on the wrong track. "The money we have been spending is dirty, the worst kind of filth that has destroyed people's lives. You have to give it to the police."

I was getting exasperated, but from past experience, I knew I needed to keep my cool.

"I didn't sell dope. Taking their money could be a

positive."

"Now you're rationalizing."

I went to the fridge for some cheese. "You don't understand. When I found the money, I was at my wit's end. I had struggled, pushed, and figured until there was no avenue left. Bankruptcy was next. If that happened, our life would change, and we would not be able to pay for Emma's school. You would be embarrassed and maybe fired at your new job. Maybe I was weak and succumbed, but if I hadn't, think of where we would be right now."

"Think of where we *are* right now."

That annoyed me, and it showed in the volume of my voice. "Goddamn it, Beth, whatever mistake I made before, it's done. I can't turn back. Don't you see? Whatever I do that does not cooperate with these scum bags puts us all at risk."

"Ask your friend Dee for help," she said in a blunt manner that made me feel like I needed to defend myself.

"I can't," I snapped. "If the drug dealers know he's involved, we all are dead. Besides, I have already incriminated myself. I could go to jail."

We'd finally come to an impasse, but mentioning Emma was in danger caused her to agree to think more about what I had said. She didn't seem to understand the train had left the station and was plunging down the mountain with no brakes.

I needed to think through how we were going to survive, how to develop a workable money-laundering plan, and at the same time run a thriving business once again. It was a relief to have Beth knowing at least most of the truth. I desperately needed someone to talk with, test my judgment, and to keep me from swerving off the road. This whole process was like a poker game where your life was in the pot. One wrong bet and you're dead.

I went to the bedroom, took off my shoes, stretched out on the bed, and stared at the ceiling. Thirty minutes later I joined Beth in the kitchen. She had a strange look on her face and came over and kissed me on the forehead. "Let's go to bed now."

She took my hand and led me to the bedroom. She was turned on. I didn't quite understand, but what the hell? I usually don't. It was great—exactly what I needed.

The next morning Beth was making sandwiches when I came from behind her, slipped my arms around her waist, and said, "I should confess to something more often."

"You should tell me the truth to start with. No telling how good it might be."

"I wouldn't be able to stand it. I'll need to keep lying."

Her face turned serious. "Scrap, even though you had a good reason to be at Sheryl's house, she's still a problem."

"Why?"

"I do trust you, but I understand women like her. She wants to get in your pants. She should be fired."

I frowned and partially raised both my hands, palms out. "I couldn't do that. I need her. She's great at her job, Beth. That's why I keep her around."

She leaned over and kissed me. "I need you, and she is a threat."

"Well, I'm sorry, but I can't fire her, especially not

now. She knows too much. Can we just disagree about her and this tainted money for the moment? I know you're sincere and morally you're right about the money, but it's my responsibility to solve this without getting us killed or making us suffer. I might have been wrong to take the money, but that's already done. We are in a much worse place now."

"You can't do this alone. You have to get Dee to help."

I walked around the kitchen island and sat on a barstool without answering. I have to admit, I had thought a great deal about calling Dee, but each time there seemed to be pitfalls.

"Try to understand," I said. "Getting Dee involved and keeping it a secret from the FBI could sink his career—and risks this mad man getting wind of it, which would put you and Emma at risk."

"I understand, but I'm not sure there isn't a way to do this without risking your life trying to deal with these people."

What she said, in a way, made sense, but I was on a different path now. Taking a deep breath, I tried again. "I'm asking you to stay with me on this, even though you don't agree."

"I will. I was wrong to doubt your fidelity, and I'm sorry I slapped you."

I tried not to show her my sigh of relief. I was making progress. "Well, if a little slap is what it takes to turn you on like last night, I'll take it anytime."

She did a mischievous smile. "You trying to get us into S and M?"

"No, your naked body is all the stimulation I can take."

She put her hand on my arm. "Scrap, talk to me. I will help."

My counseling session ended, and it was time to get back to solving problems. First, I needed to find a new and convenient way to hide money at my house. The possibility the thugs were watching me was real, which made it risky to visit my secret Live Oak ATM.

Wandering around the closed-in space under my house, I walked over to my boat in one of the garage bays. I looked inside the storage locker and moved to the external gas tank. It was about the right size.

I made a trip to Walmart and bought a new twelve-gallon gas tank. I sawed out a section of the bottom, and the cutout was reattached as a hinged door. This fake gas tank was exchanged for the old one in my boat.

Time to shake the money tree, but now I had to be cautious about a tracking device on my truck. There was a Hertz car rental just off Hamlin Road at Highway 17. I requested Uber from my home to Hertz and did a one-day rental. After taking the rental to my Live Oak Storage unit, I retrieved $500,000 and drove home. I placed the money in my new gas tank safe, the rental car was returned, and Uber took me home.

I already had a concealed carry permit and usually carried a small Kel-tec .380 automatic. Now feeling threatened, my carry weapon was upgraded to a small 9mm Glock 26.

Monday morning, I planned to work on Snake's money-laundering plan. I unlocked my secret file drawer and studied the accounts that took cash. I jotted down the numbers and studied my financials for the past six months.

My heart sank. I quickly learned my operation, as it

presently worked, was not sufficient to do what I had promised. To keep him interested, I need a plan capable of handling many more millions than was required to save my business—a scheme that would work. Snake was too smart to fall for a flawed plan.

I walked through the front office and snapped at Sheryl when she tried to ask me a question. I picked up a handful of small rocks from the drive and absentmindedly threw them into the small pond. My life depended on Snake being convinced of my value. Another source was needed to inject cash and extract taxable profits.

An idea took root. In the past, I had used a contractor's resource company conducting business for several subcontractor skills. It was effective in quickly supplying qualified subcontractors but not effective cost wise. It only added another layer of profit for the resource company. The bottom line was the concept could not be competitive unless the market became so overheated that subcontractors and suppliers were hard to find. *Yes, it'll work.* I revisited the idea, albeit in a different way.

I ran back into my office, passing a surprised Sheryl in a rush. I slammed my office door behind me, grabbed a pen, and calculated. This time, I would run the resource company. I would select subcontractors willing to accept cash for some part of their payment. It would be competitive because I would inject Snake's money to pay much of the expenses, which would allow us to extract large taxable profits. Scruggs Construction would be the resource company's best customer.

I wrote out the plan's details, which included instructions about the necessity for the ownership to belong to the entity receiving the clean, taxable profits. In other words, Snake would have to accept ownership of the new company.

Two hours later, I opened my office door and smiled at Sheryl. "I'm sorry for being rude a while ago. My mind kinda ran away."

She looked up from her work and smiled back. "You know, you're weird."

I went back inside my office and walked around like a nervous cat in a trap. It was essential to complete the plan by the time Gut showed up at my office. Of course, I didn't know if Snake would even find the plan acceptable. Not knowing exactly when Gut would show added to my anxiety.

I heard what sounded like a car—I jumped. It was nothing.

The bad part was that if I wanted to stay alive, I had to keep working the plan. I was on a treadmill with no way off.

I left for another walk but was so preoccupied I did not notice the weather. Before I could return, the sky opened up into a spring thunderstorm. The rain hit my face in sheets. The wind howled a warning of my future, lightning flashed, and thunder boomed as if the gods were furious at my moral decay.

Chapter 42

Scrap

Mt. Pleasant, South Carolina

I woke up in a sweat at 1:00 a.m. over a dream about Snake's torture room, but the victim was one of my project managers. It morphed into my neighbor's golden retriever, and I woke up. But the screaming of the real torture victim kept echoing in my head. Still awake at 2:00 a.m., I was exhausted, but the nightmare of distorted figures had destroyed all hope of sleep. Stress was taking its toll on my body. I needed exercise and hadn't run or lifted weights for several days.

A faint noise came from underneath my house where my cars and boat were parked. In the past, a rat or flying squirrel slipped through the lattice. In normal situations, I would not be concerned, but now the scratching and shuffling seemed ominous. Warm goosebumps rose on my neck, and I barely drew my breath. I picked up a flashlight from the nightstand and slipped over to the closet, trying not to wake Beth. I felt around the closet shelf for my .40 Glock equipped with night sights.

I slipped on a pair of flip-flops and moved to the center of the house. Now there clearly was a noise. To keep from alerting whatever caused the sound, I decided to use the outdoor stairs in the back that descended to a strip of land between my house and the marsh. I stepped onto the porch and smelled the familiar fragrance of pluff mud. Somewhere in the distance, a screech owl pierced the night with its reverberating pitch. Creeping down the stairs, I made no noise. The only sound was the chirping rhythm of katydids and tree crickets. I slipped around the outside of the house. There was a dark outline of an open door leading to a garage area underneath. Low voices came from inside.

Positioning my Glock in one hand and flashlight in the other, I stepped through the door. There was some sort of light down on the ground under my truck. I turned on my flashlight. A large man whirled around and drew a gun.

I centered on his chest and did a double tap. He dropped like a sack of cottonseed meal. A second man scrambled to withdraw from under my truck. Two additional shots connected. He squealed like a castrated pig, and I spoke for the first time.

"Shut up and stay where you are, or you're a dead man."

He made a low moan.

The lights came on under the house, and Beth appeared on the interior stairs holding her 9mm Lady Smith out front and in a two-hand stance. "Scrap, what is going on?"

"Call 9-1-1. Tell them there has been a shooting and we need an ambulance."

"Are you all right?"

"I'm fine, but there are two others here who are not doing well. Get the police and an ambulance."

I held the moaning invader at gunpoint next to my truck. While we waited, he begged for some kind of relief, but instead of relief, I put my gun to his temple. "Listen, sonofabitch. I have already killed your buddy. I might as well report I killed both of you. You have one chance to tell me who you're working for, or you'll never tell anything again."

"Okay, okay. All I know is he's called Gut and works for the Snake drug cartel."

I already knew, but it made my heart race anyway. A cloud of dread come over me.

The Mt. Pleasant police arrived first, followed by a county police cruiser, the ambulance, and finally the state highway patrol.

Two Mt. Pleasant police officers questioned me about what happened. They were cordial, and their body language and facial expressions indicated they were trying not to be intimidating.

"Did you know either of these men?"

"No, I don't know them, and I don't know what they were up to. What I do know is the dead man tried to shoot me."

My mind was going in all directions, trying to understand what this meant. *They worked for Snake.* Nothing was safe anymore.

The ranking police officer approached. "We will take it from here, but I would like you to come down and give a statement."

Four police cars and an ambulance arriving with sirens and lights flashing had aroused a couple of my neighbors. They were gathered in the cul-de-sac, and one of them came over. "Hi Scrap, is there anything I can do to help?"

No, Ted. I just shot a couple of guys under my house. I resisted being sarcastic. "No, Ted," I said. "Looks like two guys were trying to steal from under my house, but the police are handling it now. I'll fill you in on it tomorrow."

Beth paced back and forth on the front steps landing, her arms wrapped tightly around her thin robe.

I went over and put my hand on her shoulder. "I think it's all under control now. I need to go give them a statement."

I turned to walk away but turned back. "Thanks for the backup firepower, but I thought your rule was no violence."

"When my family is threatened, there are no rules."

I smiled, winked, and walked away. It's the mother grizzly bear thing.

At the police station I filled out some paperwork, answered a few more questions, and was told I was about done. One of the police officers got a call on his cell phone and something changed. "Sir, we need to ask you a few more questions."

"But I thought I was done for tonight. It's late, and my wife and daughter are home alone and frightened."

"I understand, and we have police still at your house. Just bear with us for a few more questions."

I was ushered into a little private room with a small desk and a chair on each side.

"Sir, please take a seat. Someone will be with you shortly."

The door closed, and I sat in the quiet. *They know about the money.*

A man I had not met entered without knocking and closed the door behind him. "Mr. Scruggs, do you know why somebody would want to track your vehicles?"

"No. What are you talking about?"

"These men were not there to rob you. They were trying to attach a GPS tracking device to both of your vehicles."

"I had no idea."

He paused, folded his arms over his chest, and turned away for a second. This was beginning to look like one of these interrogations you see on TV. He turned back and squinted his eyes. "Aren't you under investigation for a mysterious fire in your car?"

This pissed me off. "As far as I know, I'm not under any kind of investigation, and the fire was in my wife's car. What are you getting at anyway? If you think I'm guilty of something, say so."

He bristled. "Come on, Mr. Scruggs, cut through the bullshit. You killed one of these men, and you have no idea?"

"He was going to kill me in my own house."

"I'm not saying you shouldn't have shot him. I'm just saying there's more going on than you're telling us."

Another police officer walked in with a folder and handed it to the detective. "Take a look at this," he said.

The detective thumbed quickly through several pages and whistled.

"Mr. Scruggs, did you know who you were dealing with when you shot these two?"

This was going downhill. "No. Tell me."

"These are not your ordinary punks. They have long criminal records. Both of them are wanted by the FBI, and one has already been in the federal pen. Mr. Scruggs, you need to clear the air because the FBI is going to talk to you next."

"I don't have anything else to say. Either charge me with something, or I'm going home."

"Okay, go home and get some sleep, but don't go anywhere without telling us. We will be in touch."

I drove home feeling like a criminal not sure if he had covered his tracks. I parked underneath my house, closed the garage door, and went to my boat. The fake gas tank didn't appear disturbed. I opened the false bottom and breathed a sigh of relief—the money was still there. If the money were discovered, police suspicion would increase exponentially. My relief faded on realizing the police would interrogate the wounded man. I told the police I didn't know who they were. He would tell them he told me they worked for Snake.

I went upstairs. Beth had fallen asleep on the foot of the bed with her clothes on. I slipped into the kitchen, poured a shot of bourbon, and went to my porch overlooking the marsh. Daylight was coming on. I listened to the early summer sounds in the Lowcountry. Canada geese honked as they flew over from some roost out in the marsh to a daytime feeding area. Most of them had already headed to their nesting grounds in Canada. A marsh hen cackled. From an oak tree next to my house, a mockingbird tried its first magic trill of the morning.

I couldn't see them, but I imagined there must be a thousand bird eggs hatching at this moment, coyotes whelping pups, and deer feeding their newborn spotted fawn. New life springing forth. Yet three hours ago, I had destroyed a life in my own species.

Although no one had accused me of wrongdoing in the shooting, in my mind I had taken another step toward my felonious descent. I had killed a man, a killing that would not have happened if I was not involved in my other nefarious undertakings. Thou shalt not lie. Thou shalt not steal. Thou shalt not kill. My transgressions taint the essence of my being.

Chapter 43

Scrap

Mt. Pleasant, South Carolina

At 10:50 a.m., a week after the shooting, I worked on a secret spreadsheet. Next to my computer, I wrote on a legal pad full of notes, bullet points, and strikethroughs.

Sheryl's voice interrupted my concentration. "I have a gentleman here to see you. Says its official business."

It must be Gut. But then I doubted she would refer to him as a gentleman. I scrambled to close the computer and put away my notes. "Who is he?"

"Said his name was Trent Talbert...looks nice."

"Okay, send him in."

Sheryl actually opened my door and escorted him in. A well-groomed young man greeted me at the front of my desk. He had close-cut hair, was thin at the waist, and by the fit of his well-tailored, dark-blue suit coat, it was obvious he had a decent set of muscles underneath. He was polite but didn't smile. This man was not one of Snake's, but I still smelled trouble.

"Mr. Scruggs, I'm Special Agent Trent Talbert with the FBI."

My adrenalin shot up as if I had stepped on a

copperhead. I tried to act calm. I didn't acknowledge his introduction but shook his hand. His handshake was firm but not aggressively strong.

I found my voice. "Yes, Mr. Talbert, please sit down. What can I do for you?"

"I would like to ask you a few questions."

"Okay, sure."

In my effort not to appear guilty, I thought I sounded too cheery. And in my state of alarm, I thought my own handshake was too strong. *Need to be more businesslike.*

He pulled out a small notebook and opened it. "I think you have been told the men you shot in your garage were wanted by the FBI. I'm doing a follow-up on the circumstances of the shooting. Do you know why these two men would be in your garage attempting to install tracking devices on your vehicles?"

"Like I told the police, I have no idea. I was hoping you guys could find out."

Shit—a lie—he probably knew it.

"Mr. Scruggs, are you aware that your wife's SUV fire was not an accident?"

I caught myself clenching my fist. "Not an accident? Where did you get that?"

"The fire department has marked the fire as unresolved and has asked the police to investigate further."

So, there is an investigation. "It caught fire while my wife was at her exercise class. If it wasn't an accident, I like to know what it was."

He ignored my comment and clicked off more questions as if they were all leading to some conclusion. "You also have numerous unusual bank deposits, and although we see no failure to report income, we do see questionable income. All of this information warrants further investigation. It would benefit you to cooperate."

Ever since the SUV fire, I knew I was barely able to keep my nose above the water. This man was going to push me under. He knew too much. I couldn't lie my way out of this. I had a sick feeling, like a sea captain who realizes his ship is going down. I struggled internally, desperate for a life preserver. "I'm trying to cooperate, but you're insinuating I tell you something that you haven't asked."

In addition to my computer, which I had hastily slammed shut, and the legal pad I hid in my drawer, there was a clutter of pencils, other notepads, a change order, and scattered invoices on my desk. In an apparent subconscious move, he put my pencils and pens in a little pile and pushed the papers into a single stack. One document he glanced at before placing it in the stack. This pissed me off, but I was paralyzed with worry.

"Mr. Scruggs, these are not insinuations. They are facts that I would like you to comment on. The FBI isn't going away. I'll get the answers. If I get them from you, it will help your case. Are you familiar with a man named Snake?"

Oh, shit, this game is up. They interrogated the man I shot. I needed time to think. I looked out my office window, and like an omen, a spider in the corner was capturing an unwary fly in its web. It was closing in for the kill.

"Agent Talbert, I don't know what you're talking about, but you apparently have subpoenaed my financial records, and from what you have said, it sounds like you think I'm guilty of something, but you're not sure what. I cannot sit here while you fish. Give me a few days to think this through and speak to my attorney."

I could feel my shirt getting wet under my arms. I reached out and moved my papers and pencils back to their original scattered positions.

"You do that," he said. "Here is my card. I'll be back in touch. But keep in mind the FBI has some leeway in how they pursue a case. It could benefit you to establish cooperation early on."

He left me as stunned as the fly caught in a spider web in the corner of my window. Finally, I turned off my computer, slammed my fist on the desk, and lowered my head into my hands.

Damn, what kind of box canyon am I in? I was doing everything in my power and imagination to keep us from being tortured to death by a Jacksonville madman, and now I was about to go to jail. If I went to jail, surely Snake would have me killed there, or worse, have my family killed. If I cooperated with the FBI, Snake would kill my family, and I was still probably as good as dead. Give him his money, and when he gets it all, it's the same outcome—dead.

Sheryl knocked and came in to get a file. "Well, Scrap, I must say the characters that visit your office have greatly improved. That man was a true gentleman. Maybe you might share his phone number?"

"Looks are deceiving. You didn't hear what he had to say, and no way will you talk to him. He's with the FBI and not my friend."

"Oops, stepped in it again. Whatever you need, I'm

here."

Agent Talbert was another enemy, pure and simple—and dangerous. I picked up the notepad that I notice him looking at. I had scribbled reminders on it. One of them jumped out at me: *estimate Snake's needs.*

I realized I had exposed myself to additional criminal liability. I had acted like most other people when they're caught off guard: they incriminate themselves. I thought about Martha Stewart. The FBI didn't think they had a good enough case to prosecute her for insider stock trading, so they nailed her for lying to a federal agent during her interview. I had already done it. And he knew it. It was obvious Talbert had connected me to Snake.

I opened my computer back up, went on the internet, and discovered my situation was even worse than I'd thought. I could be charged, even if I had not been warned or put under oath. I did not even have to lie. If what I said was merely misleading, I might be charged with obstructing a federal investigation.

I was too agitated to sit. I left the office without speaking to Sheryl and went home to run. I ran hard, taking the path along the marsh and then out onto the sidewalk. Was that guy following me? What about that car with the lowlife spitting out the window? *Come on. Get a grip.*

It was evident now my genius plan to stay alive and protect my family would not work. There was no way I could pull off a money-laundering scheme with the FBI watching me. The only thing I still had was that Snake didn't know I was under FBI investigation, and I had to keep it that way. Now I wondered if one of Snake's spies might have seen Talbert come to my office. Somehow, I needed to keep him from coming again.

This Talbert guy was not going away. He would get me on something. I had to deter him and keep Snake in the loop, or Snake would get me. It crossed my mind—Snake needed to die. In addition to being a physical threat to my family and me, he could divulge incriminating evidence on me.

Turning back to do the second part that would take me home, I looked at my watch. I was panting hard, and my pace was way too fast. At this rate I wouldn't make the whole six miles. I slowed and could feel myself going into the zone.

I needed to figure out how to get rid of some of this stress. I thought about the jujitsu that Dee and I practiced together. One of the primary principles is to use your opponent's momentum to assist in your own attack. I pondered my dilemma. I had a drug cartel and the FBI after me. This was my overload point.

I felt like I could run forever.

Somehow, I needed to deflect one of these toward the other and away from me. Turning the FBI away from me and onto Snake would be tricky, but I had a hole card I was about to play. I had resisted it, but now I was trying to escape the fire.

It was fifty feet to the ground, and I was out of rope.

Chapter 44

Scrap

Mt. Pleasant, South Carolina

The next morning, I stepped out to the front office and asked Sheryl if I could borrow her cell phone. She raised her eyebrows, but without speaking, handed me her phone. I told her not to disturb me for thirty minutes and locked myself in my office. Using her phone, I called an unlisted, tightly controlled number in Columbia. A pleasant woman's voice answered. "Agent Boyd's office."

"I thought I was calling Assistant Special Agent in Charge, Derrell Boyd's office. AKA Big Cheese."

"Is this Scrap?"

"Linda, you're too sharp."

"You know he doesn't like titles. He wanted me to answer with just Dee's office, but the Bureau has certain formalities. What can I do for you?"

"I need to talk to Dee."

"Hang on. I have to check."

It took five minutes—no music, no bullshit recording about how the FBI has your back—just me sweating in silence waiting for Dee to answer.

Lately, it pained me to think about Dee. We both

prided ourselves on living up to what was sacred at The Citadel. The honor code: I will not lie, cheat, or steal, nor tolerate those who do. Now here I was, guilty of lying, cheating, stealing, and not only tolerating but cooperating with the worst possible violator. Dee was my best friend, but now he was a big shot in the FBI. I wondered how receptive he would be to my unlawful dilemma. I was having misgivings about my decision to call when a voice on the phone took me out of my thoughts.

"Hey, man, where you been? You must need me to arrest somebody, or are you in jail again?"

"I'm in trouble—big trouble. I need you to come down here."

"Let me guess, you finally killed those halfwits that insulted Beth."

Man, it was a comfort to hear his voice. His disposition and humor always made me relax. I was feeling better about calling.

"Dee, I'm serious. I need your advice on a real problem."

"You're my straight-arrow buddy. I can't imagine it could be too bad. You didn't kill somebody, did you?"

"Actually, I did, but it's not about that. But believe me, it's serious."

I didn't want him to get sidetracked about the shooting under my house. I would explain that, but I wanted the focus initially to be on getting the FBI off my back and figuring out how to handle Snake.

"Can you tell me something about it?"

Now I could feel the shift in his tone. He was sensing my apprehension.

"It has to do with big-time gangsters. They're after me."

"Wow, I hear it in your voice. Okay, I'll be there Saturday around 2:00 p.m. Tell Beth to fix me some shrimp and grits."

I gave a sigh of relief. "I'm afraid of being tracked. I can't take you to my house. Let's meet at the Mt. Pleasant pier."

"Man, ain't you Mr. Stealth. I ought to hire you to work for us. Okay, I'll see you there at two."

"Sorry about the shrimp and grits, and Dee…thanks, buddy."

I went to the recent calls page on Sheryl's phone and deleted the FBI number. I went back to the front office and handed back her phone. She gave me an inquisitive look but said nothing.

Following the attempt to put tracking devices on our vehicles, I was sure my house was watched and maybe bugged. I could not take the chance, so I assumed my truck was compromised. The next day, a rental car was ordered to be delivered to a parking lot several blocks from my office. I drove my truck to my office and walked out the back and over to the parking lot. The car came five minutes later, and I drove to the Mt. Pleasant pier.

At two o'clock, I walked the dock looking for Dee. I found my old friend fishing at the very end. He must have arrived early because he had already caught a nice sheepshead. I leaned against the rail and watched his line. "I forgot to bring my pole."

"Man, this is what I need," he said. "You should get into trouble more often."

I looked around, clearing the area like a spy

transferring secrets. There was only one other fisherman about twenty-five yards away. "Thanks for coming, buddy. I really need you."

"So, knob, what kind of shit you got on your shoes now?"

I kept looking at his line. "A year and a half ago, I was marsh hen hunting and found some waterproof aluminum suitcases lodged up in the marsh. They were all full of money—probably drug money—lots of it."

"Oh, boy. Whose was it?"

"I'll get to that in a minute. First, I need to explain what I did with the money."

"Well, shit, knob, I'm sure you turned it over to the authorities."

This caused me to look out across the harbor. A large container ship was easing out the channel. "Remember I told you my business was doing poorly?"

"You didn't inject illegal money into your business?"

I turned toward the other fisherman who was engrossed in eyeing his fishing line. I yearned for the simple, relaxed time of old when I could wait for a fish to bite.

"Listen, just listen," I said, feeling my face get red. "This is hard enough as it is."

"Sorry, Scrap. I'll not judge. Tell me the whole thing."

I saw a small twitch on his line. He jerked but too late. Sheepshead were famous for sucking your bait and escaping.

"I never told you that bankruptcy was knocking at my door. The construction meltdown was crushing me, and here was a solution. It worked. I saved my business, but now the crooks who lost the money are after me."

"Have you actually talked to them?"

The fisherman down the dock was hauling in a nice size sheepshead. You could tell what it was because of the prominent black and white stripes.

"Yes, I've talked to them, but that's not all. There's an FBI agent by the name of Trent Talbert who's questioning me."

"Oh boy, you really are in trouble."

Dee's eyes followed five gliding pelicans and looked at me. "How much money are we talking about here?"

I hesitated.

"All told, it's nine and a half million in nineteen suitcases."

He whistled. "Man, when you stick out your neck, it looks like an egret. And you're telling me they were just lying around the marsh."

There was a couple of healthy tugs on his line, and Dee set the hook. Up came a nice size flounder. "Well, goes to show you, sometimes you catch something you're not fishing for."

"What do you mean by that?"

He tilted his head and squinted his right eye. "I mean, dumbhead, that I caught a flounder instead of a sheepshead."

This statement bothered me, and I was quiet while he removed his fish and put it in his bucket. "Back to this money," I said. "I'm telling you that's where it was, but it took more than one trip to find it all."

He looked skeptical.

"How many trips?"

I hesitated again. "Two."

Another lie. I was not going to tell anybody about the stash at Keep Safe Storage, not even Beth. It was security for her and Emma if I went to jail or was killed. It was in a letter to Beth in our safe deposit box. It also gave me some comfort to know if the FBI or IRS stripped me naked, I would have it in reserve. Besides, if I told Dee about the stash, and he did *not* report it, his career would be jeopardized. I didn't tell him about the crash site but gave him the same story I had told Beth and Snake about finding the money suitcases in the marsh.

"What did you do with the money?"

"I kept some of it under my house and the rest was stored at a place called Live Oak Storage, which I visited, from time to time, to extract as needed."

I hated not being totally up-front, but even though I was asking Dee for help, ultimately it was my responsibility to protect myself and my family.

I told him about the threats, how the money was injected into my business, the visit to Snake, shooting the thugs in my garage, and the money-laundering plan to buy time. I did not tell him about my promise to pay Snake $1 million in cash. The reason I held this back was the payback money was a way I could get into his compound if, as a last resort, I decided to kill Snake. I had resolved to do this if necessary, and sacrifice myself, to remove the threat to Beth and Emma.

When you start lying, you start to weave a noose that eventually will hang you. Living a lifetime of honesty, I was uncomfortable lying, but it seemed in each situation, I had no alternative. Now, I worried about slipping up on whom I had told what. Snake,

Beth, Trent Talbert, and now Dee had different variations of my villainy.

"Can you call off this Trent Talbert? The thugs from Jacksonville are watching me. If they see the FBI anywhere around, they will kidnap my family."

"Well, smack, I know who this Snake guy is. He's a mid-level cocaine dealer, smarter than average. He once was a lawyer, a politician, and now a drug dealer. He's the worst kind of sociopath, known as The Acid Man for his fondness of using sulfuric acid on his victims."

He paused there, raising his brows as if to ask me whether I knew who I was dealing with.

"The Acid Man—uh—I'm not surprised. The guy's demonic. They made me witness a man being tortured to death. Come to think of it, he mentioned Acid Man when I made my visit. He seemed to be proud of the name."

"I haven't witnessed these things, but it's common knowledge within the FBI this guy has the conscience of a leopard pulling a half-eaten springbok up a tree. Not now, but later I'll need you to give me a detailed description of your contact and your trip to Jacksonville."

"I know I have broken the law. Is there any way to keep this between you and me?"

"For me to help, you're going to have to own up. I'll try to get you cleared as a cooperating witness. You're in deep kimchi, but I might be able to keep you out of jail. But it'll be tricky."

He pulled up his line and the bait had been sucked away again. "I ought to give you tours to walk because you broke my concentration, and a fish stole my bait."

"Shit, don't blame me because you just don't know how to fish," I said. "But back to my dilemma. Beth and Emma are what this is about. I have to keep them safe from this maggot, and it would be nice to stay out of jail to enjoy my family and provide for them."

"Well shit, dumbhead, it seems to me this whole thing started over your pride of providing running amok."

This last comment stung, but I knew he was right. I wondered what he would have done. "Are you judging me?"

"No, I won't judge, but we're friends, and I need to lay it out the way I see it. Now about this young Talbert. He's a hard charger, been working three years as a special agent. Around the office, he's known as a no-nonsense hard ass, respected but not well liked. Some of his colleagues call him Flinthead. Once assigned to an investigation, he's bulldog-determined to find guilt. Talbert came to the FBI after graduating at the top of his class from Penn State and serving four years as an officer in the Army Rangers. He was an Eagle Scout and a star athlete in high school."

"Well, sounds like a cadet bucking for rank. He may be tough to deal with."

"I'll try to get him to cool it for the time being until we can sort things out. Like we used to say, dumbhead, you done stepped in shit."

"Dee, this Snake, Acid Man, will kill me or my family if I don't pay back his money. Or if I do pay it back, he will kill me anyway to eliminate the exposure. My only out is to get him, and that's where you come in."

"I can't roll him up just because you say he's

laundering money. I can't even get him if you send him clean money. Besides, if I understand you correctly, you aren't actually doing the money-laundering plan yet. These guys have good lawyers. They will say it's a legal business. Don't forget, he's a lawyer."

I thought about this for a minute. I could smell the paper mill on the far bank of the Cooper River. "Okay…so what can you get him on?"

"Well, the easiest is to catch him in the act of selling his powder, but we haven't had any luck with that. If we had both the money and the drugs at the exchange site, we would have him, but this guy is cagey. He's known for keeping his distance from most transactions."

I was quiet for a spell, but an idea was forming. There was cocaine back at the crash site. My mind went into afterburner, trying to think through a plan and still stay in the conversation. This involved more guilt. I was creating another deception. No, not just a deception, it would be an outright lie.

"There's something else," I said. "When I visited his compound in Jacksonville, he mentioned that if I wanted to get on board, he could furnish me twenty-five kilos for half a mil. I was trying to buy time, so I told him I would let him know about the cocaine purchase later."

Dee looked at me sideways. I knew he could tell I was struggling with something. "He offered to sell you cocaine? Why? He usually works in much larger quantities, and besides, if you could come up with five hundred thousand, he would demand it outright as part of what you owed."

"I think he's nervous about a business deal with me

unless he knows I'm committed to a life of crime. Trading that much cocaine would do it. You said he was smart."

Dee pursed his lips in thought. He didn't seem to be buying my story. "How will you set up a drug transaction?"

"His man is supposed to come any day now to pick up the money-laundering plan for Snake to study. I'll try to arrange for a date to do the cocaine purchase when Snake's man visits. I think the big boss would feel more comfortable with me if I offered to buy the drugs before we made a deal on the money laundering."

"Do you have a certain date for the man to pick up the money-laundry plan?"

"No, but he said two weeks, and I was down there on the first of June. Tomorrow would be two weeks."

"Okay, let's see where this goes. Keep me posted. See if you can set it up and let me know. In the meantime, I'll start thinking about how to do a sting on him. It must be done so we get him in the middle of a transaction. This is going to require some finesse. We have to figure out a way to make sure he's present when the transaction occurs. Do you have access to the dirty money you haven't yet put into your business?"

"I have some at my house and some at Live Oak Storage."

"I'll need for you to provide me with the suitcase of money you'll use to buy the cocaine."

I was nervous about this. I trusted Dee but asked, "Why do you want the money?"

"'Cuz man, if I'm going to hang my ass out, I want to get paid."

"Come on, tell me why you need the money. I'm

nervous as a plebe on his first SMI."

"Provided this far-fetched plan comes together, this money will be your protection. If we put the tracking device on you, they may find it. So we'll embed it into the money."

I felt good that he was coming around to my plan, but bad for all I'd done—for all I had yet to do.

"I like that," I said. "Thanks for trusting me and for sticking your neck out."

"Hey, smack, I haven't stuck it out yet. And, Scrap, I know the answer to this, but I need to hear it from you. You were not really going to buy cocaine from this Snake guy?"

"No, I was just trying to save my ass."

The other fisherman was packing up to leave. He pulled a string of four fish out of his bucket as if to show them off.

"I know you're a hard charger," Dee said. "But let me caution: don't try anything alone."

Chapter 45

Dee

Six Mile, South Carolina

Dee drove straight from his visit with Scrap at the Mt. Pleasant Pier to his old stomping grounds at Six Mile. The official reason for his visit was to investigate Scrap's information on Fish, but he also looked forward to visiting his old home place and seeing his mother. Approaching the house, he felt a touch of melancholy mixed with some guilt over not visiting more often. Dee's father had unexpectedly died of a heart attack years back, and now his mother lived alone. Mingled with these thoughts was the warm feeling he got on entering the well-kept small frame house, where his values were nurtured.

The next day Dee set out to see if he could connect the dots in Six Mile to Scrap's story. Scrap had told him he thought Fish Blount had seen the money suitcases when they passed in the creek. Now there were rumors he had disappeared after meeting with his drug dealer.

Dee pursued his investigation in Six Mile with his usual easy style but with a local flavor. He knew the area and its people, but because it was well-known that he was an FBI agent, some locals on the shady side were leery.

He drove around but didn't see any of the old-time locals. There were a couple of people he recognized at the local dock, but they didn't fit the lowlife profile he was looking for. At noon he dropped by Six Mile Tavern to get a bite.

Bingo! Sitting at the bar was Jimmy Roe, one of Fish's running buddies. With a last name that meant fish eggs, Jimmy was known locally as Shad Roe.

Dee walked over and gently squeezed Shad on the shoulder. "Let's you and me have a game of pool."

"Man, I ain't got time. I got to be going."

Dee squeezed his shoulder a little harder. "Shad, I'm telling you up front, I ain't after nobody in Six Mile, unless he had something to do with Fish disappearing. Now come on over, I'll let you break."

Dee racked the balls, and Shad reluctantly did the break on a game of eight ball. "Tell me," Dee said, "What happened the last time you saw Fish?"

"Man, I don't know nothing."

Dee laid down his cue stick and glared at Shad. "Listen, motherfucker. Unless you want me to change my mind and drag you in for drug dealing, you better tell what you know about Fish."

"Okay, okay, I'll tell you, but you leave me out of it, and don't say I said nothing."

"You got it, man."

Dee sank three balls before a miss.

"Last time I saw Fish," Shad said, "we shoot craps. He leaves with a man I ain't seen before. Said he'd be back, but nobody ever see him again."

"Was Fish doing a lot of coke?"

Dee was relaxed talking the waterfront lingo of the locals—he was one of them—but he was repulsed by drug dealers and didn't feel kindly toward Shad. Shad tighten up. He took a shot and missed. "I don't know noth—"

"Stop it, Shad. I told you this is about finding out what happened to Fish."

Shad dropped his shoulders and took a deep breath. "Yeah man, he snort some snow and smoke some rock."

"Where'd he get the money?"

"I don't know, but boys say he found a shiny suitcase full of money in the marsh."

"Tell me one more thing, and I'll let you go. What's the word around here about what happened to Fish?"

I don't know nothing, but dudes say Fish left with big-time drug man. Most think Fish is dead."

"Eight ball in the corner pocket."

"Okay, G-man, you win, but I can't play when you got me so on edge."

Dee stored his cue. "Thanks, Shad. See you around."

No question, Scrap's situation and the missing Fish Blount were connected.

Dee called his boss, Ray Bowley. "I'm still in the Charleston area and have uncovered some interesting stuff. I think I might have a connection to our old friend, Snake. I'm onto some missing cocaine money and a possible murder."

Dee gave his boss a brief run-down on the lead from Scrap about Fish.

"So, you *are* busy. When you come back to Columbia, come by my office and let's talk about this. I know you and Scrap go way back, and I'm a little uncomfortable with you on this case."

"I understand, but don't forget if Scrap and I weren't friends, we would not be on this trail, which I think is going to be productive."

"We'll talk about it."

Dee knew he needed more corroborating evidence to get his boss on board to support a sting. "Remember back before I went to Atlanta," Dee said, "there was a decrease in cocaine prices in eastern North and South Carolina?"

"Yes, you were trying to find the cause."

"I think I may have discovered a connection to this other investigation."

"Great work, Boyd. Provided I go along, how much time do you think you'll need to develop all this?"

Time? It's not so much about time as it is about Scrap working out the cocaine purchase.

"It'll be a while. Still chasing loose ends and trying to connect the dots."

Milton Freedman once declared that cocaine trading was capitalism on steroids, and the trade certainly seemed to confirm it. The price of blow fluctuates closely with supply and demand.

The price decrease meant there was an increased supply coming from somewhere. This was added ammunition for his coming presentation to convince the Bureau to support the sting he and Scrap might work out.

Before leaving Six Mile, Dee called Scrap again. He had called him every day on a secure phone. "I'm returning to Columbia today," Dee said. "Just wanted to see if you have heard anything from your contact."

"No one's showed. I'm sorry. Do you think he got spooked?"

"No telling. He's slick. He could just be late, or he might be like a jackal, sniffing the area. Let's give it a few more days. In the meantime, think about sending Beth and Emma to Kansas."

"You think he's coming after us?"

"Well, I'm pretty sure he got Fish. I'm more worried about your family. If he interrogated Fish before killing him, you and your family might be next. This guy has no limits."

Chapter 46

Scrap

Mt. Pleasant, South Carolina

Six days following Dee's return to Columbia from his visit at Six Mile, I pulled into my office parking lot after visiting a job site. I was pissed because Trent Talbert had called Beth trying to make an appointment to interview her. Preoccupied, I entered through Sheryl's front office. There sat Gut in the reception area with Sheryl at her desk on the other side of the room.

I was paralyzed. Thoughts of his torture chamber came flooding back. I stared at him for a full five seconds before glancing at Sheryl. She nodded toward Gut. "Man still says he's a contractor. Guess they come in all sizes."

It was obvious to me he had insulted her somehow. Without further acknowledgment, I brushed past him. "Come into my office."

I motioned for him to sit, and I took refuge behind my desk. He gave me a sneer I took as his version of a smile.

"Mr. Scruggs, I believe you have an information package for me to deliver."

I paused without answering, reached into my pocket, pulled out some keys, unlocked a desk drawer, and handed him an envelope. "Tell Snake I'll have these proposed documents with me when I deliver the money I promised to pay him by first of August. Everything is explained in here, but I'll give you a brief description to pass on: the papers, which I'll have on my next visit, will contain a legal corporation with Snake owning ninety percent. I'll own ten percent. Snake's cash will come into the corporation and be used to fund expenses, which will not be shown. This will create excess profits, which will be paid to the owners in clean money."

He nodded. "And your ten percent?"

"My ten percent is a fee for running the operation. I'll keep two sets of books, one for Snake and one for the accountant. To keep Snake at arm's length, to an observer, I'll look like the sole owner."

He grunted, put the envelope in his briefcase, and turned to leave. "Okay, Scrappy, I'll be back in touch about another meeting at the snake pit."

Scrappy. Hated the sonofabitch even more. He passed through the reception area, and Sheryl vented some undisguised anger. "Listen, buster. I don't care if you're a contractor or not, but if you put your gorilla paws on me again, I'll call the police."

I looked at my office door in shock. Something like that could take our plans off the rails. It would be better to shoot him than call the police. I needed to talk to Sheryl later.

After Gut left, I called Dee on the secure cell phone he'd given me.

"The fish are biting," I said. "You need to get on over here."

He laughed. "Understand. I'll be at the fishing hole

Sunday at noon. And Scrap, your sneaky stuff is a good idea. Make sure you're not followed."

We met once again at the Mt. Pleasant pier. This time I brought my pole.

I found Dee fishing at the same spot. I put a shrimp on my hook and tossed it in. "Okay," I said, "I brought a suitcase with five hundred thousand. I had to rent another car at a different location to ensure I wasn't tracked to my money storage unit. So here I am, clean and undetected."

"Well, gumshoe, I think you done broke the code."

"Before we get into this planning session, I need to find out about what's going on with this Talbert guy. He called and tried to make an appointment to interview my wife. I thought you had put this guy on hold."

"I'm getting him involved in the sting, and he's on hold from going to the court to subpoena any more records on you, but he's eager and looking for loopholes where he can continue his investigation. I think I can stop him from talking to Beth. He's a little overzealous there. My boss is sensitive about me doing this investigation already—have to handle Talbert with kid gloves. The last thing I want is for him to leak to Bowley that I'm showing favorites with you."

He jerked his line and caught a sheepshead.

"What you using for bait?" I asked.

"Fiddler crabs. What're you fishing for with that shrimp?"

I held the fish with my foot while he removed the hook. "Whatever."

"It's my understanding from your super-secret coded message the drug sale is a go, and we can move on the sting. Once it's a go, I'll get Talbert to hold off on any of his investigations that don't support the larger operation."

"Yes…" My voice was weak. I was still ashamed about lying to my best friend. "It will take place around the first of August, but Snake needs to confirm our meeting. The contact will get in touch for the time and date to make the purchase in Jacksonville, and don't forget, at the same time, I'm to deliver the necessary paperwork for Snake to sign on the money-laundering scheme."

All of this was tentative. Not only was I lying, but I was drawing Dee into setting up a sting Snake may never give me a chance to pull off. In addition to getting me killed, a scheme gone wrong could hurt Dee's career or even get him killed. The bottom line was I had to have the best plan I could dream up to protect my family. Pretending to buy cocaine from Snake was what I needed to get the FBI on board. There was no way I could tell Dee I was furnishing the cocaine. If the FBI thought he was in on the hoax, he not only would be fired but also would go to jail.

"Who came by your office?" Dee said.

"It was the same thug who administered the pain in the torture room. He's called Gut. He's also the same one that brought the letter inviting me to visit Snake. The big bastard even tried to put the move on my secretary in my reception area. He said I would be contacted later to bring the money laundering papers…ah…both the papers and the money for the cocaine."

Dee looked skeptically at me. "I know about this Gut guy. He did a stint in the state pen and somehow got his law degree. He and Snake go all the way back to law school. Cruelty is another specialty of his, but from what I know about your secretary, he's treading on dangerous ground there. So, what do you think, will they go for your deal to buy cocaine?"

"I don't know. These guys live in a different world," I said. "But as for Sheryl, you got that right. She chewed his King Kong ass out as he was leaving."

I felt a tug on my line. It turned out to be a blue crab stealing my shrimp.

"Okay, smack, there's another item we have not discussed that we need to get out of the way. The head shed will not consider a sting operation using you as the point man without a polygraph. They're nervous about a bad sting embarrassing the Bureau. They also need it done to get on board for a lenient plea bargain."

This hit me hard. He could probably tell. Part of my plan was a lie, and I knew somebody like me would never trick a polygraph. "Man, I don't trust these things. I have heard you can be trapped into lying when you're telling the truth."

"Come on!" Dee said. "Don't try to shit an old shitter. Somewhere you're lying. If you can't come clean with me, this isn't going to work."

"Okay, okay. Listen, I'm trying to save my family and myself. For me to make this work, there are some things I can't tell because it would taint you to know. Being a criminal is enough of a burden. I can't live with the chance of taking you down with me."

"Damn it, Scrap, I know what's going on. I can't operate like this. There's something fishy about the sting setup. You're my best friend. If need be, I'll take the fall to save your ass. So, I guess there's your answer. If I'm willing to be dishonest for a friend, I would have done what you did to save your family, but I need all the information so I can think this through."

"No, I won't let you compromise yourself. We have to do it my way. I may go to jail anyhow. I may not even live through this. My bed is made. You, on the other hand, can stay above the muck. It's bad enough you're participating in this risky plan. Just listen to me."

He looked out at a huge container ship being escorted to the Wando terminal, probably full of something from China. I wondered if he might be thinking back to his own crisis at The Citadel. The comparison bothered me. His dilemma was a mistake; mine is rotten.

"Okay, dumbhead, what's the plan?"

"Tell me about these polygraphs."

Dee fumed for a few seconds before answering. "After they set up and establish your profile, they ask you a series of questions that have been determined in advance."

"Will I know what they're going to ask ahead of time?"

"Often, they want you to know the questions, but they will still know if you lie. In fact, you knowing the question in advance helps them."

There was a boat with two guys next to a Cooper River bridge abutment hauling in one fish after another. I noticed one of the guys working something in his hand. *Their catching sheepshead with oysters!*

My mind returned to the conversation. "I don't understand. I thought they were trying to catch me in a lie. How are they going to do that if I have time to think about it?"

All the deceit I had been spreading around made me nervous and worried about taking a polygraph. I was still groping for a way around it.

"You can't think about it and beat the test. The reason they sometimes want you to know about the questions is they want a true lie response, not a spike on the machine because you were surprised."

"Most of what I have told you is the truth. What if we tailor the questions to avoid my deceptive area?"

Dee looked frustrated and raised his voice. "Damn it, Scrap, I'm not sure I can make this work knowing you're not coming totally clean and trying to work around the dirty. It's not that I'm unwilling…I'm not sure it can work."

"Okay, okay. I understand, but at least let's try my way and see what you think."

"Maybe? It will be tricky, but I do have some pull. I'll have to convince the higher-ups you're sensitive about being wrongly accused. We will make it clear all parties must agree on the questions, but Scrap, don't let a question slip in you cannot be truthful about. If the question doesn't seem right, don't answer it. I'll be there to talk about it. I have some ammunition about the importance of this case and will make a strong argument for why we need to keep you on board."

"Okay, my friend, let's work on the questions I feel safe with."

It wasn't easy. Dee said they would need to ask where the money was found. I was only willing to say it was found while marsh hen hunting. Also, there was a problem with how much was found. I insisted on that day I returned with about $5 million, in ten suitcases.

This caused Dee to bristle. "You told me nine and a half million in nineteen suitcases. What the hell?"

"This is a deceptive area I can't get into. On the day I found the money, I returned with ten suitcases. Remember I said it took me more than one trip. Each suitcase had about five hundred thousand or about five million total for that day. That's the truth. Jesus, I told Snake four million, I told you nine and a half. Now we are talking five. I'm going to screw the pooch on this."

"Whoa, smack, we do one inspection at a time. I'm not giving the polygraph, and neither is Snake. You can lie to me, you can lie to Snake, but for God's sake, don't lie to the polygraph examiner."

We agreed they would not be allowed to ask about the circumstances of the discovery.

I watched an osprey flying in the distance. Completing its first circle, it dived. It rose in flight from the water, gripping a catch. *Am I that fish?*

I turned to him and changed the subject. "The money suitcase, it's a comfort for me to know you'll be able to track it, but I need to make sure I am wherever it is."

"You got it, dumbhead. The key is to always be with the money."

The plan was dependent on the FBI, but I was trying to think of a desperate backup that would not include them in case something went wrong. I had to get insurance in case the FBI sting came apart. If Snake messed with Beth or little Emma, I would kill him—even if it meant dying in the process.

Chapter 47

Scrap

Awendaw, South Carolina

Four days later Dee called me in the afternoon on my secure cell phone to set up a meeting the next day. "Let's do a different place," he said. "What do you think?"

"Okay, G-man, how about meeting me at my old place off Sewee Road. Nobody lives there now, and I still have all my shooting targets set up. We'll see if the last time you beat me was a fluke."

"You don't have a chance," he said. "Don't forget I get paid to be a professional shootist."

"Ah come on, you're riding a desk over in Columbia where the only good shooting is shooting the shit."

"Dumbhead, you're loading yourself up to be humiliated. I'll see you there at high noon."

I woke up early the next morning and, trying not to wake Beth, slipped out, and quietly made coffee. After scratching around the fridge until I found a leftover piece of sausage, I went out on my back porch to wake up.

Between our house and the edge of the marsh was a blue birdhouse, and to the delight of us all, there were babies. We had been entertained with the activity for the past two weeks. Sipping my coffee, I noticed both the male and female bluebirds, instead of feeding, were moving around the area in an agitated state. My heart sank—a snake head appeared in the hole from the inside. I went down and opened the birdhouse to view a king snake of about three feet long. I could make out three bulges in its body. I quickly grabbed the snake right behind its head and threw it in a nearby ditch. I wouldn't tell Beth and Emma about this. I'd tell them it was time for the baby birds to leave the nest.

Troubled, I closed the birdhouse and went back to the porch. Obviously, as sad as the scene was, the snake had no thoughts of remorse. It was nature's ultimate sociopath, but this was survival—part of the food chain. My mind turned to my present threat. Was this another omen? Was I a baby bird about to be devoured by that other Snake, that other sociopath?

Beth came into the kitchen. "Good morning," I said. "I thought this was a teacher's workday and you and Emma would sleep in."

"I got too many things to do."

"Speaking of things to do," I said, "Dee also thinks you should go to Kansas for a while."

This seemed to irritate her. "I can't do that right now. You know that Emma's special school has worked to develop her amazing artistic talent. We can't take her out of her summer art camp, and I have to clear things with my new job. I can't start out taking leave."

"All of this seems important, but considering the threats, you should think about going now."

"No, we need some time. We can't run our lives over your self-created crisis."

I stomped out to go to work, but by the time I drove out, I was sad.

I left the office around eleven to do my rental car switch. Even though I looked forward to seeing Dee, part of me dreaded the meeting.

He was already popping targets with his .40 Glock. I was already feeling the pressure, and I was sure what Dee was about to tell me would only increase my stress.

"Trent Talbert claims he has uncovered a lot of incriminating evidence," he said. "It was a good thing you were cautious about Snake tracking you. Seems Talbert's been tracking you, too."

This rattled me because if he had learned about either of my storage units, he surely would have a court order to search it even though Dee had put a hold on more digging into my personal business. I had told Dee about Live Oak Storage, but no one knew about Keep Safe All Night Storage, where I kept ten million. If Talbert discovered it, I could start practicing my perp walk. "I thought you had him under control," I said.

"I'm trying to call him off, but the safest way to handle this is to include Talbert in our sting. This could get sticky, but it's necessary to avoid questions from higher-ups. Talbert's original assignment was to investigate you, and he's like a snapping turtle that won't turn loose until it thunders. It's hard for him to let go of the idea of nailing you for something."

He turned his head and eyed me. "Do I need to worry about him finding something else?"

I didn't answer right away but drew my own Glock and fired at a line of five metal plates, hitting them all. "I've said all I can. Am I going to do jail time?"

"Not if I can help it, but Talbert claims he has

evidence of money laundering, misleading and lying about an FBI investigation, withholding evidence of an FBI investigation, and conspiracy to commit drug smuggling. You're going to have to plead to something, and if he finds more, I don't know. I'll be working on this back in Columbia."

At this meeting, we got into the planned sting itself. As far as Dee was concerned, it hinged on a setup to buy cocaine and present the money-laundering plan. But what it actually hinged on was a meeting for me to pay Snake his one mil and present the money-laundering plan.

The money suitcase, along with the suitcase full of cocaine, would look to Snake like I had two suitcases of money. The FBI would assume I would arrive with one suitcase. I was nervous about the plan. As of yet, I didn't even have the cocaine from the crash site. For all I knew, it was no longer there.

I think Dee sensed I was uneasy. He frowned and was more serious than usual. I interpreted this as skepticism.

"Everything," Dee said, "and I mean everything, depends on Snake contacting you again to go to Jacksonville to buy the drugs and get him to sign the money-laundering plan. How confident are you about this cocaine purchase?"

He fired at a plastic quart bottle filled with water he had set up fifty yards away. The jug exploded.

"Shit, Dee, this is your field. I don't know how reliable these scumbags are. His man, Gut, took the proposal to him. All we can do is wait for another visit to set up a Jacksonville meeting."

"But what exactly did he say about the cocaine

purchase? It all hangs on that."

Dee was pushing me deeper into my lie. "Gut said they would contact me to finalize the date for both the paperwork and the drug transaction."

"Okay, we do as much as we can until Snake pulls the trigger on the drug sale."

I was feeling the pressure. The time to pay back Snake's $1 million was coming at me like a barred owl diving on a mouse, and I needed to get the cocaine from the crash site to make my plan work, but I couldn't do that until there was an unusually high tide. I also needed to work out a plan in case the sting went wrong. The odds of this all coming together weren't looking good.

We walked together back to our cars in silence. Dee slapped me on the shoulder. "We'll get through this old friend. Together we make an unbeatable team."

"Thanks, Dee."

I drove my rental car back to the parking lot and switched to my truck. The shooting practice helped. But turning into my subdivision, I was still on edge. Alert for something else slipping up on me, I noticed a van in my rear making the same turns as me. I made a couple of extra turns and slowed. He made the same turns and slowed. I pulled off the road, and to my relief the van passed.

I arrived home earlier than usual but found no one there. Still keyed up, I paced the floor, going from room to room with no objective in mind.

After fifteen minutes of wondering where they were, the van, which I had dismissed as nothing, popped back in my mind. I called Beth. Thank God they were bike riding. Standing in the kitchen, I glanced out the window in time to see Emma pass on her bike and head down the road off of our cul-de-sac. The van—the same van—was following her.

I raced down to my truck and blasted out of the cul-de-sac but jammed on the brakes before joining the main road. I was screened by the trees on the edge of the road. The van had stopped about thirty yards up on the main road. *He's trying to kidnap my daughter!*

I jumped from my truck and ran toward the van. The driver had exited and was walking toward Emma. He didn't see me. She had stopped and appeared to be talking to him. Putting the van between the driver and myself, I drew my weapon and ran to the back of the van. I needed to be inside when he returned.

The back door on the van was unlocked. Climbing in, I could see the street through the windshield. He was walking back. Emma raced off on her bike and met Beth coming toward her. *Good girl, Emma. And now you'll get yours, buddy.*

I planned to shoot the sonofabitch when he opened the door to get in, but upon second thought, I did not want another killing investigation. I opened a toolbox in the back of the van, grabbed a pipe wrench, and waited.

A heavy-set man entered, and heaving a sigh, plopped his huge frame into the driver's seat. It was the same man that I grabbed by the balls at Snake's compound. His neck was as thick as a bull's, but I was the matador. I hit him on the top right side of his head. He grunted and fell over the console. Beth and Emma rode off, oblivious to what was going on.

Now what do I do? So, bastard, you got to live, but you were messing with my little girl. I dragged him into the back of the van and frisked for a weapon. He was carrying a Sig .45 automatic.

He stirred and moaned from my wrench to the head. *You sonofabitch, ever hear of kneecapping?* He mumbled something that sounded to me like fuck you. With his own gun, I fired one shot into the back of his right knee. He screamed and blood trickled onto the van floor. "Listen, asshole. Unless you want to be a paraplegic, you'll shut up and stay where you are."

I drove to the Mt. Pleasant hospital, which was only three miles away. Working for Snake was enough to keep him quiet, to say nothing about attempting kidnapping. I parked the van next to the emergency entry, got out, and walked away. In one hundred yards, I called Beth to come get me.

Beth drove up with Emma to meet me walking on the side of the road. "Scrap, what is going on?"

"You and Emma need to go to Kansas right away. I'll talk to you later about what happened, but please trust me on this. You have to go to Kansas."

As soon as we arrived home, Emma bounded out of the car to greet her friend in the cul-de-sac. I turned to Beth. "A man was trying to kidnap Emma."

"Oh my God. What happened? What did you do?"

"I intercepted him."

"Meaning you killed him?" She gasped.

"No, no, no. I just…shot him."

"And you brought him to the hospital?"

I was sick with concern for my family's safety, and these questions added to my stress. Things were happening fast, and I was trying to deal with them. I realized I needed to make her understand without causing undue alarm. I had a fight coming, and I needed her out of the way and safe in Kansas.

"He was going to kidnap Emma! I shot him. He's lucky; I considered killing him."

"What if he dies?"

Most of the time I liked her mind-challenging banter, but now I was finding it frustrating. Beth wouldn't accept something until she decided it made sense.

"He's not going to die. It's only a leg injury."

"But Scrap, the police will still get involved."

"Don't worry about it. He would never tell. He would be incriminating himself. Besides, I don't think he even knows who shot him."

"You're scaring me. You killed a guy a few weeks ago in our basement, and now you shot a man, and it's no big deal? What is happening to you? I know you're trying to protect us from the drug dealers, but this is getting to be too much."

"Beth"—I raised my voice—"you may be right, but the point now is you and Emma need to get away from here. Please focus on what's most important: yours and Emma's safety."

She raised her voice right back. "All right, we will leave, but not unless you level with me about your plans. I'm not leaving you here to face all the danger alone unless I know what your exposure is."

I knew she meant it, and I could not gloss over my plan. This was tough because I kept most things to myself to protect us both in case she was ever interrogated. I would soon be involved in the sting, and they would be in Kansas, so I decided it was safe to tell her most of what was going on. When I got to the part about Snake offering to sell me cocaine, she was frowning.

"You didn't agree to buy cocaine, did you?

"No, not until I was working with the FBI. Just let me finish."

I told her about taking the cocaine with me along with the money. She no longer was frowning. Her eyes were wide as if there were a puma about to pounce on my back.

"Where...oh God...where would you get a suitcase of cocaine?"

"I don't have it yet, but I know where one is. It's in the marsh where I found the money."

The question bothered me, and after an hour of conversation to convince Beth to go to her parents in Kansas, I relieved my frustration by shooting a tin can below my porch with an air rifle. Beth had opened my eyes. The idea of retrieving a suitcase full of cocaine was not only despicable but it could land me in jail.

I gazed out at the marsh, barely noticing the twenty-five or so ibis searching for fiddlers. The high-pitched shriek of an osprey on the hunt was only background noise, and the summer breeze brought me no pleasure. Trent Talbert was hounding me. Snake was hounding me. My wife and child were in danger, and despite the effort of my good friend, Dee, I feared I might die or go to jail. Each of my attempts to remedy past misdeeds escalated me into deeper felony and more serious jeopardy.

The dirty money was my first bite of the apple, and now I was in the garden, naked and ashamed. When I took the money, I thought my situation was dire, but now it was clear how spoiled I was. My family was not hungry. I was not stealing bread. It was vanity for my reputation and position in life. How many men have gone to jail for lesser crimes and been ruined trying to secure needs greater than mine had been? I felt ashamed over my past hypocrisy when I denounced all manner of transgressions from other men without knowing the torment of their temptation.

I thought about Beth and little Emma, and my perspective shifted. How virtuous was it to make decisions to assuage my guilt but were detrimental to my family? I had shaped a house where they're dependent on my success. Did I now have the right to jerk this dependency away and say they must suffer for my need to do the right thing? Which was the greater good? My family or my morality?

I went back inside. "I hate to bring this up, but you need to make arrangements at your job to be absent for at least a week."

She gave me a cold stare. "I have already talked to my boss. I told her I had a family problem and needed to go to Kansas to address it. She said she understood. I hope it won't be longer than a week."

Depressed, I went back out on the porch. My head spun with these thoughts. I tried in vain to find a plug to stop the water on my sinking boat. There was no way to deflect my trajectory toward its climax. I resolved to see it through, either to my demise or escape. I realized whatever was at the end, there would be a price to pay. Any escape I might enjoy would be purchased with the tainting of my soul.

The next morning, I called Uber to go to the airport. Beth and Emma had reservations on a flight from Charleston to Kansas City, with one stop in Atlanta. The Uber was to pick us up at the country club. With my four-door truck closed up under the house out of view, we loaded the luggage in its bed. I drove around the subdivision until I was sure I wasn't followed.

"I understand you're trying to be sure we are not followed, but why do we transfer to an Uber at the country club?"

"I can't be sure my truck doesn't have a tracking device. It's just one more precaution. Don't worry."

I rode with them to the airport in the Uber. After checking bags, we all took our place at the end of the security line. Beth grabbed me with tears in her eyes and gave me a long slow kiss right in front of God and the world.

Emma tugged at her dress. "Momma, you're taking up all the kissing. I have to kiss daddy goodbye, too."

I kissed Emma and watched them walk through security. I took some comfort in knowing they would be far away and safe, but a profound emptiness overwhelmed me when I thought about the risk of never seeing them again.

Chapter 48

Dee

Columbia, South Carolina

Dee ran into difficulties back at headquarters. First off, it was challenging setting up the polygraph with the strict limits on questions. He explained to his boss, Ray Bowley, the importance of not holding Scrap to such a squeaky-clean standard or risk losing an important asset. He tied in the drug prices in eastern North Carolina as evidence they may unravel a larger puzzle. "Ray, this could be our chance to get Snake. We need Scrap to act as a mole."

Bowley was the hard-nosed Special Agent in Charge of the FBI Columbia field office. He had been with the FBI for twenty-five years and for the most part went strictly by the book, except in his younger days as a foot soldier when he had skipped a few pages in the book to get his man. Dee was now second-in-command. They were seated inside a booth in a cheap but excellent Italian restaurant two blocks from the FBI field office. The owner liked to have them as customers because it showed the world that he was an honest businessman.

"I understand that," Bowley said, "but we still need to vet this guy thoroughly."

"The FBI isn't consistent," Dee said. "We are willing to work with hardened criminals who turn state's evidence to save their asses. We know they have done awful things in the past, and we are willing to overlook those things. Yet, because you want to nit-pick my informant, we may be passing up an opportunity to roll up a big wholesaler who will lead us to more distribution outlets. This caution is overkill. You want to make absolutely sure a man who has been honest his whole life is now telling everything?"

Bowley frowned, rolled up spaghetti on his fork, and crammed it in his mouth. He chewed and pointed with his fork. "The FBI has guidelines for a reason. Have you told your man about his exposure to prosecution for lying or misleading an FBI investigation?"

Dee tore off a piece of hot, homemade bread and slathered it with butter.

"He understands, but you know there's no perfect mole."

Bowley demurred. "I have to consider the possibility of the sting going bad if we didn't get all the information."

"No, you don't," Dee snapped. "That's my job. You just need to make sure your people are the kind who use good judgment. If you question my judgment, demote me; otherwise, let me do my job."

Bowley heaved a sigh. "Damn, don't get personal. You know very well if you get embarrassed, it will come back and bite me. I know Scrap is your friend, and I should pull you off the case for that reason alone. I already have my neck out on this."

The waiter stopped by, and it gave Dee time to

form his answer. "May I remind you that you've helped friends in the past? And I have known Scrap most of his adult life. He's a good man who's in a jam. Helping him could be a great benefit to the FBI."

"Okay, do it, but your ass is hung out on this one, Boyd, and if Trent Talbert wants to pursue Scrap for false or misleading statements, I won't stop him."

"Thanks, Ray. It's not the first time for either of us to have his ass hung out."

Two guys from a table on the other side of the room got up and walked by their booth. No wonder the food was good, they were speaking Italian.

The waiter brought the check, and they left, continuing their discussion on the walk back. They crossed the street and entered the temple of truth or consequences.

"There's one other thing," Dee said. "Before my mole gets aboard, he wants to know about a plea bargain."

"Come by my office in ten minutes. I'll have Mick there, and we'll work something out."

The door to Ray's office was open, and Mick was already seated with a pen and legal pad ready to go. Mick was the office attorney and knew all the rules and procedures. He also was a stickler for following them.

Scrap was guilty of laundering some of the cocaine money for his personal use and to save his business. The trick here was to charge him with something credible alongside a statement about his cooperation, and to hope a judge would be lenient.

"Okay, I understand Scrap will have to pay the piper in some way," Dee said. "But keep in mind I have encouraged his full cooperation based on my ability to mitigate the pain."

"I hope you haven't overpromised to help your friend," Bowley said.

The attorney piped in. "FBI guidelines would normally call for some jail time."

Dee felt his frustration building. "Come on, you guys. He's not your usual criminal. He found some money and put it to use."

Bowley sat back in his swivel chair and gave a negative nod. "Not quite. Not according to Trent Talbert, who, by the way, is pissed that he's not been included in this discussion. He says he can make a case for obstructing an investigation, bank fraud, and lying to the investigator. Until you pressured him to discontinue, he was building a case of conspiracy with narcotics operatives."

"Ah, bullshit!" Dee raised his voice. "Talbert's young and eager, but that's pie in the sky. None of that stuff would stick. Don't forget what I told you. Daniel Scruggs had an unblemished record until he found unattached, mysterious money. He's willing to hang his neck out a mile for the FBI to try to roll up one of the most despicable drug operations we know."

Mick, wanting to stay on Bowley's good side, kept looking for a hint on his thinking.

Finally, an agreement was reached for Scrap to forfeit all the money they believed he now had, both in his Live Oak Storage unit and in business cash. In addition, to confiscating the cash Scrap had on hand, he would be fined $3 million to be paid over five years. This was to recover the drug money he had put into his business. To enforce the payback, Scrap would remain on probation for the entire five years. He would be charged with accessory to money laundering but not at the level of conspiracy. A recommendation of leniency for cooperation would accompany this plea.

"Okay," Bowley said, "let's talk about this money you just waltzed into the office. It's my understanding that there's nothing to signify where it came from."

"We need to embed a tracking device in the money to follow our man."

"Hey, I understand that, but what is it?" Bowley said. "The FBI can't be throwing money around with no source or classification. Are you calling it evidence of a crime?"

"Although we know it's connected to cocaine," Dee said, "I can't call it evidence of narcotics trafficking. That might incriminate Scrap before agreement on his plea."

"Well," Mick said, "because your man was in possession and using the tainted money, isn't it criminal activity?"

"No, I'm not calling it that, either. What he gave me was money he had found. It was never put to use. It's not a crime to find money."

Bowley put his hands behind his head and smiled. He seemed to be enjoying this. "Then we call it a confiscation."

"But he gave us the money of his own free will."

"Come on," Bowley said. "You gotta call it something. You gonna say it's magic money that fell out of the sky?"

Dee had already worked this out in his mind, but this dialogue needed to play out so Bowley would be on board with the logic. Dee had not gotten to the top echelon of the FBI without being politically astute.

Steve Taylor

"I would like to call it evidence of an ongoing investigation without attaching it to an actual crime at this time."

"Okay, but keep in mind, I'm going along on this because I trust you to keep it kosher. Don't get too far out of your comfort zone."

Late in the afternoon, Dee delivered the money to the FBI lab. He instructed them about inserting the tracking device.

"I want forensics to examine the money and the suitcase itself. See if you can come up with any corroborating evidence. Check any numbers you can find on the suitcase and try to run a match. Find out who manufactured it and where it was distributed. Lastly, I want the money's serial numbers recorded for future tracking."

Inside the suitcase were twenty-dollar bills taped into ten-thousand-dollar bundles with three bundles to the stack. Dee supervised placing a tracking device in the middle bundle in a stack near the center of the suitcase. He specifically did not want it planted in the suitcase lining because of the possibility the money may be removed from the suitcase and repacked before Snake received it.

Dee was not only interested in helping his friend but also wanted to finally get Snake, and he was determined to make a successful sting out of Scrap's situation. He sensed Scrap was deceiving him about something. But they had been friends for years and felt if there was deception on his part, there was a good reason. He was determined to protect him in any way he could—even if it meant breaking FBI rules. On any drug trafficking operation leading to a takedown, Dee always tried to be at the tip of the spear. Now he was pushing the FBI, Scrap, and himself into the danger zone.

Chapter 49

Scrap

Mt. Pleasant, South Carolina

My secret cell phone chirped. "I got some news for you, smack. I'll drive over from Columbia tomorrow morning. To be on the safe side, let's change our meeting place. How about in Charleston at White Point Gardens? You know, down next to the battery."

"You think they might be on to us?"

"No, not really, but let's play the game," he said. "I'll be on the path feeding the pigeons at ten o'clock."

This was a good place, and I loved to go there. It would not be busy in the morning on a weekday, and it was a beautiful spot overlooking Charleston's historic harbor. It had gravel paths and old cannon from the Civil war.

I did my rented car switcheroo, parked in a downtown garage, and walked to the park.

Dee was already there sitting on a bench, feeding the pigeons. I surprised him when I approached from the back. "Well, dumbhead, you didn't cover your six, and I caught you doing this sneaky pigeon stuff."

"Hey, if it ain't my favorite criminal. Sit down on my bench, and I'll give you the news."

He handed me the proposed plea deal they had

worked out. I read the outline and lowered it to my lap. A couple kissed next to an American Civil War cannon. The plea wasn't good. I frowned but reluctantly agreed. Although it was open-ended, you could never tell what a judge would do. The conditions demanded by the FBI were for me to forfeit all the money I had (or what they thought I had) and pay another $3 million out of business profits over five years. As I feared, the FBI made the money part so restrictive it would have been a stretch for me to make enough extra profit out of my business to pay it. The agreement put me on probation for the entire five years I'd have to pay the money, which meant I would go to jail if I didn't make the payments.

I would survive, however, because of the secret $10 million I'd stashed at Keep Safe All Night Storage the FBI didn't know about. It made me wonder if, somehow, Dee had a suspicion I had more money. I knew he did the best he could, and I was grateful for the chance to stay out of jail, but I still had to hope for a sympathetic judge.

Dee tried to soften it. "Well, smack, I believe we can keep you out of jail, but it wasn't easy. I spent the better part of last week pulling your ass out of a crack while Ray Bowley and Trent Talbert did their best to cram it back in."

I waited for a couple to stroll past on the gravel path. "What is it with these two, anyway? I'm hanging my neck out to help the FBI."

He threw some breadcrumbs to three begging birds and looked at me.

"Ray thinks there's a lot of stuff you did that could embarrass the Bureau if it came out and they had given you a pass. Talbert thinks he almost has you dead to rights on bank fraud, money laundering, and obstruction of justice. He doesn't want to give up his *atta-boy* by agreeing to a weak plea. They both are suspicious of your visit with Snake."

"So, how did you keep me out of jail?"

"I kept hammering them with how you're taking more risk than anybody to help us put these guys behind bars. Also, I sprinkled in, from time to time, your stellar citizenship record. I schmoozed Talbert, planting the seed that he would get credit if the sting went well."

That bastard. If not for him, I would have gotten a better plea deal. Out in the harbor between Fort Sumter and the Charleston Battery, two sailboats raced with a nice southern breeze. I wished I were there and away from this stress. The one thing that gave me hope was my friend.

"I know you did the best you could, and I'm eternally grateful, but these hard assess are like negotiating with piranhas. Do they think my business will make an extra three million in five years, or is the plan to eventually put me in jail?"

The agreement even took all my working capital. I was surprised Dee didn't agonize over this. He had no questions or comments. Somehow, he suspected I have more money somewhere. As much as he would enjoy hearing about me shooting Emma's potential kidnapper, I didn't want to burden him with knowing any more of my criminal activity.

"I know you," he said. "You'll make it work."

We talked for another hour about the details and possible pitfalls of our plan. "Birdman," I said. "I'll leave you to your fowl friends. If they knew how much the FBI was paying you to feed them, these pigeons would strut even more."

He turned serious. "I'll do everything in my power to make this work, but you need to understand a sting doesn't always work the way it was planned."

I understood the failure possibility, and I also was aware that with the amount of deceit I was spreading around, this whole plan had a good chance of coming unglued. Nevertheless, departing the park, I was more optimistic, knowing I had the full power of the FBI in my corner. Also, it was a comfort to know the chances were good I wouldn't be going to jail.

I turned in the car and went back to my business, but by the time I arrived, my apprehension returned. If I were handling this alone, risks associated with a sting would be acceptable, but Snake had made it clear Beth and Emma were in jeopardy.

My employees had all gone for the day. Sitting in what had become my high-pressure chair, I studied the ceiling, trying to think of another angle to get The Acid Man. I wadded up papers from my trash can and shot baskets while my mind raced.

I figured if I died but got Snake, there would be no one left who had the incentive to kill or torture my family. Dee had talked about protective custody if I testified, but could I go into protective custody and still run my business? How would I pay the money to the FBI? It wouldn't work. If I didn't go into protective custody, and Snake went to jail, we would be looking over our shoulders while he, from his jail cell, had people searching for us. I knew Dee would see to it that my family and I always had protection, but even so, we would be like deer during hunting season.

As soon as I got home, I went out for a long run. Returning, I thought of Snake and poured a shot of bourbon. On my porch, I thought of taking the polygraph and poured another shot. I thought of Beth and poured another shot. Without her guidance I fell onto my bed and woke up hurting, dirty, and still in my clothes at 2:00 a.m. *Damn, I've got to sleep.* Tomorrow we would do the polygraph in my office.

Chapter 50

Scrap

Mt. Pleasant, South Carolina

I walked out to my cul-de-sac and picked up the morning paper. On the way back, my path was intercepted by a large black rat snake. I had always considered this snake my friend and protected it, but now it gave me chills. Back inside I poured a second cup of coffee and glanced at the headlines. My mind had been so occupied I had lost track of the rest of the world. The second part of a small headline near the bottom of the first page caused me to freeze: *Gunman Killed in Police Shoot-Out: Money Suitcases Found.*

I read the rest of the article.

According to information obtained from South Carolina Law Enforcement Division (SLED), at approximately 7:30 a.m. on Friday, July 12, Sergeant Harold Dixon, of the South Carolina Highway Patrol, stopped Mr. DeShawn Pinckney for speeding and was involved in a shoot-out resulting in the death of Mr. Pinckney. An automatic pistol suspected of having been fired at Sgt. Dixon was found near the front door of the deceased's car.

On a search of Mr. Pinckney's vehicle, two aluminum suitcases were found in the trunk containing

an undisclosed amount of cash in twenty-dollar bills.
An unidentified spokesman indicated there could be
close to $1 million in the two suitcases.

At this time, there is no information on the origin of
the cash.

I tried to understand what the article meant. Was
this cash more of Snake's money? But I thought I had
taken it all. Did Snake have other operations going on
with aluminum suitcases? Had somebody found some
of my stash? I didn't have time to address it. There
were too many pressing things to do.

At 1:15 p.m., Sheryl got a call from Freeman
Electric announcing they would arrive in ten minutes. I
went to my shop in the back and opened the large rollup
door. Soon the polygraph examiner, and none other
than Dee himself, arrived in a paneled truck with
Freeman Electric painted on the side. The truck was
fully equipped with ladders and conduit.

As the examiner was setting up, Dee got me alone.

"Have you seen today's paper about the aluminum
suitcases full of money?"

"Yes, I'm perplexed. What do you think?"

While my nerve-racking polygraph was looming, I
was still rolling over in my mind the two suitcases
found at the reported shootout.

"I'd say somebody else found some of Snake's
money," Dee said.

"Why do you think that?"

"Well, it's in the same vicinity, same type of
container, and we already know that Fish Blount had
found some. When we are done here, I'm going to pay
a call on the state police department and do some tests
on that suitcase."

"I can't think any more about it now. I'm nervous about this exam."

"That's why I'm here. If this bogs down, I'll try to straighten it out and keep things going. These questions are tight. It will be easy for an inexperienced examiner to screw it up."

Dee introduced the young examiner, who was apparently intimidated to have a high-level operative like Boyd looking over his shoulder. I told myself this should be similar to an old-time Ouija board, with all of us pushing to get a clean chart, but I wasn't sure about it.

While the examiner set up his machine in my office, Dee gave me his last-minute instructions in the reception area. "Don't answer a question if it's not exactly what we agreed to. Don't answer anything you think could register as deceptive. Don't elaborate on anything, and for God's sake, don't try to trick the machine."

"What if I don't answer a question?"

"The examiner will skip to the next question and come back to the question later, after discussing it with me."

"Will he ask anything that we haven't discussed?"

"Yes, but these questions are for him to get your profile right. They won't decide a pass or fail. He will explain these to you before the test."

Unsure and nervous, I struggled for clarity.

"Will you pipe in if this guy strays?"

"Hate to break it to you, smack, but it's not kosher for me to be in the room while he asks the questions."

He put his hand on my shoulder and guided me toward my office, which now was a place of dread.

"Dee, I need you there. I don't know how these things work. Suppose he tries to trick me?"

Even though Dee seemed optimistic, I had a feeling the exam would not go well. Without him in the room, I felt adrift on a sea of my own deception.

"He's not going to trick you. Believe me, he wants it to go smoothly. Just stay calm. You'll be fine. I'll be out front with your gorgeous secretary."

Notwithstanding Dee's confidence in me, I still had anxiety, causing an adversarial situation with the polygrapher from the start.

"I want you to relax and just follow my instructions," he said.

Fuck you. I don't trust you or your instructions.

"Okay shoot," I said.

"I'll ask you some general questions I know are true, such as: Are you sitting down? Are you in your office? etc. I'll then ask you questions about the pertinent subject. These are questions that have been agreed to in advance. In no particular order, I'll also ask a couple of personal questions you have seen earlier."

"What are the personal questions for?"

"They help establish the parameters we are working with on the charts. They won't be determinative."

I wasn't sure what he meant, but I agreed to begin, balking when he asked if I was the owner of a successful business. I was sure the machine spiked because my latest success was the result of dirty money. The examiner went out to get Dee.

"This isn't going to work if I can't establish my prelims. He's going to have to answer the general questions."

"Look," I said. "I overreacted. I told all of you I don't trust these things. I remember now this is necessary, okay?"

Dee smiled. "My magic appearance was all that was required."

We got through the preliminaries, and I could tell he was about to spring the first zinger.

"Mr. Scruggs, on a day you were out in your boat, did you find money that wasn't yours?"

"Yes."

"Did you find the money in the marsh?"

Here we go. I was afraid to answer. Technically, the hummock where I found the money was in the marsh, but that isn't the same. I had a feeling it would show deception. In my mind, I viewed picking it up in the marsh and discovering the crash as different. I sat quietly and shook my head. He went to the next question.

"Did you bring about five million in ten suitcases back in your boat on that day?"

"Yes."

"Mr. Scruggs, have you ever thought about having an affair with a woman other than your wife?"

I had seen this question and was told I needed to answer it, but I honestly didn't know how. I had been turned on and tempted by Sheryl, but I don't think I ever seriously considered having an affair. I stumbled over the answer. "No…ah, yes—yes."

"Did you know who the money belonged to that you found?"

"No."

"Did you initially store all this money in your garage?"

Once again, I was afraid to answer because I didn't know how much these people could decipher from my answer. The phrase, *all of this money*, might show I was lying.

I would not answer, so he went on to the next question.

"In your business, have you ever used accounting practices that are unethical or nonstandard?"

It wasn't clear, but I had a guilty conscience about some of what I had done. "Yes."

"Did you know a Mr. Battista Cosentino, also known as Snake, before his representative contacted you?"

"No."

"Mr. Scruggs, you did not answer two of the questions."

I thought I had failed. I asked for Dee. As soon as he entered, I complained that two questions were not what we had agreed to.

Dee was irritated. "What were the questions?"

"Did you find the money in the marsh?"

"Damn it! That isn't the question. The question is: *did you find the money while marsh hen hunting?* I have instructed Mr. Scruggs not to answer if the question isn't exactly as we have agreed. Please understand Mr. Scruggs was reluctant to do this. He thinks you'll trick him into incriminating himself."

The examiner was embarrassed, and though he did not dare show anger in front of Dee, I could tell he was pissed.

"What was the other question?"

"Did you initially store all this money in your garage?"

"That's not it. Don't paraphrase the question. It reads, did you initially store this money in your garage?"

The examiner shook his head. I knew he thought we were trying to sharp shoot the test. Dee left, and we settled back down, going back through the corrected questions two more times. I answered as best I could.

I didn't feel I had lied about anything, but I was nervous about all the lies I was not required to tell.

Dee told me normally the polygraph results would be immediate, but he wanted to take the charts back to Columbia to be analyzed.

While the examiner packed up, Dee took me to my shop in the back where the Freeman Electric truck was parked and gave me the money suitcase the FBI would use to track my movements.

"Okay, dumbhead, here is your insurance. Stay with it. It has a state-of-the-art tracking device embedded in the money."

"What happens if I can't stay with it?"

"I'm sorry, Scrap, but this is the best compromise. You and I agree we can't put the tracking device on you."

"Yes, I know," I said.

"The last time you visited these guys, you were picked up at a hotel parking lot. We will not track you and the money on the trip down to Jacksonville but will pick up the track at the designated rendezvous. When your next meeting is arranged, I'll need to know where they plan to make the switch to their car."

"Got it." I sounded confident, but I was not as confident as I sounded. Now I had a whole FBI operation hinging on another visit from Gut to set up the meeting.

Dee returned to Columbia to make the final arrangements for the sting. The next day he called me on one of my special cell phones. "Well, smack, I'm happy to announce you squeaked by on the polygraph."

"Thank God!"

The plan for the sting was coming together. Only problem was, I had heard nothing from Snake's man, and worse, I still needed to get the cocaine from the crash, which was crucial to my whole deceptive idea. After my encounter with Snake, I could imagine somehow he got suspicious of me, and the entire money-laundering plan, and would come for my family any day. Or, if he wanted to be kind, he would blow me away on some street corner.

Chapter 51

Scrap

Mt. Pleasant, South Carolina

I was running out of time to get back to the crash
hummock for the cocaine. I had been watching the
weather and tide forecast for days. Wednesday around
6:00 p.m., there would be a six-foot six-inch tide. Not
enough to float my boat all the way; however, the wind
was forecast out of the east at twelve knots, which
would help. This would give me about eight inches less
water than when I first discovered the crash site. It
would be tough, but I had to get the cocaine to make
my scheme work. To make matters worse, it was late in
the afternoon, and if there were any delay, I would be
caught by nightfall. In any case it would be dark on the
drive home.

This might be my last chance. There would be a
full moon tide at the end of the month, but that would
be pushing it too close. I would be gambling on having
a favorable wind.

Wednesday afternoon I detached the money fuel
tank from my boat motor, hooked up the real one, and
left for Garris Boat Landing around 4:00 p.m. I had
been hounded enough by Trent Talbert that I was
nervous about him trying to follow me as well as some

Bozo from Snake's operation. It had even crossed my mind that if they got careless and ran into each other, it would tip off Snake that the FBI was involved. Of course, this was all speculation or maybe paranoia because I had no evidence they were following me. If either of them did follow me, it would end in confusion once my mode of transportation was on the water and they had no boat.

It was a workday, and nobody was at the landing.

By five-thirty I had gone as far as I could with the motor. I tilted up the engine, got out, and pushed the boat through two inches of water to within a hundred yards of the island. Leaving the boat, I slogged the rest of the way on foot. With not as much water, I knew this walk would be necessary. I had on water shoes so I would not lose them in the mud.

In the two years since I had been here, vegetation had grown up around the airplane fuselage. A couple of small pine trees took advantage of the extra sunlight the crash had created and had grown partially up the side. A new cabbage palmetto fanned out next to the nose. I could still make out the favored spot for the diamondback under the old, downed palmetto log adjacent to the aircraft door. The log was still there as palmetto takes forever to decompose.

The first thing I did was poke under the hiding place with a stick. Sure enough, out came my friend—all six-and-a-half feet of him. He slithered under some fallen palmetto fronds and disappeared. There was no evidence anyone had been here since I left with my last load of money almost two years ago. The cocaine was still where I had left it in disgust. I contemplated for a few seconds. I should have left the money with the cocaine. It was as toxic as my serpentine friend hiding out there somewhere, waiting to strike. I was tested and failed the test. *Enough of this self-flagellation. I have work to do.*

I grabbed one of the two cocaine suitcases and headed back to the boat. Carrying the suitcase in the softer mud closer to the boat caused me to breathe hard.

I still had about the same water level, so once I caught my breath, the trip to the landing was easy, although nerve-racking. Having suitcases of money would have raised suspicion but possessing this much cocaine would land me in jail for sure.

The daylight faded by the time I drove away. After about ten minutes, I relaxed, only checking my rear view every few minutes instead of every ten seconds. The next time I checked, I jolted—a state police car was on my tail.

His flashers came on, and he gave a short tap of his siren.

My first thought was he knows about the cocaine, but I realized that was not rational. I pulled to the side, telling myself to keep calm.

The officer walked up to my truck window. "Can I see your driver's license, insurance, and registration, please?"

Oh, shit. I had a gun in the glove box. "Sir, I have a gun stored in the compartment with my truck papers."

"Okay, open it and hold the gun on the butt with your thumb and forefinger and hand it to me."

I gave him my 9mm Glock. He unloaded it and handed it back. I gave him the requested papers. Although I had a concealed carry permit, it was not required in South Carolina if the gun was stored in the glove box.

He studied my papers a second but did not give them back.

"Mr. Scruggs, the taillight is out on your boat trailer. I normally wouldn't stop you for this, but your tarp blew out of your boat. You need to be more careful. It could blind another motorist. I realize it will be difficult, or hazardous, for you to go back and pick it up. Remain here a few minutes. I'll bring it to you. Your documents will be returned after the tarp is retrieved."

I thanked him and once again watched in the rear view as he walked toward his car.

The officer walked past my boat, stopped, turned around, and looked directly at the suitcase. He shined his flashlight. A numb feeling engulfed me. My worst nightmare was about to happen. My God, if he found out, I was in the sausage grinder—all would be lost. I considered driving off while he was retrieving the tarp, but that option disappeared. He got to his car, stood, and turned back to look at my boat trailer. A few minutes later he returned to my truck.

"Mr. Scruggs, I'll need to run a check on your information. Please remain in your vehicle."

I sat for ten minutes with all kinds of thoughts racing through my head. I had to resist all attempts to open the suitcase. It would change everything for the worse. With all the FBI planning, the sting would not happen, and if they didn't send me to jail for lying, I surely would go for cocaine possession.

How can I head this off? What is the rule about search and seizure? The fourth, the fourth. I googled the Fourth Amendment on my cell phone.

The right of the people to be secure in their person, houses, papers, and effects, against unreasonable searches and seizures, shall not be violated, and no warrants shall issue, but upon probable cause, supported by oath or affirmation, and particularly describing the place to be searched, and the persons or things...

I considered calling my lawyer but didn't want to get others involved who would compromise the sting or complicate my plan. There would be time for a lawyer if the suitcase were opened.

Why is he interested in the suitcase? I tried to remember the police officer's name in the news article about the suitcases found in that shoot-out.

The trooper returned to my truck. I rolled down the window and looked directly at his name tag—Sgt. Harold Dixon. *That's it!*

"Mr. Scruggs, I need to ask you a few questions."

I decided to go along, hoping to deflect questions about the suitcase.

"Where have you been with your boat?"

"I put in at Garris Landing to scout for spot-tail bass." *Damn, here I go again, lying to a police officer—and incriminating myself.* I should have called the damn lawyer.

"Sir, what is in that suitcase you have in your boat?"

I balked. "Sergeant Dixon, I do not wish to continue with these questions."

A little irritated now, Dixon said, "Are you taking the Fifth?"

He made it sound like I was admitting I was a criminal.

"Yes, I am."

"Mr. Scruggs, I'm not reading you your rights. These are just routine police questions."

I turned my head and watched a motorist rubbernecking at me as he passed—probably thought how stupid to be speeding with a boat trailer. Not near as stupid as hauling cocaine.

"I do not wish to answer."

"Very well. I have to ask you to open the suitcase."

I was not going to be able to finesse or bullshit my way out. This was progressing into a full confrontation.

"Sergeant, under the authority of the Fourth Amendment, I must refuse."

He told me to stay in the car while he returned to his cruiser to check the information on my papers. At least I had thwarted his efforts for the time being.

In fifteen minutes, the officer walked back to my truck. "Mr. Scruggs, because you have stood on both the Fourth and Fifth Amendments in refusing to open or discuss the suitcase, we are applying for a warrant. Please remain in your truck."

I studied his deadpan expression for some clue. I turned and looked blankly at my steering wheel and then stared back at him with an unflinching glare. "Am I free to go?"

"No, sir, you are not. We must wait on the warrant."

"Are you detaining me?"

I could tell he was frustrated with my resistance.

"No, sir. I'm waiting on a warrant."

"Officer, the Fourth Amendment also covers unlawful detention. Either you're detaining me, or I'm free to go."

"Mr. Scruggs, are you a lawyer?"

"I do not wish to answer."

Dixon breathed a sigh of disgust and tried a different approach. "Mr. Scruggs, waiting for the warrant is a convenience for you. If you refuse to wait, we can serve the warrant at your residence. In that case, we will also need to search your house for any contents that may have been removed from the suitcase. Your home will be under surveillance until the warrant arrives."

There was a possibility he was bluffing, but I could not take the chance on a house search—not with a fake gas tank containing $500,000, and not with another aluminum suitcase, full of money tricked out by the FBI, sitting in my garage. I had done some thinking about what my move would be if they opened the suitcase. Sure, it would kill our FBI sting, but I might escape the cocaine charge. The cocaine could be explained by showing them the crash site with an identical suitcase of drugs. I would explain I was bringing the drugs to the FBI. This was weak, but enough to make up my mind.

"Sergeant Dixon, I'll wait for the warrant."

He went back to his cruiser and worked the radio for a long time. I imagined him calling for backup, returning to open the suitcase, and handcuffing me.

Once more, the officer approached my truck. *Uh-oh, here it comes.* He held my papers and glared at me. Finally, he handed over the papers. "Mr. Scruggs, you are free to go."

"What about the warrant?"

"At this time there will not be a search warrant."

I was relieved but only temporarily. Now I was on

331

the radar of the state police. I returned home with the cocaine and backed my boat into one of the parking bays. A state police car pulled into my driveway. *They got their warrant.*

Paralyzed with fear, I sat in my truck and watched while none other than Sargent Dixon got out and approached my truck. Here it comes and in plain view of my neighbors. I stepped out and greeted him. "So, we meet again."

"Mr. Scruggs, both of us forgot about your tarp that blew off. I have it in my car."

Speechless, I walked with him to his cruiser, and he handed over the tarp, now neatly folded. He drove away and I realized there was more to the timing of his arrival than giving me the tarp.

I unhooked my boat and closed the garage door. Thoughts turned to the impending threat in Jacksonville. Still worried if the sting would go bad, my mind puzzled over possible weapons. I have always been good at figuring out how to make things work. Much of my time growing up was spent creating projects that had nothing to do with school. I once built a shelter in the woods based on a Sewee Indian design, and a shooting range driven by an old lawn mower engine. By the time I entered The Citadel, I was a master at tinkering, though ill-prepared for the military discipline and academics. Now I let my creative juices flow, but whatever I came up with ran into obstacles.

I needed a way to get Snake. I had access to dynamite through my business, but what good would it do if I was not allowed to go in with anything? How was I to have a weapon if they confiscated everything? The last time I did the Jacksonville transfer, they locked my stuff in my truck. I was allowed only my keys so I could unlock my truck for my trip back home.

Would I have to go in naked, totally dependent on the FBI?

I stood up the money suitcase and studied it. I opened it and looked at the lining. I opened the cocaine suitcase and gazed thoughtfully at the disgusting contents. I sat on my weight bench, studying both suitcases on the floor as if they held a secret I needed to understand.

Chapter 52

Scrap

Mt. Pleasant, South Carolina

Tuesday morning, I got up later than usual after a restless night in the house alone. All last week I kept looking in my rear-view mirror for signs of somebody following me.

Yesterday, while standing at the teller counter in silence, waiting for a deposit-slip return, my mind was so detached I forgot where I was. "Will that be all, Mr. Scruggs?" I jumped and let out a squawk. "Ah, yes," I said. "Thank you."

I tried to walk out naturally. At the door, I briefly turned my head to glance back at the counter. The teller was still watching me. *Calm down. You're acting guilty.*

Several times a day I found myself checking my gun, which I carried everywhere.

Even though I had tried to patch up things with Beth, there was still a lot of stress between us right before she left, and now that they were gone, I remained concerned about our relationship.

I poured some water into the coffee maker and went out to get the paper. Returning to the coffee, I skimmed through the news, my mind too scattered to read anything but article headlines. On page two, my heart skipped. *Plane Crash.* I read the headline out loud: "Mysterious Plane Crash: 25 Kilos of Cocaine Found."

On Friday, July 19, the U.S. Coast Guard lowered a man to investigate a report by two 13-year-old boys, Cleat Mathews and Tray Campo, who discovered an unidentified airplane crash. The Coast Guard not only verified the crash site but found the airplane contained 25 kilos of cocaine. The cocaine was found in a waterproof aluminum suitcase. There was no sign of victims at the site.

The suitcase containing the cocaine was the same type as the two suitcases full of twenty-dollar bills discovered one week ago in the car following the fatal shootout between Highway Patrolman Harold Dixon and DeShawn Pinckney.

Both the cocaine and the money are from unknown sources, according to SLED Sgt. Harold Dixon and Coast Guard Capt. Richard Forester. There is no information on the whereabouts of the plane's missing occupants or what caused the crash. The FAA confirmed they received no report of a lost plane.

Tray Campo was bitten by a venomous snake while on the small island where the downed airplane was found. Late yesterday, he had been dismissed from the hospital in good condition.

The teens reported they discovered the crash while trying to rescue an osprey entangled in fishing line.

Along with the news article was a local map showing the exact location of the crash site. *They had found the crash.* My mind raced. What would Snake think if he found out about this? He would probably assume the money had initially been with the plane and was removed after the crash.

A week ago, the news article about finding two suitcases full of money in the car trunk of this Pinckney guy supported what I had told Snake about finding the money in the marsh. But locating the crash...he would know, or at least have enough suspicion to torture it out of me. Thank God my wife and child were in Kansas, but how hard would it be for Snake and his men to find them? Would the next trip to Jacksonville be my torture trip? I remembered I had not told Dee anything about a crash. Would he connect me to this?

Time was running out. I needed to spring the trap. This sting had to happen before Snake and Dee connected the dots. Disaster was approaching.

I turned back to the suitcases found at the shootout. Could it have come from my storage unit? I had to check. The unknowns were piling up. I should have already checked on the money suitcases but had put it off because of so much stress and work, to say nothing about the hassle of avoiding detection.

I rented another car from a different rental agency. At this point I wished I had never found the money, but now my family's safety depended on it. I shuddered to think what would happen if Snake discovered either one of my secret storage units. It was important he believed me when I told him how much I had found and where.

I first drove the rental car to Live Oak Storage, the cache used for my working capital, expenses, and where I got the money for the FBI. I had put most of the money initially stored under my house in this unit, only keeping a smaller convenient portion where I lived.

About $3.5 million were spent on my business and

for personal spending. Taking into account the million Snake took from my garage, the half-million for the sting, and another half a million in my fake gas tank, out of the $9.5 million, there should be $4 million stored in eight suitcases.

Arriving at Live Oak Storage, it was a relief to see all eight shiny aluminum suitcases sitting undisturbed. I opened two suitcases to make sure the money was still there and took the added precaution of arranging them in such a way it would be noticeable to me if they were later molested.

Relieved and in better spirits, I drove to the second storage unit, but my stress returned when I realized I had not visited it for almost six months and my last payment was expiring. My God, if I had not thought to come here today, the storage unit might have gone to one of those auctions I had seen on TV. There was no way to send me a message about overdue rent. I had given the office fictitious information. Man, this criminal stuff is tough. I could see them opening up my unit to discover $10 million. Damn, was this dumb!

I arrived at the Keep Safe All Night Storage, agitated about almost forgetting to pay my rent. I didn't stop at the office but drove straight to my unit, looking like a jackal about to steal the leopard's meal. I reached in my pocket for the key and panicked until I remembered I had put it in the truck console. I released the lock and opened the door, afraid of what I would see. The storage unit seemed to be the way I had left it.

But wait! One suitcase was at a different angle. I was almost sure they were left in a line when they were stored nearly two years ago. I counted—eighteen. Feeling numb, I counted again. There should have been twenty. No matter how many times I counted them, it was still eighteen.

The more the money got out into the market, the more likely things would unravel. This Pinckney guy had to have had the two missing suitcases, but how did he get them? If he could get it, somebody else could. Somebody knew about this money. I had to move it—now!

I took my rental car back, traded it in for a van, and returned to the storage unit by early afternoon, worried the whole time that whoever knows about the money would show up. I loaded all eighteen suitcases and left without speaking to anyone.

I pulled the van into my garage under the house and closed the door.

Now what to do? Should I bury it? It would take a big hole and be inconvenient to access. No place in the house satisfied the security needed if someone were to search.

While I was thinking of a hiding place, it occurred to me I had not looked inside any of the suitcases. I quickly opened two at random. The money was there.

Discarding several ideas, I finally came up with a temporary hiding system. My construction company had built our house with a lot of input from Beth. Coming from Kansas, she did not understand the need to protect marsh front houses from possible storm surge. She had grumbled about the difficulty of carrying groceries up the steps to an elevated house. That was enough for me to install an elevator that went from the basement level to the first and second floors. It turned out it was an unnecessary extravagance. Last summer the elevator broke between floors, and it wasn't fixed until the fall. It had occurred to me at the time if it had broken with somebody inside or even with groceries in it, we would have played hell figuring out what to do. I had worked for three hours, and it remained between floors. Finally, I had to take the motor and the whole control panel apart to discover the problem.

A plan came together for hiding my stash. I was afraid to risk another storage unit, and I had not heard anything else about a warrant to search my house. *He was bluffing.* Besides, with no evidence for a warrant, a good lawyer could put a stop to it.

I loaded $9 million in eighteen suitcases onto the elevator, closed the door, went upstairs, and punched the button for the second floor. As soon as it moved, I ran to the house's circuit breaker panel in the utility room, guessed when the car was up the shaft between the first and second floors, and tripped the circuit breaker. Next, I went to the attic where the elevator motor was located, disconnected the power, and went back to reset the circuit breaker. Now I had a broken elevator. This system should work so long as I was not subjected to an organized search. For now, at least, I had dodged that bullet.

My phone had been forgotten for two hours in the truck holder throughout my scurrying back and forth. Retrieving it, I discovered a missed call and two texts from Sheryl. Now I remembered, I had promised her I would come over to her house and help finish the work she was doing for me on the money-laundering plan, but now it was almost dark.

Snake already had the outline to study; what we were working on now was the actual legal paperwork for him to sign. Sheryl handled only part of the project. Some I had to do myself, and some an outside attorney did. Because Sheryl did not understand the whole plan, she had questions about the work I had assigned to her.

I dialed her number, and as usual, she answered with good humor. "There you are. I was worried that whoever is after you must have connected. In any case, since you are alive, I'm at a standstill with this stuff until I can talk to you."

"I'm sorry," I said. "A crisis came up this morning, and I have been working on it all day. I know I said I needed the paperwork today, but if you like, we can get it done first thing in the morning."

"Another crisis?" she said. "You need to unwind, or you'll come apart."

I sighed. "Is it that obvious?"

"It is to me."

"I'm in something I can't control. I don't know anything I can do but see it through."

"Come on over tonight. Maybe getting through some of this mysterious work will take some pressure off."

I had the fleeting recall of when I came to her house from Jacksonville—a flash of cleavage and bare thigh. "If that works for you, I'll be over in about a half-hour. I have to take a shower. I have been doing physical work all day."

"Ah, the mystery magnifies."

I arrived in her drive and saw only a lamp on in the entry. I knocked.

"Come on in. I'll be with you in a minute."

In the den, there were no lights except for the glow from a small lamp in the corner. She appeared in the doorway wearing a terry cloth robe.

"Hi, Scrap. I, too, decided to shower," she said with a devilish smile.

I noticed the robe had no sash. She held it at the waist, leaving it open at the top, the bottom revealing her upper leg.

"Sheryl...you, ah—work."

"Scrap, you aren't making any sense."

She turned loose her grip at the middle of her robe and walked toward me. I was lightheaded and couldn't think. I was in a giant whirlpool spinning toward ecstasy and disaster. The male black widow spider drawn to a mate that could eat me alive. She stopped short of making body contact and then lightly touched my arm.

I could smell her. Her touch, like a charge of electricity. Naked and smiling in front of me now—I was gone.

My phone vibrated with a text chime. It was Beth. I looked at the pop-up text on my screen and could hardly believe my eyes. It said, "I love you."

I looked at Sheryl. She knew. She pulled her robe back together.

It was time, time for the talk I had put off for so long.

"You're a beautiful woman. Sex with you would be like crack cocaine. Transport me to divine ecstasy but result in my destruction. I can't do it...I love my wife. I have loved her since the day we met. She's everything to me. This would destroy what we have. Men everywhere want you. You don't need me as a lover. You need me as a friend, and I need you...as a friend."

She smiled, stuck her hand out. "Friend."

Chapter 53

Snake

Jacksonville, Florida

Snake still had two men in the Charleston area who kept their noses to the ground for a clue on the missing money and the movements of Scrap and his wife. They had been cautioned to be careful about having another disastrous encounter. When the news article appeared about the money found in DeShawn's car, it was immediately forwarded to Snake.

Snake studied the news article, threw it down on his desk, and immediately picked it up again. His money was all over the damn place! It didn't make sense. How in the hell did it get into this fool's car? *How can I find out? The man is dead.* Scrap must be telling the truth; somebody else had found the money, probably in the marsh.

If Scrap is telling the truth about finding only $4 million, there's no point in pushing him to do something that might hurt them both.

Snake decided he should concentrate on getting the rest of the money Scrap admitted he had and pursue the money-laundering scheme. He called in Gut.

"I want you to deliver a message to Mr. Scruggs inviting him to come here with the legal papers and also the one million he promised."

Gut frowned and raised one of his thick bushy eyebrows.

"I take it you now believe Mr. Scruggs."

"I don't trust anybody. But the information indicates he may be telling the truth."

Gut started to respond but must have thought better. Ignoring Snake's trust comment, he continued. "Will all the instructions be in the letter I am to deliver?"

"No. I want to insulate myself from this. Tell him verbally he's to spend the night."

"Where will he be staying?"

"In a hotel of our choosing. This will also give us some flexibility to bring Mr. Scruggs into our compound if we decide some coercion is necessary. We must be careful, due to his personality and his FBI friend. I'll decide what happens next after he gets here. I may kill him, I may torture him, or I may do business with him."

"Yeah, but don't forget Scrap's IRA replica of a kneecapping."

It made Snake furious to think about Scrap shooting another of his boys. Counting the two shot in Scraps garage, this was the third, and so far, he had not harmed a hair on Scrap. "Pigneck was stupid. He got what he deserved. The sonofabitch is sick. He let his lust for little girls interfere with his job. You told him to be careful with this Scruggs guy, didn't you?"

"I did tell him. And furthermore, he was supposed to be *investigating* how to proceed with a kidnapping should we want him to do it. I don't know how he got himself shot."

"Make it clear to him, he's on borrowed time, and if he breathes a word about a possible kidnapping or anything else, including how he got shot, he will end up in a dumpster."

"Oh, he already knows. Believe me."

Snake believed things were coming to a head, but he didn't feel he was in control, and he got irritable. "What about this Rex guy? Find him and we'd know what happened. If Mr. Scruggs only has part of the money, Rex might have some also."

Gut pursed his lips and frowned. "I have probed all the way to the Caribbean, and the last thing we heard was he left Wilmington a year and a half ago."

Snake slammed his open hand on his desk. "Fish had my money. It was found in the back of some dopehead's car. Scruggs has some and probably Rex also.

Gut rocked back on Snake's anger. "Boss, I will keep on it. I have a feeling we will soon start to tie things together."

Snake calmed down and nodded. "Okay, get the message to Scruggs and let's see if we can develop something there. He has already admitted he has some of my money. He could be telling the truth, but I need more certainty."

"I'd love to torture the cocky sonofabitch," Gut said. "Just say the word."

Chapter 54

Scrap

Mt. Pleasant, South Carolina

Like a bolt of electricity, Sheryl's voice came through the intercom, informing me Gut was in the reception area. I responded a little too loudly. "Send him in."

His great bulk filled my office door. I felt the urge to reach into my drawer, pull out my Glock, and shoot him on the spot.

He walked right up to my desk as if it were his and gave me a smug look. We didn't shake hands.

"Mr. Scruggs, once more you are invited to Jacksonville. I am also to relay that you are to plan on spending the night. The rest of the instructions are in this letter."

I had a feeling Snake would throw me a curveball. I was still playing on their field, but a face-to-face meeting was necessary for our sting to work. This spend-the-night instruction indicated Snake's accomplices might collect the money and the business papers, leaving me in a hotel. They could take the papers to Snake to sign and return them to me the next day; I would never see him. If he opened the suitcase full of cocaine before the sting was in place, I would be dead by morning.

It was also terrifying to think of what it might mean if I had to spend the night at Snake's compound. Maybe this was it. I thought about the room of horrors. Was I being baited? A weak, let-down feeling engulfed me, and my confidence faded. It was too late to turn back. I had to take charge. *Don't let these sick bastards cloud your thinking.*

Trying to hide all emotion, I looked Gut in the eye.

"Let me make one thing clear. I have what I agreed to bring: the money and necessary papers for Snake to sign. If he doesn't sign, our deal won't happen. I'll show up at the appointed time but will not spend the night. You tell Snake I'll have the same drop-dead arrangement back here that was in place for our last Jacksonville party. Only two hours will be available to conduct our business. The two hours start when I arrive in Jacksonville and end with my departure back to Charleston."

He laid the letter on my desk. "I'll tell him, but I doubt he will agree, so be prepared to spend the night."

He winked at me and walked out.

I was afraid to open the envelope. The trap I had planned was being set for me. Spend the night? More and more it was looking like the sting could go wrong, but if I could not see Snake face-to-face, I would have no chance to get him, even if I could figure out how. There was just so much Dee and the FBI could do. Either our plan would work, or it wouldn't, but it was doubtful they would be able to save me if it went wrong.

I was developing a visceral hatred for Snake. I despised Trent Talbert, but even though he was a threat to my freedom, I knew he was just doing his job. Snake, on the other hand, was threatening my wife and child and destroying my ethics. Ultimately, he would kill me. My thoughts coalesced into a single direction: kill the son of a bitch.

The stress of not leveling with any of the people who were a part of this scheme was draining me, and although the threat to Beth and Emma was reduced, I was still worried they might be in danger. Looking at the envelope like it contained a brown recluse, I finally slit it open.

Mr. Scruggs, your presence in Jacksonville, Florida, is required on July 26 at 2:00 p.m. You are to bring all agreed-upon items along with necessary papers. Park at the front of Martha's House Inn, *10550 Balmoral Cir., West Jacksonville. Wait in your car.*

The August 1 payment date, which we had agreed to on my first visit, had been moved up six days. At least this time I had three days before I was due in Jacksonville. I wasn't sure everything was ready for the sting. Of course, Snake moved it up in case plans were being made. This guy always seemed to be one step ahead. I called Dee: "Hey, numb-nuts, there will be an inspection on July 26 at 1400 hours."

I was relieved. Dee didn't miss a beat. "Yes sir, you're on. Full-dress inspection with a parade to follow."

I gave him the transfer address listed in Snake's letter.

The morning of my departure found me closed up in the garage under our house. The two identical aluminum suitcases were placed in the cab of my truck along with a manila envelope containing the ownership papers for Snake to sign, which would create the money-laundering company.

I paced back and forth under my house, scared, trying to think of what I had missed and all the ways this could go bad. I became angry. These guys were scum, preying on ignorance to peddle their poison, wrecking lives, killing each other. And here I was, up to my neck and sinking—gasping for air.

I gave myself a little pep talk: *Take 'em on, Scrap! You and Dee are going to destroy these bastards.*

With forty-five minutes to go before it was time to leave, I went upstairs, poured a second cup of coffee, and went out on the porch. Detached and dejected, I gazed over the expanse of marsh to Dewees Island two miles away. But up close, at the edge of the marsh, on a dead red cedar, my eyes caught movement.

An anhinga. It magically materialized without me viewing the approach. The wings were half-open for drying, osculating in short strokes. The long, crooked neck and sharp, upturned beak rotated in my direction, sending its omen. The name snakebird took on new meaning.

Chapter 55

Beth

Wellington, Kansas

Beth came out of the only spare bedroom of the old frame house. The wall phone gave a jarring jingle. When her mother, Hilda Hauck, got off the phone, Beth was crying.

"Sweetheart," Hilda said, "what is wrong?"

"Nothing, Mamma. I guess I'm just nostalgic. The familiar smell of this old house brings back so many memories."

Hilda tilted Beth's head to look into her eyes and gently caressed her hair. "I think there's more. You seem nervous and not yourself. You jumped when the phone rang. Is your relationship with Scrap okay?"

"Things are fine with Scrap," Beth snapped at her mother and instantly regretted it. "I'm sorry, Mamma. Please just give me some space."

Hilda put her arm around her daughter's shoulder and gave her a troubled look. Beth turned, hugged her mother, and sobbed. "Oh Mamma, I'm so sorry. I didn't mean to sound cross. There are some things I'm troubled about, but I'd rather not talk right now. I need to get my thoughts together."

Beth would love to have her mother's counsel, but

she felt her parents would be too worried over something they could do nothing about.

"Sweetheart, when you're ready, I would like to help."

Beth noticed Bill, her father, had been listening from the breakfast area. When Hilda returned to the kitchen, he came out and touched her arm. "Pum'kin, you do seem a little jumpy, kinda like a new colt."

I've got to change the subject. "Papa, do you still have that big old shotgun."

"You mean Elsie? That's no old shotgun. That's an L.C. Smith, the finest—"

"Double barrel ever made," Beth said, finishing his sentence. "I remember, Papa. It's a 10-gauge, full choke in both barrels, bought in 1912 by my great grandfather."

"That's right."

Beth could tell he was pleased to have a chance to talk guns.

"Think I could shoot it," she said.

"You wouldn't want to shoot it. Elsie is big and kicks like a mule."

"Remember that time you took me goose hunting," she said, "and I got two big honkers in the same fly-by, and after they seemed to be out of range, you got two more with Elsie."

Bill mimicked pointing a rifle. "Oh yeah, I almost forgot about that goose hunt, but switching gun stories, what I'll never forget is you taking your first elk with the Winchester."

The rifle was one of the original Winchester Model 70s, the best big game hunting rifle ever made. It was chambered for the flat shooting Winchester .270

caliber. It had brought down whitetail, mule deer, and even three bull elk. It was the other gun Bill's father had left him.

Beth was genuinely interested in reliving these hunting stories. But the main reason was it made her feel safer to know that his old shotgun and Winchester rifle were still in good working order. She trusted that Scrap would get himself out of the mess he got all of them into and protect his family at all cost. At all cost— that's what scared her most of all. "Where do you keep it? I would like to see it."

He gave her a surprised look but then broke out in a big smile and walked toward the coat closet next to the front door and motioned for her to follow. "Sometimes I still hunt with Elsie for those big high-flying Canada Geese."

Beth admired the shotgun, broke it open, closed it, and pointed toward the living room window. It was big and it might kick, but if need be, she could fire it. *And I would hate to be on the other end.* "Where do you keep the 10-gauge shells?"

Bill gave her a long quizzical look. "I keep them on the top shelf behind a shoebox. They're all loaded with those large BB-size shot."

She handed Elsie back to him and picked up the Winchester rifle. It felt natural in her hands. She mentally ran through the steps her father had taught her. She hadn't forgotten. "When was the last time you used any of these."

"Oh, last month sometime."

"Good. That's very good."

He seemed like he wanted to ask her questions, but she was afraid she would break down and spill it all if he did. But he didn't say anything. After another questioning glance, he took the rifle and propped it inside the closet next to the shotgun. "I was waiting for Emma to get up to see the calf," he said. "But she's still sleeping. Let's go check on it now, and I'll take Emma later."

They watched the new calf attack his mother's udder with gusto as if he had been around for a month. "This may be the last of this year's crop," Bill said. "He came a little late in the season but seems to know his business."

There was a pause and Bill turned toward Beth. "You've got something to tell me, Beth. I'm ready to listen."

Tears flooded her face. "Oh Papa, I'm scared—so worried and scared."

He reached out and took her hand. "It will be much better to get it out. Tell me what's going on?"

Beth hesitated. "Promise you won't tell Mamma. She will be too upset and worried."

"I won't tell unless she has to know, or you give me permission."

She told him about the danger Scrap was in without including all the laws she thought had been violated. "Papa, these people are ruthless. I'm afraid they will find out where we are and harm us here to pressure Scrap."

The new calf was full. He playfully jabbed at his mother's udder until she grew impatient and moved away. Apparently deep in thought, Bill still looked at the spot. "Come back to the house," he said. "I have something I want to show you."

He went into his bedroom and came out with a

silver star hanging from a ribbon. "All of these years, this has been in a dresser drawer. I never told you about it because I didn't want to be reminded of the war."

"Papa, I knew you were in Vietnam."

Bill's face got serious, and his eyes had a far-away look.

"Yes, well, the North Vietnamese were about to run over us with a tank. My troops had no armament and were scared. They were about to be killed. This medal is a testament: I will not let my people be killed. I sneaked up on the tank while the commander was standing in the turret. I shot him dead, climbed the tank, dropped in a grenade, and killed the rest. Beth, I'm seventy-two but still strong. I'll protect my girls."

Speechless, Beth was shocked that this loving man could be so violent but amazed that he could be so courageous. It gave her comfort and courage.

Trying to put it in perspective, she stared through the front window overlooking a long drive that approached the house through a pasture. She imagined the thugs coming to harm them. Her eyes shifted to focus on the front closet—the closet where Elsie and the Winchester rifle were kept.

Chapter 56

Dee and Snake

Columbia, South Carolina

Dee drew a circle with an X in the middle for Snake's unknown compound. He drew a line to another circle with an A inside and then two squares with a team number in each. Filling in information around these drawings, he worried about the setup, worried about going in without knowing all the facts, and most of all, worried about his best friend. He knew Scrap wasn't telling him the whole story. It wasn't that he was concerned about embarrassing the FBI, but he wanted the facts to better plan and protect Scrap. In the past, he had tried and failed to catch Snake and was afraid his friend did not fully understand what he was getting himself into. No one got to play at Snake's level without possessing wily and treacherous skills.

He stopped drawing and focused on a block he had drawn for the hotel parking lot scheduled for the transfer. What if Snake had his boys make the cocaine swap right there? What if they took the money-laundering papers for Snake to sign and return them to Scrap via FedEx? It would fit Snake's reluctance to get personally involved in any transaction.

Dee decided to send four agents to stage at the

hotel and take down the drug dealers at the hotel parking lot if it could be determined they were making the swap and not transferring Scrap to Snake's compound. He wouldn't get Snake in the arrest, but he still might attach it to him later.

A junior agent stopped at his open door and waved a folder. "I have that information you wanted. It turns out the handles on these suitcases are unique. There's only one manufacturer that makes the hand part shaped like an eight-inch pipe."

"That's great," Dee said. "Good work. Is there anything else?"

The young agent pointed to his report. "Yes, I think you'll find this interesting."

"I'm strapped for time right now. Tell me."

"There's a small series of numbers under the handle identifying the production batch the suitcase came from. Further investigation revealed there were only four large shipments delivered of these suitcases in the past four years. Two of these happened in the two-year time frame you were interested in. One was to a warehouse in Atlanta, and the other was to a coffee company in Haiti."

"Great work. Thanks. We'll keep this on the front burner."

Dee returned to his planning. Both the deliveries were a puzzle, but he was sure they would eventually produce corroborating evidence. He had his agent drop by the South Carolina Highway Department (SLED) to take a look at the serial numbers of the two suitcases found in the deceased DeShawn Pinckney car. *Will they match any of the others?* Dee got a distant look and was quiet. *This could be interesting.*

Dee called Trent Talbert. Talbert was a thorn in Dee's side, but he had been included in the operation to keep him from further investigation of Scrap. Dee had not talked to Talbert for several days, and out of necessity, it was time to play this political game. "Trent, we have a go on the sting. The drug purchase is on, and Scrap will be making the trip on July 26, for a rendezvous with Snake at 2:00 p.m."

"That's six days earlier than what they had originally planned."

It irritated Dee to go through this, but he had to humor him. "You're right, but depend on Snake to throw a curve. It's probably a precaution to interfere with any plans Scrap might be setting up."

"Why would he give so much notice on the meeting?"

"Good question," Dee said. "What are your thoughts?"

"I think he may be hedging, so anybody that is after him will get all set up, and he can change plans at the last minute to throw them off."

Although Dee was already making plans based on this thought, he wanted to give Talbert credit. "Good point. We need to be flexible to make last-minute changes. Thanks, Trent."

Even though he was talking to Talbert to cool his jets, the conversation reinforced his thoughts. He vowed to be ready to shift his plans at any moment. Also, he would instruct his people to be as cautious as if there were trip wires and cameras. *Don't spook the coyote before he gets into the barnyard.*

He had deployed the last agents to Jacksonville and was about to leave himself when the young agent appeared at the door again. "There's a news article you might be interested in."

"Tell it to me; I don't have time."

"Seems two teenage boys discovered a crash site on an island out in the marsh. The only thing that was on the airplane was an aluminum suitcase full of cocaine."

Dee paused for a few seconds. "Okay, thanks. At this point I can't see a connection that would change anything."

The agent left, and Dee sat back down, deep in thought. He knew Scrap had not told him everything, and this complicated his planning. It became clear why it was hard to construct a polygraph Scrap could pass. It was likely all the money came from this crash site, but it could not be tied up in one neat bundle. It was still bewildering how Deshawn Pinckney had $1 million in his trunk, and what about the suitcase of money Fish had found? Finding out the manufacturer's batch number on the suitcase of cocaine found at the crash might put another piece in the puzzle.

Dee did not share the news article about the crash but filed it away in his mind.

****

In the morning after Scrap's visit was set in motion, Snake received information about yet another news article. This news was about the discovery of the crash site by two young boys. Now Snake doubted his first decision to deal with Scrap. He reconsidered whether Scrap was telling the truth.

The fact the paper reported there were no human remains compounded the mystery. *Where have they gone?* Rex and Toad had not been seen since they left to get the drugs. Was it possible for them to crash and remove all of the money without a trace? Maybe some kind of difficulty caused them to dump the money in the marsh. In that case, Scrap could be telling the truth. This scenario became more feasible on remembering about the single suitcase of money tracked to Fish. But if all of the money was jettisoned, what happened to Rex and Toad? And what about Rex's boat disappearing? Why is there only one suitcase of coke, but Two Finger Willie insisted Rex took his pay as two suitcases of cocaine?

He called in Gut to consult.

"Read this and tell me what you make of it."

Gut cast an eye over the article.

"Jesus Christ, Snake, how could the money be scattered all over the marsh if the plane went down on an island?"

"Which begs the question: how could Mr. Scruggs have found only four million?"

"Also, the money we know about was supposedly discovered south of where the airplane was yet to fly."

Snake remembered something Fish had told him in the torture chamber while peeing all over himself. Fish had found his money and saw the suitcases in Scrap's boat well south of the reported crash site shown on the newspaper's map. If Rex and Toad had thrown it out, it would have been much farther north.

Snake was perplexed and gazed unfocused on his desktop. "But Gut, the one thing I'm sure of is Fish told us the truth, and he said he found his money to the south."

"Shit, I don't know. But I say Mr. Scruggs is lying."

"Here's what I want. Forget the hotel. Bring him to the compound. I'll get the truth once and for all. Word from South Carolina is Mr. Scruggs is home alone. I want you to find the wife and little girl and hold them at a safe house until Mr. Scruggs arrives. This time I'll wring the whole story out of that cocky bastard, or he will see suffering like he can't imagine."

"What about Mr. Scruggs's threat about contacting the FBI?"

"It's not going to work this time. He would not take the chance while we hold his family. We'll have him by the balls."

"But he said the drop-dead plan would automatically trigger if he did not return on time."

Snake raised his index finger. You also told me that he said we had two hours to conduct our business. If we do this right, we can get everything we need in that time.

Gut smiled and nodded. "Okay, I see where you're coming from. Any idea where to start looking for the wife and daughter?"

Chapter 57

Beth

Wellington, Kansas

Several days went by and Beth became more relaxed. At 10:30 a.m., Beth and Hilda were drinking coffee. Emma came bounding in with Bill right behind her. "Mama, you should see the new calf. He has already learned to run."

Beth jerked her gaze toward a noise at the front door visible through the living room—it exploded open. Bill ran toward two large men pushing their way in, both brandishing guns. Beth knew. *My God, they're here.*

Even though Bill had been pushed back from the door, he still stood in their way. The man who seemed to be in charge had a long scar starting at his right ear and going all the way down his neck to his shoulder. He pointed his finger at Bill's chest. "They call me Crunch, and if you don't get your ass out of my way, you're gonna find out why."

Bill bristled and stood his ground. "Get out of my house."

"Nero, this old man needs a lesson in respect," Crunch said.

Nero wore a tight T-shirt showing muscular arms

covered with tattoos. He was big and ugly and probably outweighed Bill by a hundred pounds. He put his gun away and stepped toward him.

Bill backed up but still blocked their path through the living room. Crunch waved his gun toward Bill. "Nero, take him down."

Nero shoved Bill so hard he went sprawling across the den floor next to the kitchen.

"Grandpa, if you get up," Crunch said, "I'll blow your fucking head off."

Bill sat up but remained on the floor. "There ain't a whole lot here to steal, but you can have what there is."

"Old man, we ain't here for your piddle-ass stuff. We come for the pretty lady and little young'un."

Nero cast a lecherous look at Beth. "Yeah, sweetheart, let's me and you get it on."

Beth gave him the most disgusted look she could muster. She stood beside her mother next to the kitchen table with Emma clutching her dress. Her terror was mounting. "Don't you dare touch me!"

Nero grinned and cast his lecherous eyes on Emma. "Okay, lovely, if you don't want me, maybe I do your girl. She looks pretty good, too."

Emma's eyes got wide, and she looked pleadingly at her mother.

Bill came roaring off the floor like a charging Cape buffalo. Directly in line with the pointed .45 automatic, he jammed his right shoulder into Crunch's gut. Nero wrapped his massive arms around Bill, pulled him off, and held him while Crunch was buckled over and coughing.

Crunch recovered and pistol-whipped Bill. Hilda raced out of the kitchen and jumped on Crunch's back,

Steve Taylor

screaming and pulling his hair. "Stop it. You're killing him! You're killing him!"

Nero laughed and pistol-whipped Bill again. Bill fell limp to the floor. Hilda hung on with her legs and bit Crunch's ear.

"Get this bitch off me."

Nero yanked Hilda off Crunch and slapped her hard across the face. Beth jumped into the fray, clawing and screaming. "You scumbag! You hit my mother!"

Little Emma ran crying to her mom and tugged at her dress. Nero kicked little Emma in the thigh and shoved Beth across the floor.

Crunch turned his huge bulk toward Beth. "Listen, bitch. I'm going to shoot everybody here if you don't calm down."

They managed to put lock ties on the wrists of the females. Bill was either unconscious or dead. They left him alone on the floor.

"Nero, you dumb shit, stay away from the girl. I told you, Gut said Snake don't want no messing around and no killing. If he hadn't, I would've killed them all. The whole family's crazy. They like a stack of wildcats. Now take the pics and send them along with the other ones to Gut, and let's get the fuck out of here."

Nero took the pictures and seemed pressured to send them to somebody. He fiddled with his phone and then crammed it into his pocket.

"Drag this saucy number out and cram her into the trunk," Crunch said. "I'll put her brat inside the car."

Nero pushed Beth through the front door toward a black roadster with tinted windows. Crunch pulled Emma by the arm down the porch steps, and she cried out for her mother. "Shut up, or I'll whip your young ass."

Crunch threw Emma into the car, climbed in behind the wheel, and popped the trunk. Desperate, Beth turned on Nero, and using both her hands tied together, she grabbed his monstrous paw and bit it until she tasted blood. His big fist knocked her unconscious to the ground.

She recovered as Nero was cramming her into the trunk, but he suddenly turned her loose and faced the house. Her father staggered toward them, face contorted with anger and uttering animal-like noises. He raised Elsie toward the car. Nero reached for his handgun. The big shotgun roared, and the front tire went flat.

Nero fired and her father jerked and went down but held on to Elsie.

Beth found the jack handle, and with her hands tied in front, sprang at Nero. She caught him on the right side of his head, and he sank to the ground.

An ugly red blotch grew on Bill's chest. He strained to get back on his feet.

Crunch cranked the car and sped away with Emma inside screaming for her mother. Beth, in a panic over Emma, ran after the car. Realizing her chase was useless, she stopped and turned. Nero had recovered and aimed his pistol at her from fifteen yards away. Bill touched off a 10-gauge load of BB goose shot at twenty feet, the full force striking Nero in his right chest. He went down like a twenty-pound honker from forty yards up.

Crunch turned onto the road and Beth could still hear Emma yelling for her.

Hilda ran out of the house and to Bill, "You've been shot! We need to get to a doctor!"

With her hands still tied, Hilda tried to hold her husband, but he collapsed on the ground. He rolled over and looked at her. "We've got to stop that car," he said.

"You need a doctor!"

"Baby, my life isn't important right now. He's got Emma. Please, for once, do what I say."

A sucking sound came from an ugly wound in his chest. But Beth knew he still had one good lung, and Crunch had Emma.

Beth ran to her father. He fumbled at his right pant pocket and pulled out a pocketknife to cut the plastic ties on her and Hilda.

"Go inside and get my rifle, shells, and the binoculars. I think we can still stop him."

Hilda let out an exasperated sigh and ran into the house. Beth was now torn between saving her father or chasing down Crunch, but Bill removed any doubt. "Pum'kin, I'm going after him and nothing but death will stop me."

In mere minutes, Hilda returned to the porch with the binoculars, rifle, and shells.

Beth held her father up at the edge of the porch. He grabbed the binoculars and focused on a rise about a half-mile away from where the road curved. "I can make out the car. It looks like it has stopped. Maybe running on the flat tire has stopped him. Help me to the truck."

Beth helped her father while Hilda carried the rifle. He managed to hoist himself into the passenger seat. Beth drove and Hilda held the rifle and shells in the back seat. On the way Hilda dialed 9-1-1.

"This is Hilda Hauck. Send help! There has been a shooting and a kidnapping at our farm."

Bill motioned to stop at a low bend in the road with trees on one side blocking the view from where Crunch stopped the car. "Help me out," Bill said. "We need to work our way around 'till we have a shot."

"Papa, I can take the shot. Stay here; you're too weak."

"No, I need to be there. Help me walk."

Beth helped him through the wooded area while Hilda carried the rifle. They came to a rise where they could see the stopped car.

Bill leaned against a tree and raised the binoculars. "He's standing outside the car waiting for somebody to come along like he has car trouble. Probably shoot them, too. He's about three hundred yards away."

He tried to raise the rifle, but it dropped, and he slid down the tree. "I can't do it, but you can. It's no different than that elk when you were eighteen."

She took the rifle.

"It's sighted in to zero at two hundred yards," Bill said. "It will shoot about six inches low at three hundred."

Beth propped on a tree and sighted through the six-power setting on the variable Leopold scope. The 130-grain silvertip left the barrel at 3,150 feet per second, but it was not one of her best shots. It struck Crunch low, shattering his upper femur. He screamed, grabbed his leg, and collapsed on the ground. Without hesitation, Beth fired two more shots at the writhing figure until he was almost still. She then fired at his head, which was her best shot.

She put the gun down, and her bottom lip trembled. "He...he was taking Emma. Papa, I killed him."

"You did the right thing. We'll talk about it later."

Beth snapped out of her shock, handed the rifle to her mother, and helped her father up. "We have to get Emma and get you to the emergency room." Beth put the truck in gear, and with tires spinning and squealing, she roared up to Crunch's auto. By the time she bailed out of the truck, Emma was running to her. "Oh baby— my baby."

They piled into the four-door truck and raced to the hospital, leaving the man called Crunch dead next to his car.

Chapter 58

Snake, Scrap, and Dee

Jacksonville, Florida

Snake took slow short steps back and forth in his office. At eleven o'clock on the day Scrap was due to arrive, Gut appeared at the office door. "Boss, I just got an email from our boys in Kansas. They sent a picture of Scruggs's wife and daughter from inside a farmhouse belonging to what appears to be the wife's parents. Looks like all are being held at gunpoint. The only message they sent was 'We got them.' "

"So where are they now, still there, in route, at the safe house? These guys need to let us know what's going on. I need to keep control."

"I have already tried to confirm their first email, but they have not responded."

Snake stopped his pacing and glared at Gut. "Goddamn it. Call them! I want to know if they're at the safe house."

At noon, Gut had yet to reach the kidnappers. Snake fumed. He wanted to be up on all developments prior to Scrap's arrival. He may need more graphic pictures from Kansas to use as a torture threat to enhance his interrogation. He decided to push ahead with his plan and hope for a link-up with the kidnappers

Steve Taylor

before Scrap arrived.

He stepped outside of his office and motioned for Gut. "Prepare to do a number on the traitor we have been holding. The screaming will remind Mr. Scruggs of what to expect if he fails to cooperate. If we can get in contact with the idiots who did the kidnapping, it shouldn't take long. Mr. Scruggs could still return to Charleston in time to cancel his drop-dead plan. I'll explain to him that if he doesn't do as instructed, his wife and child will pay the price."

"What do you have in mind, Boss?"

"I'm tired of guessing about my money. What I want to do is offer Mr. Scruggs a chance to come clean in my office after I show him pictures of his family's capture. If he still resists, we take him to the discipline room and do a quick, painful number on him. Nothing permanent or disfiguring, but something simple that can also be applied to the wife in Kansas.

"I'll offer him another opportunity, but I need to be in touch with these guys holding Mrs. Scruggs at the safe house. Mr. Scruggs will be informed the same procedure will be done to his wife, and he can listen to her scream in living color on live stream. If I'm not satisfied, he will be informed his little girl will be next."

"If I can make contact," Gut said, "I will see that our guys in Kansas are equipped to do this."

"And Gut, I want that turncoat, back-stabbing prisoner screaming when Mr. Scruggs enters our compound."

"My pleasure, Boss."

At 1:00 p.m., an hour before Scrap's scheduled arrival, Snake left his office and visited the torture room where Gut and Pigneck had strapped in the sobbing turncoat prisoner for the torture display. "Have you heard from the kidnappers?" he asked.

"I tried to call again—" Gut gave a nervous shrug. "—but got nothing."

Snake was frustrated and angry. With unblinking eyes, he looked at the trembling victim. "You sonofabitch, regret isn't a strong enough word for what you're about to have."

He turned to Gut. "Those stupid jerks that did the kidnapping, do they know this is time critical?"

"Something must have happened."

Snake walked over to a pair of arm shackles hanging on the wall and studied them. He turned back toward Gut. "You need to delegate the pain management of our turncoat to Pigneck. I want you to go meet the boys making the rendezvous with Mr. Scruggs. However, keep trying to contact our kidnappers. If you get something from them, contact me on my secure phone, but Gut, don't give that number to anybody else."

Gut looked confused. "Boss, what do you want me to do at the rendezvous?"

"Call when you arrive. I'll have final instructions. I'm growing leery about this whole thing."

****

Thirty minutes out from the hotel parking lot, I got a call from Dee on my FBI-issued phone. "Scrap, I want to give you a heads-up that we have done some staging at the hotel in case Snake gets nervous and tries to do the swap right there."

The FBI would see I had two suitcases. This scenario had been a worry for some time, but up until now, I thought they would be hidden at a remote site waiting to pick up the track on the money to Snake's headquarters. "Shit, Dee, the Feds are going to spook my pick-up guys."

"Don't worry. These agents know their stuff. You won't see them, but I wanted to let you know they're there."

I decided not to say anything and wing it. At this point, what choice did I have?

Carrying enough cocaine to send me up for twenty years caused a tense drive to Jacksonville. I had no idea where Dee and his men were, but my hope was they soon would be locked on to me like a beagle on a hot rabbit trail.

I arrived at the hotel at 1:45 p.m. and parked. There was no evidence of Dee's men anywhere, and I relaxed some about them seeing the cocaine suitcase.

I jumped when my personal phone went off. The contact was due to arrive in five minutes. It wouldn't look good to find me talking on the phone. It was Beth; I had to take it.

"Beth, I can't talk right now. Things are about to get tense."

"They tried to kidnap Emma and me! Dad and I killed them before they could get away. We're safe, but Dad is in the hospital with a punctured lung. He's still in the operating room. He lost a lot of blood. I'm not sure he's going to make it."

Her voice broke into sobs. She had unloaded so much information my mind was spinning. *Should I call this off? But they will come for us again.* "Are you under police protection now?"

"Yes, except for Dad, it's all under control here. Oh, Scrap, be careful. These people are horrible."

"I know, honey. I know. I'm so sorry." Suddenly I had so much I wanted to say to her, but there was no time. "I'm not sure where this is going, but I have to do it. Remember this, I may have been wrong, but I thought I was doing the right thing for you and Emma."

"Scrap...oh God, Scrap."

"I have to go. I love you."

****

Dee and three agents were parked a quarter mile away from Scrap's rendezvous. About one hundred yards away from Dee's vehicle, agent Trent Talbert was parked with three more. Both cars contained tracking reception devices tuned to Scrap's money suitcase.

Dee had two more agents in the back of a parked plumbing van at the hotel parking lot and one inside the hotel lounge reading a newspaper. The agent in charge at the hotel was acting as a janitor. He covered the outside while sweeping the front and changing out the trash bags.

Dee got a call from the agent acting as a hotel janitor. "Something's fishy over here. The thugs never showed, and a sexy woman exchanged some kind of message with Scrap. He drove out of the parking area and is gone."

"Roger that. We have his movement. Forget the observation. They're changing the location. We'll take it from here."

Dee turned to the agent driving. "Snake's a coyote circling and sniffing. He's nervous. I was afraid of this. If he slips away today, I'll call him Eel instead of Snake."

"You think they're calling it off?"

"I don't know. Scrap's going east. He should call

me shortly. Don't get too close; they may be tailing him."

A call came in from Scrap. "Dee, they have changed the pick-up location. It's Evergreen Cemetery. I'm to park at the intersection of Woodlawn Drive and Camellia Drive inside the cemetery."

"Got it."

He turned to the driver. "Stay clear of the cemetery. They can see everything in there. This is vintage Snake. He knew we wouldn't be able to get in place at the cemetery. We'll just have to proceed without knowing what the capture of Scrap and the money pick-up looks like. Hopefully, we can follow the tracker on to the snake pit.

Chapter 59

Scrap

Jacksonville, Florida

The shiny black Sedan—it's them.

My contact arrived at the same time I reached the intersection at the cemetery. Snake must have been nervous because he was moving fast. His guys got out and approached my truck on each side.

"Mr. Scruggs, would you get out of the car and stand with your hands on top?"

One of the men reached in and grabbed a suitcase. For a minute, it looked like he was going to open it, but he returned for the other suitcase.

He pointed at the manila envelope on the front seat. "What's that?"

"A business consideration for your boss. It's part of the reason I'm here."

"You dumb shit. You don't know why you're here."

My blood turned cold. Had I made a terrible mistake? If I had fallen into a trap, it was my own stupidity.

I was thoroughly frisked, with my arms on top of the car and my car keys still in my hand. The items in my pockets were thrown into my truck console.

"Mr. Scruggs, lock your car and take the front passenger's seat in our vehicle."

Another black Sedan pulled up. The two men who had frisked me looked concerned. "Damn, that's Gut. What's he doing here?"

Gut sat in his car for a few seconds on a cell phone before approaching.

"Snake wants to split the money away from the prisoner as a precaution," Gut said. "Put it in my car along with any paperwork he brought. Make sure you are not followed. Handcuff Scruggs and put him in the trunk of your car."

I was ordered to put out my hands in front for the handcuffs. I took my last view of the outside world. It wasn't reassuring. Tombstones everywhere.

This had gone far enough. "Wait a fucking minute," I said. "I'm here for a meeting with your boss. What's this shit about riding in the trunk?"

One of the thugs pulled a gun and pointed it at my head. "Mr. Scruggs, you'll either comply with our request while you're alive, or you can comply dead. Either way, you will comply."

Reluctantly, I climbed into the trunk of the original car. I shuddered at being referred to as a prisoner instead of a guest, but that was not my biggest threat. I had been cast into the sea with no float. The money and paperwork would go to Snake, and I would go, God knows where. If Dee were indeed tracking the money, he no longer was tracking me, and now I had no phone. *Was this it? Am I slotted for elimination?*

My first emotion on being put into the trunk was shock. I didn't expect it. In all the anticipated horror of this meeting, I had not thought of the trunk. The symbolism was clear: this is what gangsters did with their adversaries. This was the terminal end. The top dog had me on the ground by the throat.

Inside, the trunk was dark, with a tiny sliver of light on the right edge of the closed lid. *What's that smell? A faint odor of something dead?* I froze with horror.

The car accelerated rapidly and proceeded with a lot of stopping and starting. We couldn't be on the freeway. They were maybe taking evasive action. Or going to a place where they discard bodies. The thought crossed my mind that they may have another torture location. I had no idea where the suitcases were going, but I knew if Snake realized one had cocaine instead of money—it was over.

They had handcuffed me from the front, so I twisted my body until, using both hands, I could feel the trunk lid for the emergency trunk release. Nothing was there. But of course, a gangster's car wouldn't have one of those. Failing with the trunk release, I felt momentary panic, like a wild animal bouncing off the walls of its cage. But soon I gathered my wits and tried to understand what the car was doing.

We quit stopping and starting. We must have been on a freeway. It was hard to keep track of time, but it seemed like this trip was much longer than last time.

I had momentary lapses into remorse. *What if my mother could see me now?* The end result of my compromised principles. The wages of sin: from a proud cadet commander, sash and shako waving in the breeze, to the inside of a drug dealer's trunk.

With time, another possibility emerged in my mind. This could be more of Snake's intimidation, a way to soften me up. If true, there would be more. Snake, *The Acid Man,* was a master of diabolical psychology. Gird up my loins for either a heinous serpentine struggle—or death. If these thugs take me to see Snake instead of my execution, I'll figure out something. Maybe the sting will still work. *Lord, give me a chance to face the bastard. That's all I ask.*

The irregular speed returned, and I imagined we had exited the freeway. We stopped. The sound of a roll-up door. We moved and the door sounded again. The trunk opened, and the light momentarily blinded me.

In a few seconds, my eyes adjusted. We were inside a garage. My two escorts, one on each side, walked me through a door. I was horrified to hear muffled screams. The entrance to the torture room opened, exposing the full sickening volume, and my heart felt like it would pound through my chest. Could I stand another episode of watching this cruelty, to say nothing of the possibility of my own torture? I felt helpless. Did Snake already know about the suitcase of drugs?

The door to Snake's office stood open, and a surge of adrenaline struck me. He was glaring, with unblinking eyes. The two men escorted me into Snake's office and left, closing the door behind them. So here I was, alone with Snake. Thank God I was spared whatever horrors were going on in the torture room, but now I was naked in the viper pit. Snake motioned for me to sit.

"Mr. Scruggs, I'm not accustomed to being told how to run my meetings."

"How's that?"

"I told you I wanted you to spend the night."

His strange eyes burned through me. Without the suitcase I was on my own. Dee would not know where I was, even if he had been able to pick up the track at the graveyard. *I need time.*

I locked my eyes on his violent gaze. "I came with your money and paperwork, but you seem to be waffling on our deal."

"Mr. Scruggs, caution is my business."

"So, are we both to self-destruct, or are we doing a deal?"

"People call you Scrap, right?"

I nodded.

"Well, Scrap, you're not in a position to talk about my destruction."

I moved my eyes to the grotesque screaming of the figure in the torture picture on the wall over his head and glared back at his unblinking eyes.

"That, Mr. Acid Man, is a misinformed calculation."

But I was losing hope. There was a knock on the door. My heart skipped a beat.

"Yes?"

"The money and paperwork have arrived."

"Bring it in."

The suitcases. The tracking device…I'm not alone. Dee knows where I am.

Gut set the two suitcases beside me, in front of the desk. He placed the envelope on top of the desk between us and left, closing the door. Snake and I were alone once more.

Snake's expression changed slightly. I hoped he could not see the elation I was desperately trying to hide. We were still playing on his field, but now, we were using my game ball.

"Mr. Scruggs, I take it these are the papers for me to view."

"If you're still interested in generating clean money."

"Before we get into that, I have something else you may be interested in."

He placed in front of me copies of pictures that looked like they had been taken at my in-laws' home in Kansas. Even though I knew my tiger father-in-law and Beth had somehow gotten the upper hand, the pictures were disturbing. I could see the anguish on their faces. And in the corner of one of the pictures was my father-in-law sprawled on the floor. It left no doubt, before the thugs experienced the wrath of Bill and Beth, the whole family had been kidnapped.

Snake did not produce other pictures—he may not know his plan had turned into a debacle.

Where is Dee? He should have been storming the building shortly after the money entered. I needed to stall for more time.

"So, you have pictures. I thought I was here to discuss business."

I focused on his face. His nose slightly flared. His right eye blinked as if a speck of dust had drifted in.

"Mr. Scruggs, this is business. This is about the business of coming clean about my money."

I knew this tone of our conversation would cause him to be suspicious, but I wanted to confuse him and stall for time, but my confidence in the sting was fading. I felt more and more this was between just the two of us. My worst fear was starting to materialize:

Dee might not make it in time.

"I told you all I know about your money. So, if you have my wife and child, it doesn't change what I have already said."

The hesitations between each of our answers became like static electricity about to spark.

"Even if you never see them again?"

I lowered my voice and locked eyes with him. "There's nothing I can do about that now, so let's get on with our business."

It seemed he knew there was something screwy about my behavior, but he couldn't figure out what. He shifted in his seat. His lips pressed together, and his eyes darted several times toward the door.

He opened the manila envelope and flipped through the papers in a distracted way. He didn't seem to be thinking money laundering. I could tell he was considering what deception I was up to. I feared he was about to order my torture.

Meanwhile, I was starting not to feel hopeful with the privileged information learned from Beth's phone call. Dee and his FBI swat team should have been kicking in the door by now. *Where the hell were they?*

Snake looked up at me, his gaze unblinking for a tense few seconds. "Let me see the money in these two suitcases."

Damn! *This is it.* I matched his unblinking gaze, reached down, picked up the cocaine suitcase and set it on the desk. Snake glanced at the latch. I moved the money suitcase to my lap—the silence between us telegraphing calamity.

Chapter 60

Dee and Scrap

Jacksonville, Florida

Agents Boyd and Talbert had tracked the suitcase to Snake's compound. A six-man team was in place, waiting for Dee to give the signal to go crashing in. Before he did so, he wanted to give Snake time to present the cocaine for the transaction so they would have all the evidence at the crime scene. His cell vibrated, the cell that only vibrated if it affected the mission.

"Boyd here."

"Sir, I just got a call from Kansas. I believe the wife and daughter have been kidnapped."

"What? Who told you that?"

"Rufus Coffey, the police chief in Wellington, Kansas."

Dee immediately knew the call was authentic. He had contacted Coffey to look out for Scrap's family while they were in Kansas.

"Oh, God...Call me immediately if you get an update."

Dee could feel the sweat popping out on his neck. Scrap's family were being held hostage. If he went in, they might be sacrificed. But his lifelong best friend was hung out. Scrap went in naked and unarmed. He held off the attack, hoping to get information— anything—to give him guidance. He estimated, unless Snake got suspicious, he had some time while Scrap presented the papers and made the dope transaction.

****

Something went wrong with the sting. Maybe the tracking system failed.

Dee isn't coming. I'm on my own.

For the first time I realized lying to Dee could be my undoing. He may delay because he doesn't know I'm actually carrying the cocaine evidence. He might give Snake time to produce the cocaine, but if Snake opens the suitcase containing the drugs, I'm a dead man. My time was running out.

Snake picked up the cocaine suitcase. I raised the tubular handle of the money suitcase in my lap, tilted it toward his chest, and slid the tiny pin back. He reached to pop the right-side latch on the drug suitcase. I quietly said, "You snake-eyed sonofabitch."

He looked up, his unblinking snake eyes boring into me, searching for an answer to this last bit of confusion. His eyes grew wide and blinked.

The homemade 20-gauge was deafening inside the office. Snake's chest exploded into a red mass. He rocked back, hovered for a second, and fell forward on the desk. Ears ringing, I retrieved a handkerchief from my back pocket. With it covering my hand, I reached over the desk, withdrew Snake's gun from its holster, and placed it on the desk next to his outstretched hand.

Doors outside were kicked in. Shouting. Gunfire. The magic words: "FBI! You're under arrest. Hands up. On the floor!"

The door to Snake's office burst open. In came, not the FBI, but Gut. He sprayed bullets in my direction. My entire left side caught fire, splinters of pain shot through my chest, my leg buckled, and I fell beside the desk. In agony on the floor, thinking he would finish me, I peeked around the desk to see him run to the far corner of the room.

Gut had picked up the suitcase from Snake's desk and was moving a throw rug from the floor. A trap door. I should have known Snake would have one. Gut disappeared into the hole with what he thought was a suitcase of money.

The room went out of focus. The shouting outside sounded like an echo. Damn, if Gut gets away with the cocaine, we don't have a case. My head was spinning. *I can't pass out. Am I dying?* I rolled onto my side, smarting from the pain…the stuff around me fading…shouting right outside the office, as if from in a giant tank. "FBI! FBI! Come out with your hands up."

I struggled to get my hand in my pocket and found my truck key fob. I punched the horn button. The whole building shook with a dull thud from deep in the ground. The echo of voices in my head grew distant—everything went quiet.

Chapter 61

Scrap

Jacksonville Hospital, Jacksonville, Florida

I opened my eyes and focused on a white ceiling overhead, a dull pain radiating through my body. I was partly dressed in white—a soft weave on my leg, side, and shoulder—bandages.

Am I in bed?

I turned my head. Cords and small hoses appeared leading to my body. Daylight peeped through blinds. I rotated my head to the other side. Dee sat silently, looking at me.

"Well, smack, I guess they don't call you Scrap for nothing."

"Dee…hey…what's going on?"

"Considering you have been shot in the shoulder, the side, and the leg, I thought a little bed rest would do you good. Speaking of what's going on, I thought *you* might shed a little light."

Then I remembered. "How'd the sting go?"

"At this point, we are puzzled. From the looks of things, you somehow took care of the major players. Of course, headquarters laments that they will not hear their story."

A nurse came in pushing a cart.

Dee stood. "Before we get into the debrief, now that I know you will live, I have some things to do. I'll leave you the morning paper. You might find it interesting."

"What about Beth and Emma? Are they all right?"

"That's one of the things I have to do. I didn't want to contact her until I knew how bad you were, and yes, they're fine. Seems this Scrap thing runs through the whole family. Your father-in-law and your beautiful but deadly wife took care of the bad guys on their end. Your father-in-law is in stable condition with a punctured lung."

Dee gave me a jaunty salute and left. A nurse came in to check my vitals. "Sweetheart," she said, "looks like somebody tried to make a sieve of your body."

"Yeah, and this sieve process hurts. Can you imagine what a shotgun would do?"

The nurse left, and I picked up *The Jacksonville Daily Reporter*. The front page told the story: *"The Sting of Death."*

In the afternoon of July 26, an FBI sting was executed on a suspected drug cartel on Jacksonville's west side. The raid resulted in the death of four and the arrest of three, all alleged drug traffickers. The FBI spokesperson, Special Agent Trent Talbert, said it was unclear at this time how two of the deaths occurred, as neither was the result of FBI engagement.

One of the deceased was Battista Cosentino, alias Snake, the suspected boss and kingpin of the cartel. He was found shot in the chest and slumped over his desk, a 9mm automatic pistol next to his hand. Talbert indicated the chest wound did not come from a pistol. He said suicide was not a consideration.

In the same room on the floor next to the office desk was an unconscious Charleston County, South Carolina man, later identified as Mr. Daniel Scruggs, who was a participant in the sting. He had been shot three times. Agent Talbert said it was believed Mr. Scruggs had not been armed.

The mystery increases with the discovery of a partially collapsed tunnel with another deceased, mutilated man holding the remnants of a suitcase suspected of containing cocaine.

Two other deaths occurred as a direct engagement of the FBI. Spokesperson Talbert reported the deaths resulted from resisting arrest. A man was also discovered hanging from arm shackles on the wall, in what appeared to be a torture chamber. The victim was taken to the hospital, where further investigation indicated he, too, was involved in criminal activity.

A suitcase containing $500,000 in twenty-dollar bills was located in the office where the drug kingpin was shot.

Agent Talbert said there was ample evidence present to justify the raid.

I had a day to mull it all over before Beth walked in to assume the responsibility of my care. She said she was tired, but to me she looked wonderful. The threat of death having been lifted, my spirit soared. I hadn't been shot at and missed, but I *had been* shot at and lived. The nurse treated me great, the hospital was great, the doctor was my friend, and my wife was the most beautiful woman in the world.

Emma was left with her Nana and Papa in Kansas, and Beth had flown to Jacksonville the day after she heard from Dee. I basked in her caring attention and tried to forget my past transgressions while my strength improved. My injuries were serious but not life-threatening, unless I caught one of those hospital infections.

"Knock," Beth said with a wide grin.

"What?" I asked. "No way, you just got your cards.

We were playing Gin Rummy on the edge of my hospital bed. She reached to gather the cards for the shuffle. I caught her hand. "Morning glory, I'm sorry for what I put you through. Will you forgive me?"

"Of course, I forgive you You're my man, warts and all. But please, from now on, keep me in the loop."

We looked at each other with wet glistening eyes. For now, I was happy, but I knew the emotional baggage would come back to haunt me.

Three days later, Dee returned in an excellent mood. "How're you feeling, smack?"

"A little pain here and there, but considering three bullet holes in my tender body, I'm in pretty good shape. Don't tell Beth that. I've been milking it since she arrived. It's great; she waits on me hand and foot and keeps telling me what a man I am."

"I'm about to be sick, but let's get to some real news. The FBI hierarchy determined the sting was a success, and I'm their rock star. But the higher-ups are puzzled and want me to get to the bottom of some unanswered questions."

"Well, ain't that some shit? I get shot, and you get an *attaboy*."

"Enough of this whining. I need information. I don't blame you, but how in the hell did you kill two armed top-level drug dealers when they more than likely frisked you before you entered their compound?"

"I'll tell you about shooting Snake because he was going to kill me. That was self-defense. The other guy, I don't know. I have been thinking about it, and I have a couple of theories. One is that maybe they had a booby trap rigged in the cocaine I was buying, so if anything went wrong, they could blow me up. My guess is they weren't all that good with explosives, and the thing went off by mistake. Gut probably tried to run off with the incriminating evidence. Another possibility is they had the tunnel rigged so they could blow it up behind them after they escaped, but somehow it went off too soon."

Dee cocked his head and grinned. "Well, Mr. Sherlock Holmes, you got it figured out. I guess the FBI can go back to Columbia."

I realized I was volunteering too much information. It made me sound guilty. I felt my face flush and tried to bluster through. "Hey, you asked me."

The awkward moment passed, but I felt better because somehow Dee seemed to know I was lying. It eased my guilt some about deceiving my friend.

"Okay, let's cover something else. Your bullet wounds are still a mystery. At first, we thought it was Snake who shot you, but as it turns out, his gun was next to his hand on the table, but it had not been fired."

"Snake was going to shoot me, but I got him with my suitcase gun."

"Your suitcase gun? Are you shitting me? Hold on, we'll get to that in a minute. Go ahead and tell me who shot you."

"This guy called Gut, the same one that did the torturing, the same one that visited me in my office. He ran into the tunnel with the coke."

"Actually, we will be able to confirm that soon. Your doctor gave me a bullet he pulled from your body. The tunnel was mostly collapsed, but one of our guys squeezed in and did some preliminary work. He found the gun, a piece of the suitcase, and enough cocaine evidence to determine it came from the suitcase. This was important to make our case that the sting caught a large drug purchase in the act."

"So has Talbert cooled his jets, or is he still investigating me?"

"Speaking of Talbert, I stayed at the compound for a while after you were shipped off to the hospital. Talbert found a set of car keys and was in the process of getting them marked for evidence when I noticed what he was doing. I recognized little Emma's good luck charm on your keys. Talbert wasn't thrilled, but I brought them with me. I know what a pain it is to replace these electronic keys. If you like, I can make him go pick up your car."

I was sipping water and almost choked. "No, no, I'll have Beth take care of it."

"Okay, I have most of what I need for my report, so tell me, how did you kill Snake?"

"Have the lab take a look at the handle on the money suitcase. I got to thinking there was a good chance your boys would not get there in time to save me, so I built a little insurance in my shop."

"The suitcase gun?"

"That's right. The aluminum suitcase has a pipe-shaped handle of about eight inches long. With parts from a walking cane gun and my mechanical genius, this handle became a 20-gauge lethal firearm. It had a trigger mechanism that fit in the corner of the pipe and the support. It would not fire unless it was cocked with a small pin on the side. This pin was not visible if the handle was folded and barely visible in the carry position. I loaded a standard 20-gauge shot shell with number 4 buckshot.''

Dee stood and walked to my room window. He looked out for a full minute and turned with a grin on his face.

"Well, if I had known you were going in to blow the thugs away, I could've stayed home. Or at the very least, I would've worried less."

I raised the hand that didn't aggravate my pain. "You know I couldn't tell you that. Talbert would have gone ballistic, and your boss would have pulled the plug."

With a stern look on his face, he shook his finger at me.

"Listen, knob. Don't act like you don't know some of your shit is already on my shoes."

"You saved my ass. Maybe when you retire, I'll tell you everything."

He pursed his lips and nodded. "Long time ago at The Citadel, when we were idealistic and sure, you saved my ass...well, I think that about covers it, doo-willy. Your suitcase gun, in a way, saved the day. It gave me what I needed to make the decision to go in. Snake's compound turned into a treasure trove of information. Computer hard drives, cell phone numbers, names of buyers, accounting info. Man, we got it all. Trent Talbert might even think of giving you a break."

"Talbert, that asshole, he wanted to nail me on a lying charge for impeding an investigation. Is he satisfied now?"

Dee chuckled. "The guy's on a tear. Thinks he's 007. We have to humor him, though. He has the ear of Ray Bowley, and don't forget, he will testify to the judge at your plea bargain."

"In that case, I'm not out of the woods yet."

"We will see," Dee said. "One more thing. I doubt it will be necessary for the protective custody, since the most dangerous is dead, or did you think of that? If you're lucky, the judge will give you a suspended sentence."

Considering how much worse it could have been, *I can definitely live with this.* "Dee, you're a true friend."

"Listen, dumbhead. You don't know how good a friend I am. I know you're bullshitting me. Be careful. Remember, you'll be on probation. One step out of line, and you'll be walking tours."

Chapter 62

Scrap

One Month Later, Mt. Pleasant, South Carolina

He said he had come for Beth's shrimp and grits,
but the real reason Dee had come was to influence my
court hearing the next day. Emma had gone to bed, and
the three of us sat around the table drinking wine.

"So, tell me, Dee," I said, "how is the sting follow-
up going? Being a wounded warrior and throwing my
intellect and body into this, I figure the FBI should give
me some kind of medal."

Dee went to the kitchen counter and uncorked
another bottle of wine. He poured three glasses. "Save
all this for schmoozing your pretty wife here. Your
cooperation and risk, however, will have relevance at
your hearing. It will be included as a contributing
benefit."

"Well, you still haven't told us how much benefit
you got."

He hesitated. "You created this domino tumble, so
I guess you're entitled to be in on the rest, but it's
important both of you understand, what I say here stays
here."

"Well, smack, spit it out," I said.

"We are about to make a roll-up on the cruise ship

smuggling system Snake used occasionally. We have rounded up several middleman pushers in eastern North Carolina. A couple of them have turned and are talking. Their testimonies, along with solid evidence from Snake's place, are putting the heat on Two Finger, a big-time pusher who works up and down the eastern U.S. We have been trying to nail him for years.

"By the way, the batch of forty suitcases we traced to the Atlanta warehouse is connected to this Two Finger Willie. It's convoluted, but we will untangle it. The suitcase of cocaine the Coast Guard found on the marsh island came from another batch of forty that was shipped to the coffee company in Haiti, so we are close to identifying the cocaine source."

"Well," I said. "Snake thought he was cool with these waterproof suitcases, but in the end, they were a liability. Never underestimate the genius of the FBI."

Dee got up from the table, stepped over to the kitchen counter, and picked up a piece of cheese Beth had cut. He turned and grinned. "There's a bit of a puzzle over the suitcase of toot we found blown up in the tunnel. Even though it was a mess down there, we managed to get the suitcase batch number from a piece of the handle. It came from the same batch of forty that had originally been shipped to Haiti. FBI's smart, but we may never figure that one out."

He cocked his head and grinned. I swallowed hard and quickly changed the subject. "What about the guys you captured at Snake's compound?"

"Right after their capture, I interrogated them in separate rooms. Taking a wild stab, I accused the weakest-appearing one of murder. I figured Fish Blount's disappearance was connected to Snake. Weak

Man babbled about the other guy, who had the refined handle of Pigneck. He said Pigneck had assisted Gut in the demise of Fish. I switched rooms and told the Pigneck guy I had an eyewitness of his involvement in murder. I let him stew for a while and then offered a deal. He gave us some good leads. There was another interesting twist. It seems this Pigneck had a messed-up leg he says is connected to you. What's that all about?"

I almost choked on my wine. "Shit, you know these guys will say anything," I said. "Especially after they get caught."

Dee grinned and winked at Beth. "He wouldn't say what he was doing, or where it happened, but in what appeared to be a slip, said he thought you did it."

I offered Dee more wine and when he declined, I emptied the rest in my glass and went back to the table. I needed to get off this subject.

"Ah, come on Dee, that's bullshit. You're pulling my leg. What about this Two Finger whoever? Is he a threat to my family?"

"Two Finger Willie. He has gone into hiding. I doubt he will try anything, although there's evidence, he knows about a lot more money that hasn't been found."

He looked at me, smiled, and continued. "Two Finger made a deal with Snake to help him find his missing money. I think we will get him soon. He doesn't have a grievance against you. It wasn't his money, so I doubt he's a threat."

At this point, Beth shifted uncomfortably. "As far as I'm concerned, this isn't over until Scrap can relax. He has been under so much pressure. And what about this fine y'all have agreed to? How can we pay?"

I put my hand over hers. "Sweetheart, it isn't a fine. It's paying back the dirty money I put into my business. They're giving me five years to do it."

I looked at Dee. He looked at his wine and said nothing.

"I have it figured out," I muttered. "Trust me. We'll talk about it later." I changed the subject quickly. "By-the-way, how did it go back at work today?"

"It went great," Beth said. "Everybody seemed to be happy I was back, and I already have some big plans in mind."

Dee raised his eyebrows. "What is this? Somebody finally figured out how smart you are and is paying big for your brains."

"Something like that," Scrap said. "She's the number two big shot in the South Carolina Department of Education."

Dee whistled. Beth blushed.

The following morning my attorney, Felix McCain, and I stood before a judge in the Charleston Federal Courthouse at 85 Broad Street. At a second table sat Dee, Trent Talbert, and a federal prosecutor. The judge looked up from his papers and asked both attorneys if they agreed to the conditions of the plea. He asked for a brief description of the charges against me.

Talbert described the charges I had agreed to accept. Dee stood.

"Your honor," Dee said, "I would like to point out that although Mr. Scruggs pleads guilty to a minor criminal offense, his benefit to the FBI investigation and society far outweighs his infraction. Because Mr. Scruggs risked his life, literally hundreds of professional criminals of the worst sort are being apprehended. He was shot three times, and it's just good fortune he's alive here today. Due to his selfless participation and courage, tons of drugs will never arrive, and tons more will be taken off the streets. The benefits are ongoing and will domino for years while Mr. Scruggs willingly serves the punishment for his transgression."

At one point, Talbert rolled his eyes. He was unequivocally pissed.

The judge told me to stand. "Mr. Scruggs, do you understand the charges?"

"Yes, sir."

Before the judge asked if I accepted the conditions of the plea, he turned to the FBI's table.

"I have studied the conditions required of Mr. Scruggs, and I find it puzzling that either side in this case finds it possible for him to remain in business with the burden of paying such a large sum out of future profits. I find this setup overly optimistic. This agreement could unravel for both sides if it becomes impossible for him to make the payments. It requires Mr. Scruggs to be on probation for the entire time he will be making these payments. He could end up in jail, and the government would be left with less money if he was forced into bankruptcy. Is there something I'm missing here?"

Trent Talbert rose to speak. "Your honor, there have been several more serious charges dropped to obtain this agreement. Mr. Scruggs has accepted these conditions. The money he will be paying overtime is what he illegally inserted into his business. What he will be immediately paying is cash on hand he has misappropriated from federal evidence."

Felix jumped to his feet. "Your honor, the money available immediately was found by Mr. Scruggs. He turns it over voluntarily. There's no law against finding money."

Talbert interrupted, and the judge put up his hand and glared at each table. "Gentlemen, this man has no prior record. He has a good business reputation. He risked his life to help law enforcement. My ruling is to accept the plea, as is, with the exception the payments will be spread over eight years instead of five. His parole time will remain at five years." With that, he picked up his little wooden mallet, slammed it onto a block, and stood.

Understandably, Trent Talbert would be upset because of the extra payback time and because the threat of jail was not included after five years. Of course, I was happy about getting extra time for the payments, especially the last three years I would not be on parole. However, it was still a stretch to expect a construction business would produce the required extra profit over eight years. Have these guys already forgotten about the last recession? I think Talbert is banking on this to get me into a jail cell. What he didn't know—and what I believe Dee had partially figured out—was I had a ton of money stashed in an elevator shaft at my house.

I grinned and winked at Beth.

Dee left the courtroom with Talbert, trying to placate him by explaining how pleased everyone was with the sting results. Exiting the building, Beth let go of my hand and ran to Dee. Talbert stood aside, looking disgusted, as Beth gave Dee a big hug. "Thanks for saving us," she said. "Forevermore you'll be my friend also."

Later Dee and I met for beer.

"Well, smack," he said. "How you like them apples?"

"I'll be beholden for life. That performance in front of the judge was dazzling."

"What makes you think it was a performance? It was true. Talbert probably will see it a little differently, but he'll get over it."

"Now going through all this," I said, "it scares me to think how many ways it could have gone wrong. You knew how risky the sting was, so why did you do it?"

"You know the answer to that, dumbhead. The Citadel taught us about grit. In FBI training I had an instructor that talked about grit. But you, Scrap, have always been my example of real grit. I had faith in you. You have always been a fighter. You'll find a way to win. I'm glad you're my friend. I wouldn't want to be your enemy."

Chapter 63

Scrap

Back On the Marsh, Fiddlers Creek, South Carolina

Once again, there was new moon tide. I put in my boat and motored out to Fiddlers Creek, the serene roots of my youth. I cut the engine and breathed the early fall fragrance of the marsh. The scent to some has no meaning and may not be pleasant, but to those who spent their formative years here, it floods the mind with a world new and wonderful. The scent of a thousand organisms cycling through life, and I am but a part of it all.

A clapper rail broke the silence with its staccato cackle and then it was quiet, except for the ripple of a mullet and the trill of red-winged blackbirds. Drifting in the tranquil water, I contemplated the scene around me—the genesis of my crime.

They never found out I embedded a half-stick of dynamite in the cocaine, complete with a cap and electronic trigger on my truck key fob. They never found out about Snake's own gun planted next to his hand so I could claim self-defense. They never found out about $9 million stuck halfway in my home elevator.

So, the creep of my moral mold was complete. I was forever left with my secrets: the secret of the money, the secret of lies, and my ultimate tainting—the secret of premeditated murder.

I'll learn to live silently with the secrets, but the mold creeps on my soul.

I arrived back at Garris Landing without my usual stress, although I did experience a slight melancholy. I tied my boat to the dock and was about to get my truck for the boat pullout. A tall, trim man walked on the dock toward me. He was dressed in shorts, a loose-fitting shirt worn outside his shorts, and boat shoes. "Mr. Scruggs?"

"Yes."

"I'm a reporter from the Jacksonville area, and I'm doing a piece on the cocaine bust a couple of months ago."

I tilted up my motor, not really wanting to talk to him. "I see," I said.

"According to my research, you were part of the undercover team that brought them down. I have also learned that a plane crash with cocaine on board was discovered somewhere not far from this boat landing. Could you please tell me what you know about that?"

I stepped out of the boat, my stress rushing back. "For the time being, while there's legal action pending for the accused, I'm not at liberty to discuss anything."

"Thank you, Mr. Scruggs, for your time. I'll be in touch with you at a later date."

With that, he abruptly turned to walk away.

"Hey," I said. "I didn't catch your name."

"Rex—Rex Morgan."

A word about the author...

This is a book of fiction; however, many events were drawn from real life. It's still painful for me to recall the construction debacle while writing about building the school observation floor. This came from my personal experience while my company was the general contractor for building an air traffic control tower. To this day, it angers me to remember being forced to give up money I had worked to earn only because it would cost more to collect it through the courts.

The part about convincing a room full of lawyers I was crazy brought me some satisfaction, and it did happen. Incidentally, my attorney's name was Alex instead of Felix. He's an excellent and honest lawyer, who still loves to tell the "Crazy Taylor" story.

When Scrap was stopped by Sgt. Dixon of the highway patrol, the gun in the glove box was an actual experience I had after being stopped myself. The procedure in the book is accurate.

The story about Beth's father, Bill Hauck, receiving a Silver Star for outstanding performance while serving as a Special Forces military advisor to South Vietnamese units, was inspired by a Citadel classmate, Wade Lovings. He, in fact, did single-handedly destroy an enemy tank, for which he was awarded a Silver Star.

Like Rex, I often sailed my seagoing Pacific Seacraft, Crelock 37. I did not suffer the breaking of the roller furling line, but once, while on an ocean sail alone, I discovered the line almost frayed in two. I shudder to think of the consequences.

The episode with a large fish setting off the depth alarm happened to me on a cruise from Charleston to Abaco with my brother-in-law, Allan Morgan.

I chose Beaufort, North Carolina, for the cocaine delivery point because I once sailed my boat into that port after a single-handed ocean crossing from Bermuda. Incidentally, I have sailed from the United States to and from islands in the Caribbean and never cleared customs going or coming.

I used my own house on the marsh with its elevated design to describe Scrap's house.

I have a twenty-five-horsepower Yamaha outboard on the back of a fifteen-foot Jon boat under my house. The hidden money in the gas tank came from a thought I had once while disconnecting the tank. I also use this boat for marsh hen hunting. Incidentally, my own boat trailer has an inoperable taillight.

This book touches on many things I know about: aviation, sailing, building construction, the military, firearms, The Citadel, and the wonders of nature where I live in the South Carolina Lowcountry. These are subjects of my life; however, I'm not an expert on the FBI, drug trafficking, or polygraphs. For these areas, I rely on the expertise of my friend and Citadel classmate, retired special agent for the FBI, Ray Bowley, and my old Citadel roommate and friend Tom Williams. Tom retired from the Office of Naval Intelligence (ONI) and is a leading expert on polygraphs.

Six Mile, Hamlin Plantation, Awendaw, Sewee Road, Garris boat landing, and Bulls Bay are real places. So far as I know, Fiddlers Creek is fictitious; I just like the sound of the name, perhaps because the street I live on in Mt. Pleasant has the word Fiddlers.

Thank you for purchasing
this publication of The Wild Rose Press, Inc.

For questions or more information
contact us at
info@thewildrosepress.com.

The Wild Rose Press, Inc.
www.thewildrosepress.com